D0123842

people she was with. Now she trained her eyes on the horizon, and then frowned. "Things are different." Her narrowed eyes explored the scenery before her, searching to discover what had changed.

"They are," Rose agreed. "The men cleared another hundred acres of woods while you were gone. It took until the end of summer to have all the stumps and roots pulled out, but the fields will be planted for next year. Moses is pleased with how fertile the soil is."

Carrie cast her a look of disbelief. "How could his men do all that work and still handle the harvest?" Her frown grew. "How could I not have noticed this before? Have I been that self-absorbed?"

"Hardly self-absorbed!" Rose protested. "You were gone for more than nine months, and the plantation has been a bedlam of people and activity since you returned home. It's little wonder you didn't notice."

Carrie appreciated her best friend's response, but her lack of observation still bothered her. "So how *did* they do it?" The last time land had been cleared on Cromwell Plantation had been before the war, and it had taken dozens of slaves laboring all through the winter to make it happen.

"Moses had Franklin hire a dozen new men," Rose said proudly. "They worked hard to get the land cleared."

Carrie turned to stare at her. "Only a dozen men?" She shook her head. "A dozen men cleared one hundred acres?"

Rose nodded. "It's amazing what people can do when they know they will be rewarded for their efforts."

"America is changing," Carrie murmured. She knew that productivity on the plantation had soared since all the workers not only received pay, but were also awarded a bonus percentage from the crop. Still, the dozen men had accomplished a daunting job during what must surely have been brutal summer heat.

"It is changing," Rose agreed, "but not enough, and not fast enough." Her voice hardened. "What is happening here on Cromwell Plantation should be happening all over the South, but despite the obvious successes with our crops, most plantation owners still insist on doing things the old way. Slavery may no longer be legal, but that doesn't change the fact they are determined to treat the freed slaves as if they are still property."

Carrie's lips thinned. "I know you're right..." Her voice trailed off before she continued. "But Moses has so much to be proud of," she said enthusiastically. "What he has done here is remarkable!" She pulled Granite to a stop and fixed her eyes on Rose's beautiful face. "How can Moses stand to be away from it? Is he happy in college?"

Rose looked away, stared out over the fields for a few moments, and then met Carrie's eyes squarely. "I don't think so," she said, and then frowned. "Not that he'll ever say anything. He knows how much Felicia and I want to be in college. He would never take that away from us, and he would never leave us."

Carrie knew that was true, and she wanted Rose and Felicia to go to college, but her heart ached for Moses. She knew how hard it was to choose to do something you weren't passionate about.

"Am I being selfish?" Rose asked suddenly.

Carrie stared at her friend, struck by the vulnerability lacing her words. "Selfish?" she scoffed. "You couldn't be selfish if you tried, Rose."

Rose didn't look away. "I'm serious, Carrie."

Carrie peered closer, recognizing the truth of Rose's words. "And so am I," she assured her. "You pushed aside your own desires and passions for years, waiting until the time was right. The doors opened for you to go to Oberlin College. Moses chose to go. I understand why he would rethink his decision, and I sympathize with how much he misses being here, but he is a grown man who made a decision for his family." She reached down for Rose's hand and grasped it warmly. "He made a decision because he loves you. That is all the reason he needs. College won't last forever," she added.

"And if I take a job in a city far from the plantation?" Rose asked softly.

Carrie took a deep breath, knowing she didn't hold the answer to her friend's question. "You'll have to cross that bridge when you come to it," she finally replied.

Rose smiled. "'Don't cross the bridge till you come to it, is a proverb old, and of excellent wit.'"

Carrie returned the smile as Rose quoted the words from a favorite poem from their childhood. "Do you remember when we read *The Golden Legend* before the war started?"

"I do," Rose assured her. "I was surprised when Felicia came home from school with a collection of Henry Wadsworth Longfellow's poems before we came here. She's been reading them constantly. She read *The Golden Legend* to me just last night."

"Did you tell her about us reading it together when we were teenagers?"

"Hidden away in your room because no one else in the Big House could know that a slave had taught herself how to read." Rose nodded. "I told her. And I told her that I probably would have been beaten if it had been discovered."

"My father did not beat his slaves!" Carrie protested. She despised the entire institution, but she also felt loyal to her father. She didn't want Felicia to see him as anyone except the man she had grown to love.

"He wouldn't have done it himself," Rose agreed quietly, "but he also didn't know all the things Ike Adams did."

Carrie understood the bitter anger that tainted Rose's reply, but wondered why the past seemed to be filling her friend's thoughts again. Perhaps it was knowing how much Moses wanted to return. "I know it was awful," she said gently. Her own memories of the old Cromwell Plantation overseer carried their own angry resentments. She could feel nothing but relief that he was dead.

Rose nodded. "I hate thinking about the past, but I don't believe it is wise to pretend it didn't exist just because slavery has been abolished. Felicia and I talked about how far blacks have come since then. We also talked about how far we have to go." She smiled slightly. "Felicia asked me what I really thought Longfellow's poem meant."

"The part about crossing the bridge?" Carrie asked.

"Yes." Rose's smile grew brighter. "I told her it meant that *they ain't no use borrowin' trouble that ain't eben be here yet.*"

Carrie laughed as Rose quoted Old Sarah, sounding just like the woman she had adored for her entire childhood. "I can imagine how tired your mama grew of telling us that over and over. We both had a habit of borrowing trouble before it got here."

Rose nodded, fixing Carrie with her piercing dark eyes. "Is that what you're doing now? You're as restless as a willow in a windstorm."

Carrie opened her mouth to refute her friend's observation, and then closed it. "You always know." She shrugged her shoulders. "I don't know what is bothering me," she finally admitted. "Everything seems to be jumbled up inside." She made no attempt to hide the frustration in her voice.

"Of course you are." Rose's voice was unperturbed, her eyes calm.

"Of course I am *what*?"

"Jumbled up and frustrated," Rose responded. "You spent nine months on a wagon train and in a Navajo internment camp in New Mexico. You experienced things you never dreamed of experiencing. You became even more of a leader." Her voice softened. "And now you're back on the plantation—back where you started—and you're wondering what is coming next."

Carrie remained silent as Rose laid out exactly what she was thinking.

"You're happy to see everyone," Rose continued, "but the last nine days have been nothing but constant activity and talk. You've gotten used to the quiet on the Santa Fe Trail. You love the plantation, but you know it's just a stepping stone to whatever is waiting."

Carrie stared off into the distance for several long moments as she let the truth of Rose's words penetrate her heart. "Cromwell Plantation will always be home, but..." Rose continued to wait while Carrie fought to give voice to her thoughts. "I thought I had found so much peace about losing Robert and Bridget..." This time her voice wouldn't continue around the clog in her throat.

"But being back here brings back all the memories," Rose finished tenderly.

Carrie nodded, knowing there was no reason to deny her feelings. "I thought it would be easier," she confessed. "I thought... after being gone for nine months that it wouldn't have the same power to swallow me."

"It *will* be easier in time," Rose assured her, "but it's still too fresh."

"It's been a year and a half," Carrie murmured.

Rose was the one to reach out and take her hand this time. "You lost your husband *and* your daughter at the same time, Carrie. Eighteen months is nothing. You have moved past the depression, and you have done amazing things since then, but that does not erase the pain or ease the ache of missing them. That will take a long time."

"How long?" Carrie demanded impatiently. She knew no one could tell her, but it didn't stop her from asking. She hated how volatile her emotions had become since returning home.

"I can't answer that for you," Rose said gently. "We all have to walk our own path."

Carrie wanted to scream when a fresh wave of frustration threatened to engulf her. She wanted answers, and the fact that no one could give them to her did nothing to make her feel better. When Granite snorted, she was suddenly certain of the one thing that *would* help. Knowing Rose would understand, she gave Granite his head and leaned forward in the saddle. Within seconds he was in a dead run, his body low to the ground as his legs flashed. Carrie threw back her head and let the wind tear at her curly, black hair tamed into a braid that would soon be in tatters.

A short time later, with no direction from her, Granite was making his way at a steady trot down the trail that led to the one place guaranteed to give her peace. Carrie took deep breaths as they wound under the glistening red and gold canopy of maples and oaks that lined the narrow path. Red berries hung from dogwood trees like ruby raindrops. Ferns, still verdant and rich, carpeted the forest floor, lifting toward the patches of sunlight that broke through the leaves. Soon, the ferns would be battling a smothering cover of leaves, but for now they were still free to dance.

Carrie felt the knots begin to unravel. When they reached the banks of the James River she dismounted, slipped Granite's saddle and bridle off, and freed him to graze. He nudged her toward the water, snorting softly, and then turned away to feed on the lush grass. Carrie watched him for several minutes. Leaving behind her beloved horse was always the hardest thing about leaving the plantation. So much had separated them—the war, school, the Santa Fe Trail. She could communicate through letters with everyone else, but not with Granite. There was just a gaping hole where her horse should have been, yet she knew he would always be waiting for her, always be happy to see her. She wished, for what surely must be the millionth time, that he could go with her every time she departed.

Granite, as if called by her thoughts, lifted his head to gaze into her eyes. Swallowing back tears, Carrie rested her hand on his muzzle. "I will miss you," she whispered. Granite sighed and dipped his head in recognition of her words, and then went back to grazing. She knew his unconditional love would always accept her actions, but it did nothing to make it easier to leave him.

A noise on the trail alerted her that Rose had finally caught up. Carrie had no doubt that Rose knew where she was headed, but had been content to canter along, enjoying the fall air and magnificent colors. Something about that suddenly irritated her. "Don't you ever need to just let go?" Carrie demanded.

Rose cocked her head, smiled, and slid from her saddle. She said nothing while she untacked Maple, certain the mare would not leave without Granite.

Finally, she turned to Carrie. "Yes, but not the way you do. It's a good thing, because if Maple suddenly took off at that speed, I would be nothing but a crumpled body in the road."

Carrie smiled slightly, but needed an answer to her question. "What do you do?" she demanded.

"How do I let go?" Rose swung around to observe the glistening waters of the river reflecting the blue of a sky unmarred by clouds. The wind had died, leaving the water a perfect glassy mirror that made the sky and water blend seamlessly. "I find quiet." Her face reflected her own troubled thoughts. "That is easy on the plantation, but it is harder to find quiet in Oberlin. I miss the wide-open spaces and the utter silence that grips the plantation every night. When my world turns topsy-turvy, I find silence so that I can hear my own thoughts and feel my heart."

Carrie considered her words. "Yes, but don't you sometimes need to blast out your feelings and do something wild?"

Rose met her eyes hesitatingly, before choosing to speak the truth. "And what good would it have done me?" she asked. "I was a slave. I couldn't race off on a horse, or go do something crazy. I couldn't even leave my room in the Big House once I started living there. I used to sit by the window and stare up at the sky, dreaming I was actually sitting *beneath* it, not forced to stare out through a small pane of glass. When I was back in the slave quarters on the weekends with Mama, I would sneak out at night so I could absorb the silence. Mama never stopped me."

"She knew you needed it," Carrie said softly. She had come to understand so much of what life had been like for Rose as her slave, but she knew she would never have a full comprehension. Rose was right; she had never had the option to go wild, so she had found solace where she could. "I'm sorry," Carrie murmured. It was one more thing to apologize for to the woman who had lost so much because of her family. She knew all had been forgiven, but that didn't change the consequences.

Rose shrugged, her eyes once again peaceful. "I love my life now." Her face became thoughtful. "Mama used to tell me that the present changes the past. I didn't understand what she meant, but I think I do now."

Carrie cocked her head, pondering the words. "What did she mean?"

"I think the time comes when you look back, but you don't find what you left behind."

Carrie thought about Rose's words as she stepped closer to the river, admiring the glowing stones shimmering beneath the clear water. "You mean, that as you change, you change how you see the past?"

Rose nodded. "That seems to be the way it works for me. What was so terrible at the time, is a reminder of how wonderful my life is now. I hated being a slave, but I can't deny it makes me more grateful for my life right this moment. The present has changed the past for me."

Carrie let the silence of the clearing wrap a blanket of peace around both of them. "That makes perfect sense. You know, Chooli's family taught me that I don't have to let my past define my future. I try to remember that every day." She sat down on the large rock that had been her thinking place for more than twenty years, and patted it to invite Rose to join her. Once Rose had settled, Carrie was content to stare into the depths of the river, doing nothing to tame her thoughts or emotions. She knew the river could handle whatever was there.

Rose was the first to break the silence. "When are you leaving?"

Carrie smiled, not even bothering to ask how Rose knew what she hadn't known herself until a short time ago. "Early January."

Rose eyed her. "Philadelphia?" When Carrie nodded, her look grew skeptical. "You're going to Philadelphia in *January?*"

Carrie grimaced. "I can't think of a worse time to be there, but I have a promise to keep to Biddy. Faith sent me a letter last week telling me how much need there is for a clinic in Moyamensing." If she were honest, her decision had been made the instant she received the letter, but she hadn't been ready to acknowledge it when she'd been home for only two days. The image of Biddy's vibrant face and glowing blue eyes appeared in her mind. "I would do anything for Biddy," she added softly. "And there is so much need for a homeopathic clinic in Moyamensing."

Rose's lips twitched. "It helps a little to know you'll be almost as cold as Moses and I will be this winter," she teased.

Carrie stuck out her tongue and turned away to gaze at the water, glad a brisk wind had risen to create dancing whitecaps. She appreciated the calm stillness, but the choppy water reflected her feelings more accurately.

"And after that?" Rose asked.

Carrie barked a sharp laugh. "Good grief, woman. I can hardly look past today. It's a huge stretch to decide to go to Philadelphia. I'm simply not capable of thinking further than that." She sobered. "I remember something your mama told me one time." She paused, remembering the brilliant shine in Old Sarah's eyes that always meant whatever she was going to say was very important. "She told me *when the present be too much, dat ya gots to look to de future. Dat I gots to make my own future.*"

Rose smiled, but said nothing.

"What's wrong?" Carrie asked after a long silence told her Rose was struggling with her own feelings.

"I don't know that anything is wrong," Rose said thoughtfully. "I just suddenly have a lot of questions swirling around. Moses and I are making our future, but I still have so many questions. I thought once I started college that the path would suddenly become clear..."

"But it's not."

"It's not." Rose said flatly, only her eyes belying the emotion beneath her words.

"I suppose we both just have to keep walking," Carrie replied. "Remember what we talked about on New Year's Day? That we have to keep walking into the unknown?" Carrie shook her head impatiently. It was obvious that Moses' unspoken discontent was worrying Rose more than she was saying. "Do you suppose *all* of life will be unknown? Will we ever *know*?"

"I have no idea," Rose answered, "but it doesn't seem too much to ask that the time might come when we have a clue about what is coming."

"Evidently it *is* too much to ask," Carrie said wryly. "All I have decided at this point is that I'm going to Philadelphia." She forced a smile. "But at least I get to enjoy the plantation for more than two months before I leave again. I've already learned how much living can be done in that amount of time, and I aim to make the most of it while I'm here." Her eyes rested on Granite, determined to ride her Thoroughbred every day she was home.

*****

Moses settled back into the rocker on the porch, grateful for the crisp breeze that cooled his aching muscles. Months of study had not reduced his strength, but hours of chopping wood were certainly harder than when he had left the plantation ten months earlier. Not that he cared about aching muscles; he had loved every minute of the hard labor. The sweat running down his body, the easy camaraderie with his men—most of whom had served under him during the war—and the satisfaction of a day's work, made it all worth it.

Annie stuck her head out the door. "You ready for some more coffee and biscuits?"

Moses grinned at his mother. "Always." It did his heart good to know his mama was here on the plantation, but his face hardened when he considered the fact there was no place in the South truly safe for blacks right now, although Cromwell Plantation was safer than most. He had refused to let anyone lower their guard during the months since the last attack. It had been almost a year, but reports of other atrocities around the South reminded him on a daily basis that it could easily happen again. Caution could mean the difference between life and death for many of them.

"Hey, brother! You're not supposed to sit around with a frown on your face. I thought you were happy to be here."

Moses pushed away his thoughts as Jeremy strode onto the porch, a wide smile on his face. If possible, he looked more tired than Moses was. His wide smile did nothing to conceal his weariness. "Hours in a factory doesn't prepare you for manual labor?" Moses teased.

Jeremy groaned as he settled into the chair next to him. "That would be an accurate assessment," he said ruefully. "They were still at it when I left. I couldn't have lifted that ax one more time if my life depended on it. Besides, they already have a mountain of firewood."

"They'll have several mountains before they're done," Moses replied. "There are more homes to keep warm now, and we have no idea how bad the weather will be."

Annie snorted as she carried a tray of coffee and biscuits out to the porch. "You been in that fancy college too long if you already not be paying attention to the signs God gives us." She put the tray down on the table, planted her fists on her ample hips, and stared down at the two men. "This winter gonna be plenty hard. Not as hard as the last two, but they's gonna be plenty of cold weather. All the signs be saying that."

Moses grinned. "Miles has been teaching you."

"Of course he has," Annie responded. "That husband of mine done know more about God's creation than any man I ever met." Her dark eyes glowed with pride.

Moses could not have been happier that his mama had found love again. She had suffered more hardship, and more loss, than anyone should ever face. To see the light of joy and love in her eyes was all he needed to make him feel content. Except that he wasn't...

Jeremy remained quiet until Annie disappeared into the house again, releasing the aromas of a delicious dinner, before the door slammed closed behind her. "What's wrong?" he asked bluntly.

Moses sighed. He thought he'd done a good job of hiding his growing discontent, but he must have been too tired to conceal it from his very perceptive brother-in-law. Still, he wasn't sure he wanted to talk about it. What good would it do?

Jeremy pushed back a thatch of thick, blond hair and let his blue eyes bore into Moses'. "You know I'm going to make you talk. You can make it hard on yourself, or easier. Your choice."

Moses met Jeremy's eyes for a brief moment before he turned to look over the pastures full of colts and fillies that proclaimed the success of Cromwell Stables. He felt the familiar twinge that Robert was not here to see the fruit of what he created, but Moses pushed it firmly from his mind. He knew he would always grieve his friend, but he had also learned that life kept rolling. "I miss it."

Jeremy watched him, his eyes narrowed and probing. "You don't want to be in college."

Moses sighed again. "What difference does it make?" He shook his head, trying to dispel the heavy feeling that had settled on him at the end of the work day. He would climb on a train tomorrow and go back to college, whether he wanted to or not. He would work toward becoming a lawyer, though he was more certain with every passing day that he had no passion for it. He supposed he believed he could help his people if he was a lawyer, but it certainly was not anything he loved.

"Does Rose know how you feel?"

Moses frowned. "I hope not," he said sharply. "And you're not to say a word to your sister."

Jeremy raised his hands in surrender. "It's not my place," he assured him. "But do you really think she doesn't know?"

Moses shrugged his massive shoulders. "What she *knows* is that I want her to fulfill her dream of a college degree. And I want Felicia to have the chance for the same. Whatever I want is simply going to have to wait." He pushed aside his vision of the lush, fertile soil of the land just cleared—the land that would certainly produce an abundant tobacco crop next season. It had hurt to not be part of the clearing; it would hurt even more to not watch the seedlings go in, to not watch them grow toward the sky.

Jeremy considered his response. "Wait for how long?"

Moses was used to Jeremy's blunt manner, but he simply didn't have any answers. "I don't know," he admitted, also admitting to himself that his inability to answer questions was the biggest source of his discontent. How long would it take Felicia to finish school? What if Rose got a job in a city? His mind was committed to enabling her to follow her dream because the country needed her as a teacher, but his heart was getting heavier with the idea of not coming home to the plantation. He stood abruptly and walked to the edge of the porch. "I don't have any answers," he growled as he looked out. "All I know is that I miss this place every minute I'm away." He allowed the fullness of his feelings to roll through him before he shook his head and turned back to Jeremy. "I'm not meant to have the answers right now or I would have them. My job is to simply live the day in front of me. I don't always have to like it in order to do it." He knew he was speaking the truth.

Jeremy looked at him thoughtfully. "I suppose that is true." He laid his head back against the rocker with a tired sigh. "My sister is a lucky woman."

"Thank you." Moses was suddenly aware Jeremy was holding back his own feelings. Now that he had released some of his own frustration, he could see the tension roiling in Jeremy's eyes. He settled back down in his rocker and reached for his coffee. "You're concerned about the baby."

"Right now, I just want Marietta to give birth so she can quit being miserable," Jeremy answered. "Her back hurts all the time now."

"Yep," Moses responded. "*And* you're concerned about the baby." For all of Jeremy's bluntness in *asking* questions, Rose's twin didn't like to answer them anymore than Moses did.

Jeremy tightened his lips and then repeated what Moses had said. "I'm not meant to have the answers right now, or I would have them."

Moses decided to cut to the chase. "What are you going to do?"

Jeremy's shoulders sagged as he met Moses' eyes, no longer able to avoid the question now that it had been stated so succinctly. "If my child is born black?" He shook his head. "I don't know."

Moses, watching him carefully, saw the flicker in his eyes. "I don't believe you."

Jeremy scowled as he took a long drink of his coffee and visibly forced himself to relax.

A long silence stretched out on the porch as the sun began to slip toward the horizon, making the fall foliage shimmer with a golden glow. Moses was content to wait, glad the focus was off him for a while, but concerned about the trapped look that had gleamed in Jeremy's eyes.

Jeremy finally began to speak. "If our baby is born black, I will not subject Marietta and my baby to life here in the South," he said slowly, forcing his words out in a heavy voice.

Moses cocked his head. "Has anyone been able to tell you the odds of that happening?"

Jeremy shrugged. "No. All I know is that my having a white father and black mother means there is a chance, even though Marietta is white."

"At least you know it can happen," Moses observed. "Can you imagine what it would have been like if you had gotten married and had a black child, not knowing the truth of your past?"

"I've thought about it," Jeremy admitted. "I can only imagine the confusion I would have felt." He grimaced. "It's impossible to imagine what my wife would have felt. As hard as all this is, I'm grateful I know the truth. I'm certain many mulattos in this country have no idea of their heritage."

"Although, most of them don't come out looking completely white," Moses said blandly. "You never had to worry about a stigma until you found out about Rose."

"That's true," Jeremy replied. "I refuse to hide the fact that she is my twin, but I don't broadcast it either. I couldn't possibly be more proud of her, but living as a white man has at least made it easier to help the black community in the city."

Moses nodded. Jeremy had done so much to aid the black equality effort in Richmond. He never hesitated to use his influence as a profitable business manager, and Marietta's position as a teacher in the black schools had made her beloved. "The black community accepts you, Jeremy, and the whites think you're a deluded Good Samaritan. They're irritated, but not threatened the way they would be if they knew the truth about your heritage."

Anger and frustration flared in Jeremy's eyes. "It's all so stupid! I hate that I even have to consider where I will raise my child."

"There are a lot of mulattos in the South," Moses reminded him. "Most of the blacks being elected into politics right now are actually mulatto."

"I know. But ever since Reconstruction started we've been lumped together with those who are completely black," Jeremy acknowledged. "It wouldn't bother me, except that now we are seen as more of a threat in the competition for jobs, land, and political power, so there is more of an effort to put us in our place."

"An increasing number of mulattos are coming down from the North to help with Reconstruction," Moses added, hoping to alleviate his frustration.

"That's true, but they are adults," Jeremy shot back. "They are making choices, knowing how they will be treated, and knowing the danger they face. They are not helpless children," he said grimly. "I know what any mulatto child will have to deal with here in the South. It's a situation that gets worse every day." His scowl deepened. "I've read several articles recently that say the South lost the war because God was punishing them for interbreeding between whites and blacks."

"That's absurd," Moses said with a snort.

"Yes, but it doesn't matter because people believe it. It's only going to make life that much harder for mulatto children." Jeremy shook his head heavily. "Things are changing, but it's going to take a long time."

"And you believe things will be better in the North?"

"Isn't life better for your family in Oberlin?" Jeremy demanded.

Moses sighed. As much as he wanted to return to the plantation, he couldn't deny that Oberlin, Ohio was a better place to raise his family. He didn't constantly worry about Rose, Felicia, John, and Hope. He opened his mouth to answer, but the front door slamming open interrupted his response.

Chapter Two

Carrie and Rose were trotting down the road, admiring the hues of the sunset, when the sound of pounding hoofbeats jolted them from their quiet reverie. Carrie stiffened immediately. Was there another attack on the plantation? She could no more stop her mind from going there than she could stop the sun from setting. She exchanged a startled look with Rose and then urged Granite into a canter that Maple could match. Now was not the time to be separated.

"Carrie! Rose!"

Carrie relaxed as she saw Amber flying down the road toward them on Eclipse, the magnificent dark bay stallion who was the foundation stud for the beautiful colts and fillies grazing in the plantation's green pastures. She would never cease being amazed at the tender relationship the spirited stallion had with the little girl, but she had long ago accepted it. The two of them almost always ended the day with a wild run down the roads. Carrie pulled Granite to a stop as Amber raced up to them. "Are you having fun?" Her question started out with a smile, but she tensed again when she saw the look on Amber's face.

"It's Marietta," Amber gasped. "She's having the baby!"

Carrie grinned, her fear dissolving with the news. "It's about time!" She reached out for Amber's hand. "How far along is she?"

Amber shook her head. "I don't know for sure. Moses ran out to the barn to get me a few minutes ago. He said Annie came to get Jeremy, so he sent me for you."

Carrie nodded. "This is Marietta's first child. It will take a little while. I'm sure she is fine because she has Annie there, but we'll get back quickly."

"You're not worried at all?" Amber asked in a voice that revealed she was worried enough for both of them.

Carrie smiled at the wiry little girl perched like an acorn on a massive oak tree. Unless you saw it for yourself, you couldn't believe such a young girl could handle a horse like Eclipse. "I'm not worried," she assured her. "Marietta is strong and healthy. Women have babies all the time."

Amber peered at her, but the worried look did not diminish. "You were strong and healthy, too," she said hesitantly.

Carrie sucked in her breath, but she wouldn't let the memory of losing Bridget in birth taint Marietta's experience. "That's true," she admitted, "but this is different." She refused to think about the wild horseback ride out to the plantation to say good-bye to her husband before he died. She had gone into labor moments after Robert closed his eyes for the last time. She gritted her teeth against the pain, forcing her voice to remain calm. The best thing she could do for Amber was keep her busy. "Why don't you go get your mama?" Polly was an experienced midwife. She would value her expertise in case there was trouble.

"Moses sent Clint after her," Amber answered.

"Of course," Carrie murmured. "Your brother will bring her back quickly." She sought for words to assuage Amber's fears, and then realized there probably were none. The little girl wouldn't relax until Marietta's baby was born. Carrie urged Granite back into a canter. "Let's get home.

*****

Carrie handed off Granite to Miles, and ran lightly up the steps of the glistening white plantation house. As she passed between the towering, three-story columns, she thought of all the births the house had seen through all the generations of her family. The realization that Marietta was giving birth to a baby whose father was the result of Carrie's own grandfather raping Old Sarah, somehow made it more special. Being able to play a part in the redemption of such a horrible act of violence felt right.

Annie met her at the door. "Miss Marietta's water done broke right before I sent Amber to get you."

Carrie nodded, her mind moving quickly as she thought through everything she needed. "How is she?"

Annie grinned. "Anxious to meet her baby."

Carrie laughed, knowing Marietta was every bit as impatient as she was. Both of them wanted everything to happen quickly. "I can imagine." She opened her mouth to ask questions, but Annie anticipated her. "We gots lots of hot water boilin', and there already be a pile of clean cloths next to the bed. Your medical bag be right there, too. Clint done went to fetch Polly. It won't be long 'fore they be back."

Carrie smiled her thanks, kissed Annie on the cheek, and ran up the staircase.

Marietta was gripping Jeremy's hand when Carrie walked into the room. "You're here!" she said joyfully.

"I told you I would be," Carrie teased. "I appreciate you waiting until I was almost home from my ride."

"I aim to please," Marietta responded, before taking a shallow breath as a spasm of pain crossed her face.

Carrie nodded to Jeremy. "It's time for the father to leave the room, please. I need to examine this beautiful woman who is about to have your baby." She opened her mouth to add words of preparation, but closed it quickly. She had no proof of her suspicions. Only time would tell.

"So, I just sit downstairs and wait?" Jeremy complained.

"You can go commiserate with Moses and Franklin," Carrie retorted. "May I remind you that you have the easy part?"

Jeremy sighed and kissed Marietta warmly before leaving the room just as Annie was bringing in the buckets of hot water.

"I got my Miles keepin' more water hot," Annie announced as she lowered the buckets. She stepped closer to Marietta and squeezed her shoulder. "You gonna do just fine, Miss Marietta."

Marietta, her blue eyes glowing beneath thick red hair pulled up into a bun, nodded firmly. "You bet I am, Annie." Her smile faltered when another contraction struck.

Carrie felt her first twinge of alarm. The contractions were coming much more quickly than they should at this point. She watched Annie leave the room, and then turned back to the expectant mother.

"Carrie?" Marietta asked in a sharp voice. "What was that look for? And don't tell me I'm imagining things."

Carrie considered making up a lie, but knew Marietta would discern anything that was not the truth. "I think your baby must be in a hurry," she said in what she hoped was a soothing voice. "How long have you been having contractions?"

Marietta closed her eyes in concentration as another spasm gripped her. "Not long," she murmured. "Maybe...twenty minutes."

Carrie focused on the positive. "It looks like you will be spared the agony of a long labor."

Marietta wasn't buying her forced cheer. "Tell me the truth," she demanded.

Carrie wouldn't lie, but she knew only what she had read. Every birth she had participated in had taken twelve to fourteen hours, or more. "I don't have personal experience with a fast labor," she admitted, willing her voice to be calm so Marietta would remain confident. "What I have read says a short labor can be more painful because your body doesn't have the time to truly prepare for the pain of giving birth."

Marietta frowned. "I've never noticed that childbirth isn't painful for *every* woman." She hesitated. "You're telling me my pain might be worse."

"It might," Carrie conceded.

Marietta considered that and smiled. "I'd rather do it this way," she said. "If something is going to hurt anyway, I'd rather sign up for the short version. Why drag it out if you don't have to?"

"Spoken like a truly impatient woman," Carrie shot back, relieved to see a confident shine in Marietta's eyes. She wondered briefly what her labor would have been like with Bridget if Dr. Wild had not been forced to do a Cesarean delivery. She supposed she should be grateful that she would never know, because the end result would still have been a stillborn baby. She closed her eyes against the pain momentarily before giving Marietta her full focus.

"Let's see what is going on here," Carrie said gently. "The important thing to remember is that most babies are born after a completely normal and uneventful labor. Rose gave birth to Hope in this same bed. It was very smooth and easy."

"And having John almost killed her," Marietta retorted as another spasm took her breath. She groaned and closed her eyes against the pain.

A soft knock announced Polly's arrival. The gentle-faced black woman took one look, locked eyes with Carrie, and then moved to take Marietta's hand. A pleasant breeze pushed through the soft blue curtains, ushering in cool air that would help with a hard labor. "You ain't never been one to waste time," she said. "Looks like this ain't gonna be no exception."

Carrie, comforted by Polly's arrival, moved into position to examine Marietta. She was shocked to see how far she was dilated. She exchanged a meaningful glance with Polly and reached for the bucket of water. "Today will most certainly not be an exception," she teased. "Have you picked out names?" It would help to keep Marietta's focus on something other than the pain.

Marietta's lips relaxed as the newest contraction released her. "Marcus Jeremy if it's a boy," she confided.

Carrie smiled, knowing how pleased Pastor Anthony would be that his grandchild carried his name. "And if it's a girl?"

"Sarah Rose," Marietta answered, pushing back damp hair from her perspiring face. "I thought about naming a girl after women in my family, but it seemed only right to name her after her grandmother and aunt on Jeremy's side." Her voice faded away as another contraction stole her breath. "Ohhhh..." she groaned.

Carrie smiled at her comfortingly. "And now you know why men don't have babies," she confided. "They could never handle the pain."

Marietta gasped and found her voice. "Then why are they trying to take over childbirth?"

Carrie was not surprised Marietta had read everything she could get her hands on about pregnancy and birth. She also knew Marietta was trying to distract herself, but Carrie's answer was interrupted when Annie reappeared in the room.

"I got the chamomile tea you asked for."

Marietta reached for it gratefully. "The tea helps control the pain by relieving tension."

Carrie grinned. "It's nice to have a patient I don't have to teach anything."

Marietta drank several gulps before another spasm forced Polly to grab the cup from her limp hand. "Oh my..."

The contraction gave Carrie time to add a shepherd's purse tincture to the table where she had placed her supplies. There was no reason to call Marietta's attention to her preparations. She hoped she wouldn't need it, but it was the best herb to stop postpartum hemorrhaging if it were to occur.

"She's been taking the blue cohosh and black cohosh for the last two months," Polly told her.

Carrie nodded. She and Polly had already discussed this, but she knew the midwife was trying to keep Marietta's mind off the pain. "And the raspberry leaf tincture?"

"Yes," Marietta answered in a strained voice. "Polly told me it would prepare my uterine muscles for efficient labor." She grimaced. "I wouldn't mind if it wasn't quite *so* efficient."

Carrie smiled, but she couldn't agree more. "Go ahead and drink some more tea," she urged, "and I'll tell you about men trying to take over child birthing."

"Oh, this should be good," Marietta managed.

"It will be pure nonsense," Polly snapped. "What do men know about women giving birth? They ain't had nothing to do with it for most of time."

Carrie made a face to indicate her agreement, her instinct telling her Marietta's child would be born soon. "Men only entered the field of childbirth about twenty years ago. Although babies have been being born for centuries with the aid of midwives, they decided their medical knowledge was far superior to that of *grubby midwives*," she said with a scowl. "Those are certainly not my words, and definitely not what I believe, but some doctors completely believe it, and they have started writing books to espouse their *superior* knowledge."

"Such as?" Marietta asked.

"Well," Carrie began, her voice dripping with sarcasm. "There are doctors who would very much disagree with me giving you chamomile tea to relieve the pain."

"Why?" Polly growled.

"Because they believe the relief of pain during childbirth removes the maternal instinct," Carrie said. "But the most important reason is that they believe it is sacrilegious to thrust aside the decrees of Providence. They believe women have been sentenced to suffer the pain of childbirth, and that to relieve their pain robs God of the deep, earnest cries which arise in time of trouble for help." She stated it exactly as she had read it. It had been so ludicrous that she had felt compelled to submit it to memory. Silence filled the room when Carrie finished speaking.

"You're *serious*?" Marietta gasped. "What about Queen Victoria?"

Carrie was impressed with the depth of reading Marietta had done.

"Queen Victoria?" Polly asked. "You mean over in England?"

Carrie smiled. "It is amazing how attitudes can begin to change when the most powerful woman in the world becomes tired of the pain of childbirth. Queen Victoria of England had already had seven children when Leopold was born in 1853. She had her doctors give her chloroform and then did the same thing for her next child, her daughter Beatrice."

"Did people throw a fit?" Polly asked, gripping Marietta's hand as a fresh contraction stole her breath. "Did they consider it a *sacrilege*?"

When the pain passed, Carrie answered. "Of course, but a man named Sir James Simpson helped convince the religious-minded people that perhaps God did not insist on suffering in birth." She smiled. "He reminded them that the first operation recorded in history was performed under anesthesia."

Marietta stared at her with confusion. "Excuse me?"

Carrie's smile turned into a grin. "Sir Simpson told people that when God created Eve from one of Adam's ribs, he caused a deep sleep to fall upon Adam." She paused. "Anesthesia!"

Polly laughed loudly, but Marietta frowned. "Carrie, Queen Victoria received chloroform fifteen *years* ago. It should not still be an issue."

"Yes, well, change does not come quickly," Carrie reminded her. "Just because someone has proved something works doesn't mean everyone is going to fall in line."

Marietta was still frowning. "I appreciate why Queen Victoria did what she did, and I don't have an ethical argument against it, but I don't think I would want to miss the birth of my child because I was passed out from chloroform."

"I couldn't agree with you more," Carrie said. "Different people want to do things their own way, and I believe they should have that right." She smiled at Marietta and glanced down, her eyes growing wide.

*****

Moses laughed when Jeremy continued to keep his eyes locked on the staircase. He exchanged a humorous look with Franklin. "Obviously a new father," he teased. "He doesn't realize nothing will happen for hours and hours." He reached over to thump Jeremy's shoulder. "You might as well sit back and relax, brother of mine. We've got a long night ahead of us."

"Not as long a night as Marietta is going to have," Jeremy said heavily.

"That's true," Franklin agreed, "but Chooli assures me it was all worth it when she was holding Ajei in her arms. Marietta will feel the same way."

Moses, feeling sympathy for the soon-to-be father, turned to Franklin. "The best thing to do is keep Jeremy's mind occupied. How far did the men get today with the firewood?" He would forever be grateful that Franklin had arrived a year ago to take over the operations at Cromwell Plantation while he went to school. He didn't know what he was going to do when Franklin took his family back to Chooli's Navajo homeland in the spring, but he pushed that thought aside. He hadn't known what he was going to do last fall either, and God had provided. Rose kept telling him he needed to trust; he was trying.

"They did real good," Franklin assured him, his long, lanky legs sprawled out in front of the fire.

The chill October air had driven them inside to bask in front of the flames. Annie, knowing there would not be a normal dinner that night, had brought them heaping plates of chicken and dumplings. Their stomachs sated, they were ready to talk.

"I figure about four more days of woodcutting ought to take care of things," Franklin continued.

"Four more days?" Jeremy asked with disbelief. "It looked to me like they already have a mountain of firewood. Moses said more was needed, but I didn't believe him."

Franklin smiled. "We're laying in enough wood to heat this house, the homes of all the men and their families, and also have a good start toward drying season next year. It's going to take several more mountains of firewood to do that, and it's much easier to cut it now than it is in the summer."

"I suppose so," Jeremy murmured.

Franklin changed the subject. "Have either of you heard anything new from Thomas about the election?"

"There is no doubt General Grant will be elected the next president," Jeremy answered.

Moses scowled, glad to have something else to think about, even if it was something that disturbed him as much as the current election. "Don't be so sure about that," he cautioned. "I know Grant has the support of Northern Republicans, but he can't count on the votes of Southern Republicans."

Jeremy stared at him. "How can you say that? Do you seriously think the black Republicans in the South won't vote for Grant? That they will vote for Seymour?"

Moses met his eyes. "You've been in the factory too long, Jeremy. It's not a matter of will or won't. It's a matter of can or can't."

"What are you talking about?" Jeremy demanded.

Moses exchanged a look with Franklin. They had spent many hours talking about the reality for black men in the South. "The South believes a Seymour victory for the Democratic Party will undo Reconstruction. They want that more than anything. They also realize the black vote could very well determine the election, so they're doing all they can to make sure the blacks don't vote." Moses was surprised Jeremy didn't already know this, but he supposed it was because the factory in Richmond was booming. Jeremy must have been too busy to be paying attention before he came to the plantation for his child's birth, but that knowledge only made what Moses feel worse. Things like this would continue to happen because people weren't paying attention.

"It's real bad in some places," Franklin said solemnly.

"How bad?" Jeremy asked.

"Merchants are cutting off credit to blacks who attend Republican meetings," Moses informed him. "Landlords are threatening to evict blacks from the plantation and their homes, where they are sharecropping, if they don't swear to never again vote for the Republican ticket."

Jeremy sucked in his breath.

"That's not the worst, though," Moses said grimly. "The Ku Klux Klan is fulfilling its mission of spreading terror. They have assassinated a number of Republican leaders, both black and white. White gangs are roaming the streets, breaking up political meetings anywhere they find them. In Louisiana, there was a mob that invaded a plantation and murdered two hundred blacks who support the Republicans. The message is coming through loud and clear that if you vote, you risk your life and the life of those you love." He continued, not attempting to mask the fury in his voice. "Black men want to vote, but I guarantee you there will be plenty of places where they don't dare to."

Jeremy sat back heavily, his face filled with sorrow. "And, so it continues."

Moses was watching him closely. "You're not surprised." It was not a question.

Jeremy met his eyes. "No, I'm not surprised," he agreed. "The Republican leadership is changing. The country is struggling economically. There is an increasing number of politicians who believe the issue of racial equality is far less important than economic concerns." He paused. "I still believe Grant will be elected, but he is far more conservative than the Republican Party that established Reconstruction. He lacks strong ideological convictions, and his earliest promoters were the conservative and commercial interests in New York."

"So, the blacks will pay the price again?" Franklin asked heavily.

Jeremy shook his head. "I don't think so. At least not yet," he amended. "While American politics are most certainly controlled by money, the business elite fear that if Seymour wins for the Democratic Party, it will reopen the whole question of Reconstruction. That will do nothing but cause fresh chaos. If Grant is elected president, they believe he will bring moderation, fiscal responsibility, and stable conditions for Southern investment." He took a deep breath. "The Republican slogan for Grant's campaign has been *Reconstruction for the South, respectability for the nation, all overseen by the man whose slogan was, 'Let us have peace.'*"

Franklin stared into the dancing flames. "Why does that not make me feel better?"

"Because," Moses retorted, "it means that black equality is only important as long as it makes economic sense."

*****

Rose slipped into the room in between a strong set of contractions. "Hope has been fed. I settled her down early for the night."

Carrie nodded and fixed her eyes back on Marietta. She kept her voice casual. "Want to give me a push?"

Marietta stared at her. "Already? I've been in labor for less than an hour."

Carrie gave Polly a meaningful glance and then looked back at Marietta. "You're not the only one who is impatient. Your baby is not willing to wait."

"You mean I almost missed the birth of my niece?" Rose exclaimed. She grinned at Marietta. "I should have known you wouldn't do anything like other women would do."

Marietta tried to manage a grin, but her face whitened with pain. "Carrie..." she whimpered, fear filling her eyes.

"Push!" Carrie commanded. "The only way to stop hurting is to have this baby. Push!"

Marietta groaned, closed her eyes, and pushed. Her scream ripped through the air.

"I imagine that got the men's attention," Rose predicted. "Jeremy will be terrified because he knows it is too soon for you to have this baby."

Carrie examined Marietta again, satisfied when she saw the crowning of a tiny head. She looked up at Rose as she gave Marietta a moment to recover. "Go tell Jeremy what is happening. Marietta is doing great, but this baby is definitely not interested in a normal birth. Explain it quickly, and then get back here so you don't miss the action."

Rose disappeared from the room quietly.

Marietta lay still for several minutes before another contraction took control.

"Push again," Carrie commanded, smiling up at Rose when she slipped back into the room, an urgent question in her eyes. "You didn't miss it," she assured her. "Push!"

Marietta didn't hesitate this time. She let loose a loud cry and bore down with all her might.

Carrie took hold of the tiny shoulders that emerged. She waited only a moment before repeating, "Push!"

With one final push, the tiny body slid into Carrie's hands. Tears of joy swam in her eyes and mingled with her smile, but she blinked them back to focus on the new life she was holding.

"Carrie?" Marietta whispered.

"You have a beautiful son," Carrie said happily. "He's perfect!"

Marietta broke into tears, her face suffused with bright joy. "A boy..."

Carrie handed him gently to Polly. "We'll get him cleaned up, and then I'll bet he's ready for his first meal."

"Oh...!"

Carrie whipped back around as Marietta's body was jolted with fresh pain.

"What is happening?" Marietta cried. "What's wrong? You told me the pain would stop when I had my son!" The look in her eyes was a mixture of accusation and fear.

Carrie looked at Polly, recognizing the old midwife had suspected the same thing she had. "You go ahead and take care of Jeremy Marcus," she said softly. "Rose and I will help Marietta bring his brother or sister into the world."

"What?" Marietta demanded, confusion replacing the fear as she blinked her eyes. "What are you saying?"

"I'm saying that you're not having just one child. You're having twins," Carrie replied. "I suspected you might but—but I wasn't certain." She settled down on the chair again, while Rose took Polly's place next to Marietta.

"Like I said," Rose whispered. "You're not willing to do things like most women."

"Twins?" Marietta gasped. "*Twins*?"

"Twins," Carrie assured her. "The next one should come fairly easily because the birth canal has already been stretched." She knew her prediction was right when a strong contraction resulted in the crowning of another little head. "Here it comes," she called. "Push!"

Marietta bore down with all her strength. It took only three strong pushes for her son's twin to enter the world.

Carrie laughed as the baby slid into her hands, and then locked eyes with Rose.

The new parents had some decisions to make.

Chapter Three

Jeremy gazed down at his son and daughter, his eyes soft with love. "They're beautiful," he whispered. He searched Marietta's eyes, knowing that the idea of what *could* happen would not compare with reality. What if she regretted her decision?

Marietta read his thoughts. "They are beautiful," she agreed. "And they are *perfect.*"

Jeremy let out his breath slowly. His eyes first devoured his son. A thatch of red hair topped a cherubic face lit by blue eyes. He was smaller than normal, but Carrie said that was to be expected since they were twins. She had assured him both the babies were strong and healthy. "Jeremy Marcus Anthony," he said quietly. "Welcome to the world."

Then he turned to gaze down at his daughter. Curly black hair topped a caramel-colored body that was very clearly mulatto. Her eyes were blue now, but they would almost assuredly change to brown. She was not as dark as her namesakes, but no one would mistake her for a white child. "Sarah Rose Anthony," he whispered as he stroked her velvety smooth arm. "Welcome to the world."

The first flicker of anxiety came to life in Marietta's eyes. "I wonder what the world will be like for our children."

"Because of their color?"

Marietta shook her head. "No, my love. Because the world is a scary place in general right now. It wouldn't matter what color they had been born. We're bringing them into a crazy world."

Jeremy relaxed again, scolding himself for fearing Marietta would feel any differently than what she obviously felt.

"We knew this could happen," Marietta said gently.

"Yes," Jeremy agreed, "but when you're the reason it's happening—when you're the reason your children will face even more challenges than the normal child—it can be a little harder to absorb."

Marietta considered his words. "I suppose you're right," she finally said, and then looked back down at the babies nestled in the crooks of her arms. "All I know is that we have two beautiful, healthy children. It's so much more than other people have. I can be nothing but grateful." She smiled when they whimpered in unison, and then she settled each of them on a breast to nurse.

Jeremy was content to revel in the beautiful sight for a long time. The flaming fire cast a warm glow into the room. The breeze that had kicked up that afternoon had grown into a strong wind that rattled the window panes and caused the tree outside to brush its limbs against the glass. He knew the cold front the wind was ushering in would drop the temperature, but he was snug with his family. Let the weather do what it wanted.

When the babies had full bellies, they snuggled into their mama, closed their eyes, and fell sound asleep. Jeremy had never felt such a strong protective urge in his life. He would do anything to protect his family. He had a sudden understanding that this was what being a father was about. "I wasn't sure I would feel it," he murmured.

"Feel it?" Marietta asked with a puzzled look on her face.

"What it feels like to be a father," Jeremy explained in a halting voice, not sure how to put words to his feelings. "My father was an amazing man, but the man who gave birth to me was nothing but a selfish bastard. He had no problem getting rid of me since a white baby created quite a problem for him here on the plantation. I think... I think I was afraid I might be more like him."

Marietta's eyes stroked his face. "There is not a cell in your body that is like your biological father," she assured him. "You are the most giving, loving man I have ever known. These babies are the luckiest children in the world to have you as their father."

"I'll do whatever it takes to give them a good life," Jeremy vowed. He let his eyes roam their tiny bodies again, and then looked back at Marietta. "We're moving to Philadelphia," he said quietly.

"Is that an order?" Marietta asked, her tired blue eyes flashing with the fire that permeated her spirit.

"I'm suggesting," Jeremy replied. "But I do believe it is the best thing," he added.

Marietta gazed down at Sarah Rose's tiny face for several long moments. "What will we do in Philadelphia?"

Jeremy hoped she wouldn't mind that he had prepared for this possibility, but he was also confident he was meant to have done it. It struck him that his stubborn and independent wife had acquiesced easily, but he shouldn't have been surprised; teaching in the Black Quarters had shown her how difficult life would be for her daughter. Perhaps her easy acquiescence, more than anything else, told him just how right the decision was. It somehow eased the angst that accompanied the decision.

Once again, Marietta read his thoughts. "It's hard to leave Richmond, but we've both had seven months to consider the possibility. We haven't talked in concrete terms until now, but little Sarah Rose deserves a better life than she will have here. I also can't deny it will be wonderful to be closer to my family," she said, her eyes drooping with fatigue. "I would like to get some sleep, but it would be helpful to know if there is a plan in place before I do. I suspect I will sleep better."

Jeremy nodded and grasped her hand. "The manager of Cromwell Factory in Moyamensing gave his notice several weeks ago. Thomas and Abby told me I could take over if needed."

Marietta's eyes narrowed. "How do you feel about that?"

Jeremy smiled. "I think it's a wonderful plan. I will miss Richmond, and miss being with Thomas and Abby, but there are many benefits." His gaze caressed the twins. "The biggest benefit is safety for our children."

Marietta fought to keep her eyes open. "There is prejudice and bigotry in Philadelphia too," she murmured.

"Yes," Jeremy agreed, "but the KKK isn't there, and it will be far easier to protect them and give them both opportunities." He paused, and then told her the rest she would want to know. "We'll buy a home at some point, but in the meantime, we will be staying at Abby's home in Philadelphia. All the medical students have moved out recently, so it is empty."

Marietta's eyes met his with gladness, then closed slowly. Her easy breathing told him she had fallen asleep. Jeremy was content to stand and watch his family. Wonder filled him as he examined the twins' tiny faces. Wispy lashes rested on their cheeks, their bodies lax on Marietta's chest. He felt love and protectiveness expand his heart until he found it difficult to breathe. He'd never known it was possible to feel this way.

The wind was now accompanied by rain cracking against the windowpanes and sizzling against the flames as a few drops found their way down the chimney. The glow from the fire wrapped his family in a golden light. It was a long time before he piled on more logs and went downstairs. He knew the others were waiting for him.

*****

Carrie looked up as Jeremy entered the dining room. She pointed toward the empty plate. "I imagine you're starving."

Jeremy grinned as he sat down. "I'm not the one who just gave birth to twins, and Annie stuffed me with chicken and dumplings earlier."

Annie pushed in through the door. "But you ain't had none of my apple pie yet," she proclaimed as she placed a huge piece in front of him. "Amber and Felicia just picked these here apples today."

"It's the best apple pie you'll ever have," Felicia assured him, her dark eyes glowing in the lantern light.

Jeremy willingly took a bite, and then nodded his head. "Since Marietta can't hear me say this, I'll admit it's the best pie I've ever eaten."

Annie snorted. "Miss Marietta don't know how to make no apple pie."

"She certainly does," Felicia replied, her eyes dancing with fun.

Annie placed her hands on her hips while she glared at her granddaughter. "Let me guess. You done gave Miss Marietta somethin' in a book that was 'sposed to teach her how to make an apple pie." Her eyes flashed. "That's pure nonsense, girl."

Felicia grinned. "It taught Janie how to make biscuits like yours," she reminded her indignant grandmother.

Annie shook her head and sighed dramatically. "What am I gonna do with you? Don't you know cookin' got to be passed down through family? You can't be learnin' everythin' in a book!"

Felicia gazed at her grandmother with sympathetic eyes. "You may not be able to learn *everything*, but you can certainly learn how to make an apple pie."

"Says who?" Annie demanded.

Felicia nodded toward Jeremy. "Ask him."

Jeremy ducked his head as if he could avoid Annie's penetrating stare.

Annie stalked over to stand next to him. "What she be talkin' about?"

Jeremy sighed, knowing this exchange wasn't going to end well. All he really wanted to do was talk about the twins, and about their coming move, but he knew Annie wouldn't let it go now that her ire had been raised. "Marietta made me a pie last week while you were over at Blackwell Plantation," he mumbled.

Annie snorted again. "Bet it weren't no good!"

Jeremy hesitated. He wanted to agree with her, but he also didn't want to be disloyal to Marietta. In truth, it had been a fabulous pie. "It was pretty good," he finally said. He raised his eyes to meet Annie's indignant ones. "You should be proud of Felicia for teaching her. They had fun that day following the recipe they found."

Annie's eyes widened as her lips thinned. "I ain't thankin' nobody for breakin' generations of tradition." She whirled toward Felicia. "You should be ashamed of yourself, little girl!"

Felicia's grin faded for the first time as she anxiously studied her grandmother's face. "I—"

Moses came to her defense. "Felicia, you have nothing to apologize for." He stood to face Annie. "I think that's enough, Mama. She didn't mean any harm."

"Then she's got to learn to stand up for herself," Annie retorted.

Moses stared at her for a long moment, obviously at a loss for words.

Only then did Jeremy see the laughter lurking in the old woman's eyes.

"What are you saying?" Rose asked, her eyes searching Annie's face.

"Land sakes," Annie declared, her face softening with compassion as she gazed at Felicia. "You goin' against every little thin' anyone done told you that you ought to be doing, Felicia. You be goin' to college, and you be thinkin' you gonna change the world for black women. If I be any prouder of you I reckon I would split wide open, but you's got to toughen up. Ain't many people gonna like what you doin' so you gots to learn how to stand up for what you believe is right. Ain't I speakin' the truth?" she demanded, leaning over to stare into Felicia's face.

Felicia slowly nodded, her eyes shining with appreciation. "That's the truth," she admitted, smiling slightly. "It's easier to stand up for what I believe in at school than it is with you, Grandma."

"That may be so," Annie agreed, "but there ain't *no* time when you gots to back down from what be right. I reckon it be harder, for sure, to stand up to the folks you love the most, but I also reckon it be the most important."

Felicia gazed at her. "Why?"

"Because they be the folks you want to love you the most," Annie explained earnestly. "It be real easy to push aside your beliefs 'cause you want folks to love you."

"So, if I expect to be able to stand up for my beliefs to everyone...I have to learn how to stand up for what I believe... no matter what," Felicia said slowly, her thoughts coming together as she verbalized them.

"You serious about changin' the world for black women?" Annie pressed, her attention solely on her granddaughter. There was not another sound in the room.

"More than anything," Felicia declared. "I know I have some growing up to do, but I know that's what I want."

Annie peered closely at her until, obviously satisfied with what she saw in Felicia's eyes, she nodded. "Then it can't matter what nobody says to you, or about you. You just gots to do what is right."

Felicia considered her words. "Then you need to hush up about me teaching Marietta how to make a pie. She wanted to learn. I taught her. She did a fine job, and Jeremy was happy. I believe that's what is important," she said with a smile.

"Humph!" Annie straightened, a look of pride shining in her eyes, and then turned to Jeremy. "Don't you be coming after me about another pie," she warned. "Tell your wife to make it."

Jeremy saw his opening. "Not even if it's a going away pie?"

Heavy silence settled on the room. The only sound was the rain tapping against the window.

Jeremy looked at everyone apologetically. "I didn't see a good way to tell you."

"So, you're leaving." Moses stated.

Jeremy nodded. "We're moving to Philadelphia. I'll be taking over the Cromwell Factory in Moyamensing."

"That's wonderful!" Carrie exclaimed. She shrugged her shoulders when everyone turned to stare at her. "I very much suspect all of us would make the same decision if we had a helpless mulatto baby upstairs that had just been born. I know I would," she said. "I'll miss Jeremy and Marietta being in Richmond as much as all of you, but I'm also glad little Sarah Rose won't face the hatred and bigotry she would here, and I'm glad her parents won't have to deal with the pain of watching her suffer."

"I won't get to see my niece and nephew when I come home," Rose said sadly.

"We'll come back to visit," Jeremy promised, "and you'll be welcome in Philadelphia any time. I'll even let you and Moses have your old room."

Rose clapped her hands. "You're moving into Abby's house?"

Jeremy grinned with relief, glad to see the light back in his sister's eyes. He had suspected she would take it hardest, but he knew he was making the best decision for his family. "We are. We'll buy a house at some point if everything works out, but I'm glad for us to have a landing place for now."

"If it works out?" Carrie asked keenly.

Jeremy wasn't surprised Carrie was the one to latch on to his comment. He took a deep breath. "I'm determined to give my children as much of a chance for a good life as possible. Philadelphia is certainly going to be better than Richmond, but I'm not against moving further north if I feel it's necessary." He shrugged. "I haven't thought on it any more than that. We'll have to see what the future holds. In the meantime," he said lightly, "we're going to be very busy with two babies."

"That you are," Rose agreed warmly, obviously trying to come to grips with the reality of him moving. "When are you leaving?"

"After the new year begins. I want to make sure everyone is ready to travel, and I know Marietta would love to spend Christmas here. I can't think of a better place for her to get used to being a new mother. The current manager of the factory won't be leaving until early February, so I'll have a month with him to get to know the operation."

Carrie was overjoyed. "So, you're staying here through Christmas?"

"If it's okay with you," Jeremy responded.

"Of course it is," Carrie exclaimed. "I'll be leaving for Philadelphia in January, as well." She looked around the room and told everyone her plans. "I will stay with Matthew and Janie so I can be with her during the last months of her pregnancy."

"And after you get the clinic established?" Jeremy asked.

"I have absolutely no idea," Carrie replied. "I can't see into the future any further than that. To make the attempt is too exhausting."

"And there is no need to," Rose added. "Every time I try to see very far ahead, I do nothing but discover I had no clue what was coming toward me," she said. "I make my plans, and then I wait to see what actually happens."

"I hear you," Jeremy said ruefully. "My father used to tell me all the time that nothing is ever wasted. I believe that is especially true at times like these."

"Nothing is ever wasted," Moses said softly. "What did he mean?"

"I didn't really understand it until I got older," Jeremy said, "but it makes perfect sense now. What he meant was there is not a single thing in my life that will ever be a waste. There are so many times I do something, or learn something, and then I don't see any results from it so I think it's a waste. I discover later—sometimes years later—that I'm using that information, or I learned something in a situation that I'm using now."

Moses stared at him for a long moment. "Does that make everything worth it?"

Jeremy considered the question, also aware Rose was staring at her husband with a calculating look. He knew Moses was not asking a casual question, and he suspected his sister knew it, too. "I think I may have to be older before I can completely answer that question," he said carefully, "but I've seen it happen enough times that it gives me peace in the midst of confusing situations."

Moses looked doubtful. "How about when you were attacked? When you were almost beaten to death? Don't you believe that was a waste?"

"No," Jeremy said immediately. "I wish it wouldn't have happened, but there are people walking around the South who are oblivious to how dangerous things are becoming because of the vigilantes and the KKK. I will never again be naïve to what is possible. I'm grateful I know enough to not be willing to have my children face that kind of hatred."

Jeremy understood the conflicting feelings racing across Moses' face, but he didn't regret speaking truthfully. He knew how much Moses wanted to come back to the plantation, but he needed to be fully aware of the danger he would be bringing his family back to. Then, when and if he made that decision, at least he would be doing so with his eyes wide open.

Jeremy was relieved when Susan came in the front door, her face creased with weariness. He hoped she was bringing a distraction with her.

"Susan!" Annie chided. "Where you been? Neither you nor Miles been in for somethin' to eat. What be wrong out there in the barn?"

Susan sighed and settled down into an empty chair. "Nothing now," she murmured, her eyes dull with fatigue. "Two of the mares came down with colic."

"Colic?" Carrie asked with alarm. "How?"

Susan met her eyes as she pushed blond hair back from her face. "Part of the fence in the new broodmare pasture came down when the winds blew a limb off a large oak tree. They got out and went into the apple orchard."

Carrie groaned. "And they ate all they could. I bet they were happy."

"Until their stomach twisted into knots," Susan said wryly. "Then, I'm sure they forgot about how wonderful the apples were."

"They're all right now?" Carrie asked. She pushed herself up from her chair.

Susan waved at her to sit back down. "They're fine. Luckily, Amber saw them when she was leaving to go home. They were already sick, but we caught them quickly. Miles fixed the fence while Amber and I walked the mares for the last three hours. They're resting now. I'm going to sleep in the barn tonight to keep an eye on them, but I believe they're fine. Amber wanted to stay all night, but I made her go home with Miles."

Annie, who had disappeared into the kitchen, reappeared with a plate of steaming chicken and dumplings. "You gots to eat somethin', Miss Susan."

Susan groaned with appreciation as she took the first bite. "Heavenly. I might just live through this night after all."

"Course you gonna live," Annie said. "You one of the toughest women I know."

Susan gazed at her, conflicting emotions on her face. "I'm not sure that is the moniker I want to be labeled with, but as long as you keep making food like this, I'll accept it."

"What's wrong with being tough?" Felicia asked.

"Nothing," Susan assured her. She opened her mouth to say more, but the thin cry of an infant, followed by another in concert, filtered down from upstairs. Her eyes opened wide "Did I hear *two* babies?" she asked.

Jeremy grinned. "Let me bring you up-to-date. While you were saving horses, we were having our lives changed."

*****

Rose, unable to sleep despite how tired she was, found Jeremy standing on the porch. He remained silent, but reached out an arm for her. She went to stand next to him, grateful for the warmth he offered. The rainstorm had passed through, and just as she had known it would, the wind had ushered in a cold front that made the temperature plummet. "We're going to have our first hard freeze tonight," she commented, not ready to focus on the reality that Jeremy was leaving the South.

"What time do you leave tomorrow?" Jeremy asked quietly.

Rose sighed. "Early. The rain will have made the roads slow. We want the kids to get a good night's sleep at Thomas and Abby's tomorrow before we catch the train back to Oberlin the day after."

Jeremy nodded and pulled her closer. "Will you be back for Christmas?"

"We will now," Rose assured him. "We had talked about staying in Oberlin since we've been here so long for this trip, but I don't want to miss the twins' first Christmas, and..." She couldn't force any more words past the clog in her throat. She counted on being able to see her brother every time she came home. The knowledge that he would no longer be in Richmond was a bitter pill to swallow. "Will life ever be more than just one good-bye after another?" she finally managed.

"I don't know," Jeremy said. "There's a part of me that is excited to move to Philadelphia because I know there will be new experiences, but we will be giving up so much. I suppose I'm choosing to be excited because I refuse to consider the option of staying here."

"You're making the right decision," Rose admitted.

Jeremy peered down at her. "Am I?"

"Yes," she said firmly, struck by the sudden vulnerability in his eyes. "I never worry about my children in Oberlin. I saw them play with white children at school here on the plantation, but that was a forced environment. Now they play with kids in their neighborhood who are white and black because it's just the way things are. I look outside sometimes and wonder if it's real."

"I don't know that Philadelphia is like that," Jeremy said doubtfully. "It's better than Richmond, but I don't see it as the bastion of equality, either."

"It's not," Rose agreed. "Philadelphia still has prejudice, as does all of the North, but you also don't have to worry about the KKK knocking on your door in the middle of the night." She frowned. "At least not yet."

Jeremy stared at her. "Surely you don't believe that could change," he protested.

Rose shrugged. "Did Moses tell you about what is happening with the election down here, especially farther South?"

"Yes," Jeremy replied, "but—"

Rose interrupted him. "If the economy is controlling things the way they are *now*, there are no guarantees what will happen in the future. The truth is that this country has no idea what to do with two million freed slaves. What was a wonderful ideal, is quite different in reality." She took a deep breath. "We talk about it at school often. Bigotry is more prominent and obvious in the South, but most white people in the North don't believe blacks should be social equals. They just don't believe they should be slaves. As we fight for more and more rights, we will become more and more of a threat. The pushback could come from anywhere."

Jeremy scowled. "So, there is nowhere safe?"

Rose searched for the right words. "You just have to live, brother. Make the best choices you know to make, and live. You'll deal with whatever comes when it comes."

"Stop thinking that!" Jeremy commanded, his eyes focused on hers. "I can see those thoughts churning around in your head."

Rose sucked in her breath. "What are you talking about?"

"You're thinking that my life would have been easier if I had never found out the truth about who I am. You're feeling bad for me because Sarah Rose looks black."

Rose gazed up at him. "Your life has certainly become much more complicated," she said gently.

"Less complicated than if I'd had a black baby *without* knowing the truth," Jeremy reminded her. "You've been dealing with slavery and prejudice all your life, while I had a very easy life as a white male. It's my turn now."

Rose looked up at him and asked the question she'd been thinking all night. "Do you wish Sarah Rose had been born white?"

Jeremy shook his head immediately. "She is my daughter, and she is perfect," he said. "I'm sure there are times I will wish for *her* that life was easier, but I suppose Sarah will be a constant reminder of who I really am, and what I'm meant to fight for." He hesitated. "I'm taking Sarah where I believe she will be safest, but I will not stop fighting for equality. I might have to do it differently, but I will fight—for our people, and for my own daughter, so that she has a better life."

"Your fight for equality won't be so different in Philadelphia," Rose replied, feeling prouder of her brother in this moment than she had ever felt. "People in the North are as determined to keep blacks in their place as people in the South are. It may look a little different, but it is still much the same. We'll be fighting for equality, all over this country, for a very long time."

Rose leaned into her brother as they both fell silent. Neither of them knew how long it would be before they had this opportunity again. They had spoken enough words. Now it was time to be silent, and let the plantation wrap them in its embrace.

Chapter Four

November 4, 1868

Amber leapt lightly from the mounting block onto Eclipse's back. Carrie smiled as the big horse looked around, almost as if the little girl's weight did not register enough to let him know she was in the saddle. Only when he was sure she was there, did he bob his head and begin to prance in place. Amber laughed joyfully before she laid a gentle hand on his neck that settled the large stallion instantly. Watching the two of them together never ceased to amaze Carrie.

Amber turned to look at her. "How many folks are going to be here tonight?" she demanded.

Carrie smiled. "I'm not certain, but it will be a lot," she promised. "Lillian has told everyone at the school, I've told everyone who has come through the clinic, and Simon and June are bringing most of the people from Blackwell Plantation."

Amber stared at her. "That's about as many people as who were here for the Harvest Festival," she said in awe. "Just for a meteor shower?"

"It's been two years since so many people came," Carrie remembered with a smile. "The Leonid Meteor shower happens every November, but it's not always spectacular. It's rather unusual for them to project another large one so soon, but Felicia's letters are very convincing. Astronomers are sure it is going to be quite a display." She glanced up at the sky, glad to see it was clear. Clouds could roll in during the day, but she hoped the weather would hold. "No one who was here that night will ever forget what they saw. Those who didn't see it, are eager not to miss it."

"I remember it," Amber said. "I thought for sure those shooting stars were going to land right on top of all of us that night. I hid my face in Daddy's shoulder during some of it," she admitted sheepishly. "I'm older now, though. I don't want to miss any of it!" A wistful look crossed her face. "Do you think Robert can see it from heaven?"

Carrie's insides tightened as she remembered the wonder of sharing that night with Robert, but a deep breath relaxed her. "It probably isn't as spectacular when you're looking down on it," she said, "but I still bet it's a great view. I like the idea of him watching it with us, don't you?"

"Yes," Amber agreed, "but I wish he was right here, instead."

"Me, too." Carrie urged Granite forward, knowing that a long ride would make them both feel better. "Let's go see what we can discover today." She was keeping her promise to Granite to go for a long ride every day. Lillian had given her students the day off from school because they would be up most of the night watching the meteor shower, so Amber was joining her.

The knots in her stomach, caused by the memories of the night with Robert watching the Leonid Meteor Shower, began to unravel as they cantered along the road. The brilliant fall foliage was being overtaken by the grayness of the winter woods, but there were still enough leaves clinging to the trees to offer a reminder of how beautiful October had been.

When they finally pulled their horses down to a walk, Carrie was at peace.

"Are you ever jealous of Rose?" Amber asked.

Carrie was surprised by the question, but she suspected Amber was leading up to something. "I don't think so," she answered honestly. "Why are you asking?"

Amber shook her head. "Is there anyone you're jealous of?"

Carrie thought about the question carefully. "There were a few girls at medical school that I guess I was jealous of," she admitted. "They seemed to understand things faster than I did, and they didn't have to study as hard as I had to."

Amber stared at her. "Did you resent them for it?"

Carrie wondered who Amber was referring to, but wanted the little girl to communicate it in her own time. "I suppose there were moments I resented it, but I realized it wasn't their fault they were smarter than me. It just meant I had to work harder, so I did." Her thoughts went to her former housemate, Alice Humphries—the petite blonde had a mind like a steel trap—but the reminder of her medical school classmate made her sad. She hated that her three housemates, Alice, Elizabeth, and Florence, had all ended their friendship when Carrie and Janie decided to pursue homeopathy.

"Didn't you get tired of having to work harder?" Amber demanded.

Carrie shrugged. "I wanted to be a doctor, so I did what I had to do," she said gently. "It would have been a waste of energy wishing it were different. In the end, I knew as much as they did." Amber turned her head away, obviously thinking about what she had said. Carrie sat quietly, wondering if Amber would tell her what had prompted all the questions.

"Felicia is a whole lot smarter than I am," Amber finally blurted.

Carrie nodded. "She's very smart," she agreed. She waited a moment and then added, "Is that hard for you?"

"Sometimes," Amber admitted. She opened her mouth to say more, but shut it again and tightened her lips.

"Do you resent it?" Carrie questioned gently, free to press harder now that Amber had revealed what she was struggling with.

"I suppose," Amber said with a ragged sigh. "I try not to, because I love Felicia, but I sure wish things came to me as easy as they come to her."

"I understand," Carrie replied. "She told me the same thing about you when she was here last month."

"What?" Amber stared at her with an expression that made it obvious she didn't believe Carrie.

Carrie nodded. "It's true. Felicia and I were out riding one day, when she saw you racing across a field on Eclipse. She told me she wished she could ride like you, but that she knew she never would be able to because she didn't know how to feel a horse like you do."

"Really?" Amber breathed. "*Felicia* said that?"

"She said that," Carrie assured her.

Amber stared off into the distance, a look of wonder on her face. A question finally sprang into her eyes. "What did you tell her?"

"I told her we all have our own gifts. I told her not everyone has a gift for horses like you do, and not everyone was going to be as smart as she is." She hoped Amber would be able to absorb what she said next. "I told her the only important thing is to be the best *you* that you can be."

Amber sat silently for several more minutes, before she turned back with shining eyes. "Is that what you're doing, Carrie? Now that Robert is gone?"

Carrie managed a light laugh. "I hope I was doing that while Robert was still alive, but yes, that is certainly what I am doing now. I pray every single day that I will be the best me that I can be."

Amber smiled brightly. "That's what I'm going to do, too," she said. Then she shot Carrie a mischievous smile. "Like right now when Eclipse and I beat you down to the end of the road." The little girl leaned forward, releasing Eclipse into a full gallop, her whoop of joy sounding loudly in the cold air.

Carrie laughed, gave Granite his head, and released herself to the joy of the race. She knew Eclipse had too much of a head start for them to catch up, and that Granite would be frustrated to be bested in a race when he used to win every competition on the plantation, but she still reveled in the run. Bright sunlight streamed down on them, melting away the remnants of the night's frost, but there was still enough to cause the surrounding grasses to dance with shining diamonds.

Bright red cardinals flitted through the branches as a large gaggle of geese flew in a perfect V formation over her head.

It was pure joy just to be alive.

*****

Susan was grooming a new mare in the barn when Carrie and Amber returned. They had walked the last mile to give their horses time to cool down. They quickly untacked them, brushed them, and turned them into their stalls to eat, before Amber dashed away to work with the colts and fillies she was tasked with training.

"Have time to talk?" Susan asked.

"Certainly," Carrie replied.

"I know you're starving," Susan teased. "I went over to the house while you and Amber were gone. There is a plate of ham biscuits waiting for you in the office."

"I love you," Carrie said fervently as she walked into the office to claim the plate. When she had polished off two biscuits, along with the lukewarm tea that still managed to taste delightful, she was ready for conversation. "What do you want to talk about?"

As usual, Susan was direct and to the point. "My offer to buy Cromwell Stables."

Carrie tensed, knowing the conversation would come up at some point, but since she hadn't yet made a decision, she had hoped it wouldn't happen for a while. She forced herself to relax. Susan was a friend. Perhaps talking about it would help her clarify her thoughts.

"It's all right if you don't want to do it," Susan said, "but I would like to know what you are thinking."

Carrie felt a flash of alarm. "Why? Are you leaving?" She couldn't imagine what she would do if Susan were not available to run the stables. Miles, Clint, and Amber were great at their jobs, but Miles was getting old, and Susan brought both experience and valuable connections. She had already more than proven her worth. Without her running the stables, Carrie's options would disappear almost completely. She couldn't imagine being able to leave for Philadelphia to open the clinic if she were also solely responsible for the stables.

Susan hesitated. "I don't know what I'm going to do," she said honestly. "I suppose I always imagined myself married by this age, but I don't see my marital status changing any time soon. Perhaps, as Annie suggested, I'm too tough to attract a man."

Carrie snorted. "That's nonsense. You are one of the most beautiful women I know. You are strong, independent, intelligent, and great fun to be around." Her eyes darkened. "The reality is that hundreds of thousands of eligible bachelors were wiped out during the war. There simply aren't enough men for all the single women in this country."

Susan shrugged, trying to look nonchalant, but failed. "Whatever the reason, I am convinced I need to plan for my future as if I'm going to be a single woman."

Carrie nodded thoughtfully. "I suppose you're right."

"It's probably for the best, anyway," Susan added.

"Oh?"

"Cromwell Stables is becoming very successful," Susan replied. "If I were to gain part ownership, I would certainly not want to risk that in a marriage." Her eyes flashed. "I would also not want to risk the money I earn here by giving control of it to a man, no matter how much I love him. The marriage laws in this country should make any intelligent woman reconsider her willingness to give up control of her life." She propped her feet up on the desk, crossing them at the ankles. "The profit percentage you give me is generous. If I keep working hard and save it, I will someday be able to start a stable of my own."

Carrie listened quietly. She knew that legally Robert could have bequeathed his share of Cromwell Stables to anyone he wanted. She could have ended up sharing the stable on her own family's plantation with a complete stranger. The marriage laws were ludicrous, but they were the law. The fact that Robert had written a will that gave her complete ownership was rare. She also knew it was a testament to her father's influence on Robert after his own marriage to his businesswoman wife. The list of things Carrie had to be grateful to Abby for was quite lengthy.

"That's one of the reasons for my hesitation," Carrie admitted.

"The fact that I might get married, and you could possibly lose ownership control of the stables?" Susan asked.

"Yes. Sometimes I long for the days when I was ignorant to how unfair the law is to women, but now that I know, it is only wise to let it mandate my decisions."

"I agree," Susan said. "I understand it is not a risk you want to take." Her eyes were both sympathetic and sad.

Carrie's thoughts whirled. She understood her reasoning, but she also understood Susan's reasoning. It only made sense that a single woman would want to position herself for financial independence. She stared off into space as the seed of an idea began to grow in her mind. She spun it, working to examine it from all angles to determine if she could spot any flaws.

The occasional snort or whinny were the only sounds that broke the silence as dust motes danced in the sunlight streaming through the window.

Carrie finally turned to Susan. "Is it ownership that is the most important to you, or is it the potential for half the income, and the surety that you would be able to continue with the stables if something were to happen to me?"

Susan sucked in her breath. Her eyes widened as she caught the meaning of Carrie's words. Still, a long silence stretched out as she considered the question. "The guarantee of income for my labor, and security for the future is what matters the most," she confirmed when she spoke. "I won't deny ownership is important to me, but not as important as the other two. Do you have something in mind?"

"I do," Carrie answered. "I haven't been sure what I thought of you buying the stables because I don't want to give up ownership—especially since Robert started the stables here on my family's plantation. I realize, however, that I don't know what my plans are for the future. I can see what the next six to eight months will be like, but beyond that is nothing but a murky shadow. I might never return to the plantation to live, but it's also a possibility that I *will* return. I also believe I would be foolish to give up the income from the horses. I realize you would buy the stables, but I believe it makes more financial sense to have it as a steady source of income for the rest of my life."

She took a deep breath, feeling better as her thoughts came together into what she believed was a solid plan. "With that in mind, I would like to propose that the two of us split the profits from the stables equally. Up to this point I have accepted all the risk and paid all the expenses. We would share those moving forward, but would split the profits between us. You will still manage all aspects of the stables, but when I'm here I will help. I will draw up a contract detailing our agreement. I will also draw up a will that makes you one hundred percent owner if I should die, as long as you draw up a will that gives the stables back to my family if we still own the plantation at the time of your death. It would never be acceptable for a stranger to have control of Cromwell Plantation property." Carrie sat back, satisfied she had spoken her thoughts clearly. "What do you think?"

Susan was looking at her with something akin to awe. "I think I had no idea you are such a savvy business woman."

Carrie laughed. "I didn't either," she confessed. "I suppose listening to all the conversations between my father and Abby, and then everything Abby taught me when Robert died, must have rubbed off more than I knew." She took a sip of tea that was now cool. "So, what do you think?"

Susan stared out the window for several minutes. They could hear Amber laughing in the distance. The rumble of wagon wheels revealed that Simon, June, and their children were arriving early, as promised, to spend the afternoon before the Leonid Meteor Shower gathering.

Carrie was content to wait. She knew Susan had a big decision to make. She opened her mouth to tell her friend she could take time to think about it, but Susan's words stopped her.

"What happens if you get married?"

"Good question," Carrie answered. "Abby was concerned about the same thing when she married my father. She loved him deeply, but she didn't want to be unwise." Susan was listening closely. "My father signed a document saying that all the assets Abby came into the marriage with would always be hers alone. Of course, the factories they have developed since then are split equally."

"You would do the same thing?" Susan asked keenly.

"I would," Carrie promised. "I will include that in the contract." She paused. "And if you marry?" She was glad they were both laying all their cards on the table. She was also surprised how much she was enjoying the negotiation. Perhaps she was more of a businesswoman than she realized.

Susan sighed. "I find that highly unlikely, but I will do the same thing. Make sure to include my commitment to it in the contract."

Carrie nodded, sure they had reached a good agreement.

Susan suddenly laughed. "Did you ever think, in your wildest dreams, that you would be negotiating business terms like a man?"

Carrie grinned, but her answer was serious. "I prefer to think I am negotiating business terms like a *woman,*" she retorted. "Abby made sure I learned how to negotiate after Robert died. I've learned from her that a woman can be as effective as any man when it comes to business."

"I've heard," Susan said with a smile. "Anthony told me he had no idea what was happening the day he met you until it was almost over, and he had paid more for a group of horses than he ever had before."

"They were worth it," Carrie said smugly.

"He agrees," Susan replied, thick admiration in her voice. "He got wonderful prices for this year's crop of foals, as well." She cocked her head. "If I agree to this arrangement, will you teach me everything you know?"

"Definitely," Carrie answered. "It only makes sense if we are going to split the profits that I would want you to make as much money as possible." She smiled. "It's time women learned what they are capable of. Most men may not think we can do anything they can, and the laws of our country may not recognize women's equality, but there are certainly things we can do to protect ourselves while we fight for our rights."

Susan straightened her shoulders. "Then, yes, I accept your offer." A brilliant smile made her face glow. "It will be an honor to be your partner," she said. She reached out her hand to seal the deal.

Carrie shook her hand firmly, and then leapt up to pull Susan into a hug. "I'm so glad! I believe this is the perfect answer for both of us." She pulled back, stretched, and nodded her head toward the house. "Simon and June are here. Let's go have some lunch. I can't wait to cuddle with Ella Pearl."

"Absolutely!" Susan replied. "I never knew doing business could make you so hungry."

Laughing and talking, the two business partners, and friends, made their way toward the house.

*****

Carrie was delighted when she walked into the house and discovered Louisa and Perry had also arrived early. Nathan and Little Simon were just disappearing out the back door, their clenched fists full of Annie's oatmeal cookies.

"Hello, you two!" Carrie called cheerfully. The two boys both grinned, raised a fist, and ran down the stairs toward the wooden swing hanging from the tall oak that sheltered the back yard. She never failed to be thrilled by the contrast of Simon's black curls and Nathan's blond locks. The two boys were the best of friends. Seeing them together always gave her hope for the future. She watched them scamper toward the swing, and then twirled toward June. "Give me that little girl," she demanded.

June smiled as she handed over her five-month-old daughter. "I'm more than happy to share. She just had her lunch, so she should be content. I predict she will be asleep soon."

Carrie gazed tenderly into Ella Pearl's dark eyes. "You are so beautiful," she crooned. She'd only had a few hours with the little girl when June and Simon had visited to tell Moses and Rose good-bye. "I was right," she announced. "Ella Pearl is the most beautiful baby on the planet."

"You're only saying that because Rose is already gone," June retorted, her eyes softening as she reached out to touch her daughter's soft curls. "Of course, you also happen to be right."

Carrie nodded. "I know I'm right. And, besides, Hope is almost three now. She isn't a baby anymore."

"And what about my babies upstairs?"

Carrie whirled when Marietta's indignant voice broke into the conversation. "That doesn't change anything," she assured her. "The twins are still *infants*. They aren't old enough to count as babies yet, so they are the two most beautiful infants on the planet."

Marietta rolled her eyes. "Do you always have an answer for everything?"

"Only when I'm right," Carrie said confidently. She grinned brightly as she lifted Ella Pearl to face level. "I'm right, little girl. You are the most beautiful baby on the planet, but the twins are going to be competition soon. Enjoy your time in the winner's circle for as long as you have it."

Everyone in the room laughed as Ella Pearl gave her a wide smile and waved her arms in delight.

Annie appeared from the dining room. "Quit your cooing at my grandbaby and get yourselves in here to eat. Once you done polished off my chicken and sausage gumbo with cornbread, there be lots of work to get ready for them folks coming tonight."

Simon patted his stomach. "I'll do anything you want if you're gonna fill my stomach with your gumbo," he promised. He looked at Perry and Louisa. "You haven't eaten until you've had Annie's gumbo."

Louisa sidled closer to Annie. "Will you teach me how to make it if I work hard this afternoon?" she pleaded.

Annie snorted. "You can quit battin' them eyelashes at me, Miss Louisa. And why you got to ask me? You mean Felicia ain't given you no recipe from a book yet?"

Carrie laughed at Louisa's confused look. "Ignore her," she suggested. "She's all bent out of shape because her oldest granddaughter is teaching Janie and Marietta how to cook from a book."

"Pure nonsense," Annie grumbled. "That's enough squawking for now, anyway. Y'all best get in there and eat 'fore it gets cold." She slid next to Louisa and favored her with a warm smile. "Iffen you be wantin' to learn how to make gumbo the right way, you come on out to my kitchen later. I'll teach you the things ain't no book ever gonna teach you."

"Thank you!" Louisa said fervently.

Carrie shook her head as she followed everyone into the dining room. She wasn't sure she would ever get used to the idea that Louisa was cooking. A life of pampered living on her family's plantation hadn't prepared the protected Louisa Blackwell for what she was doing now. Of course, *her* life as a pampered plantation daughter hadn't exactly prepared her for the reality of her life, either. Watching Louisa laugh and talk with Simon and June was all the evidence she needed that people could change.

"How are things on Blackwell?" Susan asked after she had dished up a large bowl of gumbo and piled cornbread on her plate. She laughed when Louisa stared at the amount of food she was eating. "Working hard in a barn has its benefits," she said. "I can eat anything I want!"

"Things are going really well," Perry informed her. "We had a great harvest this year, and we put another hundred acres into production." He smiled at Simon.

"Simon is an excellent manager, and he teaches me more every day."

"No trouble from the vigilantes?" Carrie asked keenly.

"No trouble," Perry assured her.

Carrie stared at him. There was something about his voice that was lacking in confidence. "Are you sure?" she pressed. She knew that right this minute there was a contingent of Cromwell hands near the front gate, and that there were some stationed in the woods near the house. She was glad Moses insisted on no one letting their guard down ever again. There had been enough death. She pushed aside the vision of Robert's laughing eyes as she focused on Perry.

Perry shrugged, his blue eyes shifting beneath his thatch of blond hair.

Carrie felt a twinge of alarm. It was obvious he was hiding something.

Louisa stiffened in the seat next to her husband. Still petite and beautiful, she pushed back a strand of blond hair and put a hand on her husband's arm. "Perry, what is it?" Her voice was calm, but her eyes flashed with anxiety.

"It's nothing," Perry insisted as he exchanged a glance with Simon.

"It's *something*," Louisa insisted. "What is it?"

A long silence stretched out before Annie broke it. "Ain't you men learned the women in this room ain't helpless? Every one of us be in this here fight together. Ain't nothin' but an insult to not tell the truth if you know there be trouble comin'." Her scowl deepened. "That be my daughter and grandbabies you got livin' on that plantation. They deserve warnin' if somethin' be wrong." She advanced on Perry, her black eyes flashing. "What aren't you sayin', Mr. Perry?"

Perry sighed and raised his hands in defeat. "I'm really not hiding anything," he insisted. "At least not anything concrete." He looked at Simon again. "We've got suspicions, but no real proof."

"Suspicions of what?" Louisa demanded. "We need to know."

Perry fidgeted. "Some of the men have been hearing things," he said vaguely.

"What kinds of things?" Louisa asked with frustration when another long silence stretched out.

Carrie's inner alarm was going off. "You have to tell us," she said urgently. "If trouble is being planned, it could just as easily come to Cromwell."

"That's not likely," Perry replied. "The vigilantes know how well guarded the plantation is, and they've already lost enough of their men to failed attempts here." He sighed heavily, and then continued. "Some of the men have received reports from other plantations that the vigilantes are planning trouble. They don't know where or when it is going to be, so we really don't have anything to go by. As far as we know, they are only rumors."

Carrie stiffened. "Will there be men at Blackwell to protect it tonight?" She had visions of the plantation left vulnerable while everyone celebrated the meteor shower.

"Yes," Perry said. "Simon and I would never leave it without a guard." He looked apologetically at Louisa. "I'm sorry. I wasn't trying to hide anything from you."

Louisa tossed her head, looking every bit the aristocratic plantation owner's daughter that she was. "Of course you were," she retorted, but her face was soft. "I love you for wanting to protect me, but the best protection you can give Nathan and me is to make sure we are not caught by surprise. Now that I know there is a threat, I will be even more careful." She looked out the window toward the woods.

"There is nothing to worry about here," Carrie promised. "I can guarantee you there are men out there right now who are watching Nathan and Simon on the swing. Nothing will happen to them."

Louisa relaxed and finished eating her Gumbo. Silence fell on the room while all of them ate the succulent meal.

"I was glad to hear Grant was elected president," Perry said when the last piece of cornbread was demolished, leaving nothing but crumbs on the huge platter.

Carrie knew he was trying to change the subject. "It was closer than anyone thought it would be," she replied.

Perry eyed her. "You received a letter from your father?"

"Jeremy rode into Richmond yesterday to take care of a few things," Carrie replied. "He brought back a whole stack of papers so we would know what is going on."

"What did you learn?" Simon asked eagerly.

Jeremy walked in the door just then. He called his greetings, accepted the steaming bowl of gumbo that Annie handed him, and settled down in an empty chair. "The field is ready for tonight," he announced. "Franklin and I, along with some of the other men, built a big bonfire. We put up long tables in the drying barns so we can put the food in there. We even built a bunch of wooden benches and put them around the bonfire so we can keep most of the folks off the ground tonight while they wait for the meteor shower. I know they will all bring blankets, but it's going to be cold tonight. People, at least the adults who will mostly feel the cold, will be more comfortable on the benches."

"Thank you," Marietta said warmly. "I'll watch it from the bedroom window tonight to be near the twins, so I know I'll be toasty," she teased. "As cold as it seems like it will be tonight, I don't think I'll miss being down there."

Jeremy shook his head. "Only twenty-four years old, and already motherhood has softened you," he pronounced sadly.

"I prefer to think it has made me wiser," Marietta said dismissively. "Something you couldn't possibly understand!"

Laughter rang through the room. When silence fell again, Perry leaned forward. "What can you tell us about the election, Jeremy?"

Jeremy scowled. "I can tell you that the KKK and other vigilante groups almost achieved their agenda," he said. "Grant won the Electoral College decisively, but the popular vote was much closer than anyone would have dreamed. Grant carried every state but eight of them, yet he received only fifty-three percent of the popular vote. It's fairly certain that Seymour carried a majority of the nation's white voters. Black voters carried Grant to victory, but Seymour won in Georgia and Louisiana." His face tightened. "Of course, there were entire counties in many Southern states where there were no Black Republican votes registered."

"None?" Simon asked in disbelief. "How is that possible?"

"None," Jeremy confirmed. "They were simply too afraid to go to the polls and vote. They were afraid for themselves, and they were afraid for their families. They've seen what the KKK will do, so they knew the threats weren't idle. It wasn't only Georgia and Louisiana, though. The Republican vote also suffered in Tennessee, northern Alabama and upcountry South Carolina."

"All KKK strongholds," Simon said angrily.

"Grant will support Reconstruction, though," Perry said. "At least he was elected."

"Yes," Jeremy agreed, "but the Republican Party is changing. Seymour might well have been elected if it hadn't been for his running mate, Francis Blair. Blair decided to embark on a speaking campaign that proved to be disastrous. Let me read you something." He stood, walked over to the table in the foyer, and chose one of the newspapers stacked there. He flipped quickly to the page he was looking for. "Whenever he got on the stage, he criticized the Republican Party for..." His voice trailed off as he searched the paper. Finding what he was looking for, he began to read. "'... *for placing the South under the rule of a semi-barbarous race of blacks who are worshippers of fetishes and unbridled lust.*'"

"More of that nonsense!" Simon growled. "Will it ever end?"

"It gets worse," Jeremy replied. "Blair ranted that racial intermixing would reverse evolution, produce a less advanced species capable of reproducing itself, and destroy the accumulated improvement of the centuries."

"And this is the man who was the Democratic candidate for Vice President?" Susan's voice dripped with disdain and horror.

"I suppose I am grateful for his stupidity and ignorance," Jeremy said wryly. "Northern Capitalists knew what kind of chaos would follow a Democratic victory. Even though many of them supported President Johnson in the past, they now endorsed Grant. President Grant's election guarantees Reconstruction will continue, but there is going to be a big change in the Republican leadership that directs it." His voice was heavy. "I'm afraid that what we have suspected is going to be true. There are politicians taking power who believe the struggle over black rights must give way to economic concerns."

"It's not all bad news, though," Carrie insisted. "Now that Reconstruction will continue, there are Republican governments in place in each state that will fight for change. We have to give them a chance to make things different. Make them better." She wasn't sure she believed her own words, but she was also not willing to give up hope. Against all odds, the slaves had been freed, and black men could now vote. That reality had assured Grant's election. It didn't matter that it had been uncomfortably close. He had won. His election gave the country more time to try to make things right.

Heads nodded around the table, but their faces reflected the same doubt Carrie felt. She glanced out the window, knowing that the biggest source of her discontent was caused not by the election, but by the earlier conversation. How long would people in the South have to wonder when the next round of violence would begin?

Chapter Five

"Carrie!" Amber yelled. "Look how many people are here!"

Carrie grinned and waved, welcoming people as they piled from wagons and dismounted from horseback. The sun had set, but the sky still glowed with the remnants of light. A cloudless horizon promised a clear night. Men guided wagons into place close to the largest drying barn. Laughter rang through the air as baskets of food were unpacked and carried into the barn. She knew that soon the tables would be groaning under copious quantities of food. Lanterns, hung from the rafters, cast a soft glow on smiling, happy faces.

Carrie entered the drying barn and stepped back into the shadows, content to watch for a few minutes. Hordes of children were accompanied by their parents. There were as many white faces as there were black. There had been so much progress made between the school children and their families before she had left for New Mexico, but the easy camaraderie that existed now between the parents was astonishing to her. She knew some white parents had refused to come, but she was also aware their refusal was prompted more by fear of what vigilantes might do, than by hatred.

"It's a miracle, isn't it?"

Carrie turned her head to smile at Lillian, the teacher who had replaced Rose at the school. Rose had already told Carrie what a wonderful job she was doing. "It is," she agreed. "Rose has told me so much about what you are doing. You should be proud."

Lillian shrugged modestly. "Rose carved the trail in the wilderness," she insisted. "All I did was follow it. I write letters to my friends in the North about what life is like down here on the plantation, but I don't think they believe me. I tried to explain it to some friends I recently visited, but I don't believe they have a point of reference for comprehending what is possible."

"It is rather unusual," Carrie concurred. "While I'm grateful for that, it also makes me sad, because it's the way it *should* be all over the South. The fact that it isn't only means the misunderstandings and violence will continue."

Lillian forced a smile. "Now is not the time to focus on that," she said decisively. "Tonight, we are going to view the Leonid Meteor Shower. We'll let the splendor of the heavens soften the reality of life."

Carrie cocked her head. "You have quite a way with words," she observed. "Do you write?"

Lillian shook her head. "I simply believe words are powerful. They should be used carefully."

Carrie opened her mouth to respond, but a loud yell interrupted her.

"*Let the feasting begin!*"

The next hour wiped the tables clean of every morsel of food that had been brought. The sun had long set, but the lanterns had turned the barn into a cozy haven of laughter and talk. Carrie moved from group to group, chatting with old friends, and meeting new families that had arrived while she was in New Mexico.

"We're lighting the fire!"

The crowd surged outside, grabbing blankets from their wagons before they moved over to cluster around the campfire. The adults settled down on wooden benches the men had built, while the children swarmed around, laughing and playing.

When everyone had congregated, Lillian stepped close to the bonfire crackling behind her and raised her hand for silence. It took only moments for the noise to fade away. All attention was turned toward the tall brunette clothed in breeches and a thick, warm coat.

Rose had told her that the Northern teacher disdained dresses, and pretty much anything else that would help her fit into Southern society. Carrie was impressed with her commanding confidence, but she also recognized the soft vulnerability flitting through her eyes. Lillian was a complicated woman who had learned to accept her power, but who was also cautious because she had been hurt. Carrie wondered if she would ever learn her story.

Lillian smiled as she began. "Felicia is not here to tell us about the spectacle you are about to witness tonight, so she asked me if I would do the honor. I am happy to tell you more about the Leonid Meteor Shower. Many of you were here to witness it for yourself two years ago. While November is the month of the year when you'll always see the most meteors, it is unusual for there to be such a grand display so close to the last one. We're lucky to know about it." She looked around the crowd. "How many of you were here for the meteor shower two years ago?"

Carrie watched as more than half the hands in the crowd went up. She was impressed how many of the children raised their hands.

"Then you know exactly what you are going to experience," Lillian said cheerfully. "And how many of you have seen a shooting star before?"

Slightly more hands went up, but it was obvious most of the new people there had never seen one. Carrie smiled. They were in for quite a treat.

"For those of you who were not here, you are about to see hundreds, perhaps thousands, of shooting stars tonight," Lillian announced.

"Them stars up there are going to drop from the sky?" one woman called fearfully.

"No," Lillian assured her. "They are called shooting stars, but they are not really stars. They are actually chunks of rocks that have broken off from a comet. A meteor shower happens when they get close enough to the Earth to be sucked into our atmosphere. They are actually rather fragile so they burn really hot and fast when that happens. What you will see tonight streaking across the sky are those chunks of rocks burning up. The most important thing to understand, though," she said confidently, "is that none of them will reach Earth. They will burn up long before that happens."

Murmurs of relief came from the crowd as they peered toward the sky.

"Now that it's dark," Lillian continued, "we'll begin to see meteors start appearing, but it is the last four hours before dawn when the most will fall." She smiled. "Many of you won't make it that long, but those who do will be sure to never forget it. I intend to watch it until dawn, which means..." She let her voice trail away to build the excitement. "Your children don't have to come to school tomorrow! We'll probably all be sleeping!"

Franklin stepped forward as the children cheered and clapped. "The fire will help keep you warm, and we're also going to light some fires in the drying barn. If you need to go inside to warm up, go ahead." He exchanged a long look with Perry and Jeremy before he continued. "If you decide you want to take your family home, we suggest you go in groups of three or four wagons."

Carrie watched as all the women stiffened and searched the darkness for their children before they peered into the shadows fearfully. She could see their shoulders drawing together as they prepared to face whatever danger might be out there.

"I'm not trying to scare anyone," Franklin said, "but we've already learned it is best to be careful. We have absolutely no reason to think anything will happen tonight, but the last years have taught us to take nothing for granted."

His confident words lessened some of the tension, but Carrie could still feel it vibrating in the air. More importantly, she could feel it vibrating inside her. She knew better than to totally trust her instincts, because Robert's murder had intensified her fears, but she also knew better than to discount what was churning in her gut. She would enjoy the night, but she would not let her guard down. She thought of Marietta alone in the house with the twins, but also knew there was a group of plantation men protecting the house right that minute.

She closed her eyes as a vivid memory of Robert sprang to life in her heart and mind. It had been two years ago in this very clearing. He had promised to stay with her for the whole night, blowing gently into her ear as he promised to keep her warm. They had danced and cheered as the meteors rained from the sky, and then cuddled under their blankets until dawn had come. Pain stole her breath as she looked around at the clusters of families. She had seldom felt so alone. It took no effort to imagine her and Robert huddled under blankets, snuggling Bridget close as their daughter peered up at the sky.

"I saw the Leonid Meteor Shower two years ago."

Carrie almost gasped with relief when a voice broke into her memories. She took a slow breath and turned to look at Chooli. Even in the darkness, she could feel the Navajo woman's excitement radiating through her. She could easily envision her black eyes snapping with the enthusiasm that seemed to infuse everything she did. Ajei, now almost thirteen months old, lay snug against her chest, the little girl's eyes turned toward the sky solemnly.

"At Bosque Redondo," Carrie said gently.

"Yes," Chooli agreed. "My people were so miserable, and so many were dying, but for that one night, it seemed anything was possible. Watching the meteors streak across the sky like rain from heaven was a sign to us." She paused as her mind obviously traveled back to the painful time in the history of her people. "At least, we hoped it was."

"And now your people are home again," Carrie said softly as she thought of the beautiful Navajo homeland that had stolen her heart. It gave her such joy to think of Chooli's family rebuilding their homes in the sacred land of their people. She felt, more than saw, the wistfulness suffuse Chooli's body. "You'll be with them soon," she whispered. "Spring is not that far away, and then you will be on your way home."

"It will take us until the end of next summer to make it home," Chooli reminded her sadly.

"Yes," Carrie agreed, "but when you arrived here, you thought you would never be able to go home again."

There was a brief pause, and then Chooli laughed joyfully. "You are right, Carrie. I'm so excited to go home that I forget that sometimes. Will you keep reminding me?"

"I will," Carrie promised.

"There's one!" someone cried.

"And another one!"

Carrie quickly ran over and laid down on the pile of blankets she had prepared next to Susan and Lillian. She lost herself in the splendor of the heavens as they erupted in a show of fiery brilliance.

*****

"Mama!" Felicia cried as the first meteors streaked across the sky. "It's happening! Do you think everyone at home on the plantation is watching the meteor shower tonight?"

Rose smiled as she looked around at the large group of students and families gathered in a field just outside of the Oberlin campus. "I do," she assured her. "I'm proud of you for making sure everyone here on campus is watching it tonight."

"No one should miss this!" Felicia crowed as more and more white-tailed meteors lit up the sky.

"Look!"

"Here comes another one!"

"I've never seen anything so beautiful!"

Cries erupted from all over the field. Rose smiled as she envisioned the same scene on the plantation. When she looked at Moses, though, her smile faded into concern. There was a broad smile on his face as John and Hope danced around with glee, but the light from the bonfire illuminated the longing in his eyes. She knew he was thinking of the plantation and missing his life there. Her heart ached for him, but they had made a decision as a family to come here. The children were so happy, she loved being a student, and she savored the feeling of safety that she experienced every day.

"Mama! Dance with me!" Felicia yelled.

Rose shoved her thoughts down. Remembering Carrie dancing with Felicia two years earlier, she laughed, grabbed her daughter's hands, and began to twirl around the clearing. She pushed aside any concerns or fears. This was a night to embrace life and joy. It was a night for dancing.

"Me too, Mama! Me too!"

Rose reached down to swoop up little Hope, her heart swelling with gladness that her youngest daughter had never experienced fear. She had been too young to remember the attacks on the plantation. All she knew now was playing with other Oberlin children in the tiny yards surrounding their homes. She found herself wishing fiercely that it would never change.

*****

Carrie was shivering, even under her layer of blankets, but she could not bring herself to leave the display of meteors that had ignited the sky all night long. Just when she thought perhaps she would go inside where it was warm, another spectacular display of brilliant shooting stars, their tails stretching across the night sky, would make her huddle back down, or get up to dance with some of the children in an attempt to warm up.

Many wagonloads of people had disappeared into the darkness, but the knowledge that she could be in her warm bed in minutes kept her where she was.

"I bet my family is watching this," Chooli murmured. Franklin had long ago taken Ajei back to their snug home on the plantation, but she had remained, joining Carrie, Susan, and Lillian beneath the blankets.

"I can imagine how beautiful it is over your homeland," Carrie replied. She thought about the singing and dancing that had erupted from the Navajo when they finally reached home after four years of exile in the Bosque Redondo Internment Camp. It was easy to think of them celebrating the wonder of nature tonight.

"Carrie..."

Carrie leaned closer to Chooli, alerted by something in her voice. "What is it?" she asked.

Chooli glanced around before she spoke, making sure there were no children to overhear her. Susan and Lillian were still in the clearing, but both of them had fallen asleep a short while before. "Do you feel anything?" Chooli finally whispered.

Carrie sighed. "I was hoping it was just my imagination," she whispered back. "What do you feel?" Spending so many months with the Navajo had taught her they had a connection with things that most people did not. She didn't know how to explain it; she just knew it was real.

Chooli looked sad. "Something bad is happening tonight. I can feel a darkness that I haven't felt in a long time."

Carrie shuddered, and then admitted, "I've felt the same thing." She peered around, wondering if it was time to go into the house. In spite of the men on guard, she knew there could still be danger.

"I don't believe it is here," Chooli said quietly, "but there is danger for people we love." Her voice grew firmer. "We must be ready to help them."

Suddenly, danger or no danger, Carrie longed for the warmth and safety of her home. "Let's go get something to eat at the house," she said, urgency tightening her voice. "I believe you when you say we're safe, but I'm ready to be warm, and the sun is not far from rising." When she looked toward the horizon, she saw the black beginning to turn a dark blue, heralding the beginning of a new day. "Please come with me."

Chooli nodded quickly. "Yes. I will come. It is good for people to be together when there is trouble. Franklin and Ajei will still be sleeping."

Carrie reached over to shake Susan and Lillian awake. Determined not to alarm them, she kept her voice light. "Since you can't see meteors with your eyes closed, I suggest we all go inside where it's warm for coffee and biscuits. Annie promised she would be up early to feed those of us who stayed up all night."

Susan and Lillian yawned and stretched their arms, then stood to roll up their blankets.

"Hot coffee and Annie's biscuits slathered with butter are an improvement over cold, hard ground," Susan said in a sleep-fogged voice. "The meteors were amazing, but I'm definitely ready for something to eat."

Lantern light glowing from the kitchen, along with smoke pouring from the kitchen chimney, told Carrie that Annie had kept her promise. Yet, she couldn't help scouring the woods for movement as the four women walked quickly up the road toward the house.

"What's wrong?" Susan asked sharply.

Carrie's eyes widened. "What are you talking about?"

"Oh, don't even try to pretend," Susan scolded. "You're as nervous as a pig in a bacon factory." She stared toward the woods. "What's going on?"

Carrie shook her head. "I don't know," she replied honestly. "I have a feeling there has been trouble somewhere tonight. I'm just being careful."

Susan stared at her, and then swung her gaze toward Chooli. "Do you feel it, too?"

Chooli nodded silently.

No one said anything else, but all four of them walked faster. They were climbing the stairs to the house when the sound of pounding hooves froze them in place. They turned toward the drive, waiting to discover what the night had brought to their door.

Jeremy and Annie, both alerted by the noise, had joined them on the stairs when the lone rider galloped into view. Carrie knew Jeremy, fully-clothed and wide awake, must have been expecting trouble.

"We need help at Blackwell Plantation!"

Carrie started down the stairs toward the man who slid to a stop in front of the house. She recognized him as one of the workers at Blackwell who had been in the clearing tonight with his family. Despite the frigid temperatures, his horse was sweating and blowing hard. They must have run the entire distance.

Jeremy beat her to him. "What's happened, Abel?"

"The vigilantes," Abel growled. "They attacked Blackwell while we was all over here. There was too many of them for the guards to hold off." He sucked in his breath before he continued, his narrow face grim with anger and frustration. "They shot three of our men, and set fire to the plantation house. That was after they set fire to the barns. We got all the horses out, but we couldn't save the barns."

"No!" Carrie gasped, her thoughts flying to Louisa and Perry. "Are the men alive?"

"They be alive," Abel replied in a thick voice, "but they ain't doing real good. Mr. Appleton done sent me to get you, Mrs. Borden."

"Are Perry and Louisa all right?" Carrie asked anxiously. "And Nathan?"

"They all be fine," Abel assured her. "Them coward vigilantes done come and gone before any of us got back to the plantation. They done know we was gonna be gone."

"And the house?" Jeremy snapped.

"There be damage," Abel reported, "but there was enough men to put the fire out before it destroyed too much. The barns burned because they be saving the house. They shot a few of them vigilantes, but they all got away."

Annie had disappeared into the house while they were talking. Now she reappeared with Carrie's medical bag, a pile of fresh blankets, a large sack, and a tray full of coffee. "You's got to drink some of this here coffee, Miss Carrie. After being up all night, you's gonna need it."

Jeremy took control. "Susan, take Abel's horse to the barn to cool it off and give it feed." He turned to Abel. "You can ride a Cromwell horse back." He looked at Carrie. "I'm assuming you'll ride Granite." He waited for her confirmation, and then continued. "A group of Cromwell men will ride back with you. I'll be behind you with a wagon. If we need to bring any of the men back to the clinic, we'll be ready."

Carrie barely listened to him finish before she raced toward the barn.

Miles, alerted to the danger by all the noise, walked out with Granite, along with another gelding. Both were tacked and ready to go, saddlebags attached to both saddles.

Carrie gave Miles a brief thanks, and then dashed into the office to change into her warmest breeches and add a thick sweater beneath her coat. There would be no blankets to huddle under to cut the chill of the frosty morning, and it would be best if anyone spotting them on the road thought she was a man. She pulled on a thicker pair of leather gloves and crammed a warmer hat down on her head.

When she ran back outside, Miles handed her a pistol and slid a rifle into her saddle scabbard. Carrie shuddered, but accepted them. She couldn't help the three men who had been shot if she couldn't reach them. She slid the pistol in her waistband and sighed with relief when a contingent of ten Cromwell men emerged from the woods and rode up beside her, their faces set and angry.

Carrie turned to Susan. "Please make sure there are dozens of blankets and pillows in the wagon that Jeremy brings. I suspect I'll be bringing all three men back to the clinic. I want them to be as comfortable as possible." Her mind raced as she thought about what she would find on Blackwell. She took comfort from the fact June would be there, but she found herself longing for Polly, and praying the men would live long enough for her to help them.

Jeremy, as if summoned by her thoughts, appeared at her side. "I've sent one of the men for Polly. I'll bring her in the wagon."

"Thank you!" Carrie replied fervently.

Annie stepped up to her, handing her an additional sack. "I'll have another one for Polly, but here be the onions and honey I know you's gonna be wantin'."

Carrie kissed her warmly on the cheek. "Thank you, Annie." She stuffed her saddlebags full, gulping down the hot coffee as she watched Abel polish off several of Annie's ham biscuits. The man must be exhausted, but his eyes were bright with determination. She knew the men who had been shot, and possibly killed, were his friends.

"I'm ready," Carrie announced, as she swung onto Granite's back. Abel nodded, leapt into his saddle, and took off at a rapid canter on Rocky, his new mount. Granite surged forward, falling into place beside him as the Cromwell men took positions behind and beside them. It was going to be a long day for everyone.

As they pounded down the road, flocks of quail exploded from the surrounding fields. Crows and ravens added their raucous calls, while sparrows tried to lend a song to the tense morning.

Carrie tried to focus on the beautiful sunrise, but her thoughts would not settle. She knew the three men who had been shot were already at a distinct disadvantage for survival because of the amount of time they were waiting for care. She prayed June was prepared with a supply of shock remedy. She had taught everyone about it before she left for New Mexico, but trauma could cause even the most capable person to forget what they knew. She wondered who had been shot, but pushed it out of her mind. She would deal with whatever she found when she got there.

No one talked as they rode. Carrie was aware every man was scanning the road and the woods for concealed danger. The vigilantes, certain help would be on the way to Blackwell Plantation, could well be lying in wait. Would they attack Cromwell Plantation while they were away? Franklin would have every man standing guard. Carrie tried to ease her worries by reminding herself the vigilantes were sure to know that. Abel had reported that some of the vigilantes had been shot, too. That would probably make the rest hole up for a while.

Puffs of white from their breath hung in the frosty air behind them as they all rode hard. If it had been for another reason, Carrie would have enjoyed the ride. The rising sun glinted off the colorful remnants of leaves, and the thick layer of frost coated everything in sight. It didn't seem possible that less than two hours ago, she had been watching meteors streak across an inky, peaceful sky. How swiftly life could change.

Gradually, memories overcame Carrie's best efforts to hold them at bay. It was impossible not to think about her last wild ride on Granite as she had rushed home, against all advice, to be with Robert as he lay dying. The pounding hooves formed a refrain in her mind. *Death is waiting... Death is waiting...*

Carrie scowled and shook off her thoughts. She refused to believe she couldn't help. She couldn't, however, keep the images from swarming her mind. Robert's white face...his anguished eyes as he told her good-bye...the ripping pain as she went into labor... the reality she had lost both Robert and Bridget. Most of the time she could keep the memories at bay, but the frantic dash to reach the injured men triggered everything she had been able to control for the last few months. Tears blurred her eyes, but she blinked hard and swallowed them. She refused to let her emotions diminish her ability to help.

Carrie was relieved when she saw Abel raise his hand and signal them to stop after an hour of riding. She dismounted quickly, glad to stretch her legs as she led Granite to the stream so he could drink. He stuck his muzzle into the bubbling stream gratefully. Carrie swallowed some of the icy cold water in her canteen, and then hurriedly ate a ham biscuit. Less than five minutes later, they were all back in the saddle, cantering down the road again.

*****

Simon was waiting just inside the gates to Blackwell Plantation when they arrived two hours later.

Carrie took one look at his grim face and felt her heart sink, but she still needed to know. "How bad is it?" she asked, as Simon fell into place beside her.

"All three of the men took a shot to their abdomen. June has been treating them for shock, but that's all she knows how to do."

Carrie almost groaned with relief. "It was the very best thing she could do," she assured Simon. "You and I both know soldiers survived for much longer on the battlefield with gunshot wounds if they were treated for shock."

Simon grunted. "All these men took bullets in the war, but that doesn't make getting shot any easier."

"No," Carrie agreed. She was calm now that she had arrived and had a task before her. "Where are they?"

"Louisa insisted we bring them into the house."

Carrie glanced at him. "It's not too damaged? Abel told us about the fire."

"Only a portion of the East Wing caught fire," Simon informed her. "My men got it out before it went any further. The part we had rebuilt from the fire five years ago wasn't touched."

"Thank God..." Carrie closed her eyes for a moment, trying to recall what was in the East Wing of Blackwell Plantation. Her eyes flew open when she remembered it was the large room where all the Blackwell Balls had taken place. She blinked away the vision of dancing with Robert the day after they had met. Now was not the time to let memories distract her. "Anyone hurt besides the three men who were shot?" The look on Simon's face said he guessed what she was struggling with, but he kept his focus on her question.

"No." Anger flashed in Simon's eyes. "The men are blaming themselves that the house was burned, but they were no match for the vigilantes."

"How many?" Carrie asked evenly, knowing conversation would keep her thoughts clear.

"About forty-five," Simon snapped.

Carrie stiffened with surprise. "Forty-five men?" she echoed.

Simon nodded grimly. "They were serious."

"Your men must have been more serious," Carrie said in astonishment. "How in the world did just ten men stop forty-five?"

Simon shrugged. "They had the element of surprise on their side. The vigilantes were stupid enough to think Blackwell would be left completely unprotected. I suspect they had no idea how many men were actually shooting at them from the woods. The woods also gave my men protection. The vigilantes were out in the open with no cover. They managed to shoot three of ours, but my men figure they got a bullet into at least a dozen of the vigilantes. No one came off their horse, but they lost their appetite for a fight pretty quick. The house was burning when they took off out of here like scared rabbits, but my men got it out right fast. Thank goodness the well is close to the East Wing. The barns weren't so lucky. There weren't enough of my men to put out the fire in the barns, and also save the house."

They reached the house just as Simon finished the story. Carrie was out of the saddle the moment they stopped.

June and Louisa appeared on the porch, their hair in disarray and their eyes fatigued. "This way!" Louisa called.

"Go," Simon urged. "I'll be right behind you with your bag."

Carrie raced up the stairs. She gripped Louisa and June's hands, but no words were spoken as they led her toward a bedroom on the lower level.

"In here," Louisa said, pain dripping from her words.

Carrie, knowing it would be bad, took a deep breath before she entered the room. She glanced at the men, recognized they were all unconscious, and then turned to June. "Talk to me," she commanded.

"All three were shot in the abdomen," June replied. "The gunshot wounds are bad," she said grimly. "I believe I stopped the bleeding, and I gave all of them the shock remedy. Their feet are elevated."

Carrie nodded and smiled slightly. "You did the right things," she assured June. It had taken only a brief look to discern that all three of the men had fevers, which meant infection had already taken hold. She approached the first man, and carefully pulled the bandage away from his wound. Her lips tightened as she examined the large hole in his stomach. The surrounding edges were already swollen and red. It was impossible to tell if any more organs had been damaged. "How long ago was he shot?"

"Abel says the attack happened around one in the morning," June answered. "We got here around three o'clock. They were already in shock, but their breathing stabilized pretty quick after we gave them that concoction of water, honey, apple cider vinegar, and cayenne pepper." She shook her head. "It was like watching a miracle, seeing how fast it helped them."

Carrie grimaced. She was glad the shock had been reversed, but almost eight hours had passed. Still, she had seen much worse cases coming in from the battlefield. She quickly examined the other two men, and then turned to her friends. "All the bullets will have to be removed," she said, "but I can't do it here. They'll need to come to the clinic."

June sucked in her breath. "Will they make it that long?"

"I can't be positive," Carrie admitted, "but I think their chances are good." She looked at Louisa. "We need to make a poultice of onion and honey to fight the infection that has already set in. I have some in my saddlebag."

"We've already made it," June informed her. "I just wasn't sure if we should pack the wounds before you had a chance to look at the injuries yourself."

Carrie hesitated. She would have preferred the wounds had been packed right away so infection could have been avoided, but there was only one person in the room with true medical experience. June was the reason these men were still alive. "You did great," she said, as she resolved to give more medical education to women in the area. Living in the country meant you needed to know how to take care of your loved ones. "Let's get the wounds packed."

*****

Carrie and June were just finishing applying the onion and honey poultice when Louisa appeared at the door.

"Jeremy is here with the wagon," Louisa reported, her usually bright eyes dull with fatigue.

"You need to get some rest," Carrie urged.

Louisa lifted a brow. "And you?"

Carrie shrugged. "I'll rest once the men are stable. If having you stay awake would help anything, I would ask you to do that, but since it won't, one of us may as well get some sleep," she said lightly.

When Polly appeared at the door, Carrie wanted to cheer. She filled her in quickly, glad Polly would be in the wagon with the men on the way home.

"The wagon be ready, Mrs. Borden. Me and the men are here to do whatever you want."

Carrie smiled at the man who appeared at the door, and then directed the group who carried the patients out to the wagon. Within minutes they were in makeshift beds created from pillows and blankets. She recognized Polly's work. When she was convinced they were as comfortable as possible, she waved Jeremy toward Cromwell.

Jeremy peered at her. "You're up for riding Granite back?"

"I'll be fine," Carrie said. "The men and I will follow along in a few minutes. I'll be there if the patients need anything, but Polly can probably handle whatever comes up." Louisa, ignoring the advice to get some rest, was waiting on the porch when Carrie turned around. "I'm sorry about your house, Louisa," she said softly.

Louisa shrugged. "It's only a house," she said dismissively. "It can be fixed. It's been fixed before. I'm just sorry anyone was hurt protecting it."

Carrie looked at her closely, noticing defeat mixed with the fatigue in her friend's eyes. "How are you?" she pressed.

Louisa stared back, her shoulders slumping for the first time. "I'm tired of living in fear," she admitted, raw pain coating her words and filling her eyes. "I love Blackwell Plantation, and I love the dreams we have, but I don't know if the price is worth it." She shuddered. "What if Perry and Nathan had been here? What if..."

Carrie knew the sentence she hadn't finished. *What if they had been killed like Robert?* "They weren't here," she said gently.

"They could have been," Louisa insisted in a weary voice. "As long as we run this plantation the way it ought to be run—treating our black workers as valued employees—the vigilantes are going to come after us. It's not a matter of *if*, it's a matter of *when*. When will they burn the entire house? When will they hurt or kill Perry or Nathan? What about June...or Simon...or Little Simon." Her voice rose. "I couldn't stand it if anything were to happen to any of them."

Carrie wanted to argue, but she understood her fear all too well. "What would you do if you leave here?" she asked.

"You're not going to tell me I shouldn't feel this way?" Louisa's look was full of suspicious astonishment.

"And if I did?" Carrie asked.

Louisa smiled tightly. "It wouldn't matter."

"Precisely," Carrie replied. "Besides, I know exactly what you're feeling."

Louisa lowered her eyes, a look of shame crossing her face. "I know you do, Carrie. I'm sorry."

"There's no need to apologize. I truly understand."

"How did you handle the fear?" Louisa blurted.

"I'm still dealing with it every day," Carrie admitted. "When things like this happen, it brings back the memories of Robert's murder, and of losing Bridget..."

"How do you stand it?" Louisa murmured, her eyes soft with sympathy.

"I don't know," Carrie replied. She turned her focus to the blackened boards encasing the East Wing. "I suppose I simply refuse to let them win. If I do what I think I should do, which is to leave, then I give them the victory. I believe Robert would tell me to keep fighting for the plantation, and for the right to live my life the way I'm meant to live it. There is going to be hatred in this country for a long time. I can't run away from it, so I guess I've decided to face it where I live."

Louisa listened carefully, but shook her head when Carrie finished. Her gaze remained fixed on the horizon. "I don't know what we will do," she finally said.

"You'll do what's best for you and your family," Carrie responded in a gentle voice. "That's all any of us can do." She started down the steps toward the group of men waiting for her. "I have to get back to Cromwell," she said over her shoulder.

"Be safe," Louisa called.

*****

Annie had lunch waiting for Carrie when she arrived back at the plantation. "I don't have time to eat," Carrie insisted. "I need to change clothes and go to the clinic."

Annie stepped in front of her, blocking her way to the staircase. "You ain't doin' no such thing until you done had something to eat," she said firmly, her eyes shining with compassion.

Carrie knew she must look exhausted. "But—"

"But nothing," Annie said calmly. "Polly be with them men. Another few minutes ain't gonna mean their death, is it?"

Carrie took a deep breath. "I don't believe so," she acknowledged. When she had last checked on the men, shortly before arriving at the plantation, none of them had seemed any worse. Polly had reported all three had regained consciousness for brief moments before passing out again.

"Then you gonna eat," Annie repeated. "I got you some good chicken soup and bread waitin' for you. You can eat it quick, and then go on over to the clinic. You prob'ly take better care of them men anyhow if you ain't starvin' to death."

Carrie reluctantly acknowledged Annie was right, and she couldn't deny how wonderful soup and bread sounded. "You win," she conceded.

"I ain't never had no doubt about that," Annie retorted. "You go eat. I'll have you some hot coffee in just a minute."

Carrie was shoveling in the delicious soup when Marietta appeared in the door, a baby cradled in each arm.

"You look exhausted," Marietta murmured, as she took a seat across from Carrie.

Carrie fastened her eyes on the two adorable infants. "They're beautiful," she said softly. Seeing their innocent faces somehow eased the worst of the pain and exhaustion.

"They are," Marietta agreed.

Carrie continued to gaze at them. "I'm glad you're getting them out of the South."

Marietta nodded. "I am, too. I have hopes that someday the South will be a safe place to raise black and mulatto children, but it's not now. I know there are many people who don't have the option of leaving, and I feel lucky and privileged all at the same time. There are moments I feel guilty that I'm not trapped here, but mostly I feel gratitude."

Carrie cocked her head as she considered Marietta's words. "You have nothing to feel guilty about." She would never forget the slaves who had escaped Cromwell. Miles had told her the stories of the long months hiding and suffering to make it to Canada, where they could be free. "Anyone who truly wants to leave can find a way. There are no options right now that are *easy.* I believe we make our choices, and then we do what it takes to live with our choices the best we can." She reached out to stroke Sarah's black curls, running a finger down her velvety, caramel-colored cheek. "Sarah deserves a chance to live without fear. Her grandma would tell you the same thing," she murmured. She raised her eyes to meet Marietta's. "And you deserve a chance to not constantly worry about what might happen to your children."

Marietta looked back at Carrie for several long moments. "Thank you," she whispered.

Carrie ate the rest of her soup quickly, stuffed several pieces of bread into her pocket, and then stood. "I need to change so I can go dig bullets out of the Blackwell men," she said flatly. "I long for the day when I don't have to do that, but it's not here yet."

*****

Carrie was beyond exhausted when she finished extracting the last bullet. The final one had required extensive probing before she discovered it, and she was grateful her patient was still unconscious. She carefully sewed up the wound, packed it with onion and honey poultice, and wrapped it carefully. Finally, she stepped away. Her eyes were burning, and her lower back ached from hours of being on her feet. She was stunned when she looked outside and realized it was dark. Had it really been just the night before that they had all gathered to watch the meteors. It seemed a lifetime ago.

Polly caught her expression. "You've been working a long time, Carrie," she said softly. "It's time for you to be done. I've got Gabe waiting outside with the wagon to take you home."

"I should stay here with these men tonight," Carrie protested, even while knowing she didn't have the strength to stay awake.

"You're not doing any such thing," Polly insisted. "I'm staying here with them tonight, and I've got some other women coming in to check on them. They'll be fine."

Carrie slowly agreed. "If they wake up, they need to be given the white willow tea you fixed for fever and infection."

"I know," Polly said patiently.

Carrie managed a smile. "I know you know," she replied sheepishly.

"You get on home," Polly scolded. "And I don't want to see you back here until lunch tomorrow." She raised her hand to stop Carrie's protest. "If something happens that we need you for, I'll make sure someone comes to get you. But we both know the only thing gonna help these men is time. We'll give them the white willow tea, and make them drink as much water as we can get in them once they wake up."

Carrie nodded. "I do believe they'll all make it." Her mind traveled back to her patients in Chimborazo Hospital during the war. "I've seen men in much worse condition recover fully."

Polly nodded. "I've sent word to their families. I suspect their wives will be here tomorrow to take over their care."

"That will be the best thing for them," Carrie agreed, stifling a yawn with her hand. She was suddenly not sure she could continue to stand.

"Go," Polly commanded. "Not one more word from you." She glanced at the window, gave a wave, and moved to open the door.

Her husband, Gabe, appeared in the doorway and took Carrie's elbow. "Time to go home, Miss Carrie," he said gently.

Carrie looked at him numbly and gave a short nod. She allowed him to help her to the wagon, climbed into the seat, and then slumped forward, hoping she could stay upright until she got home.

*****

Carrie was grateful for the cozy warmth of her room when she made her way upstairs. Annie had already pulled her covers back.

"I'll have a bath brought up for you in the morning," Annie declared, "but I reckon all you need now is some sleep."

Carrie nodded, not bothering to resist when Annie pulled off her boots, undressed her, and slid a flannel nightgown over her head. She felt like a child, but she was so tired, the ministrations were welcome. "Thank you," she whispered, as she slid between the sheets.

She was asleep before Annie slipped out of the room.

Chapter Six

Marietta, happy to leave the twins in their father's care for a couple hours, pushed into the kitchen. She stopped to breathe in the delicious aromas, welcoming the blast of moist heat that enveloped her. There was something about a warm kitchen on a cold winter day that created so much comfort. She smiled as she envisioned the twins running into her own kitchen in the future. The vision caused her lips to tighten and her eyes to fire with determination.

"What you doin', Miss Marietta?" Annie looked up from rolling out a huge lump of biscuit dough.

"I want to use my time here to learn more about cooking," Marietta said. Then she hesitated. "I've learned a lot from the books Felicia gave me, but you seem to have a secret ingredient." She made her voice pleading, not sure if Annie had forgiven her for baking her first apple pie from a cookbook recipe.

"What about your mama or grandma? They didn't teach you how to cook?"

Marietta shrugged. "They tried," she admitted. "I thought I had better things to do than be in the kitchen, so they finally gave up."

Annie eyed her. "Hmph! So, when did you get this burnin' desire to cook?"

"Ever since the twins were born," Marietta admitted. "I want them to be able to run into my kitchen, smell delicious things, and build memories of the foods cooked there. I've seen how happy your cooking makes people. I want to make my family happy that way. I love teaching, but I can find time for cooking, too – especially now that I won't be teaching again until the twins are older."

Warm understanding replaced the skepticism in Annie's eyes. "It's a gift for your family, sure 'nuff."

"So you'll teach me?" Marietta asked. "*Really* teach me?"

Annie scowled. "What you mean by that?"

Marietta didn't back down. "I've heard what the others say," she replied. "You say you're going to teach them how to make something, but you don't teach them all of it. That way, no one cooks as good as you." She stopped, a little nervous of incurring Annie's wrath, but if she was going to learn how to cook, she wanted to do it the right way.

"That's what they say, do they?"

Marietta, staring into Annie's face, saw a glimmer of humor and appreciation. It gave her courage to press forward. "Yes, ma'am, that's what they say. If I'm going to cook for Jeremy and the twins, I want my food to be as good as yours." She hesitated briefly. "If you're not going to teach me the right way, I'd rather not learn at all."

Annie narrowed her eyes before releasing a deep chuckle. "I reckon you got more guts than any of the other women 'round here." She nodded her head. "I'll teach you to cook, Miss Marietta, but you's gonna do it my way, and there won't be no back talkin' or tellin' me it ought to be done another way. This here be *my* kitchen. I better not be hearin' 'bout nothin' you read in some book." She cocked her head as her black eyes flashed. "You got that?"

Marietta shoved down her desire to dance around the kitchen. She settled for nodding her head, while she smiled so big she thought her face might split. "Yes, ma'am," she said fervently. "I've got it." Then she frowned. "The only thing I haven't got is a lot of time. We're leaving in a few weeks."

Annie frowned. "Don't be remindin' me that you's gonna be takin' them babies away from here," she snapped. She reached behind her, grabbed an apron and tossed it toward Marietta. "The thing you got goin' for you is that this here house gonna be fillin' up with folks for Christmas. They's gonna be a lot of cookin' goin' on. And I got me a lot of cookin' to do today so I's can fill up the wagon headin' over to Blackwell Plantation tomorrow. I ain't no use in buildin' them new barns, but I figure I can send lots of food. You can't be leavin' them babies for very long right now, so you's can help me cook."

Annie looked thoughtful as she walked over to a large closet at the back of the kitchen. "You ain't the first Cromwell woman to have babies to tend while they be cookin'. Most times slave babies were kept down in the quarters while their mamas be in the kitchen, but there be times they's got to be with their mama. When them times happened, I reckon they put them here in this crib while they be workin'." She opened the closet and hauled out a large wooden crib.

Marietta gaped. "I never knew that was in there!"

Annie nodded with satisfaction. "It be just what you need for the twins. They can learn what real cookin' ought to smell like from the very first," she proclaimed.

Marietta laughed and clapped her hands. She donned the apron, twirled with delight, and then turned to Annie. "Jeremy has the twins for a little while. What can I do?"

"You can finish rolling out these biscuits," Annie answered. "I want a round that is a half inch thick," she ordered. "You'll have to pat a little flour on the rolling pin, and maybe a little on the dough. Don't push down real hard...just firm enough to roll it out or you'll end up with tough biscuits."

Marietta reached eagerly for the rolling pin.

Annie pulled it back, her eyes dancing. "Don't you be messin' up these here biscuits," she warned. "I'll come after you with this rollin' pin iffen you do."

"I promise," Marietta said earnestly. "When I roll these out, will I cut them into biscuits?"

"Yep, but you's gonna take one step at a time. Most folks get impatient. They be so eager to make it to the next step, that they mess up what they's doin'. You just roll that out the way I tole you. Then I'll show you how to cut them." She smiled slightly. "When we done with that, we's gonna make more dough. I gots to make a whole lot of biscuits!" She laughed as she handed Marietta the rolling pin.

Marietta took it carefully and turned to the counter. Annie had agreed to teach her how to cook! She was determined to do everything just the way she was told. She hummed happily as she envisioned the twins blasting in through the kitchen door in a few years, their eyes bright with excitement to discover what their mama had cooked. If she could keep her focus there, perhaps she could shove aside her other thoughts.

*****

Carrie savored the deep contentment she felt as she mucked out stalls. She had insisted Miles and Clint go over to Blackwell Plantation a day early, while she promised to help Susan and Amber with all the stable chores. She knew how much there was to be done at Blackwell in order to be ready for the horde of workers that would soon descend to build the barns burned by the vigilantes a month earlier. At least half the Cromwell men had already joined in efforts during the last weeks to scour the woods for rocks to build the massive foundations, and to cut trees to be planed into lumber.

Truth be told, Carrie enjoyed mucking out stalls. She had never been allowed to do any actual work in the stables as a young girl because it didn't fit the image of a proper plantation owner's daughter. She chuckled as she envisioned her mother's expression if she could see Carrie now. The hard work kept her warm in the cold winter air, and she enjoyed the smells of the barn as she listened to the horses munch the grain she had given them earlier. It would be dark soon, and she knew Annie and Marietta were making a hearty beef stew. The very idea of it made her stomach growl.

Granite's whinny alerted her to a presence in the barn a moment before a voice broke into the quiet. "Would you like a little help?"

Carrie narrowed her eyes as she leaned on her pitchfork handle to peer into the nearly dark barn. The lanterns provided enough light for mucking, but little else. "Anthony Wallington?"

"I'm glad you still recognize my voice after all this time."

Carrie shook her head in disbelief as Anthony's tall, slim frame materialized in the gloom. "What are you doing here? Should we have been expecting you?" She was surprised to discover how happy she was to see him.

"No," Anthony assured her. "I got into Richmond a few days ago. Thomas and Abby invited me out for Christmas, but when I discovered what happened on Blackwell Plantation, I decided to come early to help with the barn raising tomorrow."

"How wonderful!" Carrie said. "I don't think it's ever possible to have too many people when it comes to building a barn in a day—especially one the size of what burned on Blackwell."

Anthony stepped closer. "I heard about the three men who were shot. How are they?"

Carrie grinned. "I sent them all home four days ago. A couple of them presented some problems with infection, but they're fine now. They won't be helping tomorrow, but they are well enough to order people around."

"You can never have too much of that," Anthony said, his green eyes dancing with fun under his sandy blond hair.

Carrie appraised him for a moment. "It's good to see you."

"And you, too," Anthony said sincerely, his deep voice filling the barn. "You look wonderful."

Carrie blushed under his warm scrutiny. They had corresponded before her New Mexico trip, but she hadn't seen him since the previous fall. "Thank you," she murmured. Feeling flustered, she stepped back and waved him toward the rack of pitchforks. "I only have two stalls to go, and then we can go inside out of the cold for dinner."

Anthony grabbed one of the pitchforks. "I was in the house long enough to know something smells delicious. Let's get this done."

Silence reigned in the barn again as Carrie attacked the last stall. It disturbed her just how happy she was to see Anthony. She thought back to the day, more than a year ago, when he had offered his friendship, proclaiming that neither of them were ready to consider anything else because their losses were still too fresh. Anthony had lost his wife and small son during childbirth three years earlier. He had been hugely instrumental with helping her put together her trip to New Mexico, but it had all been done from a distance. She worked harder, unwilling to analyze what she was feeling at that moment.

The wind was picking up when Carrie and Anthony left the barn, latched the doors securely, and started toward the house.

"Glad to be home?" Anthony asked.

"Very glad," Carrie said. "There are things I miss about being on the Santa Fe Trail, but I'll admit it's nice to sleep in a warm bed every night."

"I bet," Anthony agreed, with the laugh she had come to associate with him.

"You're here for Christmas?"

"Yes. Abby made it sound so wonderful I had to come see for myself." Anthony glanced at her. "It wasn't hard to convince me, however."

Carrie understood the deeper meaning in his words, but didn't comment on it. "How is business?" she asked, determined to keep the conversation on ground she felt comfortable with.

Anthony went along willingly. "It couldn't be better. I could probably do nothing but sell Cromwell horses and make a good living, but the success I've had with your horses has opened the door to more business. Of course, it's been a challenge to find horses of the same caliber to satisfy my clients."

"Of course," Carrie agreed smugly.

Anthony laughed and reached over to tuck her hand in his arm for the last hundred yards to the porch.

Carrie stiffened, but didn't pull away. They walked the remaining distance in silence. She drew a deep breath when they entered the warmth, surprised by feelings of both relief and disappointment.

"Anthony!"

Anthony strode into the parlor to greet Jeremy. "I would shake your hand, but both of yours seem rather full," he said with amusement.

Carrie, watching him closely, saw the wistful look in his eyes. She understood. She loved the twins with all her heart, but she couldn't see them without wondering what Bridget would have been like. Far too often, her emotions were bittersweet.

Jeremy grinned down at Sarah Rose and Marcus. "Besides the pure joy of holding my children, this is my contribution to Marietta becoming a great cook. I can assure you the sacrifice is worth it."

"What?" Marietta's eyes flashed as she entered the room. "Are you saying I wasn't a great cook before?"

Jeremy cocked his head. "Can I get away with saying there was slight room for improvement?"

Marietta swatted at him as she rolled her eyes, and then gave Anthony a hug. "It's wonderful to see you again, Anthony. May I offer you some advice?"

Anthony, his eyes bright with laughter, nodded. "Of course."

"Never give your wife's cooking anything but praise."

Anthony was the one to cock his head now. "So...lying is preferable to the truth if it is less than flattering?"

Marietta burst into laughter. "I forgot you had eaten some of my first attempts at biscuits." She reached for Sarah and pulled her daughter close. "I can promise you they are much better now."

"I'm relieved," Anthony said solemnly.

Carrie joined in the laughter, and then plucked Marcus from Jeremy's arms. "My turn."

Jeremy moved closer to the fire. "I thought you would be here next week with Thomas and Abby."

"My plans changed when I found out what happened at Blackwell Plantation. I'm looking forward to helping tomorrow," Anthony replied. "Have they found who did this?"

Jeremy looked grave. "No, and I'm sure they never will. The vigilantes all wore bandanas around their faces. A few of them had hoods."

"Cowards!" Anthony growled.

"Cowards that are growing in number," Jeremy said grimly. "They haven't come on Cromwell or Blackwell again, but there have been reports of black homes being invaded. Men have been beaten. Women..." His voice trailed off.

"Women have been raped," Marietta said angrily. "Even children have been hurt." Her anger faded as fear shadowed her expression.

"We're getting out of here, dear," Jeremy reminded her.

"I know," Marietta said with a heavy sigh. "And I know it's the right thing to do, but I still hate that we are being separated from our family because our children won't be safe. It's wrong."

"It is wrong," Anthony agreed, "but you're making the right decision."

"I know," Marietta repeated.

Carrie felt a surge of concern as she watched Marietta. Her blue eyes held a weariness she had never seen in her spirited friend. The same woman who had thumbed her nose at violence in Richmond because she was so determined to teach her black students, suddenly seemed defeated. She came to life in the kitchen, and Carrie knew Marietta was attempting to appear strong, but the light in her eyes was growing dim. Carrie's concern grew as she thought of Marietta alone in the house with the twins during a Philadelphia winter, while Jeremy worked hard to take over management of Cromwell Factory. Marietta's family was near Philadelphia, but winter forced most people to stay close to home.

"Why are you staring at me?" Marietta demanded.

Carrie blinked, not realizing Marietta had been aware of her scrutiny in the dim light. She pulled Marcus closer, breathing in the little baby scent that she loved so much. Suddenly, she knew what she needed to do. "I was thinking about asking you a question," Carrie lied.

"Since when did you ever hesitate to ask me a question?"

Carrie was struck again by Marietta's attempt to be spirited, while being weighed down with fatigue and fear. "Since I'm not sure it's right to ask you and Jeremy if I can live with you while I'm in Philadelphia starting the clinic," she retorted. Marietta would never agree to her plan if she thought it was just to take care of her. She was far too independent.

Marietta narrowed her eyes. "I thought you were living with Matthew and Janie."

Carrie breathed a prayer for forgiveness as she lied again. "Matthew and Janie are just down the road," she said casually, grateful for that reality. She wanted to be close to Janie for the last months of her pregnancy, but her instinct told her Marietta needed her more. "Their house is wonderful, but it's much smaller than Abby's. I'm afraid my staying there would be something of an imposition." She paused, and then shrugged. "I thought it was at least worth asking. I'll understand if it would be too much."

"I would love it!" Marietta said enthusiastically. She looked toward Jeremy.

"Absolutely," he agreed.

Carrie knew from the look in Jeremy's eyes that he suspected what she was doing. She read nothing but glad gratitude. "Thank you!" she exclaimed. She held Marcus up to stare into his blue eyes. "You're going to be stuck with me a while longer, little man." She laughed when Marcus gurgled and batted his hands toward her.

"He's as glad as I am," Marietta declared. "It will be wonderful to have you there for a few months."

Carrie was happy to see the haunted look was not so strong. Only then did she understand how Marietta really felt about going to Philadelphia. "You won't be stuck with me all day," she said lightly. "I'll be working to start the clinic, but you'll have to put up with me more than you'll have to put up with Jeremy. At least until the factory is running smoothly again."

"I suppose I'll endure it," Marietta replied with a dramatic sigh, her eyes dancing with genuine life again.

"It's settled then," Jeremy said.

"And dinner is ready," Annie announced from the doorway.

When Carrie looked up and saw the approval in Annie's eyes, she knew the woman had been standing there long enough to hear the exchange. In spite of her gruff exterior, she knew Moses' mother had one of the biggest hearts she had ever known. Her approval always made Carrie feel good.

Carrie looked up and saw the light in Anthony's eyes. The expression on his face revealed he knew her ulterior motives as well. She smiled at him brightly, and slipped her hand through the crook of his arm as she stood and went into the dining room. She was suddenly very, very glad that Anthony Wallington was on Cromwell Plantation.

*****

Carrie's mouth dropped open in astonishment when they reached Blackwell Plantation that morning. They had left before dawn, determined to be there to begin work with everyone else. It was the *everyone else* that had her so astonished.

Leaving behind twenty of the Cromwell men to provide protection for the plantation, they still had almost seventy men with them, many of those from other plantations who had heard of the attack and wanted to help. Most of the women had stayed behind to care for the youngest children who were not in school, but there were still ten wagons full of food that had been prepared. Twenty wives had joined them to serve food to the workers.

All the Blackwell workers were present as well, but what really surprised Carrie were the fifty white men who had come to work. She realized all of them were parents of the schoolchildren, the same who had been watching the meteor shower the night Blackwell had been attacked.

Carrie dismounted from Granite and walked over to the group of men standing off to the side waiting for direction. "Good morning, Alvin."

Alvin Williams smiled broadly. "Good morning, Miss Carrie. It's going to be a fine day to build a barn," he said cheerfully.

Carrie gazed at him, hardly able to remember the angry man she had met almost two years earlier when his wife, Amanda, had brought their two children to the clinic, gravely ill with pneumonia. "How are Silas and Violet?"

He bobbed his head. "Real good. They both are growing like weeds, and they're getting smarter every day." He chuckled. "They're already smarter than their daddy!" he boasted.

"Lillian tells me you are in school, too," Carrie said warmly. The confidence shining from his eyes made her almost forget the limp sleeve where an arm used to be, and the wooden peg protruding from one of his pant legs. He had lost both limbs during the war, but had managed to conquer the bitterness and depression that had threatened to consume him.

Alvin flushed slightly, but met her eyes evenly. "Miss Lillian convinced me the only way to make it in the New South is to get myself an education. She's holding classes at night for the men so she can teach us what we need to know." He shrugged. "I reckon I lived through that war for some reason. If I'm gonna make life better for my family, then I got to learn some things."

"What are you doing now?" Carrie asked.

Alvin shrugged. "Some of this, and some of that," he said evasively. "I find work wherever I can find it. I want to move into the city, but Amanda don't want to take the children away from their school." He frowned. "We may have to, though. Jobs are hard to come by in the South now, but they are harder to come by outside a city. I'm going to learn as much as I can, and then I'll have to figure out what comes next."

Carrie nodded, well aware of the struggle Confederate veterans were facing daily. The struggles they faced in the defeated South were many times as difficult as the struggles of the freed slaves. They had come home to a ravaged economy, a decimated countryside, and a government that had no idea how to help them rebuild their lives. She laid a hand on his arm. "If you decide to go to Richmond, please let me know. I'm sure my father would have a place for you at Cromwell Factory."

Alvin's eyes shone with appreciation. "Thank you, ma'am. I'll remember that." A distant call made him swing his head around. "I've got to go. The barn raising is about to begin."

Carrie nodded. "Thank you for being here. I know it means so much to Perry and Louisa."

Alvin met her eyes. "What them vigilantes did was nothing but wrong. Not all white men are as ignorant as them. The only way to make the South different is for everyone, both races, to show they know the right thing to do. If I want my kids to have a better country to live in someday, then I have to do my part, too."

Carrie smiled and squeezed his arm, then headed for the porch where Louisa was standing.

"Good morning, Carrie."

Carrie climbed the stairs to stand beside her friend, looking out over the throng of men milling around in the yard. "Astonishing."

"Yes, it is," Louisa said softly.

Carrie gazed at her, happy to see the defeated look in Louisa's eyes after the attack was gone. "Jeremy told me a mountain of stones have been gathered for the foundation." She looked in the direction of where she knew the barn was, but the thick border of cedar trees kept her from seeing anything.

"Actually," Louisa reported, "the twenty men Franklin sent over from Cromwell, already laid the foundations for all the barns."

Carrie gasped. "*All* of them?"

Unshed tears glimmered in Louisa's eyes. "The main horse barn, the cattle barn, and three tobacco drying barns. It's been remarkable how hard everyone has worked."

"It's what happens when you treat people right," Carrie said, her heart swelling with gladness for her friend.

Louisa took a deep breath. "You're right, of course." She smiled. "We're staying," she announced.

Carrie sighed with relief as she grasped Louisa's hand. "I'm so glad."

Louisa nodded. "I'll probably still worry every day about what might happen to the people I love, but we have decided we're not going to let ignorance and bigotry destroy what we're working so hard to accomplish. We're going to keep treating our workers the way they should be treated. We'll deal with what comes."

Carrie squeezed her hand more tightly. She recognized the fear lurking in the defiant statement, but that only made her prouder of Louisa's stance. True courage could only be experienced in the face of fear. "I'm proud of you," she murmured.

Louisa turned to stare at her. "We have you to thank," she replied. "I was ready to leave. I had no idea where we would go, but anywhere seemed better than here. Then you reminded me that we can't run from the hatred, but we can decide to face it where we live. Perry and I have decided to do that."

Their conversation was stopped when Perry and Simon climbed on top of a small platform that had been hastily erected.

"Thank you for coming," Perry called, his loud voice snapping through the frosty morning air. He glanced up at the sky. "We all know those clouds are threatening snow, but some of my men have assured me it won't come before tonight. Since this southern Georgia boy doesn't know a lot about snow, I've decided to believe them." He waited for the laughter to die down.

"We's got time iffen we get to work," one of the men called. "You just tell us where you want us!"

Perry began shouting instructions. It was only minutes before groups of men broke off to go toward the areas where the barns would go up.

Carrie watched them depart before turning to Louisa. "What can I do?"

"We're going to make sure those men have all the food and hot coffee they need to keep going on such a cold day." She looked toward the line of wagons. "June is already getting everything put together. Simon had the men build a big cooking fire this morning near the barn area. We'll keep it going for as long as anyone is still here." Louisa turned back toward the house. "We have a few minutes before we are needed." She raised a brow. "Who was that tall good-looking man who rode in with you this morning?"

"That was Anthony Wallington," Carrie murmured, knowing it would do no good to pretend she didn't know who Louisa was referring to. "He's the man who handles all the transactions with the Cromwell horses. He has relocated to Richmond, and is living with Father and Abby when he's not traveling." She kept her voice deliberately casual.

Louisa narrowed her eyes. "That's all?"

Carrie shrugged. "What more do you want to know?"

"You could attempt to explain why he was watching you the whole time he was waiting for the work to begin."

Carrie blushed, but had no answer. She hadn't been aware of Anthony's scrutiny, but she couldn't say she was surprised.

Louisa waited a few moments, her eyes narrowed on Carrie. "All I can say is that it's a good thing I'm married this time."

"Oh?" Carrie asked lightly, intrigued by the amusement lurking in Louisa's eyes.

"Yes. Since I'm happily married, we won't have to fight over Anthony like we did Robert," she said demurely.

Carrie was surprised when the mention of Robert's name didn't cause a flash of pain. Instead, she was able to remember the intense jealousy Louisa had experienced with amusement. "Thank God for that," Carrie teased. "You were quite the shrew."

Louisa laughed. "The whole world should be grateful I finally grew up," she admitted. She linked her arm through Carrie's. "June will be bringing in women soon to take out the huge urns of coffee we made this morning. Let's go get everything ready."

Carrie was happy to get to work, relieved Louisa was too preoccupied to say anything more about Anthony.

*****

The ride back to Cromwell was mostly weary silence, but every single person had a look of deep satisfaction on their face. All the barns had been erected in record time. It would take the Blackwell men another day to finish off the inside work that still needed to be done, but by tomorrow night, the horses would all be back in their stalls, and all the equipment would be back in the storage rooms. Cromwell men would drive wagons over with enough hay to take care of their animals through the winter. The second-story loft in the new barn was watertight and ready to receive it. The hay supply would be tight on both plantations, but there was no thought of doing anything else. They would all do the best they could, and pray for a short winter so the pastures would turn green sooner in the spring. If necessary, Carrie would pay to have more hay delivered. It was a sacrifice she was more than willing to make for her friends.

Within a few minutes, the sun, obscured all day by clouds, had sunk far below the horizon. Darkness swallowed the road, but all of them knew the way home. Clouds that had been present all day thickened and began to swirl overhead as the winds picked up.

Carrie shivered and burrowed deeper into her coat. She thought longingly of her bed and the crackling fire she knew would be waiting in her room, but there were still hours to go before she would feel anything but numbing cold.

She wasn't aware Anthony had ridden up beside her until she heard his voice.

"Long day."

"I had no idea a city boy could work that hard," Carrie teased, glad for something to take her mind off her discomfort.

"*City boy?*" Anthony asked indignantly. "I was raised on a farm."

"Which was a couple decades ago," Carrie reminded him with a laugh. "Now you're just a city businessman." She was certainly not going to reveal that she had watched him for most of the day, impressed with his energy, strength, and knowledge.

Anthony barked a disbelieving laugh. "And here I've been under the impression you were more intelligent than the average woman," he said solemnly. "It hurts to discover how wrong I was."

"Oh," Carrie said casually, "you were right about me being more intelligent. I'm intelligent enough to realize men have very fragile egos. I apologize for pointing out to you what a city boy you are."

"Hmmm..."

Carrie waited for Anthony to say more, but several minutes passed in silence while they trotted down the road. "It's not usually so easy for me to have the last word," she taunted.

Anthony chuckled. "You're only showing your lack of intelligence again," he said calmly. "There is no sense in debating a woman whose brain is obviously fogged from the cold. I will take pity on you for the night, but be prepared. When I have been unjustly accused, I always find a way to get even."

Carrie let the silence stretch out again before she replied in a proper, demure voice. "I look forward to the challenge, Mr. Anthony Wallington. I look forward to the challenge..."

Chapter Seven

Carrie reached out a hand and groaned, quickly burrowing back under the covers when she woke late the next morning. Marietta, as promised, had made sure there was a fire burning in all their rooms when they returned home last night, but the flames had long since died down. Carrie knew she would see clouds of her breath if she emerged from the cocoon of her bed. She cracked the covers just enough to peek out, not surprised to see snow clinging to the branches of the guardian oak outside her window.

The first snowflakes had begun to fall a few minutes before they arrived home. Normally, she was thrilled by the first snowfall of the year, but she had been too exhausted to do much more than lift her face to the flakes before trudging up the stairs to the house. Annie had met them with warm milk and cornbread, but Carrie drank only a few swallows before she climbed the stairs and collapsed into bed.

She closed her eyes and considered going back to sleep, but then she remembered Thomas and Abby were arriving today with Moses, Rose, and their family. The thought was enough to make her scramble out of bed, throw on warm woolen clothes, and dash downstairs to the kitchen. She pushed in through the door, ravenous for the bacon and eggs tempting her with their aroma.

"About time you got up."

Carrie peered at Anthony sitting in a chair in front of the blazing fire. A cup of coffee was in his hands, a plate of cinnamon rolls balanced on his lap. "Cinnamon rolls?" she breathed.

Anthony looked at Annie with a forlorn look on his face. "I thought she would never get up," he complained. "It's sad how much becoming an important doctor has softened her."

"*Softened* me?" Carrie scoffed. "Only in your wildest dreaMiss"

"The evidence would indicate otherwise," Anthony continued in a sad voice. He looked at Annie. "Does she always sleep so late?"

"No," Annie agreed readily. "You might just be right, Mr. Anthony."

Carrie glared at Annie. "What are you talking about? Whose side are you on, anyway?"

Annie shrugged her shoulders innocently. "Ain't on nobody's side," she protested. "Just makin' an observation."

Amber pushed through the back door before Carrie could respond. "Carrie! Carrie! You've got to come outside and see this. I promise you ain't never seen anything like this."

Carrie yawned and sipped the coffee Annie had poured for her. She reached for a cinnamon roll. "Can it wait until I eat?"

Amber sighed and looked at Anthony. "I guess you were right," she murmured.

"Right about what?" Carrie demanded as she cast a glare at Anthony. He merely smiled benignly and lifted a shoulder.

"I came looking for you earlier. Anthony explained you were still sleeping because you've gotten soft now that you're an important doctor," Amber answered with twinkling eyes.

"He what?" Carrie sputtered, pushing aside her coffee. "That is complete nonsense." She shoved back her chair. "What do you want me to see?"

"It's right out here," Amber said eagerly.

Carrie looked longingly at her coffee and then marched to the back door. She had only taken a few steps down when she felt strong arms grab her from behind and lift her into the air. "What in the...!"

"This is what is called getting even," Anthony murmured in her ear.

Carrie shrieked as he ran to a deep snowdrift and dropped her. Cold whiteness encased her body, sliding down her neck and freezing her hands. "I'll get you back for this!" she cried as she scrambled to push herself up from the ground, dodging his groping hands. She flew back up the stairs before he could stop her.

She raced to stand in front of the fire, and then whirled around to stare daggers into Annie. "And *you.* You went along with this scheme." She watched out the window as Anthony gleefully shook Amber's hand. "And Amber? How could she betray me like this?"

Her words were hanging in the air as Anthony pushed back into the kitchen. "You'll find that women can't resist my charms," he said with a laugh. "Once I explained to them how you callously insulted me after a day of hard labor for our friends, they came to my side." He paused. "It was the right thing to do."

Carrie glared at him for several long moments before she doubled over in laughter that almost stole her breath. When she could finally stop laughing, she raised her eyes to his. "Let the war begin," she vowed. She looked back at Annie. "Don't think you're forgiven, either."

"Don't need to be forgiven for doin' the right thin'," Annie responded. "You gonna up and say things like what you said…" She shook her head. "Well, you gots to learn to live with the consequences." Her eyes were bright with mirth.

Anthony smiled serenely. "And you heard her declare war, didn't you, Annie?" He turned his teasing eyes to Carrie. "Be careful you don't start something you can't finish."

Carrie rolled her eyes and snorted a very unladylike snort. "I promise you I can finish anything I start." As she reached for her coffee and cinnamon roll again, she realized she couldn't remember the last time she'd had so much fun.

*****

Rose studied Moses carefully as they approached the gate to Cromwell Plantation. She couldn't miss the look of peace that suffused his face as they rolled in through the brick pillars.

Felicia and John cheered, and jumped up and down in the carriage. "We're home!" they hollered. "We're home!" Hope shrieked and clapped her hands happily, her face barely visible above the pile of warm blankets.

Rose smiled as their excited voices rang through the frigid air. The snow had been deep enough to slow them down, but not enough to stop them. Now that they had arrived, she hoped there would be more snow. It was Christmas!

The train ride from Oberlin had been brutal in the crowded cars, but they'd been able to rest at Thomas and Abby's the night before. It still amazed Rose that they could come home so often. She knew it was only the income from the plantation that gave them the financial freedom to return when they wanted. She turned her face toward the sky, reveling in the crisp, fresh air after two days on the train and a night in Richmond, a city daily growing more crowded and clogged with smoke. Rose knew growth was inevitable after the war, but she was surprised to discover how much she did not want to be in a big city. She frowned, wondering how that would impact her desire to teach, and then shoved it to the back of her mind. All she wanted to do was enjoy the next two weeks. She and Moses had already decided they would not return to the South again until the following summer.

"I love it here so much," Abby said softly.

Rose turned to gaze at her. "I don't know how you stand to be in Richmond. The city is so clogged and dirty now."

Abby sighed. "I know, but it's where the factory is. There are so many people who depend on us for their jobs."

Rose was sure Thomas and Abby had accumulated enough money to stop working. "Don't you sometimes want to walk away from all of it?"

Abby met her eyes. "Of course," she replied honestly. "But the economy in Richmond is just starting to rebound. With Jeremy leaving, we don't have anyone we trust to take over the factory. We encouraged him to leave, and the factory in Moyamensing will benefit from his management, but it will take time for things to stabilize here. We have great hopes for the new manager we've hired, but only time will tell if we can trust him. Now is simply not the time to walk away."

Rose turned to Thomas. "Do you want to come home?"

"Every day," he admitted, his eyes sweeping the landscape they were rolling through. "But, my beautiful and brilliant wife is right—now is not the time to make a change."

Rose narrowed her eyes, but her questions were squelched by cries of welcome from the house. She laughed when she saw Carrie, Annie, Jeremy, Marietta, Anthony, Susan, and Lillian lined up on the porch, waving wildly. She was surprised when she felt tears prick her eyelids. It had been less than two months since they left, but she was thrilled to be home.

*****

Carrie breathed in deeply when she entered the house on Christmas Eve Day. The last week had flown by in a medley of horseback riding, snowball fights, long walks, and hot chocolate by the fire. Annie and Marietta had kept a steady supply of food coming from the kitchen, and Carrie had to admit Marietta's Irish oatmeal cookies were as good as Annie's. The fact that even Annie admitted it, was something akin to a Christmas miracle.

Carrie peeked into the parlor, thrilled to see the Christmas tree in its place, towering tall enough to touch the fourteen-foot ceiling. She smiled when she remembered the hordes of children who used to decorate the tree. Her smile faded quickly as she wondered what had happened to all the slave children from Cromwell. She prayed they were safe and warm somewhere, finding a way to live the life of freedom they had been granted.

Felicia looked up and caught sight of her. "Carrie! Come in and help us decorate!"

Carrie nodded but turned toward the kitchen. "As soon as I get some of whatever smells so good," she replied. "I'm starving."

Anthony walked out of the kitchen just then. "I do believe you eat more than I do," he said good-naturedly.

Carrie eyed him with a smirk. "Which only goes to prove that I work much harder than you do, city boy." She shrugged. "Of course, I already knew that."

Anthony chuckled. "I counted. I cleaned out ten of the stalls today. You only did eight."

"Because I also fed all the horses," Carrie protested.

Anthony shook his head. "Which is far easier than mucking stalls," he pointed out. "I did the extra stalls because I knew the doctor lady was feeling weak."

Abby stepped from the dining room. "Do you two ever let up?" she asked with a laugh.

"You can't feed a man's ego by letting him think he has won," Carrie said primly. "I know it is proper Southern protocol to give them a sense of victory, but I say they have to earn it. So far, I don't think Anthony has."

Abby laughed harder and reached out to squeeze Anthony's shoulder. "She's a hard nut to crack, city boy."

"*City boy?*" Anthony echoed. "You're going to label me with that ridiculous moniker, as well?"

Abby shrugged. "I'm just evening the scales. You seem to have pulled Annie, Amber, and Marietta over to your side. The Cromwell women have to stick together."

Carrie grinned and reached over to pluck Abby's hand from Anthony's shoulder, tucking it through her elbow. "I say the Cromwell women go find out what smells so good."

Amber blasted through the kitchen door then. "It's sugar cookies!" she cried, balancing a heaping plate as she moved toward the parlor.

Carrie reached out a hand, but Amber dodged away with a laugh.

"You only get sugar cookies if you help decorate," she insisted. "We need help, Carrie. Come on!"

Carrie followed obediently. "I'll do anything for Annie's sugar cookies."

"They are not *Annie's* sugar cookies," Marietta announced, as she stepped from the kitchen, her apron and cheeks smudged with flour. "I made them."

Carrie froze in place. "Are they safe?"

Marietta glared at her, and then called into the parlor, "Carrie has dared to question my cooking. She is not allowed to have any cookies!"

Carrie turned away. "Sorry, Amber. If I don't get any cookies, I'm not going to help."

"Wait!" Amber cried. "Miss Marietta, we need help real bad in here. How about if I give Carrie the cookies I was going to eat?"

Marietta pretended to consider the question, and then grinned. "I suppose that will be acceptable."

The banter continued as Carrie grabbed a handful of cookies and began to hang decorations on the tree. She beckoned Anthony to join them. "We need your height," she pleaded.

Anthony cocked his head. "I'm supposed to help with the yule log," he protested.

"They don't need your help," Carrie replied. "Moses used to carry it in here all by himself years ago. He has Jeremy and my father to help him." She looked at him pleadingly. "Please?" She hid her grin as she batted her eyelashes, well aware of the effect she would have on him.

Anthony gazed at her appraisingly, a slight warning light in his eyes, but then nodded and moved into the parlor. "Tree decorating, it is."

Carrie knew she was playing with fire, but it had been so long since she'd felt like teasing and flirting. She hadn't taken the time to analyze her feelings; she was simply having a good time. She laughed and joked with the children as they decorated the tree. When they finally stood back to appreciate their labors, Carrie sucked in her breath.

"It's beautiful," Felicia whispered.

"Pretty!" Hope squealed.

"Now, it's Christmas," Amber said, deep satisfaction in her voice.

"I bet it's the best Christmas tree ever," John boasted.

Carrie couldn't have agreed more. With the exception of the war years, Christmas on Cromwell Plantation was all she had ever known. Each year brought its own kind of magic. As she grew older, she became increasingly grateful for the Christmas traditions that didn't change, no matter what the world threw at them. She closed her eyes as she thought of Robert, her mother, Old Sarah, Sam... Their faces, now claimed by death, would forever hold their place in her Christmas memories. There were so many things from the past that she wanted to sink her roots into, never letting them go, but she was also keenly aware she needed to continue to release the pain still lingering in her heart so that she could look to the future.

"A penny for your thoughts," Anthony said quietly.

Carrie opened her eyes and gazed into the green ones watching her. Flashes of Robert's eyes overlaid Anthony's, but she refused to look away. She wasn't sure what she was feeling, and she certainly had no idea what she intended to do with any knowledge once she had it, but she could no longer deny she was attracted to Anthony Wallington. The acknowledgement was a source of both comfort and deep confusion.

Anthony gazed at her steadily, seeming to read her feelings, but he remained silent.

Carrie thought back again to their conversation a year earlier. Anthony was keeping his promise to be a friend. She'd certainly had a wonderful two weeks with him, but she was uncertain how to act on the feelings that fluttered through her. She was certain Anthony would step out of the role of friend if she were to offer him the slightest encouragement, but it would be unfair to do that when she was still so confused. She smiled, but kept her voice neutral. "I'm just glad everyone is here for Christmas."

Anthony was careful to keep his expression as neutral as her voice, but she didn't miss the flicker of disappointment in his eyes. It made her more certain than ever that she owed him nothing less than complete honesty.

Abby appeared in the doorway. "Everyone wash up for dinner. Annie says it's almost ready."

Carrie, relieved at the reprieve, dashed up the stairs to freshen up. She changed out of her barn breeches and into an emerald green gown, then undid her long braid and carefully coiled it into a bun. She stared at her reflection for a long moment, recognizing the shine in her eyes. She bowed her head as she thought of Robert. What would he think of her if he knew she was attracted to another man? She struggled with the question, but tossed it aside with a sigh. It was time for Christmas Eve dinner.

*****

Rose was waiting outside for Carrie when she emerged from the house later that night. "Hello," she said quietly.

Carrie jumped. "Rose? What are you doing out here? I thought you had gone upstairs with the children."

"I did," Rose replied, "but then I came back down when you were still in the dining room."

Carrie wished she could see Rose's eyes, but she didn't detect trouble in her voice. Still... "Is everything all right?"

"That's what I came to find out."

Carrie was completely puzzled now. "What are you talking about?"

Rose answered with another question. "Are you headed out to the barn?"

"Yes. I decided to check on the horses one more time before I go to bed."

"Checking on the horses, or needing some time to think?" Rose asked.

Carrie should have known Rose would sense the turmoil she thought she had concealed so well. She tucked her hands deep into her coat pockets, and then walked down the steps, Rose at her side. "Both, I suppose," she admitted.

"Anthony?"

Carrie managed a small smile, sure the full moon resting high in the sky would reveal it. "Anthony," she agreed.

Rose remained silent until they reached the barn and lit some lanterns. She joined Carrie as she checked all the stalls, speaking quietly to the horses, and then walked over to sit down on a large trunk. "Talk to me," she invited.

Carrie sank down on the trunk next to her, trying to make sense of her thoughts. She wasn't sure she was ready to talk about it, although she was sure Rose would help her figure it out. It had always been that way, and she didn't expect it was going to change. She sat silently for several minutes, knowing Rose wouldn't rush her. "I like Anthony," she began.

"That's easy to see," Rose replied.

Carrie flushed, not sure she was comfortable with that realization, but acknowledging she had never been good at hiding her feelings – especially from her best friend. She grappled with what to say next.

"It's Robert," Rose prodded.

Carrie was grateful to Rose for putting it into words. "Robert was my love," she said, blinking back hot tears. Just saying his name brought his face vividly to mind.

"And you were his," Rose murmured. "He loved you so much, Carrie. Do you really think he would want you to be alone?"

Carrie shrugged. "Isn't that what people always say when they're trying to justify a new relationship?" she asked in a flat voice. She realized too late that she had as much as admitted she was considering a new relationship. It wouldn't do any good to try to hide the truth, because Rose could always see through her attempts at subterfuge.

"I don't know," Rose replied. "If the roles were reversed, would you want Robert to be alone?"

Carrie shook her head. "How can I know that? I'm not the one who is dead." She knew she was being deliberately contrary, but she was also speaking honestly.

Rose chuckled. "So, let's pretend you're the one who died. What do you *think* you would want?"

Carrie sighed. "I know I should say I wouldn't want him to be alone, but perhaps I'm selfish enough that I would want him to pine for me all the days of his life."

Rose remained silent.

"Fine," Carrie grumbled. "I wouldn't want him to be alone," she admitted. "But that's not the only thing I'm struggling with in regard to Anthony."

"What else?" Rose asked.

"I suppose I might be ready for love again someday, but right now I want to focus on being a doctor. I don't want any restrictions or expectations from anyone else," she blurted. "I loved Robert with all my heart, and I would give anything if he were still here, but I'll admit it made choices about my career more challenging. The months on the Santa Fe Trail showed me how much I truly love being a doctor." She took a deep breath, her thoughts crystallizing as she spoke them. "I'm looking forward to going to Philadelphia to establish the clinic Biddy financed. And after that?" Carrie shrugged. "I don't know what comes after that, but I find the freedom to make whatever choices *I* want to make is quite exhilarating."

Rose listened carefully. "You don't care about a husband or a family?"

Carrie hesitated, knowing Rose's whole world revolved around Moses and her children. "If Robert and Bridget were alive, I would take joy in creating a life with them at the center." She closed her eyes for a moment. "They're not alive," she said huskily. "I don't feel the need to enter another relationship just for the sake of having one. I know that is the proper thing for a woman to do, but there are many more single women in recent years because so many men were lost during the war." Her thoughts flew to Susan. "Being single won't carry the same stigma." She smiled tightly. "Not that I've ever been known to let that bother me. I have a whole future stretching out before me. This time last year, I was struggling to find reasons to stay alive. I've come a long way since then."

Carrie stood and then paced over to stand beside Granite's stall. He stuck his nose out and bumped her shoulder, nuzzling her. She patted his neck absently before she turned back to Rose. "I want to see how far I can go," she declared. "Is that so wrong?" she added defensively. "Is that so horrible?"

Rose looked at her for a long minute. "I'm very proud of you," she finally said.

Carrie stared at her. "What?"

"I said, I'm very proud of you," Rose repeated. "You've been through something that would have broken many people—not just women, but many men, too. You have fought your way through to a position of strength." She smiled. "Not many people could have done that, so yes, I'm very proud of you."

Carrie breathed a heavy sigh of relief and returned to the trunk to sit next to her friend. "Thank you."

Rose reached out to take her hand. They sat silently for a long time before they finally walked back through the deep snow and entered the house that was now quiet and dark.

Chapter Eight

January 1, 1869

Rose was sitting on the bank of the James River with Carrie, Abby, and Felicia, celebrating the arrival of 1869. Felicia had begged to be able to join them. Carrie and Abby had both agreed readily.

"So, am I a Cromwell woman now?" Felicia asked earnestly, her gaze fixed on the horizon as she caught her breath after several minutes of wild dancing on the snowy riverbank with the other women. She had required some coaxing, but had joined in eagerly when she discovered it was part of the tradition.

Abby nodded. "You are indeed, my dear. You know, I've only been a part of this tradition for a couple years."

Felicia smiled. "I know. Mama and Carrie have been doing it since they were younger than me." She turned to Rose. "Except for the war years. Right, Mama?"

"That's right," Rose agreed, catching Carrie's eyes over the top of her daughter's head. She knew what they both were thinking—that they were thrilled to be passing the tradition down through the generations. She wondered how long it would be possible for Cromwell women to celebrate the New Year together. What did the future hold for all of them?

The four of them sat silently as the sun climbed higher in the sky. The snow-covered ground and the laden trees glimmered in the sun. Rose had been granted her wish for more snow; at least a foot blanketed the ground, but a warm breeze blowing in from the south promised it would melt away in time for them to leave for Richmond in two days.

"It's going to be a good year," Abby said softly.

Rose turned, remembering the question that had been gnawing at her since they had arrived at the plantation. "Abby, may I ask you something?"

"Always."

"When we were driving into the plantation two weeks ago, you mentioned that now was not the right time to walk away from Cromwell Factories. There was something in your eyes that I didn't understand. Will you tell me what it was?"

Abby eyed her with surprise. "You've been thinking about that all this time?"

"It's just been niggling at my brain. I kept pushing it back because of all the celebrations, but I thought about it again when you said it was going to be a good year."

"You want to leave the factory?" Carrie interrupted, her eyes wide with surprise. "Since when?"

Abby shrugged. "I've worked very hard for a long time. So has your father. We talk often about how wonderful it would be to move back to the plantation," she said wistfully.

"I know it's not because of money," Rose said. "Is it really just about Jeremy leaving?"

Abby nodded her head slightly, and then stopped. "No, that's not true," she admitted.

Carrie cocked her head. "What am I missing here?"

Abby smiled. "It's not that you're missing anything, Carrie. Most people in America have no idea what is happening, including most business owners." She took a deep breath. "I believe America is headed into a financial crisis," she finally said. She gave a short laugh. "I'm quite sure business owners all across the country would disagree with me."

Rose eyed her. "Will you explain what you're talking about? I can't help but think it's important since I haven't been able to quit thinking about it for two weeks."

"That *is* rather odd," Abby mused. "I've never known you to have a thought for financial matters."

"I still don't," Rose said lightly, "but I do have many thoughts for *you*. What I saw on your face that day has stuck with me."

"I don't want to put worry where there is no need for it," Abby protested. "There are quite enough things in America to be concerned about already."

"Hiding from things doesn't make them go away," Felicia said earnestly, her intense eyes boring into Abby. "I would like to know what you're thinking, too." She hesitated. "I don't believe I'm too young, so don't hold back because I'm here. If I'm going to be part of the Cromwell women, I need to be treated like one."

Abby smiled tenderly. "You are most certainly not too young, Felicia. You'll have to deal with the consequences if I'm right."

Rose sat silently, warning Carrie and Felicia with her eyes to do the same. She knew Abby needed to gather her thoughts.

Abby spoke after a long silence. "Have any of you heard about the 'Year Without A Summer'?"

Rose shook her head. She was surprised, however, that Felicia also remained silent. "There is something my daughter doesn't know?" she teased.

Felicia made a face at her, and then turned back to Abby. "What was the year without a summer? I've never heard of it."

"I grew up hearing about it," Abby said. "It happened in 1816, two years after I was born. My family almost lost everything that year. A few years later, they actually did. It took them a long time to rebuild." She shook her head. "Let me explain...at least the best I can, because no one really knows why it happened."

Carrie looked as mystified as Rose was sure she did. "I'm afraid I have no idea what you are talking about, Abby," Rose said.

"And I'm doing a horrible job explaining it," Abby muttered. She straightened her shoulders and shook her head. "I'll do my best to help you understand what I'm thinking. I should start at the beginning, though. War usually brings a post-war economic surge. It was no different after America's War of 1812. People were celebrating the win, and feeling positive." She paused, her soft, gray eyes growing contemplative. "I know *my* family was. Two of my uncles were killed in the war, but the rest of my family was working hard on our Virginia plantation during the summer of 1816. No one knew there was such a big problem in the beginning, they just thought we were having a cooler than usual summer. They were actually enjoying it...until people started arriving from New England with terrible stories."

"Stories about what?" Felicia demanded.

"Snow in June and July. Hard frosts all summer long. Crops failing. People starving."

"What?" Carrie gasped.

Abby nodded. "Anyone who could leave, was leaving. They couldn't feed their families. Farms were going under faster than anyone could keep track of. My family tried to help. We were having a good crop year, so they took in several of the families. My folks gave them jobs, and let them plant gardens. The stories they had told about the Northeast all seemed far away until August twentieth and twenty-first of that year."

"What happened?" Felicia breathed.

"There were two nights of hard frost that destroyed almost all our crops."

Carrie stared at her. "Frost? In August? Here in Virginia? That's not possible."

"It was possible," Abby said somberly. "It hurt everyone. Thomas Jefferson had retired from the presidency and was farming at Monticello. He sustained such staggering crop failures that he went further into what was already massive debt. It was a debt he never recovered from. When he died, his estate, his possessions, and his slaves were sold at auction."

"President Thomas Jefferson?" Felicia pressed. "The author of the Declaration of Independence?"

"The same," Abby replied. "Most people don't know that aspect of his life." She shook her head. "I'm getting far off track. People suffered all over New England, Canada, and Europe because of crop failures. It was only a small part, though, of all the pieces that would eventually make 1819 a reality."

Rose chose to remain silent, letting Abby tell the story in her own way.

"It was just the one year?" Carrie asked.

"Just the one year," Abby agreed. "Perhaps there will be answers someday to why it happened, but for now we just know it happened, and we hope it never happens again." She stood and walked to the edge of the river, staring out over the glistening water for several moments. "Like I said, that summer was merely one piece of the puzzle. There was a complete financial collapse in 1819."

"Fifty years ago," Rose murmured.

Abby nodded. "Yes. I'm trying to figure out how to explain this by using terms you'll understand. I've spent years studying finance since taking over Charles' business, but it's still hard to comprehend." She paused. "Let's just say that it proved very challenging for America to transition to an independent economy once all the fighting with England finally ended. There were so many boom and bust cycles that I don't think anyone really had a handle on what was happening. Then, the banks started making very poor decisions, at the same time our country started doing excessive speculations in public lands."

"Excuse me?" Felicia said. "What does that mean?"

"The government wanted Americans to migrate west, though west was still this side of the Mississippi River at that point. They decided to offer public land at two dollars per acre. Many of the people who lived through the Year Without A Summer decided migrating west was a wonderful idea, so they moved."

Carrie frowned. "Public land they took from the Indians?" She couldn't help thinking of all the suffering she had witnessed during the last year.

"Yes," Abby agreed regretfully. "You could buy one hundred and sixty acres for three hundred twenty dollars, but you had to put one quarter down to get it, and then pay equal payments for four years to pay it off. If you didn't pay it in full, you lost it." She paused.

"Without going into great depth, the banks making the loans for this land didn't have the resources to back it up. They simply kept making loans, and the bigger banks kept printing money to take care of the problem, but that only made it worse." She shook her head ruefully. "It finally all collapsed on them in 1819. It took several years to get things back on track."

"But they learned how to do it right?" Felicia queried.

"I'm afraid not," Abby said with a sigh. "Our country has continued to go through cycles of financial crisis."

"But why?" Felicia pressed. "That doesn't make sense."

"Because men get greedy," Abby said flatly. "Everyone wants to make money *right then*, for themselves. They are not willing to consider the long-term consequences. There was another crisis in 1847, and then another in 1857."

"Just a few years before the war?" Carrie asked with surprise. She had been alive, but far too young and protected on the plantation to have any knowledge of it.

"Yes," Abby acknowledged. "Things were already on shaky ground, but then the *SS Central America*, now known as the *Ship of Gold*, sank in a hurricane. There were four hundred twenty-five souls who lost their lives, and almost twenty-one *tons* of gold lost with them. It was gold the banks in New York were waiting for to stabilize everything that was faltering in the economy. When it didn't come, things crashed again. This crash was big enough to affect economies all over the world. It didn't really recover until the war started, at least in the North."

"Hurrah for war," Carrie said sarcastically.

"Did *your* business suffer?" Rose asked. "During the last crisis?"

"It was impacted," Abby replied, "as was every business, but I wasn't hit hard."

"Why not?" Felicia asked.

"Because my husband, Charles, made sure he taught me about the dangers of reckless investments. He taught me that far too many business people, when the economy seems to be going well, will invest beyond their ability to pay. Then, when the next crisis hits, they have no money to fall back on. They fall further into debt, with far too many of them going bankrupt."

Rose understood now. "You believe another crisis is coming."

"Yes," Abby admitted. "I used a very long explanation to teach you a financial lesson." She stared hard at all of them. "Carrie, you must be very wise with the stables. Rose, you need to talk to Moses so he will be prudent with the plantation." Then she looked at Felicia. "Young lady, I have no idea what you will be doing when things finally collapse again, but you can never have too much knowledge. Men aren't going to teach you this, so I hope you have listened well."

"I've listened to every word, Aunt Abby," Felicia said earnestly. "My *Kinaalda* taught me how important it is to learn from women who are older than me. I'm going to read as much as I can so I will understand it better."

"When do you believe it will crash?" Rose asked anxiously, thinking about the years to come.

"And why do you believe we will have another crisis soon?" Carrie added.

"I can't predict exactly when it will crash," Abby said immediately, "though I can tell you I'm not willing to make any risky moves right now. As far as why I believe we will have a crisis? I'm watching the same things happen now that have happened before. There is high inflation, and there are massive speculative investments being made, especially in railroads. It won't take much to tip the scales so that there is a massive strain on the bank reserves. Combine that with a growing trade deficit, and it's only a matter of time before we have another financial crisis."

Rose was confused about something. "But why not leave the factories now? Wouldn't it be smart to leave before a crisis hits?"

Abby considered the question for a long moment before she answered with a question of her own. "If you and Moses had more money in the bank, would you walk away from the plantation now?"

Rose knew she needed to think deeply before she responded. "No..." she finally said.

"Why not?" Abby asked gently.

Rose closed her eyes as she thought about all the black families who were living a life they couldn't have even dreamed of before the war. "Because it would impact so many people," she murmured. "Not just them, but their families, and probably their families to come. The Cromwell workers are getting to create a life for the first time."

Carrie smiled. "The *Bregdan Principle*. Everything has an impact for generations to come."

Abby nodded. "That's right. The factory in Richmond has hired so many former slaves, and also white veterans who have returned to a destroyed South. My first factories in Philadelphia have hired record numbers of women, and they are being paid fairly for the first time. The Moyamensing factory is finally giving the Irish a way to make a good living. If we were to close all of them, or even sell them to people who would not carry on with our values, we would lose what we have worked so hard to accomplish."

"You can't work forever, though," Rose argued, not able to forget the wistful look in Abby's eyes the day they arrived on the plantation.

"No," Abby agreed, "but now is not the time. To walk away now, when we're certain another financial crisis is imminent, would be very unwise. Protecting our investment is certainly one part of it, but it's far more important to know that whoever is running the factories does it from a place of integrity. It would not be fair to put them into a business that is getting ready to go through extremely hard times."

She looked back at the river as a Great Blue Heron swooped low into the water, came up with a glistening fish, and then flew off again. "I would trust Jeremy with the Moyamensing Factory, and I see the day coming when we will hand it off to him, but I don't have the confidence with the other factories. No," she said as she shook her head decisively, "now is not the time. I believe we'll know when the time is right. In the meantime," she said, "we'll come out to the plantation every chance we get."

"What should we do?" Carrie asked. "To be ready for the next financial crisis?"

Abby smiled. "I'm so glad one of you asked," she teased. She gazed at Carrie. "You've already learned so much about business in the last two years," she said, her voice thick with pride. "I talked with Susan about your partnership arrangement." Her look was full of admiration. "You put together a very fair and profitable deal for both of you."

"Did you have time to read the contract?" Carrie asked eagerly. "I didn't want to ask over Christmas."

"I did. It's clear and fair," Abby said. "It's set up for both of you to share equally in the challenges *and* the profits. My only caution is to make sure Susan understands what we talked about today. Partnership problems usually come when business values aren't shared, or when one wants to take more risks than the other."

Carrie opened her mouth to ask a question, but closed it when Abby raised her hand.

"I already know what you're going to say. Risk is a wonderful thing, and I've taken more than my share of them, but you have to understand timing. I knew the economy was going to thrive in the years right after the war. That's why I invested so much in the horses that started Cromwell Stables. It was a risk I could afford to take, but," she warned, "it's not a risk I would take now. Generosity is a wonderful thing, but you first have to make sure your primary business stays solvent if you want to continue giving."

Carrie nodded. "I understand."

"And the plantation?" Rose asked.

Abby regarded her thoughtfully. "We'll talk on the way back to Richmond. There are many things to be considered in the future. Thomas and I have talked about it a great deal. We had already planned on talking to you and Moses about it when we got back to Richmond." She suddenly stood and stretched. "But right now, I believe we have a New Year's Day Brunch that should be ready soon. We all know Annie will have our hides if we're not there for it."

"Annie and *Marietta*," Felicia said with a grin. "She's getting as possessive of that kitchen as Annie is. I had no idea what I was starting when I gave her that cookbook so she could make an apple pie."

All four of them were laughing as they entered the tunnel that would take them back to the house.

*****

"Where to?"

Carrie looked up at Anthony. "Anywhere I want to go?"

"That's what I said."

Carrie grinned up at him, hardly able to believe this was her last day in Richmond before she boarded the train for Philadelphia. The last five days in the city had passed in a blur. Most of it had been spent roaming the town with Anthony. She wouldn't deny she'd had tremendous fun. She leaned forward now, and smiled up into Spencer's face. "I want to go to Opal's Kitchen."

Spencer grinned at her, his eyes glinting with pleasure. "Opal going to be pleased as punch to see you, Miss Carrie."

"And I'm so excited to see her," Carrie replied. "My stomach is hungry for some of her cooking."

Anthony raised a brow. "Who is Opal? And could her cooking possibly be better than May's?"

Carrie and Spencer both laughed and rolled their eyes. "If you are going to live in the South, Anthony Wallington, you have to learn not to compare black Southern cooks," Carrie scolded.

"She's right," Spencer said seriously. "You just tell all of them that their cookin' be the best in the world. It don't matter none if they believe you or not, 'cause you done said the right thing. You wouldn't never catch me comparin' my wife's cookin' with someone else's. May might be a kind woman, but them be fightin' words for her."

Anthony nodded soberly, his eyes dancing with fun. "Thank you for the advice. I certainly don't want anyone coming after me with a rolling pin. I already had that happen with Annie."

"It's true," Carrie confirmed to Spencer. "Anthony made the grievous error of telling Annie that Marietta's cooking was as good as hers."

Spencer sucked in his breath. "You got some kind of death wish, Mr. Anthony?"

"Evidently," Anthony conceded. "I thought Annie would be pleased since she taught Marietta how to cook, but I quickly learned she took it as an insult." He rolled his eyes. "Women talk about male pride, but as far as I can tell, we don't have anything on Southern cooks."

Spencer laughed outright as he narrowed his eyes at Carrie. "I do believe Mr. Anthony has figured out things nicely."

Carrie waved her hand. "You're both ridiculous. Now," she said briskly, "if the two of you have finished talking nonsense, I would appreciate going to Opal's Kitchen," she said imperiously.

Spencer picked up the reins and moved the carriage forward, but he was shaking his head. "Mr. Anthony, you can know for sure that you got too close to the truth for Miss Carrie when she gets that tone of voice and changes the subject. When she waves her hand, that means you really got to her."

Anthony nodded gravely. "Thank you, Spencer. Perhaps you and I can talk more later. I suspect you would be a fount of knowledge about Mrs. Borden."

Mrs. Borden. Carrie hid her frown behind a playful smile, but the words hit her strongly. She *was* Mrs. Robert Borden. Robert may have died, and she may possibly believe he wouldn't want her to be alone, but she still struggled with feeling unfaithful to his memory.

"Carrie?"

Anthony's quiet voice broke into her troubled thoughts. "Yes?" she asked a little too brightly.

Anthony's eyes said he knew something was bothering her, but he wouldn't ask her in the carriage. "Who is Opal?" he asked instead.

Carrie's smile was genuine this time. "Opal used to be one of the Cromwell slaves. I helped her escape the plantation shortly after the war began. She has been through so much..." She briefly told him of how Opal's cousin Fannie had died in an ammunitions explosion at Tredegar Ironworks. "Fannie's husband, Eddie, was arrested as a spy the same day, so Opal took charge of their four children, bringing them back out to the plantation until the war ended. She and Eddie fell in love after the war, and then moved up to start a restaurant in Philadelphia." Her face darkened as she remembered the fire at their thriving business, but she decided not to tell him about all the deaths that day. "They returned to Richmond to be closer to friends and family. Opal opened her restaurant about a year ago. She's one of the finest cooks you've ever seen," Carrie said fondly. "This is my first chance to eat there. I hope the restaurant is doing well."

"It's doing real well," Spencer assured her. "There ain't hardly an empty seat in that place, from the minute they open to the minute they close."

Carrie smiled. "So, Abby's idea of putting her restaurant outside the Black Quarter was a good one."

Spencer shrugged. "Them white people might not want us on their street cars, and they might hate us being able to vote, but they sure enough do love Opal's cooking." He grinned. "They are making a right lot of money off them white folks. A lot of it is going back into the Quarters."

Carrie laughed. "I'm glad to hear that."

Fifteen minutes later, Spencer pulled to a stop in front of a cozy storefront on Broad Street. "This here be it," he announced.

Carrie, too eager to wait for Anthony to assist her, jumped down from the carriage. Moments later, she was stepping into the restaurant's cozy dining room. She had planned their arrival so they would miss the midday rush, but almost every table was full. Laughter and talk filled the air, and food was disappearing fast. The air was redolent with the smell of fried chicken and sweet potato pie. She looked around with delight.

"Miss Carrie!"

Carrie's face split into a broad grin when a young man came rushing toward her. She shook her head with disbelief. "Carl?"

"That's me!"

Carrie kept shaking her head. "You weren't as tall as me the last time I saw you." She gazed up at the boy who stood almost as tall as Anthony. "When did this happen?"

"I reckon Opal's good cooking made me grow," Carl replied. Then he reached down, picked Carrie up, and swung her in a circle.

Carrie was aware of dark looks and murmurs of disapproval from many of the white patrons, but she couldn't have cared less. She merely laughed and gave him a hug when he set her down.

"What's all the commotion out...?"

Carrie swung around just as Opal's voice sounded behind her.

"Land sakes! Is that you, Carrie Borden?"

Carrie laughed as she held her arms wide. "It's so good to see you, Opal!"

Opal gave a glad cry as she rushed forward to wrap her in a hug. "Aren't you a sight for sore eyes!" she exclaimed. "What are you doing here, Miss Carrie?"

"I came for lunch, of course," Carrie replied. She knew the instant Opal spotted Anthony standing slightly behind her.

"And who is that?" Opal murmured, her eyes narrowing as she looked over Carrie's shoulder.

Carrie beckoned Anthony forward. "This is my friend, Anthony Wallington."

Anthony smiled warmly. "Carrie has bragged on your cooking, Opal. She has also told me what a fine woman you are."

Opal gave him a long appraisal. "Welcome to Opal's Kitchen," she said graciously. "We'll make sure you don't leave hungry."

Carrie, aware Anthony had passed Opal's inspection, smiled. "Where are Eddie and Amber Lou?" She glanced at Anthony. "Amber Lou is their thirteen-year-old daughter."

Carl answered for Opal. "My little sister can't be pulled away from school to do much *work*." His voice was complaining, but his eyes shone with pride. "She's set on going to college, and said she doesn't have time for restaurant work. Daddy is out getting supplies. He'll be back soon enough."

"Carl! You know your sister works hard here when she can," Opal scolded. "If we could only get you to spend more time at school, you wouldn't have to work so hard here, either."

Carl shrugged and grinned. "I like working in the restaurant. As long as I can find as good a cook as you when I want to open my own restaurant, I figure I will do just fine."

"Good luck with finding a cook as good as Opal," Carrie teased. "We're starving," she added. "What do you recommend?"

"How about if I just send out my special today?" Opal asked.

"Perfect," Carrie replied. "Whatever it is, I know it will be delicious."

Carl led them over to a small table next to the window that looked out onto the bustle of Broad Street. "You in town for long, Miss Carrie?"

"No," Carrie answered. "Actually, I'm leaving for Philadelphia tomorrow to start a homeopathic clinic."

Carl nodded, his eyes saying he was impressed, and then leaned in closer. "Didn't I hear you took off to the West?"

"I did," Carrie answered. "I spent nine months on the Santa Fe Trail, and in New Mexico last year."

Carl's expression was thick with admiration and envy. "I figure that's where I'll be heading one day," he confided.

"Oh?" Carrie asked in surprise. "Why the West?"

Carl dropped his voice to almost a whisper, obviously not wanting to be overheard by the white patrons who filled the restaurant. "I don't figure things in the South going to be that much better for a real long time. I hear things are a lot better for blacks out in the West."

Carrie eyed him. "I suspect you would find it easier," she agreed softly. "I'm sorry it has to be that way."

Carl shrugged. "It is what it is. Hatred ain't going to stop me from living my life, but it doesn't mean I can't make things a little easier."

Carrie smiled. "Your family will miss you."

Carl grinned again. "Amber Lou is fixed on going to college, but I'm hoping I can talk Opal and Daddy into going with me when it's time. I already know I'll never find a cook better than Opal, so I figure I ought to take her with me."

Carrie laughed. "You're a very wise young man, Carl."

Carl ducked his head briefly and then looked back up. "Wait until you try the new potato chips, Miss Carrie."

"What's a potato chip?" Carrie had never heard the term before.

Carl shook his head. "You have to taste one before I tell you the story." He turned away when the bell over the door rang again. "I'll be back with your food, but I have a new customer to seat."

Carrie watched him as he straightened his shoulders and walked with confidence to the door. His manner was both self-assured and respectful. She was sure Eddie and Opal had drilled the behavior into him since they had decided to open Opal's Kitchen in the white part of town.

"He's a fine young man," Anthony said quietly.

"He's very special," Carrie agreed. "He was only nine when his mama died. He was one scared little boy when he came out to the plantation the first year of the war."

They watched the traffic on Broad Street and chatted easily until the food arrived. Carrie smiled when she saw a big plate full of fried chicken, okra, and green beans. "Now this is eating," she said happily.

"Not until you've had these." Carl pulled a basket from behind his back and set it down on the table.

Carrie stared at the contents. "What are those?"

"Potato chips," Carl said proudly.

Carrie eyed them dubiously. "Are you supposed to eat them?"

Carl snorted with laughter. "Don't be such a chicken, Miss Carrie. Try one."

Anthony reached forward. "They look wonderful!"

Carrie grimaced as she studied them. "I'm figuring they're made from potatoes since they are called potato chips, but I don't know why someone felt the need to smash all the life from them."

Anthony chuckled as he bit into one and handed her another. "Don't be such a chicken, Miss Carrie," he taunted while Carl laughed.

Carrie made a face at him, but bit into one of the potato chips, surprised when she instantly loved the crunchy, salty taste. "Oh my..." she murmured, as she reached for another one. "Tell me the story of these," she commanded. "Did Opal create these?"

Carl shook his head. "No, ma'am, but as far as we know, Opal's Kitchen is the first restaurant in Richmond, maybe in all the South, to have these."

Carrie took another chip as she listened to him, certain she could eat nothing but the potato chips for lunch.

"Matthew came by with his brother, Harold, when you were in New Mexico," Carl explained. "He told us about this fellow named George Crum who lived up in Sarasota Springs, New York. You know, that's where Mr. Harold used to live."

Carrie smiled and nodded.

"Well, Mr. Crum is both Black and Indian, not that it really matters much. Anyway, they serve this thing up there called French Fries."

Carrie nodded. "I had some when I was in New York City. They came over from Paris. I believe it was Thomas Jefferson who first served them here in America at the White House during his presidency."

Anthony stared at her. "And you know this how?"

Carrie smiled. "When you have Felicia around, you learn all kinds of things that most mere mortals know nothing about." She reached for another potato chip. "Back to your story, Carl."

Carl grinned. "French fries were real popular at the restaurant where Mr. Crum worked, but one of the diners complained they were too thick. Mr. Crum made a thinner batch, but he still complained. Mr. Crum finally made fries too thin to eat with a fork, just so he could annoy the fussy man."

Carrie ate another one. "He ended up loving them," she guessed.

Carl nodded. "The potato chip was born that day! Mr. Harold told us about them, so Opal played around with the potatoes until she thought they were just right. When Mr. Harold told us she finally had it, we put them on the menu." He looked around the restaurant. "Everyone loves them."

Carrie glanced around, surprised to see that almost every table had a basket of potato chips. She sighed happily as she reached into the basket again. "You might want to bring another one of these for Anthony," she suggested. "I plan to eat all these chips myself."

"I don't think so," Anthony scoffed, as he reached forward to snatch a chip.

Carrie laughed and pulled the basket closer.

Carl chortled with laughter. "I'll bring you another basket, Mr. Anthony," he promised. "I learned a long time ago that it's best to not get between Miss Carrie and her food."

Carrie smiled serenely. "I told you Carl is a wise young man."

*****

The sun was setting when they arrived back at the house. They had spent the afternoon roaming the streets of Richmond after polishing off their lunch at Opal's Kitchen. The winter air was cold, but they were getting a reprieve from the bitter temperatures that had encased Richmond before Christmas.

"Want to sit outside for a few minutes?" Anthony suggested.

Carrie nodded, but was suddenly nervous. Unsure of what to say, she blurted out the first thing that came to mind, waving her hand at the towering magnolia tree that guarded the porch. "This magnolia tree is very special to me. My father presented me with the one flower that was blooming the day I married Robert." As soon as she spoke the words, she wondered why in the world she would bring Robert into their conversation.

Anthony regarded her steadily for several long moments before he replied. "I know how much you loved Robert, Carrie."

"I know," Carrie answered with a sigh, and then fell silent. She didn't know what else to say.

"May I speak honestly?" Anthony asked.

Carrie wanted to say no, but it wouldn't be fair to him. "Yes."

"I love you, Carrie Borden."

Carrie opened her mouth to protest, but she couldn't think of what to say.

Anthony held up his hand. "You don't have to say anything. I just want you to know my true feelings. I know you're not ready for another relationship. I understand, and I respect that. I simply wanted you to know, so that if the time ever comes when you *are* ready, you'll know I want to be in the running."

Carrie gazed at him, still searching for the right words. "I..."

Anthony raised his hand again. "I will give you all the time you need, because I love you that much. I fell in love with you the first day we met, when you manipulated me into paying more for a group of horses than I ever have." He smiled. "If you never return my feelings, that will be my problem, not yours." He reached over to grasp her hand. "I promised to be your friend. I will always be that."

Carrie stared at him, her heart swelling with what she knew was love. *Still...* She pulled her hand gently away. "Anthony, we have never been anything but honest with each other, so I can admit to you that I do love you." She held up her own hand when his eyes brightened. "But, that does not mean I want to get married." She struggled to find a way to express herself, and then thought back to her conversation with Rose in the barn.

"I may be ready for marriage again someday, but right now I am focused on being a doctor," she said. "I loved my husband with all my heart, but being married meant my career was not my priority. I want the freedom to pursue my career without expectations or restrictions," she said. "My time on the Santa Fe Trail reminded me how much I truly love being a doctor." She took a deep breath and met Anthony's eyes evenly. "I'm looking forward to establishing the clinic in Philadelphia," Carrie continued, "but I don't know what comes after that. I'm finding the freedom to make my own choices is exhilarating."

Anthony nodded. "I would be surprised if you felt any other way," he murmured.

Carrie stared at him. "Excuse me?"

Anthony smiled. "America is changing, Carrie. It was already changing, but the war made it change faster. Women found out what they are capable of, and they're not willing to take steps back. I agree with that." He took her hand again.

This time Carrie didn't pull away.

"I won't deny that I wish I could go to bed with you every night," he said warmly.

Carrie blushed, but she didn't look away as his green eyes gazed into hers.

"I can wait," Anthony repeated. "I'm wondering, though..." He let his voice trail off.

Carrie smiled slightly. "You're wondering what?"'

"Well, now that you know how I really feel, is it acceptable to say I'm courting you?"

Carrie wanted to nod enthusiastically, but she took her time in responding. She liked Anthony too much to be anything but completely honest. "As long as you understand I may never change my mind," she said softly. "I might decide having your devotion is enough for me as I pursue my career. I wouldn't want you to grow to resent me."

Anthony tilted her chin up. "There is no danger of that," he replied. "I appreciate your honesty more than you know, but," he added in a playful voice, "you need to know I'm going to do my best to change your mind. I won't pressure you, but I intend to make myself completely irresistible."

Carrie grinned, not willing to tell him how easy that might prove to be. "This should be interesting," she said instead.

Anthony smiled, and then lowered his head to claim her lips with his own.

Carrie stiffened momentarily, unsure the rules of the game included kissing, before she melted into him.

Chapter Nine

Carrie wondered if it was too late to change her mind about opening the clinic in Philadelphia. She huddled under a thick layer of blankets in the carriage, but they seemed to be doing nothing to cut the blustery wind blowing inland from the Delaware River. The Santa Fe Trail had been brutal, but Philadelphia in January was somehow worse. Blinking her eyes against the cutting snowflakes, she prayed the traffic would clear so they could make better time. She pulled her collar higher, grateful for the thick gloves and warm hat Abby had presented her with before she left Richmond. In an attempt to keep her mind off the cutting cold, she examined the city as they moved forward through the clogged roads. The clang of a streetcar made her glance up as it rolled by next to her. Her eyes opened wide.

"There are blacks on that streetcar!" Carrie exclaimed.

Her driver, a portly black man who had introduced himself as Sarge, glanced back at her. "You have a problem with that, ma'am?" His voice was courteous, but his eyes were steely.

Carrie took no offense. "Absolutely not. I think it's wonderful! When did it happen?" Her delight almost made her forget the cold.

Sarge tightened his lips as he calculated. "It'll be two years coming up pretty soon, ma'am. It was back in March of sixty-seven." He glanced at her and then continued. "There were a lot of folks who weren't too excited."

"There are stupid people in the world, Sarge," Carrie said sadly. "I suppose that will never change, but I hope things can get better." Sarge nodded, still watching her closely in between paying attention to the road. She understood. Her driver didn't know anything about her. Michael, her usual driver, had left the city to move further north. Even with progress being made, it was only wise for Sarge to stay cautious. She was surprised when Sarge asked her another question.

"You ever heard of Octavius Catto, ma'am?"

Carrie nodded, trying to remember where she had heard the name. "I have...I believe he is a highly respected teacher in the city?" She brightened. "Was he also the one who organized a lot of the black soldiers who served during the war?"

Sarge stared at her with astonishment. "How do you know that?"

Carrie smiled. "My best friend was one of the first black teachers in the contraband camps," she explained. "Her husband was one of the first spies for the Union Army, before he joined one of the units to fight and became a leader."

"That right?" Sarge's voice was skeptical.

Carrie gazed back at him steadily. "That's right."

Sarge still looked dubious. "Your best friend is a black woman?"

"That's right," Carrie repeated, slightly unsettled by the hard look in his eyes.

"Ain't that a *Southern* accent, ma'am?" he pressed.

"That's right," Carrie repeated, suddenly irritated that he could intimidate her. She sat up straighter, forgetting the cold as anger flared through her. "Do you have a problem with that?" she snapped. "Not everyone in the South fits the stereotype people like to put on us." She paused. "Any more than black people do," she added in a firm voice.

Sarge looked uncomfortable, but his eyes were still hard.

Carrie felt a surge of sympathy as she looked past the hardness in his eyes and saw the truth. "Where were you a slave?" she asked softly.

Sarge's eyes widened briefly before he seemed to deflate. "Down in Mississippi, ma'am," he admitted.

"And it was terrible."

Sarge stared into her eyes, but the hardness was gone, replaced by the pain of memories. "Yes, ma'am, it was terrible," he agreed.

"I'm sorry," Carrie said. "How long have you been in Philadelphia?" She innately knew that if she wanted to dissolve his hardness, he needed to know she cared about him as a person.

"Ever since the war ended," Sarge replied. "I fought through the war once them soldiers came down and set me free from the plantation in '62." He took a deep breath. "Captain Jones, my commanding officer, was a good man."

Carrie gasped. "He still is," she said warmly.

"You know the captain?" Sarge asked with surprise.

"I do, indeed," Carrie replied. "He is a very good friend. His sister, Susan, is my business partner in my horse stables."

"You own a stables, ma'am?"

Carrie grinned, understanding his skepticism. "I do," she assured him, her tone growing somber. "My husband and I owned it together, but he was killed by vigilantes on our plantation in Virginia. It's mine now."

Sarge whistled. "Your husband be killed by the vigilantes?" His eyes darkened with anger and fear. "I'm real sorry to hear that."

"Thank you," Carrie replied, and then had a thought. "Do you know Moses Samuels?"

Sarge chuckled outright. "Moses Samuels? Well, of course I do. Ain't nobody who ever met Moses could forget him. He's too big to be forgot. I didn't serve in his unit, but he knew Captain Jones, too. How you know Moses?"

"He's my best friend's husband," Carrie confided, "and also one of my best friends." She paused, wondering how much she should say, and then decided there was no reason to not reveal everything. The only way people in America would know that things could be different is if they were to see it *being* different. "He also happens to have become half-owner of the plantation my family has owned for generations."

Sarge took a deep breath as his eyes widened. "You really think I'm gonna believe that?"

Carrie shrugged. "I don't really care if you believe it or not. I'm just telling you the way it is." She decided to not go into the revelation that Rose was also her father's half-sister. There was only so much the poor man could take.

Sarge focused on his driving for a while, and then turned back to her. "Why you tellin' me all this?"

Carrie smiled. "Because people of every color need to know things can be different if we truly want them to be." She paused while she thought, grateful their conversation was keeping her mind off the cold. "And not just black people," she added.

"What you mean?" Sarge asked.

"There are many people here in America that are not equal," she answered. "Women should have the vote," she said firmly, "and husbands shouldn't have control of their wives." Her thoughts crystallized as she spoke. "And it's not only blacks who have a hard time in America. The Irish have been treated terribly, as have other ethnic groups." She shook her head. "We talk about America being the land of the free and equal, but sometimes I think it only applies to white men."

Sarge was staring at her. "You get into a lot of trouble talking like that, ma'am?"

Carrie chuckled. "Sometimes," she admitted. "But it's true. And, it needs to be said."

"You really know Moses Samuels?"

"I really do," Carrie replied with a smile. "He and Rose are at Oberlin College right now. One of his men from the army is running the plantation while they're gone. Most of the Cromwell workers came from his old unit. Moses is studying to be a lawyer, and his wife, Rose, is preparing to be a teacher."

Sarge went back to studying her. "And you really believe things can be different?"

"I *have* to believe it," Carrie replied, almost surprised to realize how desperately she felt that. "I know things are still very difficult for you, but isn't it better than being a slave?"

Sarge nodded emphatically. "That be the truth."

"It took a long time for that to change, but it did. I'm sorry to say I believe it will be a long time before blacks are truly equal, but there are a lot of people fighting to make that happen, too. If you give up believing, then you have no reason to fight." Carrie thought about the question that had started the conversation. "Why did you ask me about Octavius Catto?"

Sarge chuckled. "I already done forgot about that. Remember your surprise that the streetcars got black folks on them now?"

Carrie nodded, waiting for him to continue.

"There be a woman named Caroline LeCount. She be Catto's fiancée." He paused. "I didn't finish telling you about Catto, though. I should do that first. He's not all black, like lots of black folks. He's from some fancy mixed-race family down in Charleston that was free, but his daddy brought them up here. And, he ain't just a teacher. He also a real fine baseball player," Sarge boasted. "He's done turned Philadelphia into a major hub for Negro league baseball."

"Baseball?" Carrie asked in surprise.

Sarge nodded. "He helps run the Pythian Baseball Club here. They went undefeated two years ago, back in '67."

Carrie could tell how much pride Sarge felt. Then she had a thought. "Do you play baseball, Sarge?"

He shrugged modestly. "I might have been on that team," he said dismissively, then went back to his story. "Anyway, back in March of '67, the General Assembly of Pennsylvania passed a bill saying black folks can be on the streetcars. Well, three days later, Caroline LeCount, that be the woman engaged to Catto, tried to get on one of them cars. She also be a real fine teacher, by-the-way. Anyway, the conductor weren't about to let her get on—told her we wasn't allowed to ride on the cars. He was real rude to her. Now, most people would a probably just let it go 'cause they don't want to draw attention, but not her," Sarge said proudly. "She went to a magistrate first, but they weren't gonna be no help, so she went all the way up to the office of Secretary of the Commonwealth right here in Philadelphia, and got herself a copy of the legislation that said she *could* get on that streetcar. Well," he said with a chuckle, "that conductor done got arrested and had to pay a hundred dollar fine." He smiled in satisfaction. "And the Blacks been riding the city streetcars ever since."

Carrie clapped her hands. "What a wonderful story! And what an extraordinary woman. All of us have to demand that things be different if we want them to be." She thought about what Sarge had told her. "So Catto is mulatto?"

"Yep."

"Where does he teach?"

"Over at the Institute for Colored Youth," Sarge answered. "Why you want to know?"

Carrie was relieved there was no suspicion in his look, just mere curiosity. "The couple I'm staying with while I'm here in Philadelphia are very good friends." Again, she didn't feel the need to go into all the details. She was still appalled and embarrassed by what her grandfather had done to Old Sarah. "Jeremy is mulatto," she revealed, "though he looks completely white." She hesitated, wondering how much she should say, but quicly decided it didn't matter, because no one could ever miss Sarah Rose's mixed heritage. "Jeremy's wife is white. They recently had twins. One came out white, while the other looks more black."

Sarge whistled. "I didn't know stuff like that could happen."

"It can happen," Carrie assured him. "Anyway, I think Catto could be a very good connection for Jeremy. He fought hard for black rights in Richmond. I know he wants to continue that fight here in Philadelphia."

Sarge nodded. "He didn't stay down there in Richmond 'cause of how his mixed baby gonna be treated," he said shrewdly.

"That's right," Carrie agreed.

"What's Mr. Jeremy do?"

"He's taking over as manager of the Cromwell Factory in Moyamensing," Carrie revealed.

Sarge shook his head. "Well, if that don't beat all."

Carrie waited for him to continue.

"Catto grew up down in Moyamensing once his daddy brought the family up here. That be a real poor part of town," he revealed.

Carrie remained silent, wanting to know what else he was going to say.

"Just the poor blacks and the Irish lived down there. Catto went to a place called the Lombard Street School. Back then it was the only grammar school for blacks. He and his friends got real used to sprinting down Lombard Street through all them Irish boys." He shook his head. "It weren't real safe."

Carrie could easily imagine the fights that had broken out among the boys.

"When they opened up the Institute for Colored Youth, Catto went there. He did real good. And now he teaches there." Suddenly his eyes widened. "Ain't I taking you down to Moyamensing?"

"That's right," Carrie agreed. "I'm going to visit a friend."

Sarge seemed to accept that. "I heard some good things about that factory," he said. "I wish they were hiring more black folk, but I figure it's making things down there better anyway, now that they be hiring the Irish. They ain't got so much reason to hate us." He paused, thinking. "You know, those Irish be one of the biggest reasons it took black folks so long to get on the streetcars. They didn't want black men to be able to get rides down to the wharf where they could take their jobs."

"Life is hard for a lot of people," Carrie said sympathetically. "Fear makes people do things they might not normally do."

"You figure your friend Jeremy is gonna hire some black folks down in Moyamensing?" Sarge pressed.

Carrie considered his question. "I don't know," she answered honestly. "Cromwell Factory was started in Moyamensing to give the Irish a chance for a fair-paying job. There seem to be more opportunities opening up for blacks elsewhere in the city since the war ended, but there's not much for the Irish." She paused. "I do know, however, that Cromwell Factory down in Richmond has hired about an equal number of whites and blacks. If the factory here is able to expand, I suppose I could see that happening." When she finished speaking and saw the expression on Sarge's face, she realized she had probably said too much. She didn't feel the need to hide her identity, but she preferred to keep it low key.

Sarge was staring at her. "You sure do know a lot about Cromwell Factory."

Carrie sighed. She didn't want to renew his earlier suspicions because she was being evasive. She wanted Jeremy to get an opportunity to meet Octavius Catto. Looking up, she held Sarge's gaze, amazed that he could still continue to maneuver the carriage through the crowded streets when he didn't seem to be paying much attention to his driving. "My name is Carrie Cromwell Borden," she said. "My father and stepmother own the factories."

Sarge whistled. "Seems like that be somethin' you should be shoutin' from the rooftops so that people know how important you be."

"Being their daughter does not make me important," Carrie protested. "They are the ones who have created the factories and the opportunities." Knowing that her influence had helped make it happen in Moyamensing was quite enough for her.

Sarge was staring at her with an assessing look. "So what do you do, Mrs. Carrie Cromwell Borden?"

Carrie smiled. "I'm a doctor."

Sarge whistled again. "A lady *doctor*?" He shook his head. "For real?"

"For real," Carrie assured him, and then she stiffened. "Watch out!" she cried.

Sarge whipped around in the seat just in time to pull the carriage around a large wagon that had suddenly turned and almost blocked the road. "Land sakes," he hollered, shaking his fist at the other driver, who merely scowled in return.

Carrie was relieved when Sarge decided to focus more closely on his driving. She was warmer, but she was no less eager to reach Biddy and Faith's house. Her heart saddened when she allowed herself to focus on the fact that Biddy was gone. She could hardly believe it was a year ago that she had held Biddy's hands while her friend died. She took a deep breath, remembering all their wonderful conversations, and how coming to grips with her own Irish heritage had launched Cromwell Factory in Moyamensing.

"I miss you, Biddy" she whispered. Indeed, she knew she always would. Biddy had become the grandmother she'd never had. All she had to do was close her eyes to see Biddy's sparkling blue ones, full of kindness and compassion. Suffering losses that would have crushed most people, Biddy had become more determined to make a difference. Carrie prayed she would do the same thing every day of her life.

"It won't be long now," Sarge called back over his shoulder.

Carrie was relieved when she realized they had finally broken through the worst of the traffic and were very close to Moyamensing. She was confident the cold snow would have everyone inside. No one but Faith was expecting her, and her heavy layers of clothing concealed her identity. She normally loved being greeted by all the Moyamensing children, but today her heart wasn't in it. She was focused on fulfilling the mission Biddy had given her.

Ten minutes later, the carriage rolled to a stop in front of the impressive home Biddy and Faith had shared. Carrie was glad she'd gotten an early start that morning. She handed Sarge enough money for a good lunch. "Will you return in four hours?"

"You bet, Mrs. Borden," Sarge answered. "I'll get you home before dark." He cast an eye at the sky. "But what if it keeps snowing? I'll have a hard time getting through these roads."

Carrie cast a practiced eye at the sky. "It won't snow much longer," she said confidently. "I believe we'll be fine." She laughed at Sarge's dubious look. "I'm a plantation girl," she reminded him. "I know you didn't have much snow in Mississippi, but I learned how to read the weather signs when I was a little girl. We'll be fine."

Sarge shrugged. "Whatever you say. I'll be back in four hours."

Carrie jumped from the carriage and ran toward the house, giving a cry of delight when Faith appeared in the doorway. "Faith!" Her delight faded when she got closer to the slender, elderly black woman. She was still thrilled to see her, but she was alarmed at how much Faith had aged in twelve months. Always slender, Faith now looked almost skeletal. Carrie kept the smile fixed on her face as she clasped her friend's hands, stepped inside, and pulled the door closed against the cold. "It's so wonderful to see you."

Faith pulled her close. "Carrie..." she murmured.

Carrie held her in a warm embrace until she felt Faith relax. Only then did she step back. "How are you?" she asked quietly.

Faith sighed. "We both know I don't look very good." She shook her head. "I know Biddy would probably be disappointed in me, but I've been kind of fading away ever since she left us. I've got lots of folks around here who check on me, and I'm very grateful, but living without Biddy in this big house is very lonely."

Carrie nodded with sympathy. She understood grief. She also knew Faith was almost eighty years old. She was convinced it was Faith's companionship that had kept Biddy alive until ninety-eight. What was going to keep Faith alive? An idea that had been germinating in the back of Carrie's mind suddenly sprang to full-blown life. She knew though, that she would have to approach it carefully. She lifted her head and sniffed. "Do I smell cookies?"

Faith smiled, her eyes brightening a little. "Did you really think I wouldn't have cookies for you?" she demanded.

"I didn't want to have expectations," Carrie murmured.

"Since when?" Faith scoffed. "Every time you walk through that door, you're expecting my cookies."

Carrie was happy to see a flash of Faith's old spirit, and she was suddenly certain her idea was a good one. "Guilty as charged," she said with a laugh. She hooked her arm through Faith's and walked with her to the kitchen, glad to find it warm and cozy.

Faith interpreted the look on her face. "Arden comes by every morning to build up the fires," she told her. "Biddy's grandson has been very good to me in the last year."

"I'm glad," Carrie replied. "He knows how much you meant to Biddy." Her heart filled with sadness as a look of desolation filled Faith's eyes. It was time to put her plan into action. "Let's take the cookies into the parlor."

Faith piled a plate with cookies, added a pot of steaming tea and two delicate Davenport china cups, and then led the way.

Carrie had to battle tears when she spotted the chair where Biddy had taken her last breath. She watched as Faith carefully avoided looking at it, and then settled into a chair that would keep her eyes trained in a different direction. Carrie doubted Faith used the room very often. She pushed aside her own grief as she poured the tea, adding a little bit of cream and sugar. "So, it's time for the clinic," she said cheerfully.

"It is," Faith said, seeming to draw energy from Biddy's last request. "I found a place a block or so from here that I believe will be the perfect location. It's in the center of Moyamensing, and it's large enough to handle the amount of people I believe will come."

"And they'll let us rent it?" Carrie asked. "It can be difficult to find spaces for a homeopathic clinic run by a woman."

Faith snorted and smiled her first genuine smile. "Oh, they'll let us," Faith said confidently. "I found out recently that Biddy owned the building. Since I was put in charge of all her property until I pass on, and then Arden after me—who wouldn't dare deny Biddy's request—we don't have anything to worry about."

"That is wonderful news!" Carrie paused, making sure her face and eyes showed the correct amount of concern. "We still have a problem, though."

Faith's eyes sharpened. "And what would that be?"

"Well," Carrie said, "I have an idea of who I would like to run the clinic once I have it established, but I would want them to live in Moyamensing so they would be close to their patients." She sighed heavily. "Lodging around here can be hard to come by, and I would want them to be comfortable, especially if they're a single woman." She looked at Faith. "Do you have any ideas about that?"

Faith stared at her for several long moments before she answered. "You want them to live here."

Carrie couldn't tell if Faith was annoyed, but she wasn't going to let that stop her. Still, she shook her head quickly. "Not if it would be an inconvenience in any way," she assured her. "I do like knowing, however, that the woman running the clinic that was Biddy's last request, would be in a safe, warm place." She tried to keep her voice neutral, but she was aware she might be going a little overboard.

Faith narrowed her eyes. "Do you have someone in mind?"

Carrie shrugged. "I know who I hope will do it, but I haven't spoken to her yet. I'll be meeting with her later tonight."

"Tell me about her," Faith invited.

Carrie smiled. "Her name is Carolyn Blakely. She was the first person I met at the Homeopathic College, and she went with me to New Mexico last year."

Faith's interest was sincere. "All of those letters you sent when you returned home were fascinating. I remember you talking about Carolyn."

Carrie envisioned the older woman with salt and pepper hair that topped lively, light blue eyes. "She was invaluable on the trip," she confessed. "All of my team was wonderful, but Carolyn brought a maturity and steadiness that none of the rest of us had."

"How old is she?" Faith queried.

"I don't know for certain, but she is in her mid-fifties."

"And just finishing school to be a doctor?"

Carrie nodded. "Her husband died a few years back. She had always wanted to be a doctor, so she decided to use this time in her life to do it. I believe the people here would find it easy to trust her."

Faith nodded thoughtfully, and held Carrie with her direct eyes. "Don't think I don't know what you're doing."

Carrie blinked innocently. "What do you mean?"

Faith rolled her eyes. "You think I don't know that you're trying to put someone in this big old house so I won't be alone?"

Carrie considered denying it, but grinned instead. "Is it working?"

Faith glared at her for a moment, and then chuckled. "I suppose it is," she finally said. "I wouldn't want someone young, but this Carolyn seems interesting."

Carrie held her breath, wondering if Faith would make the connection that there was about the same age difference as there had been between her and Biddy. She could tell by the soft expression on Faith's face that she had.

Faith's eyes darkened as the memories swelled through her. "And she won't care that she will be living with a black woman?"

"I can assure you she will not," Carrie said. "It will take her only moments to realize she will be living with a very *special* woman." Faith took a sip of tea and turned to stare directly at Biddy's chair. Carrie held her breath, knowing somehow that Faith was asking permission of her old friend.

Faith nodded her head slowly. "I'm not saying yes, but I'm willing to meet her."

"That's wonderful!" Carrie said enthusiastically. Now, she could only hope Carolyn would consider running the clinic here in Moyamensing. They hadn't talked about Carolyn's plans when she finished school in the spring. She could be planning on moving to a completely different part of the country.

Faith rolled her eyes. "You think I don't know you're trying to put someone in this big old house so I won't be alone?"

Carrie considered denying it, but grinned instead. "Is it working?"

Faith glared at her for a moment, and then chuckled. "I suppose it is," she finally said. "I wouldn't want someone young, but this Carolyn seems interesting."

Carrie held her breath, wondering if Faith would make the connection that there was about the same age difference as there had been between her and Biddy. She could tell by the soft expression on Faith's face that she had.

Faith's eyes darkened as the memories swelled through her. "And she won't care that she will be living with a black woman?"

"I can assure you she will not," Carrie said firmly. "It will take her only moments to realize she will be living with a very special woman." Faith took a sip of tea, and then turned to stare directly at Biddy's chair. Carrie held her breath, knowing somehow that Faith was asking permission of her old friend.

Faith nodded her head slowly. "I'm not saying yes, but I'm willing to meet her."

"That's wonderful!" Carrie said enthusiastically. Now, she could only hope Carolyn would consider running the clinic here in Moyamensing. They had not talked about Carolyn's plans when she finished school in the spring. She could be planning on moving to a completely different part of the country.

*****

Sarge was right on time, and Carrie was waiting for him. The snow had stopped, just as Carrie predicted, but there was a fresh bank of clouds on the horizon that had her concerned. Combined with the shift in the wind, which was now blowing in from the west, she was fairly certain they were in for a large snowstorm. The flakes this morning had been nothing but a harbinger of what was coming.

Sarge was staring at the sky, too. "What do you think, plantation lady?"

Carrie chuckled as she climbed into the carriage, and then turned to give Faith a final wave. She hated the forlorn look that had already settled in her friend's eyes, but if all went well, that would be changing soon. "I think we have just enough time to get back to my house," she said cheerfully. "But," she added, "tonight is going to bring us some real snow."

Sarge pulled his hat down further on his head, picked up the reins, and urged the horse forward. "Let's go, girl. We'll all be warm soon if you get us back quickly." The mare pricked her ears as if she understood, and took off at a brisk trot.

Carrie snuggled down into the blankets. She'd had enough talk for one day. All she wanted to do now was think about her conversation with Faith, and finalize the plans they had discussed.

Chapter Ten

Marietta hummed contentedly as she carried warm water to the water closet to give the twins their bath. She missed Richmond, but she loved Abby's house, especially the coal furnace in the basement that kept the house cozy. After living her whole life hauling wood and building fires to keep a house warm, this was sheer luxury. Micah took care of keeping the fires burning in Thomas' Richmond house, but she had never gotten over feeling guilty about it. Even though Micah was no longer a slave, and was paid well for his job at the Cromwell home, it was still hard for her. She had loved Richmond with all her heart, and missed it, but there was a large part of her that was glad to be back in the North. After fighting so hard for equal rights, and after spending the last four years as a teacher in the war-torn South, her heart was evidently ready for a break.

She poured the water into the basin, and then went into her and Jeremy's bedroom to fetch the twins. She could hardly believe Marcus and Sarah Rose were already two months old. They were still small, but growing fast. Their little personalities were also becoming quite obvious. She chuckled when Sarah Rose waved her fists in the air as soon as she walked into the room. Her daughter's dark eyes followed her progress, a toothless grin almost splitting her face. Sounds of delight burst forth.

Marcus, on the other hand, was completely content to lay quietly and watch her. His blue eyes regarded her steadily, but he didn't make a sound. She might have worried, except for the complete contentment that suffused his face. She couldn't help but think about how Jeremy and Rose would have compared to each other if they hadn't been separated at birth.

"Come here, my darling," she crooned as she swept Sarah Rose into her arms, laughing when the cries of delight from her daughter's lips grew louder. "It's time for your bath, little one."

Marietta frowned as she glanced out the window and saw dusk was falling. Her concern grew as she saw the thick clouds hovering over the city, pressing down lower with each gust of wind that rattled the windowpanes. She hoped Carrie and Jeremy would be home soon. It was obvious the snow would not hold off much longer. All the signs said it would be a big storm; she wanted all her family where they would be safe and warm.

She turned away from the window, undressed Sarah Rose, and lowered her into the bath water. Her daughter waved her arms and her eyes grew wide. Sarah Rose loved her baths. Marcus merely tolerated them with the same calm that seemed to encompass his entire little being.

As Marietta bathed her little girl, she thought about how drastically her life had changed since having the twins. She hoped to go back to teaching someday, but for now, she was content to be a mother. She was also willing to admit that as much as she missed Richmond, she was happy to not have to constantly worry about what would happen to her children. She wasn't naïve, however. She knew Sarah Rose, and Marcus by association, would still face bigotry and racism in the North, but she prayed violence wouldn't accompany it here in Philadelphia.

*****

Carrie drew a deep sigh of relief when Sarge pulled the carriage to a stop in front of the house. "Thank you!" she called. "Now, get back to the stable as fast as you can," she urged. "I want you and Nellie out of this cold."

"No more than we do," Sarge answered with a brief smile. Then he paused. "You be a fine woman, Mrs.

Carrie Cromwell Borden. I enjoyed taking you to Moyamensing today."

Carrie reached up and laid a hand on his arm. "And you are a fine man, Sarge. I'll be in touch. Before long, I'll be going to Moyamensing every day. I would love it if you would be my regular driver."

Sarge nodded, his eyes bright with pleasure. "I would be my honor, ma'am."

As Carrie waved a hand, turned and ran up the stairs, the first flakes began to fall, swirling in the dim light of the streetlamps that were just beginning to glow.

"You're home!" Marietta called. "I'm in the kitchen."

Carrie hung up her hat, coat, and gloves on the coat tree in the foyer, held her hands over the furnace for a few moments, and then dashed to the kitchen. She took a deep breath as she pushed open the door. "Chicken soup," she said happily. "There is no better food for a cold, snowy night." She looked around. "Is Jeremy home yet?"

Marietta nodded. "He arrived a few minutes ago. He went up to kiss the twins. I've already put them down for the night."

"Will they sleep through the night?" Carrie asked curiously.

Marietta stared at her with disbelief. "You can't be serious. I haven't had a full night of sleep since those two little angels were born. One wakes up crying to be fed. As soon as that one is satisfied, the other one wakes up demanding food. It's as if they have an inner signal that tells them it's their turn." She paused. "I'm not sure I'll ever know what it means to sleep through the night again."

Carrie eyed her. "It must not be *that* bad," she said unsympathetically. "You look happy."

Marietta grinned. "I've never been happier," she agreed. "I'm learning how to sleep during nap time."

Carrie walked over to smell the soup, and then opened the woodstove to peer in at the golden biscuits. "You're definitely conquering the cooking," she said. "I'm as spoiled here as I was on the plantation."

"Better than the food you had on the Santa Fe Trail last year?" Marietta teased.

Carrie made a face. "Hard biscuits and hot mush got old quickly," she admitted. Then she grinned. "I'm so excited to see everyone tonight. It's hard to believe it's been three months since I last saw my team."

Marietta nodded as she dished up bowls of soup. "Do they know the reason you're here?" She slid the pan of biscuits out of the oven, smiling her approval at their fluffy perfection.

Carrie shook her head. "I don't think so. But for tonight, I'm just thrilled to be with all of them again." She looked out the window at the swirling snow. "If they can make it here," she said in a worried voice. "I think we're in for a big storm."

Marietta raised a brow. "Aren't these the same people who survived a blizzard on a wagon train?"

Carrie laughed. "Yes, but that wasn't exactly a choice."

"Really?" Marietta drawled. "I didn't see anyone holding a gun to your head to make you decide to travel the Santa Fe Trail in the dead of winter."

Carrie laughed again. "That's true, but I'm not sure I would be willing to go out on a night like tonight if I had the choice to stay warm and dry."

Jeremy pushed into the kitchen. He reached to grab a biscuit, but ducked away when Marietta swatted at him. "How can you deny a starving man?" he protested.

Marietta eyed him. "I'm sure you'll survive until I get it on the plate," she retorted.

"Perhaps," Jeremy conceded. "What can I do to help?"

"Tell me the twins are still asleep, and that I'll be able to eat a meal in peace." Marietta placed the bowls of soup on the table as she spoke, and then dumped the biscuits in a basket.

"They were sound asleep when I went in," Jeremy assured her. "I left the door open so we'll hear them if they cry."

Marietta sighed with relief. "You have just earned the right to eat," she announced happily.

Carrie moaned with pleasure as the first spoonful of soup slid down her throat. "I will forever be grateful that you made Annie teach you how to cook. This is delicious!"

Jeremy stopped spooning soup into his mouth long enough to cut open a hot, steaming biscuit and slather it with butter. "I am a blessed man," he murmured. "There were times I thought I might starve to death before I reached old age, but you have come around nicely, my dear."

Marietta scowled at him, but chuckled. "I know my cooking wasn't the best."

Jeremy opened his mouth to respond, then shut it again. He merely nodded, a sly grin on his face.

Carrie turned to Jeremy. "I found out something interesting today." She told them about Sarge, and about Octavius Catto.

Jeremy listened closely. "I'd like to meet him," he agreed when she finished. "I'm, of course, interested in furthering equal rights, but..." His voice trailed off. "What I really want to do is play baseball!"

Carrie and Marietta laughed.

"Since when?" Marietta asked.

Jeremy shrugged. "For a long time," he admitted. "Richmond has some amateur teams that started playing right after the war, but I was too busy at the factory to think about joining."

Carrie cocked her head. "What team would you play for? I suspect you're a little too white to play on Catto and Sarge's team."

Jeremy frowned. "Too white for some. Too black for others." His face darkened, but he shrugged. "I suppose it's time to make it known that I'm mulatto. One of the reasons for coming to Philadelphia was so that I wouldn't have to hide—and so that I don't have to hide the twins. I'll talk to Catto. If they'll have this white boy on their team, I'll play." He glanced at the window as a strong gust of wind pressed the snow flat against the glass. "Once the ground doesn't have snow on it, that is."

"Will you have time when summer comes?" Marietta asked. "I would love to bring the twins to the games," she said eagerly.

"I think so," Jeremy responded. "The factory's old manager has done a fine job. Everything is running smoothly, and it's so much like the Richmond factory there isn't much to learn. I'm just focusing on meeting all the workers. They are a fine group of people."

Carrie thought about her conversation with Sarge. "Do you think you will be expanding operations?"

Jeremy looked thoughtful. "Possibly. There is a building next door that can be purchased, but I'm not sure now is the time to do it. I've communicated with Thomas and Abby about it. We've decided to see how things go in the next year. Business is excellent, but..."

Carrie nodded. "But financial trouble could be coming because of things happening with the economy."

Jeremy eyed her. "You've been talking to Abby."

"I have," Carrie agreed. "I understand you have to be careful, but I know how much it would mean if you could expand operations and hire more people."

"I agree," Jeremy replied. "But if we take too much risk and end up shutting down the existing factory, we'll do nothing but hurt people."

"You're right," Carrie murmured, then changed the subject. "How is George doing?" Carrie had not communicated with her old friend during the year she had been away.

"He's great," Jeremy said enthusiastically. "I appreciated our office manager in Richmond, but George has an innate business talent. He sees things our Richmond manager didn't see, which definitely makes my job easier. I actually gave him a raise two days ago."

Carrie grinned. "That's great!" It was hard to remember George as a frightened young woman who had decided that going to war disguised as a man with her brother was better than being left alone on their farm. Georgia's decision to continue living life as a man because of better opportunity, had obviously been a good one. Jeremy and Marietta didn't know the truth about George, and there was no reason for them to know. Carrie couldn't wait to see him.

*****

Three days passed before the roads were clear enough for carriages and wagons to resume travel. The snowstorm had indeed kept her Santa Fe team from coming to the house, but Carrie had enjoyed the three days holed up with Jeremy, Marietta, and the twins. They had played countless hours of chess and backgammon, and Marietta had kept them supplied with hot soups and Irish oatmeal cookies.

Carrie loved every minute with the twins, taking them from Marietta every chance she could. There was something both healing and haunting about their smooth, fresh skin and delicious smell when they came out of their baths, and she was content to rock them for hours in front of the fireplace. Somehow, it was easier to think about Bridget when she was holding the twins.

"Does being with the twins make it harder?" Marietta asked one day as she stood in the doorway and watched Carrie with Marcus and Sarah Rose.

Carrie understood immediately. "Actually, no. I thought it might," she said softly, "but a part of me heals every time I hold one of your adorable children. I may not ever be a mother, but there are so many children in the world to love."

"Never be a mother?" Marietta protested. "Surely you will be!"

Carrie lifted a brow. "No one knows what the future holds," she said calmly. She was amazed how much she meant it.

"You'll marry again," Marietta argued.

"Perhaps," Carrie answered, unable to keep her thoughts from going to Anthony.

Marietta took a deep breath. "Anthony loves you, you know."

Carrie merely looked at her friend.

Marietta nodded her head. "It's obvious that he does," she said.

"Yes," Carrie agreed. "He told me."

Marietta stared at her. "He *told* you? When?"

"Before I left to come here." She paused, knowing the questions racing through Marietta's mind. "I told him I wasn't ready." She then repeated what she had told Anthony, more certain than ever that she had made the right decision.

Marietta considered her words, and smiled. "You'll know what to do," she said.

"Yes," Carrie agreed, nuzzling Sarah Rose's soft, downy hair. "I'll know."

*****

Carrie raced to the door when the first knock sounded. She threw it open, waved a hand to Sarge who was just rolling away in the carriage, and then pulled Carolyn Blakely inside to give her a hug. "Carolyn! It is so wonderful to see you."

Carolyn laughed and returned the hug. "And it is marvelous to see you, Carrie. Having to push through snow to get here was reminiscent of where we were this time last year. The streets are mostly clear, but the snowbanks are massive."

Carrie laughed with her, even more assured Carolyn was the perfect person to run the clinic. As she gazed into her dancing eyes, she knew Carolyn would connect with the Moyamensing residents. She was eager to talk to her, but another knock at the door told her she would have to wait.

"Nathan Gaffney!" Carrie cried as she gripped his hands, and then hugged him, gazing up into blue eyes crowned by thick red hair. He was as tall and wiry as ever. "Did you have trouble getting here?" She knew he had little money, so she suspected he would have walked, though she had sent him a telegram informing him she would send a carriage.

Nathan shook his head, answering in the thick Irish brogue she never tired of listening to. "Not a bit of trouble," he assured her. "There wasn't a blizzard blowing, and the snow is not nearly as deep as what we dealt with last year. A year ago, I would have complained of this being a mighty storm. Now it seems like nothing more than a wee bit of snow," he said cheerfully.

"I know what you mean," Carolyn replied, stepping forward to give him a hug.

Within a few minutes, Randall Bremerton and Melissa Whiteside had joined them, rubbing their hands over the furnace after they shrugged out of their heavy coats.

"Thank you for sending the carriage," Melissa said gratefully. "I know I could have walked through the snow, but after nine months on the Santa Fe Trail, I have discovered an even greater affinity for the small luxuries in life."

"You and me, both," Randall agreed. "Three years in the army during the war, and the months on the Trail, have convinced me I have done all the 'roughing it' that I have any desire for." He stood close to the furnace. "I won't mind if I'm never cold another day in my life."

"You are living in the wrong city," Carrie said with a chuckle.

"Perhaps," Randall agreed. "There was a time I thought I would live in the South, but the idea of slavery kept me in the North." He shook his head. "Now that the war is over, I find it is still not a place I want to live."

"I understand," Carrie said sadly. "I hope the chaos will settle down, but I believe it will take some time."

Marietta walked out of the kitchen holding a large tray. "Can I interest anyone in Irish oatmeal cookies?" she asked.

Carrie made the introductions, including Jeremy as he walked down from checking on the babies. Time flew as the group talked and laughed, reliving the experiences they had shared, and talking about what was going on with them now.

Nathan was the one to ask Carrie the direct question she had been waiting for. "So, what *are* you doing here in the dead of winter, Carrie? Why aren't you down on your plantation with your horses?"

Carrie smiled. "I have a job to do up here first."

"Graduation, perhaps?" Carolyn asked. "Dr. Strikener told me they had approved you to receive your doctor's degree."

Carrie nodded. "I will be graduating," she agreed, still not used to the fact she was actually done with school. "But that is not the reason I'm here..." She let her voice trail off mysteriously.

Randall cocked his head. "Are you going to tell us, or just leave us guessing?"

Carrie grinned. "I'm going to tell you, because I hope all of you will be involved." She was thrilled when they all looked interested. "I've been given a mission to accomplish by a very special lady." She told them about Biddy, choking up at times with the memories that surfaced. "I loved her like she was my grandmother," she said softly. "Besides the fact that she was a good friend, and a remarkable woman, she filled a very special place in my life."

Nathan was listening closely. "She was the one who gave the building for the factory down in Moyamensing, wasn't she?"

"She was," Carrie agreed. "She was so excited to be doing something for her people there."

Nathan nodded his head. "That was only one thing she did," he replied. "My mama has talked about Biddy Flannagan for years. It seems she was the reason I got to go to school when I was a boy. I wouldn't be in medical school now if she hadn't given me my first opportunities."

Carrie's eyes misted. "She would be so happy to know that."

"What does she want you to do?" Carolyn asked bluntly.

Carrie smiled. "One of her final requests in her will was that I start a homeopathic clinic in Moyamensing," she revealed. "A building has already been secured, and the funding is in the bank."

"That's wonderful!" Carolyn cried. "But, you here in *Philadelphia*? I didn't think you wanted to live here."

"I don't," Carrie replied. "I have agreed to start the clinic, and then I'm going to pass it off to someone else to run it."

Silence met her announcement before understanding began to dawn in their eyes. The group remained silent, however. Carrie knew they were going to wait to hear what else she had to say. "I've thought about this a great deal," Carrie continued. "I only want people I know and trust to work in the clinic. After nine months on the Trail, and then in Bosque Redondo, I know I can completely trust all of you." She paused. "I would like to hire each of you to work in the clinic on a part-time basis."

Heads nodded eagerly, but still no one had spoken. Carrie smiled to herself. Her team had learned to let her communicate fully before they had a reaction. She turned to look into Carolyn's eyes. "Carolyn, you are finishing school in a few months. I would be honored if you would consider working closely with me, and then taking over the clinic when it is time."

Carolyn gasped and laid a trembling hand over her mouth. "Really?" she whispered.

"Really," Carrie assured her. "I believe you would be a perfect fit for Moyamensing."

"Why?" Carolyn asked with her usual blunt honesty.

"May I answer that?" Nathan asked eagerly.

Carrie smiled with delight. "Please do." Nathan knew Moyamensing better than anyone since he had grown up there.

"Moyamensing can be a challenging place," Nathan began. "The Irish have learned not to trust many people because it's the only way they've been able to survive. They've gotten used to being treated badly." He glanced at Carolyn and Carrie. "Then you two came down and started treating folks for cholera. You know, my parents were saved during the epidemic. One of you is responsible for saving their lives." His eyes warmed as he looked at Carolyn. "You've not been back much since then, but I can assure you not a folk has forgotten you.

They wouldn't have to learn to trust you because they already *do* trust you." He nodded his head. "I can tell you for certain sure that as soon as the Irish of Moyamensing realize who is running that new clinic, they will be coming in droves."

Carrie watched as confidence built in Carolyn's eyes. Then uncertainty flickered.

"Droves?" she asked. She looked at Carrie with disappointed eyes. "I still have this term at school. I'm not sure I can give what you need to the clinic."

"That's where everyone else comes in," Carrie said, turning toward the rest. "Nathan, Randall, Melissa...would you be interested in working at the clinic part-time while you are in school? You will be paid, of course."

"I would work there for free," Melissa said eagerly. "I learned more during the nine months of our trip than I ever have, even though my father is a homeopathic physician. The answer is yes for me!"

"Me, too," Nathan replied. "I can't think of anything more satisfying than being able to help my friends in Moyamensing. I'll give all the time I can." He paused. "Besides the fact that I can help my friends, it will be a tribute to Biddy Flannagan for changing my life."

Randall nodded too, his blond hair glowing in the lantern light. "I'm definitely willing to help. I agree with Melissa that I have never learned so much about homeopathic medicine as when we were on our trip last year. I'm intrigued by what I learn from the books in class, but when you see it working, it makes all the difference in the world."

Carrie clapped her hands with delight. "Thank you all."

Marietta stood. "Now that Carrie has gotten what she wanted, which I actually had no doubt she would, I'm going upstairs to check on my babies." She winked at Carrie and glanced around the room. "It was wonderful to meet all of you."

Nathan held up a hand to stop her. "May I ask you a question before you leave?"

"Certainly," Marietta said graciously.

Nathan fixed his blue eyes on her. "Your Irish oatmeal cookies taste just like the ones Miss Faith used to cook." He glanced at Carrie. "I never got to see Mrs. Flannagan very often, but all the boys used to go to their back porch for some of Miss Faith's cookies." He narrowed his eyes. "I heard she never shared her recipe. My mama tried many times to talk it out of her."

Carrie squirmed. "I believe that may be my fault," she admitted. "I talked Faith into giving me the recipe for Annie." She briefly explained about Annie being Moses' mother, as well as the cook for the plantation. "I assured her that since we were in Virginia, the recipe would never be divulged."

Marietta's eyes widened. "You never told me!"

Carrie shrugged. "Annie had already taught you how to make the cookies. She couldn't *unteach* you."

"And you wanted to make sure you kept getting those cookies," Marietta said shrewdly.

"That might be possible," Carrie admitted sheepishly.

Nathan shook his head. "Can I give you a little advice, Marietta?" He waited for her nod before he continued. "Don't serve those cookies if Miss Faith comes to visit."

Marietta chuckled. "I will most certainly heed your advice," she assured him.

*****

Carolyn was still sitting by the furnace when Carrie waved good-bye to Melissa, Nathan, and Randall. Carrie returned to the parlor and settled down in the chair next to her, certain there was more her friend wanted to say. "What is it?" she asked quietly.

Carolyn stared into her eyes for a long moment. "Thank you," she finally said.

"For recognizing the perfect person to fulfill one of the last requests for a woman I adored?" Carrie asked. "You're welcome."

"Can you tell me more about it? There are so many questions rampaging through my mind," Carolyn admitted.

"Of course there are. I was counting on us having more time to talk when the others left. The building where the clinic will be is in the heart of Moyamensing. It is large and will be perfect for a clinic. It will need a little work, but the renovations have already begun. It was owned by Biddy, so there is no concern about it ever not being available."

"Does it include housing? I like where I live, but I wouldn't want to make such a long trip every day to go to work, and I imagine there will be some long days."

Carrie took a deep breath as she prepared to lay out what she hoped would be the remedy for Faith's loneliness. "There isn't housing at the clinic, but I have what I believe is the perfect solution." Carolyn remained silent, watching her closely. "You heard me talk about Faith, who was Biddy's best friend and her housemate for thirty years."

"Yes," Carolyn murmured.

"Well, Faith has taken Biddy's death very hard." Carrie had not been able to push the image of Faith's empty eyes out of her mind. "Biddy's house is quite large–much too large for just one person to live there. Faith is very lonely. I suggested to her that you might live there with her for as long as you run the clinic. There would be no cost to you, and you would have a ready supply of Irish oatmeal cookies," she said playfully. "She would like very much to meet you."

"She already knows you want *me* to run the clinic?"

"She does," Carrie confirmed. "I've told her there is no one else I want to do it."

Carolyn absorbed that statement, but her eyes were still troubled. "And you think we would get along well?"

"I do," Carrie replied, "but you always have the freedom to make another choice if you are uncomfortable in any way."

Carolyn nodded thoughtfully.

"And," Carrie reminded her, trying to lighten the moment, "you would have that endless supply of Irish oatmeal cookies. Assuming," she added sternly, "that you never reveal Marietta's secret."

Carolyn chuckled. "It seems like you're thought of everything." The tension was gone from her face, replaced by a glimmer of excitement.

"At least enough to move forward," Carrie answered. "I'm quite sure we will discover challenges, but I also believe we'll work through them."

Carolyn nodded again. "I believe you're right. I have to process all this, but I'm smart enough to know I have been given a remarkable opportunity. Thank you from the bottom of my heart!" She hesitated briefly. "May I ask you another question, about something totally different?"

"Of course."

"I seem to remember that when you first started at the Homeopathic College, you mentioned living in this house with several other roommates. Do you mind me asking what happened?"

Carrie's eyes darkened.

"I'm sorry if that is too personal and nosy of a question," Carolyn said quickly. "Don't feel you need to answer."

Carrie shook her head. "No, it's quite all right." Her mind traveled back in time. "I actually met Biddy through one of those women. It's quite a long story, but Elizabeth Gilbert's mother was a friend of Biddy's. There was a night when we found ourselves in danger in Moyamensing. Biddy's grandson, Arden, rescued us and took us to his grandmother's house. It wasn't too long before Biddy made the connection of who Elizabeth was. That night changed my life in so many ways," she murmured, shaking her head. "Anyway, there were three other women who lived here with Janie and me. Elizabeth Gilbert, Alice Humphries, and Florence Robinson. Alice was not from a medical family, but both Elizabeth's and Florence's fathers are physicians." Memories swarmed through her mind as she talked.

She sighed, trying to focus on what needed to be said, not on all the memories of the good times. "All was well until Janie and I decided homeopathic medicine more closely fit our beliefs and ideals. When we dropped out of the Women's Medical College to enroll at the Homeopathic College, the three of them declared they could no longer be our friends, and most certainly could not live with us. They moved out the next day."

"Really?" Carolyn asked with a gasp. "I never knew about that."

Carrie shrugged. "There was no reason to talk about it. We followed our convictions. They did the same. They just didn't happen to mesh."

"It must have hurt terribly," Carolyn murmured.

Carrie closed her eyes for a moment. "It did," she said softly. "I think Elizabeth's friendship may have been the hardest to lose." Now that she was talking about it, she was eager to get it out. "She is passionate about making a difference as a doctor. *Italian* passionate," she added with a laugh as she envisioned Elizabeth's round face, black hair, and dark Italian features that always flashed with life.

Carolyn smiled. "I imagine the two of you were quite close friends if you shared the same passion."

"We were," Carrie admitted. "It's over, though. There has been no contact since they left the house. Janie and I used to dream they would see the error of their ways and want to renew the friendship, but we were wrong." She sighed. "All I can do is follow my own path and wish them the best."

Carolyn reached over to squeeze her hand. "I'm sorry, Carrie."

Carrie took a deep breath and stood. "You need to get home before it gets any later." She looked up to see Jeremy coming down the stairs. "Jeremy is going to walk you home," she said firmly. "No arguments."

"No arguments given," Carolyn replied. "One of the benefits of old age is wisdom. I'm wise enough to not want to roam the streets of Philadelphia at night alone."

Carrie walked to the foyer and grabbed Carolyn's coat. Just as Carolyn finished donning her winter clothing, there was a knock at the door. Startled, Carrie looked at Jeremy. He shook his head to indicate he wasn't expecting anyone.

When Carrie opened the door, all she could do was stand there and gape.

Chapter Eleven

"Hello, Carrie."

Carrie finally found her voice. "Hello, Elizabeth." She remembered her manners and stepped back. "Won't you please come in?"

Elizabeth Gilbert, her cheeks flushed from the cold and her eyes darting with nervousness, entered into the foyer.

Carrie tried to fix a smile on her face, completely shocked to see her old friend. She wondered if Carolyn's and her conversation had somehow conjured her. "I'd like to introduce you to Carolyn Blakely and Jeremy Anthony." She was sure she should say more, but she was coming up empty. She was aware of Jeremy's curious gaze, but she was too stunned to think clearly.

Carolyn stepped in to rescue her. "It's nice to meet you, Miss Gilbert. I was just on my way out, and Mr. Anthony is being so kind as to walk me home. I hope you have a nice night."

Carrie flashed her a grateful smile, realizing Elizabeth was as uncomfortable as she was.

"It was nice to meet both of you, too," Elizabeth murmured.

Carrie watched as Carolyn and Jeremy walked down the stairs, resisting the urge to call them back so she wouldn't have to be alone with Elizabeth. *Stop it,* she scolded herself. *You've been hoping she would walk through the door again someday. Someday is here. Find out what she wants.*

"May I pour you some tea?" she asked graciously. "It's a brutal night."

"It is," Elizabeth agreed. "And, yes, I would love some tea." She took a deep breath before continuing. "I'm sure you're wondering why I'm here."

"The thought has crossed my mind," Carrie admitted with a small smile as she quickly poured two cups of tea. Hurt was still a hard knot in her stomach, but she also couldn't miss the desperation in Elizabeth's eyes. "What's wrong?" she asked quietly.

Elizabeth twisted her hands in her lap as she looked around the room that had once rang with the laughter of five friends. "I need your help," she blurted, blushing crimson. "I know I've done nothing to deserve it, but I had to come ask."

"Help with what?" Carrie asked, completely mystified.

"It's Alice," Elizabeth cried, her eyes filling with tears. "Her husband has put her into an insane asylum!"

Carrie gasped. Of all the scenarios she could have imagined, this was not one of them. "What?" Then she was reminded how much time had passed. "Alice is married?"

Elizabeth's eyes flashed with a terrible fury. "She's married to the most horrible man alive."

Carrie shook her head. "I'm afraid you need to start at the beginning." Her mind was whirling at the thought of Alice in an insane asylum. Sweet Alice, with her blond hair, blue eyes, and gentle manner. Carrie couldn't hold back her shudder. "Please tell me what happened."

Elizabeth slumped, her fury replaced by confused fear. "I don't know how it happened," she whispered. "I got a letter from one of Alice's friends in New York that she had been spirited away in the night to an insane asylum. Her friend is frantic to help her, but doesn't know what to do."

Carrie was horrified, but still confused. "And you think I can help? How?" She would have to get the whole story later.

Elizabeth straightened. "I remember that you told us one time that Abby, your stepmother, is friends with Dorothea Dix."

"That's right," Carrie agreed.

"Well," Elizabeth said, "Dorothea Dix has been very involved with improving conditions in insane asylums I'm hoping she can get me in to see Alice." She reached out and grabbed Carrie's hands. "Carrie, we have to help her. I know that we disagree on some things, but I hope we can agree that sweet Alice doesn't belong in an insane asylum!"

"She certainly does *not*," Carrie said vehemently. "You have to tell me everything you know. I promise I will contact Abby in the morning so that she can connect us to Dorothea Dix."

"I don't know much," Elizabeth moaned. "Alice got married about six months ago." Her face softened for a moment. "She was so happy. Sherman is very wealthy, quite good-looking, and seemed to dote on her. He also seemed to support her decision to be a doctor." Her face darkened. "Until they actually got married. He let her come back to school, but she had to return to New York several times at his command. It greatly impacted her studies, but she was determined to catch up with everyone else. Then he started telling her he didn't want his wife to be a doctor because some of his business connections felt it was wrong, and because it kept her from fulfilling her role as his wife." Her eyes flashed. "The last time he telegrammed her to come back, a few weeks ago, she was quite irritated, but didn't feel she had any choice but to return. He insisted he needed her badly."

Carrie sat quietly, letting Elizabeth tell the story in her own way, but her insides were seething.

"I received a letter from Alice about a week ago. I suppose the deed had already been done before I got the letter. She said she was scared what Sherman might do, because he was quite determined she would not receive her medical degree. Dear Alice loves to please, but she was also certain she should be a doctor, and had reminded Sherman that he was aware of this when they married."

"And Sherman was not pleased," Carrie guessed.

Elizabeth shook her head. "Alice said she was afraid." She groaned and covered her eyes with her hands. "I'm sure she never imagined he would put her in an insane asylum..." Her voice trailed off as it thickened with tears. "Carrie, I am having constant nightmares. I can't imagine Alice in one of those terrible places."

Carrie listened grimly. She couldn't either.

*****

Alice Humphries Archer hunched her shoulders and tried to close herself off from reality as another scream ripped through the dark. She shuddered as tears coursed down her face. She tried to be strong during the day when light exposed her weakness, but at night she couldn't hold her terror at bay. She shrank back against the wall, huddled as far in the corner as she could, hoping that being as small as possible would keep her safe. She felt terrible for the five other women who shared her cramped room, but she knew they were completely unstable and could become volatile at any moment. She bit back the sob that wanted to escape her lips, determined that no sound would awaken one of her roommates.

Her thoughts whirled as she struggled to bring her emotions under control.

Alice, you are nothing but an embarrassment to me. You are my wife now, and you must do what I say. My business colleagues have made it clear how they feel about my wife becoming a doctor. They question my fitness for business if I would sanction my wife taking on such an unwomanly profession. I will simply not allow it.

Sherman's voice boomed through her head, as real as if he were here in the room with her. Just as real was her response.

But Sherman, you knew I wanted to be a doctor when we married. I have only one term left to finish. I'm sorry your colleagues are disturbed by my choice of profession, but I will not allow them to change my path.

Her voice had been firm and unyielding. In spite of Sherman's many demands for her to come home from school, she had been sure he would listen to reason.

Being a doctor is who I am meant to be. I love making a difference for people, especially by making them well. I have worked so hard, and I'm so close. You've told me many times that you want me to be happy. This is what makes me happy.

His eyes had grown hard and flashed at her with a fury she didn't know he was capable of.

And so, because of your selfishness, my career must suffer? I never knew you were so uncaring. You don't care that I am embarrassed by my own wife? His lips had curled into something very closely resembling the snarl of an angry wolf. *You have no choice, Alice. I have tried to reason with you, but obviously I have failed. Now I am simply telling you. You will not become a doctor.*

Her own temper had flared then. Alice very rarely expressed anger, but what Sherman was demanding of her was simply unacceptable. Equally unacceptable was his belief he could simply demand how she would live her life. She had drawn herself up to her full height, still quite diminutive next to his towering size, and had looked him square in the eye.

Yes, I will become a doctor. You cannot stop me. I have worked hard for this, and I will be a physician. If our marriage must end, so be it.

She had surprised herself with her own determined courage, but she had faltered when she saw the cold hatred pouring from his eyes.

You would attempt to divorce me?

Alice still trembled at what she had seen in his expression. *If I must*, had been her only reply. She had wanted to scream and cry at his lack of understanding, but she had remained stoic, somehow knowing that to admit fear would only make her more vulnerable.

The words that came next had shocked her, but she had not taken them seriously.

You will either do as I say, or I will see to it that you can never become a doctor.

She had looked at him with contempt, turned her back, and walked from the room.

The very next night, catching her completely unaware, three men had entered the study where she was catching up on the time she had missed at school, and carried her away to the insane asylum where she was now locked up. She had fought them, but had been no match for their strength. She had tried to cry out to get the attention of neighbors, but they had covered her mouth to muffle her screaMiss

Alice sagged even further back against the wall, hoping it would swallow her to take her away from the reality of the asylum, but the cold hardness mocked her. She had been sure, during her first few days in the asylum, that it would be quickly discovered she was far from insane, and they would release her.

It was true many of the women locked in the ward with her were clearly not in their right mind, but there were several, like her, who were merely traumatized and terrified, committed by their husbands. They made it clear no one was interested in her sanity, or lack thereof. Her husband had assured the asylum that she was indeed insane. His connections in business had somehow secured the confirmation of two physicians whom she had never seen, that Alice Humphries Archer was insane. It was all that was needed to make sure she stayed locked up for as long as he wished. She had no idea how that could possibly be true, but she also knew she had no way of finding out.

As Alice thought about it now, the first sob burst from her lips. She could no more hold it back than she could harness the waves of the sea.

"Shut up!"

Alice broke into a sweat as a snarl sounded from the bed above her.

"Shut up!" The cry grew louder. "Shut up! Shut up! Shut up!"

Suddenly, other cries rose from the room as the first woman woke the rest.

Alice grabbed a blanket and pulled it over her head, praying with all her might that one of the women wouldn't attack her.

Shut up! Shut up! Shut up!

Alice gasped with relief when the door was flung open, a bright lantern illuminating the room.

"What's going on in here?" The ward matron stormed in, swinging the light to illuminate every face. When it landed on Alice, who had lowered her blanket just enough to peer over the edge, the light stopped for a brief moment.

Alice, watching from her huddled position, was sure she saw a flicker of sympathetic understanding in the woman's eyes before she looked away. The light calmed the panic in the room as the women settled down to groans and sighs. When everything was under control again, the matron turned, left the room, and closed the door.

Alice bit her lip when she heard the lock snap into place. She would not make one more sound.

Chapter Twelve

Moses stared out the window of their small, wood-framed Oberlin home at the swirling snowflakes dancing among the barren limbs of the trees. The snow from shortly after Christmas had melted away, but he had felt a big storm coming in the last few days. The dark nimbostratus clouds on the horizon earlier that morning had told him this was the day. When he was coming home from class, the wind had carried the clouds lower and lower, seeming to push them together in a more menacing mass as they came. He had picked up John and Hope from the woman next door who cared for them while they were in class. They had all been in the middle of cookies and hot chocolate when the first flakes had begun to fall.

Felicia pushed in through the door, brushing snow from her hair as she hung her coat. "I should have listened to you this morning," she said. "I didn't really think it would start snowing, so I didn't take a hat. You were right."

"Your father is always right," Moses stated.

Felicia glanced at him, her lips twitching. "Whatever you say," she teased. Then her eyes brightened. "Is that hot chocolate?" When Moses nodded, she rushed over to the stove to pour a cup. "I learned the history of hot chocolate today."

Moses cocked a brow. "Hot chocolate has a history?"

"Of course it does, Daddy," Felicia responded as she sat down at the table and grabbed a cookie.

"What is his'ory?" Hope demanded as she took a big bite of her cookie.

Felicia grinned at her. "It's the story about how something happened." She held up her cup. "Like the story of hot chocolate."

"Like story!" Hope replied, her little face crinkling with an expectant smile. "Tell story!"

"Yeah," John exclaimed. "Tell the story of hot chocolate."

Moses listened as Felicia began to talk, amazed as always that her small head could carry so much knowledge.

Felicia held up her cup. "Daddy made this by shaving part of a chocolate bar into hot milk and adding some sugar. Well, chocolate bars have only been around for thirty years." She paused. "They weren't invented until 1839. And it was only ten years before that, in 1828, that some Dutch guy figured out how to make cocoa powder by taking out all the cocoa butter."

"Really?" Moses was intrigued. If he had ever stopped to think about it, he would have imagined that chocolate bars had been around for quite a long time – much longer than just thirty years.

Felicia nodded eagerly. "Chocolate actually starts as cacao seeds that grow in pods on a cacao tree. They ferment the seeds, then dry them, and then roast them. Once they take the shells off, they have something called cacao nibs. They crush the nibs into a thick paste called chocolate liquor." Her eyes brightened. "That's what people used to mix into water to make a drink."

Moses made a face. "No sugar? Sounds bitter."

Felicia laughed. "Yes, but it was a very *manly* drink," she assured him. "I love hot chocolate because it tastes so good, but a lot of old civilizations consider chocolate to be very sacred. Usually only the elite were able to drink it. Well," she amended, "the elite and the soldiers."

"Soldiers?" John piped in. "Like Daddy used to be?"

"Yes," Felicia agreed. "Chocolate used to be a part of daily rations because it gave soldiers so much energy. They believed the chocolate would make them fight harder and longer." She looked at Moses. "Daddy, did they ever give it to you in the war?"

Moses shook his head. "Perhaps to some troops, but not the black troops."

Felicia frowned. "Well, it was introduced to Europe in the seventeenth century. It was known as a luxury, and a drink of the elites. Coffee, on the other hand, was something that was consumed by lower and middle-class people," she revealed. "If you drank coffee, you were looked down upon."

Moses shook his head as Felicia lifted her nose and looked at him haughtily. "You better not let your mama hear you say that. You know how she is about her morning cup of coffee."

"You too, Daddy," Felicia giggled.

Moses nodded solemnly. "I love a good cup of hot chocolate, but it's best if you don't get in the way of my morning coffee."

Felicia giggled again as the door opened, letting in a rush of cold air. Rose stomped into the kitchen, her eyes lighting with delight when she saw them all seated around the table.

"Do you want some hot chocolate, Mama?" John called. "It makes you better than when you drink coffee."

Rose removed her coat and advanced on him. "Who told you such a terrible untruth? Are you saying my coffee is a bad thing?" she demanded.

John chortled at the mock glare in her eyes. "Not me, Mama. Felicia said it."

Rose swung around to glare at Felicia. "Is this true?"

Felicia jumped up and backed away to the stove. "I'm merely telling history," she protested, her eyes wide with innocence. "You can have all the coffee you want, but..." she paused dramatically, "...if you really want to be elite, you will drink more hot chocolate."

Rose sighed with relief. "It's settled then. I couldn't care less about being *elite*. I simply want to start every day with my coffee. However," she said playfully, "I'm happy to *pretend* to be elite on a snowy afternoon." She poured herself a cup of hot chocolate and reached into the cupboard to pull out a plate of scones.

"That's where those are," Moses exclaimed. "I couldn't find them, so I brought out the sugar cookies."

"That's because I hid them from you," Rose retorted. "I wanted there to be some left for dinner tonight."

"You think I would have eaten them all?" Moses demanded.

Felicia smiled and laid a hand on his arm. "You do eat a lot of food, Daddy."

"I'm a big man," Moses protested.

John jumped up and reached for a scone. "And I'm a big boy," he declared as he grabbed a scone. "Someday I'm going to be as big as Daddy. My teachers told me so."

"That's true," Rose said with a sigh. "I don't know how anyone expects me to feed all of you."

"Grandma Annie doesn't seem to mind," John answered around a mouthful of scone.

"Don't talk with your mouth full," Rose scolded, and then took another sip. "Grandma Annie is a saint," she replied. "She actually loves cooking for all of us."

"Not you, Mama?" Hope piped in. "No love to cook?"

Rose paused. "I love feeding my family," she responded, "but I certainly don't love to cook the way Annie does."

Moses pushed aside his feelings as Rose smiled and bit into a scone. Now was not the time for anything but gratitude for being with his family like this on a snowy day.

*****

Moses finished reading John his bedtime story before he went downstairs. Hope was asleep, and Felicia was in her room studying. He was very much looking forward to some time to be with Rose. He stopped at the door to the parlor to admire the sight of his beautiful wife, curled under an afghan in a chair pulled close to the fire.

"Is John asleep?" Rose asked, her hair glowing in the flicker of the flames.

"He was asleep before I finished the story," Moses answered. "He was asking about little Simon tonight."

"Oh?"

Moses nodded. "He wanted to know if Simon would still remember him since he didn't live on the plantation anymore. I assured him he would always remember his best friend."

"John misses Patches, too," Rose said quietly.

Moses didn't see any reason to deny it, so he remained silent. John lived for the times he could go home and ride his black and white pony. Moses had a story he had made up about Patches that he used to tell his son as a bedtime tale, but it always made John sad now, so he had stopped telling it.

"You miss the plantation," Rose said next.

Moses sighed. Again, there was no reason to deny it, so he shrugged his broad shoulders. "You know I do, but that doesn't change the decision we made for our family. There is plenty here to be grateful for."

"Yes," Rose agreed thoughtfully, "but I can feel your discontent growing."

Moses sighed again. "I'm sorry. I thought I was doing a better job of dealing with it. How I feel about things is my problem. I don't want to make it your problem, too."

Rose gazed at him. "You think it can possibly *not* be my problem? You're my husband."

Moses shook his head. "It shouldn't be your problem," he insisted. "You're going to be a teacher. You have to go to college, and I would never consider leaving my family."

"And I love you for that," Rose said softly.

They sat quietly for a few minutes. Moses stared into the flames, wishing the conversation had not happened. He didn't want his struggles to make Rose feel bad about her desire to be in school. Talking about how much he missed the plantation only made it more difficult.

"You don't want to be a lawyer, do you?"

Moses stared harder into the flames. Where were all the questions coming from? He thought about lying, but he was certain Rose already knew the truth. "Not particularly," he admitted, "but I'm going to get my degree. It's what I'm here for. Jeremy assured me that nothing we ever do in life is wasted. I'm choosing to believe that."

Rose knit her brows together, and then asked yet another question. "You received a letter from Franklin yesterday. Did it have any news about finding someone to take his place?"

Moses bit back the heavy sigh of worry he wanted to make. "No," he said simply.

"Are you worried?"

Moses looked back into the flames. Of course he was worried. "I reckon I have to trust the right person will come, just like it happened when Franklin arrived. He and Chooli aren't leaving until early April."

"And what if no one comes?"

Moses stared at her. "Rose, where are all these questions coming from? We've made a decision, as a family, to be here in Oberlin. We knew there would be challenges, and I suspected I would miss the plantation. I can't change how I feel, but it certainly is not going to dictate how I make my decisions. We have to trust that things will work out."

Rose nodded again, but her eyes were unsettled. Another long silence stretched out into the room. The only sounds were the crackling of flames, the hiss of the tea kettle, and the wind against the windowpanes.

"What if I miss the plantation, too?" Rose asked softly.

Moses swung his head to gaze at his wife. "Do you miss it?" He refused to read anything into her simple question.

"I do," Rose admitted, her voice indicating the words were hard to say.

"Well, I suppose it's natural to feel a little homesick after spending the holidays with everyone. It will pass as we get further into the term," Moses assured her.

"I don't think so," Rose replied.

Moses finally turned to stare deeply into her eyes. "Rose, what are you saying?"

Rose took a deep breath, and then reached out to grasp his hands. "I'm saying I want to go home."

Moses took a deep breath, and then shook his head. "I don't understand. What about being a teacher? You can't give that up."

"I won't have to," Rose revealed, her eyes taking on a shine for the first time since they had started the puzzling conversation. "I spoke with the administration today. I have made top grades in all my classes, and I'm teaching many of the students. They agree they really don't have anything more they can teach me."

Moses pushed down the hope soaring in him. "But you must have your degree," he said firmly.

"And they are going to give it to me," Rose revealed. "I will finish this term, and I will graduate a year early." She hesitated. "If that is what we want."

Moses sucked in his breath. "And you will have a degree that will let you teach anywhere?"

"I will."

Moses still wasn't convinced. "You want to teach in a big city," he said.

"Not anymore."

"I don't understand," Moses responded. "What has changed?"

"It's simple," Rose replied with a smile. "*I* have changed. It *is* the prerogative of a woman to change their mind, dear." She jumped up and began to pace the room. "All I have ever wanted to do was make a difference. I realized when I was home in October, and over the holidays, what a difference the school at Cromwell is making. I found myself yearning to continue what I began."

"What about Lillian?" Moses asked.

Rose smiled. "Lillian is a wonderful teacher. The school has grown enough to need two teachers, and we can afford to keep paying her from the money we make at the plantation. I would be honored to work with her." She stopped in front of the flames and met his eyes. "Why are you not excited?" she demanded.

Moses met her eyes evenly. "I'm afraid to be," he confessed. "I don't believe you have considered everything, and I don't want to get my hopes up."

"What haven't I considered?"

Moses sighed. "The reality of being back in the South," he said bluntly. "You feel safe here. You know the children are safe here. Things are getting worse everywhere in the South." He knew it was better to be honest now. Going home would put all of them in danger. Suddenly, he wasn't certain *he* was willing to put his family back in that kind of danger. His mind flashed to the attack on Blackwell Plantation. It was probably a matter of time before it happened on Cromwell again—or the school would come under attack again. The vigilantes were becoming more aggressive, not less...

"I know," Rose answered. She returned to her chair and sat down, staring into the flames again for several minutes.

Moses waited for her to speak.

Finally, she looked up. "Moses, I have mixed feelings about it. I hate the thought of putting our children in danger, but I also don't want them to learn to let fear control their actions. All of life is a risk, no matter what we do. God has protected us this far." She took a deep breath. "I have to believe that will continue."

"And if something happens to one of them?" Moses hated to ask the question, but he knew he must.

Rose sucked in her breath. She looked trapped for a moment, but shook her head. "I know I can't let fear stop us," she said. "Carrie had to deal with losing Robert. I pray with all my heart that I won't have to face losing you or one of our children, but I can't let that fear mandate my decision if I believe we are truly meant to go back."

Moses felt hope surging through him, but he still wasn't done. "And what about Felicia? We can't take away her chance to go to school."

"You're right," Rose said. "We'll have to talk to her. I've spoken with her favorite teacher, Mary Ferguson. She's told me how much she would love to have Felicia live with her if we return to the plantation."

It was Moses' turn to abruptly stand and pace the room. The thought of leaving Felicia in Ohio on her own was not something he was willing to consider. "Leave her here by herself? I can't bear the thought of that."

"Shouldn't she be the one to make that decision?" Rose asked softly.

Moses shook his head.

"I want to stay, Daddy."

Moses whirled around when the soft voice sounded in the room. Felicia was standing at the base of the stairs, looking at him with wide eyes. "How much of this did you hear?"

"Most of it," she admitted. "I'm sorry. I came down to tell both of you good night, but I heard you talking and didn't want to interrupt. When I realized what you were talking about, I just kept listening," she said sheepishly. "I'm sorry," she repeated.

Moses took a deep breath. "You don't have to apologize," he replied. "If it had been me at your age, I would have done the same thing." He sat down and pointed at the chair between him and Rose. "Have a seat."

Felicia sat, her face as earnest as when he first realized she was there. "I want to stay and go to school."

"And be here all by yourself?" Moses demanded. "What if you need us?"

Felicia straightened. "I'm almost fourteen, Daddy. I'm a woman now." She smiled slightly. "You already know I'm more mature than most girls my age. And I love Miss Ferguson. It won't be like living with you and Mama, but I want to stay in school." Her eyes met his squarely. "I *have* to, Daddy. It's the only way I can do what I'm meant to do. I have to finish my education." She looked at Rose. "Mama knows what she is supposed to do, and she wants to do it. I'm not sure yet exactly what I am meant to do with my life, but I know it will require me getting an education. There is no place better in the country for me to do that than here in Oberlin."

Moses couldn't deny that was true, and he also couldn't deny Felicia's certainty. He looked at Rose. She was gazing at her daughter with deep love in her eyes.

"I can't bear the idea of you staying behind," Rose finally said, "but I understand why you want to."

Felicia returned her look of love, and then shifted back to Moses. "Can I come home anytime I want to?"

"Of course," Moses said, "but I will not have my fourteen-year-old daughter, no matter how mature you are, on a train by yourself. It's not safe." He hated the troubled expression that filled Felicia's face, but he wasn't going to bend on his decision. He had saved her on the streets of Memphis. He wasn't going to knowingly put her in danger now.

"I believe I can provide the solution to that," Rose said.

"You can, Mama?" Felicia breathed, hope springing back to life in her eyes.

Rose nodded. "Many of the students have said how much they would love to visit the plantation school. If we arrange for one of them to accompany you each time you want to come home, then you'll be safe, and they will get a tremendous experience."

Moses nodded when Felicia swung around to stare at him. "I would approve of that."

Felicia leapt up and jumped into his lap. "So, I can stay?"

Moses met her eyes. "You believe we should go back to the plantation?"

"Of course, Daddy," Felicia said impatiently. "Anyone can see how much you miss it. Mama wants to go home. All John wants is Patches and Grandma Annie's cooking, and Hope is too young to know anything other than that she wants to be with her mama and daddy." She hesitated. "I will miss you terribly, but I believe this is right."

Moses took a deep breath. "I will miss you, too." The idea he could go home was slowly sinking in, but the knowledge of leaving Felicia behind was tearing at his heart.

"Daddy, the time is coming soon, anyway," Felicia said with confidence. "I'm growing up. You can't keep me home forever, and besides, now is the best time to go back to the plantation."

Moses heard something in her voice he didn't understand. "Why is now the best time?"

"Because you don't want the plantation to be in turmoil when Franklin and Chooli leave," she replied. "I've been reading up more on business and finance since Abby talked to us on New Year's Day."

Moses managed to mask his expression of amazement. Thomas and Abby had talked to him and Rose before they left for Oberlin about their concerns for the future. He had listened closely, but had not found time to dig deeper. He shouldn't be surprised that Felicia had. He had never seen anyone with such a hunger for knowledge. "What have you learned?"

"Well, I still have a lot to study, but Abby is right that the banks are making bad decisions, and they are giving too many loans to people buying land out West. They can't support the loans, and it's just a matter of time before things crash," she said frankly. "It's best for you to be back on the plantation so you can manage things. I'll be happy to keep sending you information about the things I learn."

Moses smiled and pulled her close in a hug. "I'd appreciate that. I love you, you know," he murmured, relishing the feel of her lithe body in his arms. Memories of the frightened little girl who had returned from Memphis after seeing both parents murdered swarmed through his mind.

Felicia snuggled close. "I love you too, Daddy."

Moses looked over her head and met Rose's eyes. "When?" he asked.

"This term ends at the beginning of April. I will graduate, and then we can return home." Rose gave him a brilliant smile, her eyes sparkling with joy and anticipation.

Moses stared at her. He finally allowed his face to explode in a grin that matched hers. "Home," he repeated. "We're going home."

"Home," Rose said firmly.

Chapter Thirteen

"Have you heard from Abby yet?"

Carrie looked at Janie. "Not yet, but she would have only just gotten my letter. It's too soon to expect a reply. I would like to have been able to explain it all in a telegram, but it wasn't possible." Her eyes sharpened as she examined her friend's tired face. "Are you as uncomfortable as you look?"

"Probably," Janie admitted, but her smile was bright. "This baby has to come soon, doesn't she?"

"According to when you think you got pregnant on the Trail, you should deliver mid-February. If this baby decides to come on time, you have about two weeks to go."

Janie stroked her swollen belly. "Please, little one, come on time. I can hardly wait to meet you, but mostly I want you outside of me."

Carrie watched her closely. "What hurts?"

"Oh, my back...my feet...my legs..." Janie smiled ruefully. "All the normal things you would expect from a pregnant woman." She eyed Carrie. "Quit looking at me that way. What I am feeling is perfectly normal!"

"I know," Carrie murmured. "I just want everything to go smoothly."

"No more than I do," Janie said fervently, "but this pregnancy has been completely normal."

Carrie knew she was right. She also knew Janie wouldn't do anything crazy, like galloping for hours on a horse. The pain of the memory tightened her heart.

"Stop," Janie said, reading her thoughts perfectly. "You know, now that Matthew and I are married," she continued gently, "I would have done the same thing." Her eyes darkened. "I couldn't imagine letting him die without me there." Her eyes filled with tears. "I would have ridden Granite home, too."

Carrie sucked in her breath. "Really?" She wasn't sure it was true, but Janie saying it helped more than she could have imagined. Watching both Janie and Marietta have normal pregnancies both thrilled and mocked her.

"Really," Janie said firmly. "Every day I feel so much joy that I'm about to bring a child into the world. And every day I feel sadness that you had that joy robbed from you." She held up a hand. "We will never know whether Bridget would have survived even if you hadn't ridden home, but that doesn't change my feelings that those vigilantes murdered two special people that night."

Carrie was saved from having to respond by a knock at the door.

"I have a telegram for Mrs. Carrie Borden," the slender young man said when she opened the door.

Carrie reached for it. "I'm Mrs. Borden."

"Sign right here," he said firmly, not relinquishing the telegram until she had.

Moments later ,Carrie was seated in the parlor, tearing into the telegram.

"What is it?" Janie demanded. "Is it from Abby?"

"It is." Carrie read the contents carefully. "She received my letter. A longer letter is coming, but she wants me to know she has telegrammed Dorothea Dix. She has also telegrammed a lady by the name of Elizabeth Packard. Abby discovered she is in Philadelphia, and wants us to meet with her."

"Who is Elizabeth Packard?" Janie asked.

"I have no idea," Carrie answered, "but Abby wouldn't suggest meeting her if she didn't believe it would be helpful."

Janie nodded. "That's true. When will you meet?"

Carrie smiled. "She is coming over tonight. Evidently, she will not be here in Philadelphia much longer, so she agreed to make time to meet with me."

"Can you get Elizabeth Gilbert here in time?"

Carrie stood and reached for her coat. "I'm going by her home right now. She and Florence live only a few blocks away. I'll leave her a note if she's not there."

Janie frowned. "How do you feel about all this? After what Elizabeth and Florence did? And Alice?"

Carrie shrugged. "It doesn't matter how I feel. Whatever has happened between us pales in comparison to the idea of Alice in an insane asylum. I promised Elizabeth I would do whatever I could, and that's what I'm going to do."

"You're a good woman, Carrie Borden."

"You'd do the same thing," Carrie said. She raised a brow when Janie opened her mouth as if to protest. "And don't even try to pretend you wouldn't. You're a much bigger softy than I am."

Janie nodded. "I suppose I would do the same thing," she admitted, but there was still a stubborn expression on her face. "Have the two of you talked about your differences?"

"No. There hasn't been time, and quite honestly, I don't feel the need. It doesn't reflect on what we are trying to do for Alice."

"But can't they get in trouble for colluding with the enemy?" Janie quipped, her eyes bright with indignation.

Carrie chuckled. "I suppose it's possible, but that's hardly my problem. They are the ones who came to me for help." She finished buttoning her coat, put on her hat and gloves, and then opened the door. "Stay as long as you like. I should be home soon. Right now, all I want to do is deliver this message and then meet Mrs. Packard. I'm intrigued to see what she has to say."

Janie nodded. "So am I. Is it okay if I'm here, too?"

Carrie grinned. "You're willing to collude with the enemy?"

"Oh, I'm fine with it," Janie retorted. "I believe it's what Shakespeare was referring to when he said 'kill them with kindness'." She smiled. "I have nothing to feel guilty for, so I have no problem making Elizabeth feel guiltier for ending our friendship."

Carrie laughed. "I have felt the same way," she agreed. She waved her hand, and started toward the door. "Mrs. Packard should be here at five o'clock." She fixed Janie with a stern look. "You are not to walk by yourself on these snowy sidewalks in the dark. I don't care that it's only a few houses. It's not safe."

Marietta's voice sounded from the stairs. "Jeremy will be home by then. I'll send him to get her."

Carrie smiled with satisfaction. "Perfect! I'll be back soon."

*****

Carrie was privately hoping no one would be home when she arrived at Elizabeth's house and knocked. She had prepared a note to leave on the door. Her heart sank when she heard footsteps, but she straightened her shoulders and held her head high. She was dismayed when it was Florence Robinson who opened the door, but she kept her expression neutral. "Hello, Florence."

Florence's blue eyes widened beneath her red curls that were as unruly as always. Her tall, angular body was rigid with surprise. "Hello, Carrie," she murmured.

Carrie held out the note. "I came to deliver this to Elizabeth. My stepmother has arranged a meeting with a woman by the name of Elizabeth Packard tonight. She believes she will be able to assist us in helping Alice. I thought perhaps Elizabeth would like to be there." She knew her voice was formal, but she quite simply didn't know how to act after all that had transpired between the one-time friends.

Florence reached for the note. "Thank you." She hesitated. "Won't you please come in?"

Carrie shook her head. "Thank you, but I really must be going." The forced politeness was wearing. She could still remember Florence's blazing eyes when she attacked Carrie and Janie about their decision to attend the Homeopathic College. She turned to leave, but Florence's next words stopped her.

"Please come in, Carrie. I really would like to speak with you."

Carrie turned back and met her eyes evenly. "Why?"

Florence flushed, but did not look away. "Because I want to tell you how sorry I am for being such an idiot."

Carrie continued to gaze at her as she repeated Janie's earlier words. "Wouldn't my coming in be considered colluding with the enemy?" She tried to keep the anger from her voice, but she knew she had failed by the way Florence flinched.

"Possibly." Florence, in spite of her flustered face, managed to keep her voice calm. "Still, I would appreciate a chance to speak with you."

Carrie hesitated, but finally decided she would have to face it at some point. It might as well be now. She doubted Florence, who had never been known for her tact, would do anything but heap coals on top of a still simmering fire, but Carrie would at least listen. "All right," she said quietly.

Florence smiled with relief and held the door open wider. "I just finished preparing some tea. Will you please join me?"

Carrie nodded. "Yes, thank you."

Florence poured the tea, sat down, and got straight to what she wanted to say. "Carrie, I was an idiot," she said bluntly. "I wanted to come talk to you before, but I was too embarrassed."

Carrie's eyes widened. "Why the change of heart?"

"My mother almost died last year," Florence began. "My father and I did everything we knew to do for her, but she continued to get worse."

Carrie remained quiet. She knew some of the remedies they would have tried, and also knew just how pointless they were.

"We were quite sure she was going to die," Florence continued. "I love my mother deeply, so it was breaking my heart."

Carrie felt her own heart soften with compassion. Regardless of what had transpired between them, she knew the pain of losing a loved one.

"Anyway, a close friend of Father's told him he was being a fool to not at least try a homeopathic remedy. He ridiculed him for being too stubborn to give his wife a chance to live."

Carrie's eyes widened. In the past, Florence had told her enough about her physician father to know exactly how he would have reacted.

"Father was furious, of course, but he also truly loves my mother. He allowed a homeopathic physician to visit the house and treat her. Within a week, she was out of bed. She now has more energy than ever," Florence reported.

"I'm glad," Carrie said. "I'm sure you were greatly relieved to get your mother back."

Florence nodded. "I was," she agreed. "But, I also realized how my pride and arrogance had cost me two good friends."

Carrie's mind was on something else. "What did your father do after your mother was healed?"

"Father?" Florence smiled widely. "He is now a homeopathic physician. He completely changed his practice when he realized how much it had helped my mother."

Carrie bit back a gasp of astonishment. "And you?" she asked.

Florence met her eyes evenly. "I am finishing at the Women's Medical College, but only because my father and I believe there is a place for both disciplines. I think you and I would agree there are times when surgery is necessary. I want to know how to help people in that way. When I am done, my father and I are going into practice together. I am studying homeopathy on my own while I finish school."

Carrie stared at her with surprise, and then smiled. "I'm glad to hear that."

Florence leaned forward. "Carrie, can you ever forgive me?"

Carrie searched for words. She knew she should offer open-hearted forgiveness, but something was holding her back. "How does Elizabeth feel about what you've done?"

Florence shrugged, and sat back with a disappointed expression. "Elizabeth and I have agreed to disagree," she replied. "She had much the same reaction to me that she had to you in the beginning, but we finally decided we had already lost too much by our stubbornness. We didn't want to lose anymore. We decided that, as women, we didn't have to follow the dictates of men. We will never agree with everyone in life, but that doesn't mean we need to destroy relationships because of our differences."

"I see," Carrie murmured, moved by the words despite herself.

"I am so very sorry," Florence murmured. "So very... very sorry."

There was something in Florence's voice that melted the last reserve in Carrie's heart. Her face broke into a genuine smile. "And you promise to never be so stupid again?"

"I do!" Florence breathed, hope blazing in her eyes. "Will you forgive me?"

"I will," Carrie said softly. "I've missed you terribly."

"Not as much as I've missed you!" Florence cried.

The two friends stood and embraced.

When they stepped back, tears shining in both their eyes, Florence pointed toward the seat. "Will you please sit back down and tell me what has been going on in your life? How is Janie? And Robert?"

Carrie looked away a moment. "Robert is dead."

Florence gasped and covered her mouth with her hand. "What? Robert is dead? How is that possible?"

Carrie stared down at her cup of tea. "He was killed by vigilantes on our plantation, almost twenty months ago."

Florence was shaking her head slowly. "Carrie, I'm so very sorry. I didn't know."

Carrie didn't feel the need to point out that she couldn't have known since she had ended their friendship. She decided to reveal it all since it would come out at some point. "I was seven months pregnant," she continued. "My daughter was stillborn a few minutes after Robert died." She managed to keep her voice calm, but she couldn't help the tears filling her eyes.

Florence reached forward to grab her hands. "Carrie..."

Carrie suddenly realized how much she had missed her fiery, red-headed friend. "I had a rough year," she stated, "but I have somehow found a way to move forward with my life." There was so much to talk about, but it would come out in stages.

Florence seemed to understand what she was feeling as she changed the subject. "And how is Biddy? I think of her often. Both Elizabeth and I do."

Carrie smiled sadly. "Biddy is gone, too. She was ninety-eight when she died last January." Her voice softened. "Faith and I were with her when she took her last breath. She was at peace."

"No," Florence whispered, deep regret filling her eyes. "So, because I destroyed my friendship with you, I missed spending more time with a fabulous woman before she died."

Carrie remained silent, but she squeezed Florence's hands. She understood the regret of decisions made too late. "I'm actually here doing something for Biddy."

"Oh?" Florence's voice was thick with pain.

Carrie explained Biddy's last request. "I am starting the clinic in Moyamensing. A fellow student at the Homeopathic College will take it over when it is up and running smoothly."

"You're done with school already?" Florence asked. "How is that possible?"

Carrie flushed and explained Dr. Strikener's decision. "I spent most of last year on the Santa Fe Trail, and at an internment camp for the Navajo Indians called Bosque Redondo. It fulfilled the requirement for my degree."

Florence stared at her with astonishment. "My heavens!" she stated in an awed voice. "So much has happened to you..." She frowned. "My life has been quite boring by comparison."

"Hardly," Carrie assured her. "You almost lost your mother, and you're getting ready to take a stand against the entire medical establishment by going into business with a homeopathic physician. You'll be glad life has been a little boring once you jump into the middle of that maelstrom!"

Florence laughed. "I suppose you're right. Carrie, I've missed you so much." Her eyes darkened. "My heart breaks for you about Robert and your daughter."

"Thank you," Carrie whispered. "There is not a day that goes by when I don't miss them, and wonder what life would have been like if they were still alive, but I'll never know. I wanted to die for a long time, but I finally chose to live. I'm trying to make the best of it, and there are increasing moments when I feel genuine joy." She shook her head and changed the subject. "I really do have to get back. There is some paperwork I need to do for the clinic, and then Mrs. Packard will be arriving at five o'clock. Will I see you then?"

"You will," Florence agreed. "It will almost be like old times." She frowned. "Without Alice, of course."

Carrie sighed. "We'll be able to thank her for bringing us back together when we get her out of that horrid place."

Florence fixed her eyes on Carrie. "You really believe we can?"

"Of course," Carrie said firmly. "It's not possible for her husband to lock her up there without cause. Dorothea Dix will get us in, and then we'll bring her home."

*****

Carrie and Janie finished final preparations for the meeting while Marietta and Jeremy put the twins down for the night.

"What do you think it's like in an insane asylum?" Janie asked in a troubled voice.

Carrie shuddered. "I can't imagine it's anything but horrifying, especially when you aren't insane." She shook her head. "I know virtually nothing about it, but I'm quite certain Alice doesn't belong there."

Carrie was putting out the last tea cup when a knock sounded at the door. A wagon, having just discharged its passenger, was pulling away from the curb as she ushered Florence and Elizabeth inside. Carrie had time to register the sympathetic look on Elizabeth's face before she turned to welcome Mrs. Packard.

"Welcome, Mrs. Packard," she said warmly.

"Hello, Mrs. Borden."

Carrie was immediately drawn to the woman standing in front of her. She was dressed rather severely, but ringlets of brown hair framed a kind face dominated by caring and compassionate eyes. "I appreciate you coming on such short notice."

"Of course," Mrs. Packard replied. "I have devoted my entire life to women who find themselves in a situation like your friend Alice Humphries."

Carrie had so many questions, but she remembered her manners enough to usher Mrs. Packard into the parlor, introduce her to the rest, and get her settled with a hot cup of tea. Marietta and Jeremy came downstairs just as they had all sat down, so she made fresh introductions.

"I made an apple pie," Marietta murmured. "It's the last apples of the season. May I entice anyone?"

Carrie squirmed with impatience as Marietta and Janie served the pie. Politeness was a wonderful thing, but with Alice confined in an insane asylum somewhere, Carrie wanted to get down to business. She turned to Mrs. Packard as soon as etiquette allowed.

"Mrs. Packard, at the risk of being rude, I'm afraid I know nothing about you. There was not room in the telegram for anything but an announcement you would be here tonight. You mentioned at the door that you have devoted your entire life to women who find themselves in situations like our friend Alice. May I ask why?"

Mrs. Packard took a sip of tea before she began. "My answer is quite simple. I used to *be* your friend Alice. My husband declared me insane and had me locked away in an asylum in Illinois for three years, from 1860 to 1863."

Carrie, as well as everyone else in the room, gasped and leaned forward.

"But why?" Elizabeth stammered.

Carrie waited for her answer. It was obvious to everyone in the room that Mrs. Packard was sane. Her eyes shone with clear, calm intelligence.

"Because he could," Mrs. Packard said flatly. "We don't have much time this evening, so I won't bore you with the whole sordid tale." She reached into the bag resting by her side and pulled out a thick book. "This book was released last year. It will answer most of the questions I will not have time to address tonight."

Carrie reached for the book eagerly, looking up with surprise when she read the cover. "You wrote this!"

Mrs. Packard nodded. "I did, indeed," she agreed. "I have several. The first was published in '64, the year after my freedom was finally obtained. The book you are holding, *The Prisoner's Hidden Life, or, Insane Asylums Unveiled,* is my latest."

"I don't understand," Janie murmured. "How could your husband possibly have had you committed to an insane asylum?"

Mrs. Packard took another sip of tea. "The most important thing I can help all of you understand tonight is *why* he was able to do it. You see, my husband is a minister in the Presbyterian Church. He is quite staunch in his beliefs. When I dared to question those beliefs, and began to ask questions for further understanding, he took offense. He was at first understanding, but when some of the members of his church became alarmed by the influence I was having with my questions, he forbade me to continue and demanded I apologize for my wrong thinking."

"Which of course you didn't do," Florence said indignantly.

Mrs. Packard gazed at Florence for a moment. "You are correct. I was quite certain of the rights I had in regard to religious freedom as a citizen of the United States." She held up a hand to stop further questions, and continued. "As Florence surmised, I was not willing to relinquish my religious freedoms. A friend, who is also an attorney, assured me I had the freedoms I believed I had."

Carrie could feel a sickness beginning to churn in the pit of her stomach.

Mrs. Packard smiled slightly. "I continued to believe that, up until the day Mr. Packard spirited away my six children and had me locked in an insane asylum."

"Six children?" Marietta hissed. "He took you away from six children?"

"Yes. My oldest was almost eighteen. The youngest, was only two years old." Sadness filled her eyes.

"That's horrible!" Elizabeth cried. "All because you had differing religious beliefs? How could he deny your rights that way?"

Mrs. Packard sighed. "Because I had none."

Carrie shook her head. "I'm afraid I don't understand."

"Neither did I," Mrs. Packard responded. "I had a conversation with Mr. Packard on the way to the asylum. I asked if I did not have a right to my opinions. He assured me that I did, as long as my opinion was right. That, of course, meant as long as my opinion was the same as his."

Carrie felt her anger building.

"I then asked him," Mrs. Packard continued, "if the Constitution does not defend the right of religious tolerance to all American citizens."

"It certainly does!" Carrie exclaimed.

Mrs. Packard turned sad, but knowing eyes, on Carrie. "His response was that I was correct that the right extends to all American citizens, but that I am not a citizen. He assured me that while I am a married woman I am a legal nonentity, with absolutely no say in the law." Her lips twisted. "He told me I was dead as to any legal existence while a married woman, and that I therefore had no legal protection." She sighed. "That was my first lesson in the very true reality that a married woman has no legal right to her own identity or individuality."

Stunned silence filled the room.

Carrie grappled with what she was hearing. "That is truly the law?" she demanded. "Everywhere in America?"

"Until two years ago, it was the law in thirty states. I had the law changed in the State of Illinois in 1867, but it still remains the law in most of our country. I assure you I was not the only woman in the asylum who was quite sane, but put there by her husband anyway."

Elizabeth took a deep breath. "Is it the law in New York?"

Mrs. Packard met her eyes. "I'm afraid it is."

Carrie felt sick at the idea of Alice trapped in an insane asylum at the mercy of a husband who owned her identity. "How did you get out?" she demanded. "Somehow you obtained your freedom."

"Yes, but it was not easy," Mrs. Packard said. "I was held at the asylum for three years, until my oldest son reached the age of twenty-one. He had tried many times during the three years to get me released, but his father thwarted him every time. My son had promised me since my imprisonment, that as soon as he became a man, he would set me free."

"And he did?" Marietta asked eagerly.

Mrs. Packard looked pained. "He tried. Oh, how he tried, but his father is quite a deceptive man. His father knew of my son's desire to free me, you see. My son, Theophilus, had gone to his father and told him he would like to remove me. He promised he would cheerfully support me in his home if his father would but agree." She sighed. "What my son didn't know was that the asylum had told his father he must remove me anyway. They had pronounced me incurably insane, and they would no longer be responsible for me. They had tried their best to get me to change my stance on my religious freedoms, but I refused."

Carrie stared at her, wondering if she would have had the courage to stand so strong in the defense of her beliefs. "What happened?"

"My son was so excited to take me away from the asylum, but I knew the law still held me subject to my husband. My son had no liberty to protect my freedom. His ability to do so depended on the promise of my husband, which I knew to be no good. I suspected he wanted to kidnap me again, because I had learned about his communication with another asylum in Massachusetts, which would take me even farther from my children and everyone I knew."

"Dear God," Jeremy muttered. "What kind of man is he?"

"Quite an evil one," Mrs. Packard replied calmly. "I negotiated with the asylum to let me stay there in a private room where I could continue working on my first book. I figured I would have it done in six weeks, and would thus have a form of defense in my hands. I had no idea that I would ever be able to use it in legal proceedings, but I wanted to have my experiences written down. The asylum agreed with my plan, formally discharged me, and then left me to my writing."

"Something went very wrong," Carrie muttered.

"Yes, something went very wrong," Mrs. Packard agreed. "I'm still not quite sure how it all happened, but the trustees of the asylum, prompted by Mr. Packard, declared me their prisoner and ordered me into the custody of my husband four weeks before I was going to leave to join my son. I knew nothing about it until my door was forced open, all my belongings stolen, and I was once again taken into custody by men I could not resist."

"This is unbelievable!" Elizabeth cried angrily. "And you say this is happening to other women?"

"To *many* women," Mrs. Packard replied, her eyes flashing with anger.

"Did you end up in another asylum?" Janie asked in a hushed voice.

"No," Mrs. Packard revealed. "Mr. Packard must have believed it was not possible, because he locked me in the nursery of my house, took away all my clothes, and boarded up the windows to shut me off from the world. None of my children were allowed to see me."

Carrie's horror deepened. "He could *do* that? Was there no end to the atrocities?"

"His actions ended up being my salvation," Mrs. Packard said stoically. "While he *could* legally lock me up in an insane asylum, he could *not* legally lock me up in my own home. I did, however, through careful listening, ascertain that he was plotting to get me locked up in another asylum as a case of hopeless insanity. If he had succeeded, I would be there to this day," she said gravely. "After about six weeks locked in the nursery, I managed to push a letter through one of the slats of my window boards. A transient who was using our water pump found it and took pity on me. She took it to a nearby judge who came to the house and demanded that Mr. Packard bring me to his office. There, the judge decided that I must be given a fair trial. He gave me permission to seek refuge in a friend's home, where I stayed until the trial."

Carrie inched forward to the edge of her seat with horrified fascination. "You were declared sane."

"Yes," Mrs. Packard agreed. "But I lost so much else. Mr. Packard did his best to prove I was insane, but the courthouse was packed with two hundred women supporters, and there was overwhelming evidence in my favor. It took the jury only seven minutes to come back with the verdict that I am, indeed, quite sane." Her eyes darkened. "When I returned home the next day, I discovered Mr. Packard had rented out my home, sold our furniture, taken all my belongings, and disappeared with my children."

"No!" Marietta cried, bringing her fist to her mouth. "How could he?"

Mrs. Packard met her eyes. "Because legally he could. As long as marriage robs women of their personal rights and the right to their children, there are men who will continue to abuse their vows."

Her words hung in the silence for several minutes.

"How long was it before you saw them again?" Elizabeth finally asked.

Mrs. Packard smiled sadly. "I still have not."

Carrie shook her head, unable to believe what she was hearing. "You have not seen your children in almost nine years?"

"I have seen my two oldest sons who were able to defy their father and visit me at the insane asylum, but I have yet to see my other four children."

Carrie blinked back her tears. "And will you ever?"

"I should know fairly soon," Mrs. Packard said in a more hopeful voice. "I have not been idle since my release, and my declaration of sanity. I made a vow to help as many women as I could. I have published many books to bring attention to the issues of women's rights, the rights of people committed on grounds of insanity, and the harms of religious absolutism. The press has paid much attention. Laws have changed in Illinois and Massachusetts that restore rights to women. A husband can no longer commit their wife to an insane asylum without a trial to prove her sanity, but there is still so much work to be done."

"But you said you might see your children soon?" Carrie asked again. Her mind was spinning. How could this woman have been free for six years and still be kept from her children?

"Yes," Mrs. Packard replied. "I have recently gotten more bills passed in Illinois regarding female rights in child custody. I have a hearing in one month to regain custody of my children. My lawyer assures me I have a very good chance of winning because of how well known my case is." She took a deep breath. "If all goes well, I will gain custody of them, and they will join me in Chicago." She blinked her eyes. "We will all be together for the first time in nine years. Theophilus is now twenty-seven, but my three younger children are still teenagers. My youngest will turn twelve this summer. I will have a chance to raise my children," she said happily. "My older sons have made sure they know how much I love them, and how hard I am fighting for them."

Carrie smiled, but her fears bloomed even larger for Alice. "You say there are no laws that have been passed in New York?"

The smile faded from Mrs. Packard's face. "That is true, Mrs. Borden."

"So, our friend Alice has no hope of getting out of the insane asylum?"

"There is always hope, my dear," Mrs. Packard said gently. "I am proof of that."

"Yes," Carrie said impatiently, "but Alice has no children to fight for her."

"No," Mrs. Packard replied. "But she does seem to have very good friends."

"Yes, she does," Elizabeth said. "We'll do whatever we can to help her."

"Then we need to come up with a plan," Mrs. Packard answered.

Chapter Fourteen

Carrie opened the window in her room, relishing in the almost balmy feel of the breeze ruffling the curtains. It was still cold, but the temperature had risen substantially from the sub-zero blast they had just endured. Since it was early February, she knew they would have more snow before the winter was over, but she was thrilled for the reprieve between storms. She sighed as she settled down on the window seat, thinking of all the long hours spent studying in this very location. It was hard to believe she was done with school. She would never be done with study and learning, but she was thrilled there would no longer be pressure attached to it. She lifted her face to the weak sun filtering through the high, thin layer of clouds, frowning as she noticed the dark bank of cumulus clouds hovering on the horizon in the west. They might not have long before the next snowstorm after all.

A knock at the door startled her out of her reverie. "Come in," she called.

Marietta opened the door and eased into the room, Sarah Rose snuggled against her chest. "A telegram came for you," she announced.

"A telegram? I didn't hear anyone at the door."

"I had stepped outside to sweep the porch when the delivery boy arrived."

Carrie fixed her eyes on the telegram, but smiled. "Isn't it a little difficult to sweep while holding your daughter?"

Marietta laughed. "She was sound asleep when I went downstairs. When I came up here to give you the telegram she was wide awake, so I grabbed her before she could wake Marcus."

"Smart mama," Carrie murmured. Her eyes were fastened on the telegram, but she didn't reach for it.

Marietta cocked her head. "Don't you want it?"

Carrie nodded slowly. "I do...but I'm afraid to read what it says. What if Dorothea Dix can't get us in to see Alice?"

Marietta's eyes were sympathetic as she held out the telegram. "There is only one way to find out." Her voice grew firmer. "We can't give up hope, Carrie. We have a plan in place. Now we have to make it happen."

Carrie stared at the envelope, reached for it, and then carefully opened it. "Yes!" she cried happily. "Dorothea Dix was able to get us in!" Her eyes sharpened. "Wait..." She read the entire telegram carefully, and then stared up at Marietta. "They only allow one person in to visit a patient. She insists that it be me, since she is doing this from Abby's recommendation."

Marietta's eyes widened. "You have to go into the insane asylum by *yourself?*" She shook her head vehemently. "Carrie, that can't possibly be safe. You can't do it!"

Carrie was quivering on the inside, but she maintained a brave front. "Why?" she asked. "At least I don't have a husband who can commit me as a patient. I'm sure it will be fine." She was not at all sure of that, but she knew she would do it anyway. Alice must be terrified and feeling so terribly alone. She met Marietta's eyes. "Wouldn't you do it for me?"

Marietta sighed heavily. "Of course, but..."

"But nothing," Carrie replied. "I don't believe Miss Dix would recommend this course of action if she thought it was unsafe. I suspect it will not be pleasant, but it is far better than what Alice is experiencing every day."

Marietta's mouth drooped with defeat. "When?"

"I have a scheduled meeting with Alice in three days," Carrie revealed, her thoughts speeding ahead. "I will travel to New York City by train tomorrow, stay with the Stratfords, and then travel out to the asylum."

"The Stratfords?"

"Yes. Nancy Stratford is a close friend of Abby's. Her husband, Wally, is very successful in real estate. Their son, Michael, is a New York policeman. At least he was the last I knew. His parents would love it if he would choose a different profession, but he believes he is needed." She glanced out the window, her mind whirling with plans she would have to make before she could leave. She would want a day at the Stratfords' before she went to the asylum. "I've stayed with them before. They are lovely people."

"And you're really going to go by yourself?"

"I am," Carrie said firmly. "I'm sure Michael will at least ride out to the asylum with me. I doubt they will make an attempt to imprison me when there is a New York policeman waiting for me," she added wryly.

"I suppose that is true," Marietta conceded reluctantly.

Carrie moved over to her wardrobe, and pulled out a light blue, patterned satchel. "I'll need to leave in the morning," she said briskly. "Since we have company coming for dinner tonight, I had best pack now." She smiled at Marietta. "Please don't look so concerned," she scolded. "We have a plan in place. The good news is that my need to go alone won't change our plan. It may not be comfortable to be in there by myself, but we all agreed we would do whatever it takes to make sure Alice doesn't have to endure what Mrs. Packard did."

Marietta straightened her shoulders as she forced a bright smile. "You're right," she said staunchly. "I'm taking Sarah Rose downstairs to work on supper while you pack."

*****

Carrie looked around the dining room table with delight. To have so many of her favorite people all together was wonderful. She had helped Marietta with the cooking, but the gleaming china and silverware were all due to Marietta's hard efforts. Her earlier concerns that her friend would find it difficult to endure a Philadelphia winter had all faded away. She was absolutely thriving on being a mother and housewife. Carrie knew she also kept a stack of books handy in every room of the house. Whenever the twins were sleeping, she would spend time reading about teaching and current affairs.

George eyed the platter of chicken and potatoes. "That looks wonderful, Mrs. Anthony."

Marietta clucked. "You will certainly not call me Mrs. Anthony, George. My name is Marietta. My husband tells me he could not run the factory without you." She smiled warmly. "That makes you family as far as I'm concerned. It's such a pleasure to have you here tonight."

George flushed with pleasure. "Thank you, Marietta."

"You're welcome, George." She eyed him appraisingly. "I can only hope my red-haired, blue-eyed son will grow up to be as handsome as you."

Carrie grinned and turned to Janie, their eyes sharing the fun of their secret, and then her smile faded. "You have to promise you won't have this baby in the next four days," she said sternly.

"Why?" Janie demanded as she narrowed her eyes.

"I have to leave for a few days," Carrie revealed. She wouldn't deny she was nervous about Janie having her baby while she was gone, but she was certain she had to take advantage of this opportunity to visit Alice.

"Why?"

Janie's voice was calm, but Carrie saw the tension in her eyes. Carrie explained the situation. "I have to go," she finished in a pleading voice.

"Of course you do," Janie responded. "Women have babies all the time. I will be fine," she said bravely.

Matthew walked up in time to hear her final sentence. "What will be fine?" he asked, his blue eyes bright with concern.

Carrie turned to him and smiled. "I'm counting on you to convince your child to wait at least four days before making its entrance into the world."

Alarm flared in Matthew's eyes. "Why?"

Carrie bit back a sigh. She hated to leave town so close to Janie's delivery date. She didn't feel she had a choice, but she struggled with the feeling she was letting her friends down.

Janie saved her from making another explanation by making it herself.

When she finished, Matthew nodded his head firmly. "You're doing the right thing, Carrie."

Carrie peered into his eyes, searching for a hint of disappointment or condemnation. She breathed a sigh of relief when she saw nothing but determined confidence and belief. "Thank you," she said.

"I would go with you if Janie weren't so close to having our child. I've already gotten clearance from the newspaper to do a series of articles on insane asylums, especially with regard to what is happening with women. I've met with Mrs. Packard, and am in the process of reading all her books." His eyes darkened. "You've got to get Alice out of there."

Carrie knew he was right, but the intensity of his gaze deepened the pressure she was already feeling. "I know."

"What time do you leave?" Janie asked.

"I catch the train tomorrow morning at eight o'clock. I'll spend the night with the Stratfords. I've telegrammed them about my arrival, and asked them to speak with Michael about whether he can accompany me."

Matthew nodded gravely. "That would be wise."

Alarm flared in Carrie. "Why? Do you believe I'm in danger?"

"No," Matthew insisted. He hesitated briefly. "I believe you will probably be quite upset when you have to leave Alice behind. I think it will be a good idea if you aren't alone."

Once again, Carrie was sure he was right. She prayed Michael would be able to go with her.

*****

Dessert had been served when Janie held up her hand to stop the easy flow of conversation around the table. "I have an exciting announcement!"

"Please tell me you have not just gone into labor," Carrie murmured.

Janie laughed lightly. "No, but it is actually something as exciting, because it is a birth of sorts."

Silence filled the room as all eyes turned to her expectantly. Janie opened her mouth to speak when a knock sounded at the door. Jeremy stood immediately.

"Are we expecting someone else, dear?" Marietta asked.

"Not that I know of, but you might want to get another slice of chess pie and another coffee cup. As long as they are friend, and not foe, I will invite them in."

Jeremy walked from the room to answer the door, as the rest exchanged looks of curiosity.

"Is it too late to intrude upon a friend's home?"

Carrie's eyes widened when she recognized Anthony's voice. She didn't miss Marietta's knowing smile as she slipped into the kitchen to get more pie.

Jeremy's voice boomed through the house. "Anthony Wallington! What a pleasure. It's never too late for *you* to intrude." Moments later the two men walked into the dining room. "Look who the wind deposited on our doorstep."

A flurry of greetings was exchanged through the room. Jeremy pulled up an additional chair as everyone scooted closer together to make room for Anthony.

Carrie was not surprised when Jeremy placed the chair beside her, and she made no effort to conceal her delight when she turned to greet him. "This is indeed a pleasant surprise," she said warmly. "To what do we owe the pleasure of this visit? I thought you had sworn off Philadelphia during the winter time."

"I did," Anthony assured her, "until Abby received a telegram from Dorothea Dix this morning that revealed she had gotten you into the asylum, but that you would have to be in there by yourself."

Carrie felt a surge of joyful hope, but waited to hear the rest of his announcement.

"She and I decided you should at least have someone to accompany you, and since we couldn't be certain Michael Stratford would be free, we decided it would be me." Anthony's eyes shone with satisfaction.

"You did, did you?" Carrie asked, hoping her voice did not reveal how thrilled she was. She had not resisted Anthony's declaration that he was going to court her, but Marietta was the only person in the room she had spoken with about it. She could feel Janie's eyes on her, but she refused to meet them. Carrie loved Anthony Wallington, but she was no closer to wanting to marry him than she had been when she left Richmond a month ago.

"I left the house immediately and caught the first train," Anthony continued. "I just arrived."

"You must be tired," Carrie said.

"Not particularly," Anthony replied, his sparkling eyes revealing much more than his words.

Carrie blushed and looked away, determined to do something that would take everyone's attention away from her. She finally looked at Janie. "I believe you were about to make an important announcement. I'm dying to know what it is," she said brightly.

Janie's eyes bored into her with the promise they would have a long conversation soon, and then her face lit with a fierce pride. Matthew looked down at the last crumbs of his chess pie as she pulled out a book and held it up for everyone to see. "Matthew's book, *Glimmers of Change*, has been released!"

Cries of congratulations and excitement rang through the room.

"That's incredible!" Carrie cried. "Let me see it," she demanded.

Janie grinned and handed it to her, but Marietta snatched it out of the air. "My dinner party," she said smugly as she caressed the cover of the book. "I get to see it first."

"You only brought one copy?" Carrie complained. "You knew we would all want to see it."

Matthew was laughing now. "It's just come off the press. It's not even in the bookstores yet. Be grateful I was able to spirit away the one copy."

"His publisher said they had already had an impressive number of pre-orders," Janie boasted. "They believe it will be a bestseller."

"Of course it will be a bestseller," Carrie said matter-of-factly, her eyes fastened on the book longingly. "Our country needs the hope these stories can bring. All we hear is the bad news. It's beyond time someone told the good stories." She looked at Matthew. "I'm so proud of you, Matthew. Does Harold know?"

"I sent him a telegram," Matthew assured her. "I also wrangled a copy for him that is now in the mail."

"You can't hog it to yourself, Marietta," Carrie said with mock sternness. "You at least have to read something from it."

Marietta smirked at her and riffled through the pages. Her eyes widened when she got to a section about halfway through the book. She stopped, scanned the page, and looked up. "All of you have to hear this one," she breathed. "I had no idea this kind of thing happened during the war. Listen..."

Man or Woman?

Stephanie was just sixteen when war exploded through the country. Orphaned at the age of ten, she had only her brother, Seamus, who was one year older, for family. Somehow, the two children managed to survive, and through endless hard work, they purchased a small farm in the mountains of Georgia the year before the war began.

Small and delicate, Stephanie worked as hard as her brother to create a life for themselves. Slowly, but surely, they began to carve a living from the land they had purchased. The days were endless, but the satisfaction, and the beauty of their farm, made it all worthwhile. The two were certain they were beginning a new chapter of their life that would give them great joy.

They made plans for an additional house on the land, so that even when they both married, they would have a home, and they would remain close for all their lives. Everything was going according to plan until...

Until the first shots were fired on Fort Sumter.

Suddenly all their dreams were disrupted as the cry went up for loyal Southerners to bear arms for the new Confederacy. Stephanie will never forget the day when Seamus returned home from a trip into the nearest town.

"I got to fight," Seamus said grimly.

"No!" Stephanie cried. "You can't leave. We've just begun to create the farm. What will I do without you?" Having no idea of the reality of the war, it never crossed her mind that something bad could happen to her brother. She just knew the idea of staying alone on the farm was unbearable, but she also knew, even before she spoke, what Seamus would do. She had seen that look on his face so many times—the look that said he was determined to take a course of action he believed was right.

"I got to go, Stephanie," Seamus said. "The South is at war."

"About what?" Stephanie cried. "Who are we fighting?"

Seamus frowned then. "I don't know that I rightly understand it. What they be saying is that the Northern part of the country is trying to tell all of us in the South how we done got to live. They told me they are gonna come down here and destroy all our farms and kill us."

"Why?" Stephanie gasped. "Mama always told us she emigrated from Ireland because America was a free country where folks had a chance for a good life."

"I know," Seamus agreed heavily, "but it seems it ain't that way anymore. Anyway," he continued in the firm voice she knew so well, "I got to fight to save our land. All the guys are going. I have to." He forced a smile. "But don't feel too bad. It ain't gonna be much of a fight, they say. I figure I'll only be gone a month or two. We've already plowed all the fields, and I ain't leaving until next week. We'll go ahead and plant everything, and then I'll be home in plenty of time for most of the work and the harvest."

Stephanie listened quietly, and then went off for a walk in the woods. The next morning, she informed her brother there was no reason to plant the fields because she would not be there to tend them.

"What are you talking about?" Seamus asked with astonishment.

"I won't be here," Stephanie said stubbornly.

"Where are you planning on being? We need you to stay here on the farm."

Stephanie shook her head. "I ain't staying here all by myself." She hated the tears that filled her eyes, but she dashed them away. "I'm going with you."

Seamus stared at her, and then started laughing. "You can't go with me, Stephanie. I'm going to war. They only let men fight in a war."

"I know," Stephanie said, fighting the fear threatening to engulf her. "I'm gonna dress up as a man and go fight with you. You said the war should only last a month or so. We'll go together, and we'll come home together."

"You're crazy!" Seamus shouted as he glared at her. "I won't let you do it."

Stephanie's Irish temper flared. "I'd like to see you stop me!" she yelled back.

In the end, Stephanie had her way. She cut off all her hair, rubbed dirt on her face and nails to attempt to cover her delicate features, and enlisted in the army. Whether she was that convincing, or simply because the South was desperate for recruits, she was accepted with her brother into a company from Georgia.

As everyone knows, the war did not end in a month or two. As the fighting stretched out, Stephanie had no choice but to continue her masquerade as a man. She fought hard. She worked hard. And she did whatever it took to hide her true identity.

And then disaster struck.

In May of 1864, Seamus died during the horrific Battle of the Wilderness. He had been wounded, but very possibly could have been saved if his fellow soldiers could have reached him. With the flames of fire licking toward him, and after hearing the screams of *other soldiers consumed by the flames, Seamus shot himself to avoid the same horror.*

Stephanie was watching.

She tried to reach her brother, but she had been shot herself. Losing consciousness was a blessing. Now she hoped for death.

Instead of death, Stephanie ended up in a Confederate hospital. When she regained consciousness, she was horrified to discover she was scheduled for surgery that afternoon to try to save her arm from the infection ravaging it from the bullet wound.

She would sooner lose her arm than have her true identity revealed.

Her salvation came in the form of a Confederate nurse who took pity on her when she learned the truth. Instead of judging and condemning her, she managed to spirit Stephanie (known for the last three years as Stephen) out of the hospital and into her private home.

Stephanie was nursed back to health, but perhaps of equal importance, she was taught to read, and she was accepted for who she was.

When her recovery was complete, instead of deserting the army or reverting back to female, she chose to return to the fight. Part of the reason was that she didn't know any other way to live by this time. The bigger reason was that living as a man had taught her how limiting it was to live as a woman. She would rather risk her life than lose the freedom of being a man, even one who had to be a soldier.

Stephanie died during the long march from Richmond to Appomattox.

You may be asking how such a tale came to be included in a book filled with stories of supposed hope. So now I'll tell you the rest of the story...

Stephanie did not die. Amid all the confusion surrounding the end of the war, it was reported that she...well, he...had died. Stephen Cummings was listed as a casualty of war.

When Stephanie discovered this fact, she decided it was a blessing. She had no family to return to. There was no one waiting for her. Because their farm was in the path of Sherman's March across Georgia, she knew there was nothing to go back to. And now that Seamus was gone, she had no desire to return to farming on her own.

Secure in her identity as a man, Stephen Cummings headed north. Armed with a sharp mind, and with his ability to read, Stephen secured employment in a factory. It wasn't long before his abilities and hard work made him stand out. He has moved to a few jobs, advancing every time.

As of this writing, Stephen Cummings has a secure, well-paid position. He is happy in his identity as a man, and has no intention of changing.

Questioned as to whether he misses the potential of marriage and children if he were to revert to being a woman, he is quick to assure me he does not. While he admits it can be lonely at times, he has no interest in returning to the limited freedoms that American women are granted. He has the right to vote, he is allowed to own his own business, and he is free to make decisions for his own life—all things that women, especially married women, are not allowed to do.

He has chosen the life he wants for himself, and has found happiness. I believe that reality should give us all hope.

Marietta looked up. "There is a postscript to this story," she breathed.

Since this interview, I have discovered there were hundreds of women who served as men in the military. Stephanie was certainly not the only one. These women served for many reasons. I hope the time will come when all their stories will be told.

*****

Silence filled the room when Marietta finished reading. Carrie wasn't quite sure how she should respond, but she needed to say something. She had been watching George carefully through the whole reading, but had done her best to not make it obvious. She had seen him stiffen when Marietta began reading, but other than that, he had shown no emotion.

"That's incredible," Marietta said, holding the book in her hand and staring down at the pages she had read.

Carrie and Janie exchanged a brief look.

"That's one of my favorite stories," Janie confided. "I can only imagine the courage it took to conceal your identity to fight in a war you didn't have to fight in."

"Courage or insanity," Anthony said flatly. "She watched her brother die and still went back to fight?" His brows drew together as his lips thinned.

Carrie watched him closely. She was curious as to how he would respond. Robert had never discovered the truth about Georgia, now George. She didn't know how he would have reacted if he had discovered one of the men in his unit was actually a woman. George had begged her not to tell, and Carrie had conceded. She respected George's wish for his secret never to be known, and she knew the biggest courage had been exhibited when he agreed to tell his story to Matthew for his book.

Anthony remained silent for a moment before continuing. "I think perhaps this story, more than any I have ever heard, tells me how horrible life is for women in America," he said thoughtfully. "When a woman would choose to give up the chance to ever marry or have a family, simply because it is so difficult to be female, there is something terribly wrong."

Carrie bit back her sigh of relief. "You're right," she said. "I'm fighting for the right of women to vote, but until Alice, I didn't truly understand how the rights of women are being trampled on. To be considered nothing more than property once you are married is wrong on every level."

Anthony met her flaming eyes. "It should make one very careful whom they marry," he acknowledged.

"It's not only husbands that make it easy for women to end up in insane asylums," George stated quietly.

Carrie turned to him, eager to escape the challenge in Anthony's eyes. She was not willing to think about marriage. "What do you mean?"

"I've been doing some reading since I found out about your friend Alice," George replied. "I suspected we would talk about Alice at some point tonight so I brought something to read to all of you." He reached into his pocket and pulled out a sheet of paper. He carefully unfolded it and spread it out on the table. "This is a list of reasons women can be admitted to an insane asylum. It was put together by medical doctors," he said grimly. He looked down and began to read:

Intemperance and Business Trouble
Kicked in the Head by a Horse
Ill Treatment by Husband
Hysteria
Immoral Life
Jealousy and Religion
Laziness
Marriage of Son
Masturbation for Thirty Years
Novel Reading
Overaction of the Mind
Parents Were Cousins
Religious Enthusiasm
Politics
Death of Sons in War
Desertion by Husband
Excessive Sexual Abuse
Suppressed Masturbation
Time of Life
Superstition
Small Pox
Grief
Hard Study
Feebleness of Intellect
Female Disease

George stopped reading and refolded the paper. Then he looked up and waited for everyone's response.

Carrie stared at him. "That's real?" she asked with disbelief.

"It's real," George assured her. "There are actually one hundred and twenty-five reasons, but I decided not to read them all. The list is quite extensive."

"Dear God..." Marietta muttered. "Every woman in this room qualifies for an insane asylum," she added in a shocked voice.

"I rest my case," Anthony said harshly. "If I had been Stephanie, I would have chosen to live as Stephen, too."

"I would have made the same choice," George agreed.

Carrie registered his comment, but was still too stunned by what George had read to appreciate the humor of the moment.

"How is this possible?" Janie demanded. She shuddered visibly. "Just how many women are locked into asylums who have no reason to be there?"

"Thousands of them," Matthew stated, his voice tight with anger.

Silence fell on the room again as everyone considered what they had heard.

"*Why?*" Everyone turned to look at Marietta. Her eyes were blazing, and her face was tight with fury. "Why do men believe they have the right to control women in this way? Why do they believe women should have no voice?" She stared around the table, raking Jeremy, Matthew, Anthony, and George with her fiery gaze. "*Why?*"

Carrie wondered which of them would have the courage to address the question, but she wanted to know the answer as much as Marietta did. "It's a fair question," she added. "Why?"

Chapter Fifteen

Matthew was the first to respond. "I agree that it's a fair question, and I have thought about this a great deal since I began the research for my articles," he said. "My career as a journalist has introduced me to many very intelligent, accomplished women, beginning with Abby. I was raised to believe men were always supposed to be in control, because women could not take care of themselves, but my experiences have taught me that's not true." He paused, obviously being careful to think through his words before he spoke them. "I believe men have been taught that if women win, men lose. They are afraid of being powerless, so they work to subjugate women to make themselves feel stronger."

"That's stupid," Janie snorted.

Matthew smiled briefly. "I agree, my dear, but I'm doing my best to answer Marietta's question as to *why* men feel they have to maintain control of women."

"You're right," Janie muttered. "I'm sorry. I do want to hear what you have to say."

"Men have an irritational fear of women," Matthew continued. "Over the years, I have wondered if it is nothing more than a man's innate need to always win. Culture has taught men they are superior." He raised a hand. "Please do not attack the messenger," he pleaded. "I am smart enough to not believe that, but there are far too many men who do." He paused again. "Alice's husband is a good example of that. He believes he is superior to Alice, so he uses his strength and connections to control her. I'm quite sure Alice is more intelligent than him, or any of the men who kidnapped her, but she was no match for their brute strength. So, they won."

"Not for long," Carrie growled.

"And that's where women have the advantage," Matthew pointed out. "You will use your intellect to outthink your opponents."

"So far, we don't seem to be winning," Marietta said angrily. "Our superior intellect has not won us the right to vote, or even to have control over our lives."

"That's not true," Jeremy argued. "It's a battle, but Mrs. Packard has gotten laws changed for women. She is close to regaining custody of her children, and she is committed to changing laws in every state."

"That's true," Marietta acknowledged. "But every single right shouldn't be such a battle."

"Perhaps, but that will not change reality. You can't quit fighting," Matthew said firmly. "Take Janie, for instance. The only reason we are married is because the laws changed enough to allow her to divorce an abusive husband. There were times that wasn't possible," he reminded everyone. "Men are not going to change. Oh, there are enlightened ones, like the men in this room, but most men are never going to see things the way you see them. They are afraid of losing, but that is exactly what will have to happen—they will have to *lose*. Women can't wait for men to view things their way, because men will never want to lose their power."

"It gets so exhausting," Marietta complained.

"Yes," Carrie agreed, "but then I think about how long slavery existed in America. It took a lot of people willing to fight for a very long time to change that. I have to believe that if we refuse to give up, someday it will change." She thought back to the almost identical statement she had made to Sarge the day they met. She was determined to be one woman who would never give up.

Janie laid a hand on her stomach. "It has to change," she said fiercely. She exchanged a long look with Marietta. "If I have a daughter, I'm determined that someday she will have the right to vote, and to have a say in the control of her own life."

Marietta nodded. "And I have determined the same thing for Sarah Rose. Even if I never have the right to vote, I will never quit fighting for *her* to someday have that right."

"And then we pray they take advantage of it," Carrie added.

"What do you mean?" Janie demanded.

"Sarge took me to the clinic this morning," Carrie explained. "Like always, we talked the whole way. He is discouraged by how many black people are not taking advantage of their freedom. They are not going to school. They are not trying to get better jobs. They seem to think because they are free now, that things should *get* better, instead of them *making* them better." Carrie thought through her next statement. "The slaves wanted their freedom, but most of them didn't know how to fight for it, or they couldn't. Suddenly, one day, they were free. They appreciate it, but they don't know what to do with it." She frowned. "From what Sarge said, many of them are doing nothing with it."

Marietta nodded her head thoughtfully. "And you think women might do the same thing," she stated.

Carrie shrugged. "There are a lot of women who are fighting for the right to vote, along with other rights, but there are far more who seem oblivious to the whole issue. They either don't know how to fight for it, they are too afraid to, or they simply don't care." She paused. "Either way, if you suddenly end up with something you had no part in achieving, I wonder if you attach as much value to it as we would." Her thoughts continued to whirl. "And then, what about our daughters? And our granddaughters? Will they value it? Will they know what battles were fought to win their rights?"

Thoughtful silence filled the room.

"I'll make sure Sarah Rose knows what it took," Marietta vowed. She opened her mouth to say more when a demanding cry floated down the stairs from above. Moments later, another joined the chorus. Marietta smiled. "The twins are saying this dinner party has ended. At least my part in it. The rest of you are welcome to stay as long as you like."

George pushed back his chair. "I've got to get home. I have a boss who will not be pleased if I'm not at my best in the morning." He grinned at Jeremy, glancing at his pocket watch. "My rented carriage will be arriving any moment." A rattle of wheels on the pavement outside confirmed his statement.

"I'll walk you to the door," Carrie said.

"Thank you," George replied. He put on his coat and stepped outside.

Carrie joined him, grabbing her own coat as they walked onto the porch. She held up her hand to indicate to the driver to please wait. She shrugged into her coat and then turned to George. "How are you?" she asked quietly.

George chuckled. "I will admit it was a shock for Marietta to pick my story from that book, but when it became obvious that no one had a clue it was about me, it was rather fun. I loved the conversation it spurred about women's rights."

Carrie thought of something. "George, if women get the right to vote, and win other important rights, would you revert to living as a woman?" she asked, careful to keep her voice low.

George looked at her sadly. "I hate to burst your bubble, Carrie, but I doubt we will live that long." He squeezed her hand, walked down to the carriage, and stepped in.

Carrie watched until he was out of sight, hoping with all her heart he was wrong.

"Is it too late for a walk?"

Carrie whirled around when Anthony's voice sounded behind her. "A walk?"

"I realize it's cold, but I have always loved walking through the city in a snowstorm."

Carrie glanced up. "I hate to state the obvious, Anthony, but it's not snowing."

"Yet."

Carrie shook her head. "It's not going to snow."

"Would you care to place a bet on that?" Anthony teased.

Carrie stared up again, looking for the stars she had seen earlier. She was astonished to discover they had been swallowed by thick clouds so low they reflected the street lamps. "Oh my," she murmured. She realized she was shivering. "I was dreaming about spring this afternoon. I had my window open."

Anthony chuckled. "That wasn't a dream, Carrie. That was a delusion."

Carrie laughed. "I know, but a woman can hope. I realize winter has not loosened its grip on Philadelphia yet." She stared up again. "But I was at least hoping for a break in the weather so I can get to New York." Alarm quickened her breath. "I have to catch that train in the morning."

Anthony nodded. "*We* have to catch that train. I don't think it's going to be a heavy snowstorm, but I believe we'll have a few inches by morning. Have you made arrangements for a carriage to take you to the station?"

"*Us* to the station," Carrie corrected, suddenly very glad he was coming with her. She smiled when his green eyes glowed brighter. "And, yes, Sarge will be here at six thirty tomorrow morning."

Anthony held out his arm. "It doesn't have to be a long walk," he said persuasively.

Carrie considered. "A short one," she agreed. "But I need to get my hat and gloves in case your fantasy of snow actually happens."

Anthony grinned, pulled his other arm from behind his back, and handed over her hat and gloves. "At your service, ma'am."

Carrie couldn't contain her smile as she donned the hat and gloves, buttoned her coat the rest of the way, and slipped her hand through his offered arm. They were less than a block away from the house when the first flakes began to fall.

Anthony leaned in close to her ear. "Good thing you didn't make that bet."

"I am not a gambling woman," Carrie replied serenely. "I never make a bet unless I am one hundred percent sure I'm right. If I ever agree to bet with you, you should walk away from it."

"Is that a challenge?"

"It's information," Carrie retorted with a smile. "If you choose to ignore it, I will be more than happy to accept your money."

Anthony laughed and tucked her hand more securely into his arm. "I have been forewarned," he said solemnly.

Nothing more was said for a long time. Carrie appreciated that Anthony understood she needed to settle her thoughts before leaving for New York in the morning. The snow and the lateness of the hour had driven people inside for the night. The quiet of the empty streets, save an occasional carriage rumbling past, soothed her soul.

They were on their way back before Anthony spoke. "How is the clinic coming?"

"Wonderfully!" Carrie said, eager to talk about it now. "We have equipped it entirely. We've seen a few people who wandered in, but we're not really accepting patients until a week from now. We're still setting up our procedures and protocols."

Anthony cocked a brow at her. "And how do you know how to set up procedures and protocols for a homeopathic clinic? Is that a required class?"

"It should be," Carrie said, "and I've encouraged Dr. Strikener to mandate it, but right now it isn't. Thankfully, Florence's father was willing to assist me in setting up an office. He has been invaluable."

"Florence?"

Carrie explained the situation with her former medical school friends.

"Amazing," Anthony murmured. He pulled her to a stop and gazed down at her in the dim light of a street lantern. "You are quite a woman, Mrs. Carrie Borden."

Carrie didn't flinch this time when she heard Robert's surname. "I feel rather the same about you, Mr. Anthony Wallington."

Anthony's eyes settled on her lips, but then he glanced at all the houses surrounding them. "Do I risk destroying your reputation if I kiss you openly on the streets of Philadelphia?"

Carrie chuckled. "Have you still not figured out I'm not concerned about risking my reputation?"

Anthony's answer was to wrap her in his arms and silence her with a kiss.

*****

Carrie was tired when she and Anthony stepped out into the dark, frigid morning, relieved to see Sarge waiting patiently in the carriage. She handed him a hot cup of coffee and a napkin filled with two ham biscuits. "I figured you would appreciate these this morning."

Sarge reached for the cup eagerly. "You're a good woman, plantation girl," he said gruffly before taking a drink. His eyes closed with pleasure.

Anthony eyed her. "Plantation girl?"

Sarge finished drinking and then nodded. "She's right good at telling when snow be coming."

"Not last night," Anthony replied. "She missed this snow entirely."

"A woman can't always be right," Carrie said lightly, loving the banter. "It only makes the men in her life more insecure."

Sarge and Anthony both hooted with laughter, and then Sarge picked up the reins to urge his mare forward. "Get up, Nellie," he called. "There be a train to catch."

*****

One hour later, Carrie and Anthony were settled into their train car, watching as the station bustle disappeared behind them. Carrie sighed and dropped her head back against her seat.

"Tired?" Anthony asked.

"Exhausted," Carrie admitted. She narrowed her eyes at him. "But you must be, too. It took you all day to get to Philadelphia from Richmond yesterday. Now we'll be on this train until late afternoon."

"Yes," Anthony agreed, "but I find being with a beautiful woman always gives me energy."

"*Any* beautiful woman?" Carrie teased. She knew she was flirting shamelessly, but she was also having great fun. Most women would have been appalled at her brash behavior. The idea made her smile more broadly. She had never cared what people thought, so why should she start now?

Anthony returned the smile. "Definitely not just *any* beautiful woman," he said. He patted his shoulder with his hand. "Care for a shoulder to sleep on?"

Carrie leaned her head into him and allowed the rocking of the train to lull her to sleep.

*****

Carrie was more rested than she had anticipated when she and Anthony rolled into the New York station. She had slept for the first several hours, nestled on his strong shoulder, and had then spent the rest of the time talking with Anthony and reading Elizabeth Packard's book. Her horror at what Alice must be going through had intensified with each turn of the page and each click of the train wheels. She was determined to do all she could to free Alice from the horrible asylum.

Anthony picked up their satchels and began to worm his way through the throng of people waiting on the platform. "Let's go find a carriage," he called over his shoulder.

Carrie stayed close behind him, grateful for his height and size that paved the way for her. They made their way outside the station to where the carriages waited for passengers. Anthony raised his hand to wave one over.

"Carrie Borden!"

Carrie whirled around as the voice sounded behind her. "Michael Stratford!" She grinned with delight as he swept her into a hug, his dark brown eyes gleaming with the good humor she associated with him. She was relieved that being a policeman in New York City had not diminished the light. "What are you doing here?"

Michael gazed down at her. "Did you really think my parents would let you take a carriage on your own?" he chided. "They sent me here to pick you up."

Carrie pulled Anthony forward. "I'm so grateful you're here, but I'm not alone. I didn't have time to get a telegram to your parents. Michael, this is Anthony Wallington. Anthony, this is the wonderful Michael Stratford."

Michael eyed Anthony, and then stuck out his hand with a smile. "Any friend of Carrie's is a friend of mine," he said graciously. "Welcome to New York City."

Anthony shook his hand firmly. "I've heard great things about you, Michael. It's a pleasure to meet you."

Michael nodded. "Let's get out of this madhouse. Mother has prepared a special meal for you tonight. I guess I'll have to eat less to make sure there is enough for you, Anthony."

Carrie knew he was teasing, but was embarrassed nonetheless. "I'm sorry. I should have sent a telegram before we left this morning. I don't want Anthony's presence to be an inconvenience."

"Nonsense!" Michael hollered over his shoulder as he plowed through the crowd. "I'm playing with you. You know Mother always has enough food for twice the number of people she is actually feeding." He remained silent until he reached his carriage, loaded their luggage, and climbed into the driver's seat. Only then did he turn around to talk to them. "I, for one, am very glad Anthony is with you. It turns out that I can't go with you tomorrow because of work." He scowled. "I doubt any of us would have let you go out there by yourself."

Carrie held her tongue. She knew there was nothing that would have kept her from visiting Alice, but since Anthony was with her, there was no reason to argue the point. She was, however, alarmed by the grim look in Michael's eyes. "It's that horrible?" she asked.

Michael took a deep breath, looked off to the horizon for a moment, and then nodded. "It's that horrible."

They were settled down at the dining room table before they broached the subject of what had brought Carrie and Anthony to New York City.

"What happened to Alice?" Nancy asked, her blue eyes glowing with distress. "I simply can't believe that sweet, gentle soul is in an asylum."

Carrie told them everything she knew. She held back her belief that Alice was in terrible danger, suspecting they would fight to keep Carrie from going to visit if they thought she might also be putting herself in danger. Her intuition was rarely wrong, but she didn't always have to voice it.

Wally Stratford listened carefully, his eyes flashing with anger. "What is her husband's name?"

"Sherman Archer."

Wally walked over to a table in the foyer, pulled out a sheet of paper, and then returned to the table. "What does he do?"

Carrie shook her head. "I'm afraid I don't know," she answered. "I'm hoping to get more information while I'm here." She turned to gaze at Michael with an appeal in her eyes.

"I'll do the best I can," Michael promised. "From what you said, he must be fairly wealthy."

"That is the impression I have gotten," Carrie agreed. "I believe he is involved in business of some sort. I'm here to visit Alice, but also to find out as much about him as possible." She hesitated. "I'm afraid I don't have much time, however."

"Why?" Nancy asked. "You know you and Anthony are welcome to stay here as long as you desire. We have plenty of room."

"Thank you," Carrie said warmly, "but I don't know how long Janie will wait for me."

Wally cocked a brow. "Wait for you?"

Carrie smiled. "Janie is due to give birth any day now. She has a very capable midwife assisting her, but I want to be there just in case." She knew she didn't need to say anything else. The Stratfords were well aware of what had happened with Robert and Bridget.

"Of course!" Nancy said quickly. She smiled brightly. "Janie will make a wonderful mother. She must be very excited."

"She definitely is," Carrie agreed, and then turned the topic back to Alice's situation. "Wally, do you think you might help me find out who Sherman Archer is, as well? Since you're so well known in the New York business world, I'm hoping there may be connections that will tell us more about him."

"I'll be happy to help, Carrie," Wally said promptly. "One of the benefits of being in real estate is that I can almost always find people."

"At least those that aren't in the tenements," Michael said darkly.

Carrie understood. New York City was a confounding mixture of flamboyant wealth and desperate poverty, all crammed into one bustling city that continued to grow daily.

"What do you hope to accomplish if you discover who he is?" Nancy asked. "I thought you were here to see Alice?"

Carrie nodded. "I'm here to see Alice, so that she'll know she's not forgotten, but I can do nothing to actually get her out of the asylum. Only her husband can do that."

"Alice has rights," Nancy objected.

Carrie scowled. "You would think so, but it's not true." Shocked silence fell around the table as she filled them in on all she had learned from Elizabeth Packard. When she finished, the only sound in the room was the carriages rolling by on the cobblestone streets below.

"It's the law here in New York?" Nancy asked in a horrified whisper.

"It is," Carrie assured her. "There are many wives who are locked up in insane asylums simply because their husbands want them there."

"I don't know what to say," Nancy murmured. She swung toward her husband. "Wally, we have to do whatever it takes to get Alice out of there. And then we're going to help Elizabeth Packard with whatever she needs when she fights the law here in New York."

Wally nodded immediately. "Of course we are. And, I'll find out who Sherman Archer is," he promised. He locked eyes with his son. "Michael and I will do it together." He paused for a moment. "Since you are going to see Alice, won't she be able to tell you about her husband?"

"I hope so," Carrie responded, "but I'm afraid to count on that. There is still a possibility they won't let me in to see her." She opened her mouth to say more, but then closed it. There was no reason to talk about the fact she was concerned what condition she would find Alice in. Mrs. Packard had warned that a month spent in the insane asylum could alter someone completely.

Wally eyed Carrie, seeming to see into her dark thoughts, but merely nodded. "I'm still uncertain what you plan to do with the information."

Carrie met his eyes. "Once we find him, I'll continue to need your help to force him to set her free."

Wally cocked a brow. "I'm listening."

"All of us in Philadelphia discussed this at length with Mrs. Packard. We've come up with a plan. We believe Sherman Archer must be a businessman. As such, he relies on other business connections for his income. We don't know enough to be certain, but we're hopeful our investigation will reveal some valuable business dealings we can use as leverage."

A smile glittered in Wally's eyes. "So, when I find out who he is, I use my connections to block some valuable business deals because of the horrible way he is treating his wife. The business will be blocked until he releases Alice from the asylum."

"And agrees to divorce her," Carrie added. "As long as she is married to him, she is considered nothing but property. He could decide to lock her up somewhere else, and we may never know where she is the next time. He must divorce her," she repeated. "Elizabeth assures me that men who stoop low enough to do what he has done are prompted by greed and power. If that is threatened, they will do what it takes not to lose it."

Wally nodded thoughtfully. "I'd say Elizabeth's assessment is correct."

"We'll find him," Michael stated, his quiet voice filling the room.

"Now," Wally continued, "we need to talk about the asylum." He turned and gazed at Anthony. "How do you feel about Carrie going in there by herself?"

Carrie bristled. "What Anthony feels will not change my decision," she said. "I *am* going."

"Oh, I know you are, my dear," Wally said, "but if it were my Nancy going into that hideous place, I might need to be in the asylum myself before she came back out. Not knowing what she was going through would probably drive me quite mad," he finished.

Carrie opened her mouth, but Wally stopped her with a raised hand.

"I realize you have said nothing about a deeper relationship with Anthony, but I am not blind—or dumb," he continued. "Whatever your feelings for Mr. Wallington, it is quite obvious what his feelings are for you. I'm merely trying to prepare him."

Carrie blushed and snapped her lips shut. She refused to look at Anthony, knowing she would see nothing but amusement in his eyes.

"Well done, Father," Michael said with a laugh. "I don't believe I've ever seen anyone able to silence Carrie."

Carrie scowled at him, but then smiled reluctantly. "Go on," she murmured.

Wally fastened his eyes on Carrie. "People are not allowed in to visit patients at the asylum," he began. "The only reason you are getting in is because of Dorothea Dix. She has gained quite an influence because of all she has done to try to create change in the asylums, but I'm afraid the vast majority of people don't know the real truth about what happens in those places. People want to believe the insane are cared for kindly and properly. If they hear stories of abuse, they dismiss them as wildly exaggerated."

"But why?" Carrie cried, thinking of all she had read in Elizabeth Packard's book. "There are truly horrible things happening."

"Yes," Wally agreed immediately, "but if people acknowledge the horror of reality, then they either feel compelled to take action, or they feel guilty because they turn away from the suffering. It is easier to choose denial over fact."

"How do *you* know the truth about what is happening?" Anthony asked keenly.

Wally's lips twisted. "I fear I know only a portion of it, but what I know is bad enough. I was out to a meal with business colleagues several months back. I overheard talking from another table. Two of the men were doctors from the Women's Insane Asylum. I doubt they realized they could be so well heard, but they might not have cared either way. They talked in very harsh terms of the women held there, laughing at the treatment they received."

Carrie trembled. "They were *laughing*?"

"I'm afraid so," Wally replied. "I heard one of them say the women are so insane they aren't even aware of how terrible their treatment is." His lips thinned.

Nancy stood abruptly, paced around the room, and then turned to her husband, her eyes flashing with fury. "Why have you not told me this before?"

Wally spread his hands. "And what would you do?" He met his wife's eyes. "You are fighting for women's rights. As am I. Until women have more rights, I doubt there is much that can be done."

"But we have to try!" Carrie wanted to scream the words at the top of her lungs, but somehow she managed to control her voice. She could feel Anthony's eyes on her. She glanced at him, relieved to see nothing but sympathy.

"I agree," Wally said. "That is why Michael and I are going to find this Sherman Archer and discover all we can about him. We may not be able to change life for most of the women in the asylum, but if we can get Alice out, at least I'll feel we will have done *something*. And then," he added, "we will help Elizabeth Packard with the laws here in New York." He turned to gaze at Carrie. "Prepare yourself the best you can, Carrie. It will be one of the hardest things you have ever done, to leave Alice tomorrow. I promise you, I will not rest until we have a way to get her out."

Chapter Sixteen

Try as she might, Alice could not stop shivering. The two blankets she had started her imprisonment with had been taken away as punishment for her unwilling attitude toward the attendants. Now, huddled against the hard wall, wrapped by darkness, the cold was eating away at her. She stared listlessly into the dark, wondering if this mindless existence was all she would ever know. Her body craved sleep, but her mind feared what would happen if she allowed herself the vulnerability of slumber during the night. While she didn't dislike any of the other women in her room, she knew she was not safe from their volatility. During the daylight hours, she contrived to find ways to communicate with them, and she seemed to be getting through to them in many ways, but when the terror of night descended, their reason seemed to flee.

She gritted her teeth when a moan struggled to escape her lips. She had managed to stay silent since that night when she had allowed a sob to burst forth. She refused to make that mistake again.

"Help!"

Alice straightened when the cry for rescue sounded outside the door of their room. She longed to rush out to help, but the large lock prevented her, and she knew there was nothing she could do to stop whatever was happening. She put her hands over her ears, but it could not block the noise.

"Get your hands off me!" came another cry.

Alice recognized the voice of a new patient who had arrived on the boat just that day. She had known the instant she laid eyes on the delicate woman that she was as sane as she herself was. She longed to warn her that her sanity would only make her treatment worse, but there had been no opportunity before they had been locked in for the night.

"Shut up!" the attendant growled.

Alice closed her eyes when she recognized Mrs. Bartle's harsh voice. The stout Irish woman was someone she had learned to quickly dread. Alice had done her best to stay clear of her, but the very effort had caused some of the punishments she had endured, because Mrs. Bartle demanded compliance from everyone.

"Help me!" came another piteous cry, followed by a yelp of surprise and then a moan of pain.

Alice squeezed her eyes closed tightly, but she knew too well what was happening. Some of the attendants were actually kind, doing their best to help the patients they felt such pity for. Others, like Mrs. Bartle, took perverse pleasure in making the patient's existence as terrible as they could. Unfortunately, those attendants were the majority.

"I said shut up!" Mrs. Bartle said roughly. "You need to learn your place here."

Alice could see nothing in the dark, but the charge in the air told her that her roommates were awake, listening to the exchange outside the door. She could feel the fear growing in the dank air. She bit her lip, trying to prepare for whatever was coming.

When she heard the sound of dragging feet, she knew the helpless patient was being pulled by her hair to the bathroom. Her cry for help faded away, and was replaced moments later by a scream of terror as she was plunged into a bathtub of icy, cold water reserved for non-compliant patients. Seconds later, there was only silence.

Alice counted silently, wondering how long Mrs. Bartle would hold the woman under the water. How long would the delicate woman struggle? How long before she realized that only by ceasing her struggling would she be allowed up for air? Would she pass out, as others had, before she was released? Silent tears coursed down Alice's cheeks as she imagined the terror the poor woman must be feeling. Alice prayed she would realize quickly the futility of her resistance.

Alice bit back her groan as the woman in the bed beside her began to move restlessly. Moments later, another woman, Susannah, swung her legs over the bed and moved toward the door, muttering in agitation. When she raised her fists to pound on the door, Alice sprang into action. If Susannah beat on the door, Mrs. Bartle's wrath would turn on them. Alice had vowed to protect these defenseless women as much as possible.

"No," she whispered, grabbing Susannah's fist just before it hit the door. "It will only bring trouble," she whispered into the skinny woman's ear. "Please don't, Susannah. I promise to take care of you."

Susannah hesitated long enough for Alice to hope. The middle-aged woman with wild eyes responded well to her during the day. Alice had washed Susannah's hair that day—probably the first time it had been washed since her imprisonment. Susannah had actually relaxed while Alice brushed it out. "Shh... I promise to take care of you," Alice said as soothingly as she could.

She breathed a sigh of relief when Susannah lowered her hand and leaned into her slightly. "That's right," Alice said quietly. "Let's go back to bed now." As she turned to lead the woman back to her hard, narrow bed, another woman leapt up.

"Shut up!" the other woman yelled. "Shut up!"

The sound of her angry voice destroyed Susannah's slender thread of composure. She stiffened and jerked away from Alice. "Ahh!" Susannah screamed.

Knowing she should retreat to her bed, Alice made one more attempt to bring the situation under control. "Shh... It's all right. It's all right, Susannah." She reached for the woman's shoulder again, hoping her touch would bring comfort.

"No!" Susannah screamed.

The darkness gave Alice no chance to dodge the blow she could sense coming, but could not see. She groaned and crumpled into a heap on the floor when Susannah's fist connected with the right side of her face. Though skinny and malnourished, the troubled woman still had an impressive amount of strength.

The lock turned and the door flew open. Suddenly, the room was illuminated by bright lantern light. Alice held her hand to her throbbing face as she peered up into the light, hoping against hope that she wouldn't see Mrs. Bartle glaring down at her. She breathed a sigh of relief as she stared up into the concerned blue eyes of another of the attendants, Miss Wade.

"Quiet," Miss Wade called, keeping her voice both calm and assertive. She swung the light around the room, knowing the illumination would calm the distress of the other women. When silence once more consumed the women huddled on their beds, their eyes gazing back with fear, the attendant crouched down beside Alice. "What happened?"

Alice sighed. "I tried to keep them quiet," she said ruefully, biting back the sobs that wanted to escape. The pain radiating through her face told her she had been badly hurt.

"You shouldn't have done that," Miss Wade scolded, "but I know you can't help yourself. I've watched you help the other women since you've been here." Her voice held both admiration and dismay.

"Is it bad?" Alice asked.

"Yes," Miss Wade said with a sigh, her concerned eyes revealing the truth. "It's bad. We've got to get it looked at."

Alice shivered at the thought of going to the medical clinic in the middle of the night. She was certain it was bad at any time, but she knew she would be far more vulnerable to the men who staffed the clinic during the night hours. "No!"

Miss Wade understood immediately. "I'll be with you. I promise not to leave you alone."

Alice shook her head again, her thoughts racing. "Is my face cut? Is there blood?"

Miss Wade held the lantern high. "No, but it is quite bruised and already swelling. You won't see out of that eye in the morning."

Alice delicately probed her face, grimacing as each touch increased the pain, but was relieved to discover nothing was broken. "No bones are broken. There is nothing they can do for me in the medical clinic," she announced. "If you would be so kind as to get me some cold water and a rag, I will do what I can to control the swelling."

Miss Wade stared at her. "And just how do you know this?"

Alice peered up at her. "I'm a doctor," she said quietly.

Miss Wade gasped. "You are a *what*?"

"I'm a doctor."

Miss Wade stared at her. "Is that your craziness talking?" she asked suspiciously.

Alice smiled despite the pain. "I think you know that isn't true. My husband had me put here because he does not *want* me to be a doctor. The laws of New York say I have no rights since I am a married woman, so here I am."

Miss Wade whitened and stared at Alice for several moments. "I will bring you the cold water," she said softly.

*****

Alice ached all over, and her whole face was swollen when dawn finally chased away the worst of the dark in her room. Fear and pain had kept her awake all night as she held cold compresses to her face. She longed for arnica, but knew asking for it would be pointless. Even if they had it, which she was certain they would not, they would not give it to her. As much as she hurt, she did not regret her decision to stay in her room.

Miss Wade appeared early, unlocking the door and carrying in a fresh pan of icy water. She stared at Alice and shook her head. "Your right eye is swollen shut," she announced. "Your left eye is almost as bad. Your face must hurt like the dickens."

"I have felt better," Alice admitted, knowing she must look terrible. She had managed to wash at least her upper body every day she had been locked up, making sure she kept her hair clean in an attempt to maintain sanity, but there would be no such effort this morning. All she wanted to do was curl up in her bed and finally go to sleep. Now that it was daylight, the other women would be taken from the room.

Miss Wade looked at her with pity. "I wish I could let you stay in bed today, but the director is coming through. If he sees you in bed, you will pay for it."

Alice shuddered. She knew what *paying for it* meant. She hauled herself to her feet, biting back the groan, and made her way into the main room. She was in pain, but the damage done to her face was not fatal. She paused for a moment to stare at the weak light filtering in through the bars of the narrow window. She had always considered herself rather weak. The last month had taught her she had more strength than she imagined. She doubted it would keep her from slipping into insanity if she were to be kept here for life, but somehow it gave her a momentary feeling of pride.

The morning slipped by slowly. Alice kept applying cold compresses to her face. The other women from her room had not approached her. They sat in a huddle, muttering among themselves as they peered at her. Susannah refused to look at her, but merely sat wringing her hands as she stared at the floor.

Sympathy twisted Alice's heart. She didn't know what had reduced Susannah to the pitiful mess she was now, but Alice was certain that at some point in her life, this demented woman had been a happy child looking for love. Whether she had entered the asylum in this state, or had turned into an insane person because of the treatment she had received, Alice couldn't help but feel sorry for her. "Susannah?" she called softly.

Susannah lifted her head enough to peer out from under her long, blond hair, still clean from the previous day's washing.

"Would you like me to brush your hair?" Alice asked tenderly. Somewhere in Susannah's mind, she knew there was regret for what she had done. Alice knew the woman could not be held responsible for her actions.

Susannah stared blankly for a moment, and then shuffled over to where Alice sat. "Hurt?" she muttered.

Alice managed a smile. "I will be fine." She patted the floor in front of her. "Sit down and I will brush your hair. Remember how much you like it?"

Susannah nodded and settled down like an eager little girl.

Out of the corner of her eye, Alice saw Miss Wade staring at her. She ignored her and gently began to brush Susannah's hair. She had learned early that the best way to maintain her own sanity was to give in every way she could to the others in worse shape than herself.

*****

"Alice Archer!"

Alice jerked awake when her name was yelled. The movement made her wince. She had finished Susannah's hair, and fallen asleep sitting in her chair. The exhaustion from the long night had finally caught up with her. She looked up, relieved she could still see something from her left eye. The relief turned into immediate dismay when she realized it was Mrs. Bartle glaring down at her. "Yes?" she asked quietly.

"They want you upstairs," Mrs. Bartle barked.

Alice was certain she saw a brief flash of sympathy in the woman's eyes when she took in her battered condition, but it was quickly replaced by her usual disdain. Alice smoothed her disheveled hair the best she could, straightened her shoulders, and followed the broad woman from the room. Every eye was on her. She wondered if she was about to undergo some new kind of punishment, but she was too tired to even worry about it. The reality of that acknowledgment *did* worry her, because she knew it was another step closer to giving up, but she just couldn't find the energy to care. Another sleepless night was coming. She wondered how many more she could endure. There were moments when she envied the truly insane women housed here. They were miserable, but she didn't believe they could fully comprehend their situation.

"Sit down," Mrs. Bartle barked.

Alice sat.

"You will wait here," the attendant ordered, and then walked from the room.

Alice gazed around the best she could. The room was plain, but was certainly in better condition than any of the rooms in her ward. It didn't look like a torture room. She sighed and rested her head back against the seat, relishing the fact that this room wasn't as brutally cold as the ward with all its open windows. She would find out what she was doing here soon enough.

Alice didn't know how much time had passed before she heard the door open. She straightened, placed her hands in her lap, and turned. She was surprised when Dr. Tillerson walked in. She gazed dispassionately at his hawk-like features, feeling the same disdain for his cold haughtiness as she had the one other time she had spoken with him. Her attempts to explain her sanity, when she had first been admitted, had been met with a curled lip and silence. He had held up his hand after five minutes, looked at his nurse, declared Alice incurably insane, and walked from the room.

"Mrs. Archer," Dr. Tillerson said coldly.

Alice gazed at him, but didn't reply.

"I see you are doing well in our fine facility," he said snidely.

Alice stiffened, but was determined not to give him the satisfaction of seeing her squirm. She remained silent.

"I am here to give you an opportunity for release," he continued.

Alice's heartrate quickened. Had Sherman finally come to his senses?

Dr. Tillerson paused. "Have you nothing to say?" he taunted.

"I'm listening," Alice said quietly.

Dr. Tillerson smirked. "It's really quite simple. Your husband is a man of honor."

Alice barely contained her snort of disgust, but forced herself to remain still.

"He wrote me yesterday with an offer that will secure your release." He paused, obviously expecting Alice to demand more information.

Alice clenched her fists, watching him cautiously.

Dr. Tillerson scowled, frustrated that his ploy for power was not being received as he had hoped. "As I said, it's really quite simple, because your husband is a man of honor. You are aware of his displeasure at your choice of career. He is quite confident that your time residing in our pleasant establishment has granted you the opportunity to reconsider your position. He has offered for you to come home to his tender care if you will but renounce your intention of becoming a doctor." He paused. "Now, or at any time in the future."

Alice ground her teeth, but outwardly remained calm. More than anything in the world, she wanted to be released from this house of horrors, but she was quite certain returning home to live under Sherman's control would be just as horrible in its own way. Her mind whirled as she considered her options. Finally, she knew what her course of action must be. Trying to keep the pain and fear from making her voice tremble, she shook her head. "No."

Dr. Tillerson froze. "What did you say?"

"I said no," Alice replied, the confidence in her decision growing. "I will not move from one prison to another by my own accord. I have rights as a woman. I am being held here against my wishes, and in contradiction of my rights. At some point, this will become known. I am quite sane. Sane enough to know that to return to Sherman Archer would be as terrible as remaining here in your *pleasant establishment*." She made no attempt to hide the sarcasm in her voice.

Dr. Tillerson laughed harshly. "No one has explained to you that as a married woman, you have no rights?"

Alice lifted her head and met his derisive eyes. "At some point that will change," she said. "I will wait." She tamped down the trembling that fought to take control.

Her voice remained steady. "I shall not do as Mr. Archer wants."

"You are a fool!" Dr. Tillerson snapped.

Alice felt renewed strength as she made the decision that gave her a small amount of control over her own destiny. Her body may be imprisoned, but she was declaring freedom for her soul and mind. "Perhaps."

A long silence passed in the room.

"That is all you have to say?" Dr. Tillerson demanded.

"What more would you have me say?" Alice asked wearily. "You have presented your offer. I have declined."

Dr. Tillerson stared at her for several long minutes, and then stood abruptly. "You will wait here," he said harshly, before he turned and left the room.

Alice, suddenly exhausted beyond words, sagged back against the chair. She might have just confined herself to the asylum for the rest of her life, but the idea of returning home, defeated, to the man who had put her here was equally unfathomable.

She swallowed back tears as she waited for an attendant to return her to her ward.

*****

Carrie and Anthony stepped off the boat that had just navigated the gray, choppy waters of the East River. Carrie shivered as she pulled her coat to her more closely. The dark day mirrored her feelings of dread as she stepped onto the wharf of Blackwell's Island.

"You're going to be all right," Anthony said quietly, squeezing her arm reassuringly.

Carrie gazed up at him, grateful beyond words for his presence. "I'm frightened," she admitted.

"Of what?"

Carrie appreciated Anthony's willingness to let her talk through her feelings. The closer she had gotten to the island, the more her fears had grown. "I'm not afraid of what will happen to me in there. I believe the letter from Dorothea Dix will make certain I come to no harm..." Her words trailed off, but Anthony remained silent. "I'm afraid," Carrie finally said, "that I won't know what to say to Alice." Her words tumbled together as they rushed out. "I'm afraid I won't know how to help her. How to give her hope." Her voice trembled. "Anthony, I have not seen her in two years. She ended her friendship with me because of my belief in homeopathy. What if she won't see me?" Her voice sharpened. "What if, despite the letter from Miss Dix, they won't *allow* me to see her?"

"That's a lot of things to be afraid of," Anthony said. "Where would you like to begin?"

The calm easiness of his voice somehow cut through Carrie's fear the way a warm knife cuts through butter. She chuckled. "Thank you," she said quietly.

Anthony cocked his head.

Carrie looked up at him. "You do have a way of helping me put things in perspective. It's only normal to be afraid, but we both know I'm going to walk into that asylum and see Alice. I'll do the best I can. It will have to be enough," she said. "It will just have to be enough."

*****

Alice, too exhausted to stay awake in the warm room, had drifted off. She didn't know how much time had passed when she heard footsteps, followed by a key turning in the lock. She yawned, realized she felt marginally better after some rest, and then straightened. There was no way of knowing what would come next, but she had to attempt to be ready.

When the door creaked open, Dr. Tillerson strode into the room.

Alice blinked, surprised to see him again. Had he returned to force her to change her mind? And why was Sherman anxious to have her home again?

"You have a visitor," Dr. Tillerson announced, displeasure evident in his voice.

Alice took a breath, readying herself for Sherman to walk through the door with an attempt to bring her under his control once again. If nothing else, her month in the Blackwell's Island Insane Asylum had convinced her she would never spend another moment with the man who had wooed her to become his wife, only to control her, and then entrap her in this horrible place.

*****

Carrie thought she was ready for anything when she stepped through the door of the room where she was to meet Alice, but nothing could have prepared her for the pitiful sight that met her eyes. She wanted to cry out and run to her, but she maintained a rigid control.

She turned to the man standing by her side. "Thank you, Dr. Tillerson. I will let you know when we are finished."

Dr. Tillerson scowled. "I cannot leave you alone with this patient," he said. "She is quite insane, and quite volatile."

Carrie maintained her composure. The beaten woman sitting in front of her could not possibly be a danger to anyone, sane or insane. "I will be left alone," she said, unwaveringly. She held up the letter from Dorothea Dix. "This letter clearly states I have been granted clearance to spend private time with Alice Humphries." She couldn't bring herself to use Sherman Archer's surname.

"You mean Mrs. Archer," Dr. Tillerson retorted, his eyes flaring with anger.

Carrie remained silent, meeting his eyes steadily. In truth, she felt no fear. The farther she had walked into the asylum, the more her anger had grown. Her first glimpse of Alice had stoked the anger to full-blown fury. She made no attempt to hide it.

Dr. Tillerson looked away. "Fine," he snapped. "But don't say I didn't warn you. There will not be anyone to save you if you need assistance."

"I'm sure I will be fine," Carrie replied in a cutting voice. After reading Elizabeth Packard's book, she knew what kind of man she was dealing with.

Dr. Tillerson glared at her for another moment before turning to leave the room, pulling the door behind him, and locking it with finality.

Only then did Carrie run to Alice, dropping to her knees before her. "Alice. Dear Alice! What have they done to you?"

Alice stared at her with shock and confusion. "Carrie? Carrie Borden? What are you doing here?"

Chapter Seventeen

Carrie swallowed tears of rage and sorrow as she gazed at Alice. "What has happened to you?" she asked softly. Her eyes narrowed as she took in Alice's swollen and bruised face, already starting to purple. Her mind flashed to her medical bag, wishing she had been able to bring it in, but they had made her take it back to the carriage, accusing her of attempting to bring contraband to a patient. "Who did this to you?"

Alice shook her head. "It wasn't one of the attendants. It was a patient I was trying to help last night. I know it looks bad, but nothing is broken." She reached out and gripped Carrie's hands. "What are you doing here?"

Carrie realized Alice had no idea how terrible she looked. Her once immaculate, petite friend was down to a skeletal weight, her skin was pale and sallow, and her hair hung limply. She fought her fury, knowing she had to focus on the purpose of her visit. "Elizabeth told me you were here, Alice."

"Elizabeth?" Alice asked with a gasp. "I didn't think anyone knew I was here." Tears began to slip down her cheeks. "How did she know?"

"Your neighbor, Sophia, had taken her dog outside when the men came and took you away. She waited until your husband went to work the next day, went inside to find Elizabeth's address, and sent a letter. She was terrified for you, but didn't know what to do." Carrie hesitated. "She also seemed to be rather frightened of Sherman."

Alice nodded. "Most people believe Sherman is who he wants them to believe he is, but Sophia has seen the way he treats me. She had come to visit one day when he arrived home unexpectedly. She remained in the parlor when I went to see what he wanted." She shrugged. "He went off on one of his tirades, leaving again before he realized Sophia was in the house. He would be horrified if he knew."

Carrie gripped her hands more tightly. "Alice, I don't know how long we're going to have today. In spite of the letter I have from Dorothea Dix, they could make me leave. Why did Sherman do this to you?"

Alice sighed. "He doesn't want me to be a doctor. He said it was ruining his reputation in the business world. When I refused to give up my career and told him I would divorce him, he informed me he would make sure that I would never practice medicine. The next night, I was brought here."

Carrie was rigid with anger, but managed to keep her voice calm. "What does Sherman do?"

Alice shrugged. "Does it matter?"

"It does," Carrie said urgently. "We have a plan to get you out of here, but we need to know more about your husband."

Alice stared at her. "*You* can get me out of here?" Hope flooded her voice. "I've been told I have no rights since I am his wife."

"Technically, that is true," Carrie agreed. "But there are other ways to make him sign your release."

"Sherman sent a message today saying I could come home if I promise not to be a doctor, now or in the future," Alice said bitterly. "Dr. Tillerson brought me in here to tell me shortly before you arrived."

Carrie stiffened. "How did you reply?" She could well imagine that Alice was desperate enough to agree to anything to escape the asylum.

"I told them I would not exchange one set of prison walls for another."

Carrie chuckled, relieved beyond words to see Alice's spirit had not been crushed. Then she sobered. "Tell me about Sherman. Everything you know."

Alice pursed her lips. "Sherman is involved with the railroad," she revealed. "I know he is very high up with the Pennsylvania Railroad company. He is extremely secretive about what he actually does, but his image is everything to him."

Carrie nodded. "Does he work from a particular office?"

"I'm afraid I don't know." Alice sighed heavily. "I'm sorry I can't be of more help." Her body sagged. "Does this mean I can't get out of here?"

Carrie's heart ached to hear the forlorn defeat lacing Alice's words. Her earlier show of spirit seemed to have sapped all her available energy. "Of course not," Carrie assured her. "I have Wally and Michael Stratford searching for any information they can right now. We will find what we need," she said confidently, praying she was right. "And when we do, we will leverage his greed and power to make him realize he must free you, or lose his business success."

"You can do that?" Alice asked, skepticism and hope warring in her eyes.

"I believe we can." Carrie knew the greatest gift she could give Alice right now was hope that she would get out of the asylum.

Alice stared at her for a moment, and then dropped her eyes. "I'm so sorry, Carrie..." Her voice trailed off. "I can't believe you are trying to help me after the things I said to you the last time we were together."

Carrie realized more than ever that none of it mattered now. "It's all right," she said soothingly. "Elizabeth, Florence, Janie and I are all good now. We are working together to get you out of here. The past is the past. We are friends."

"*All* of you?" Alice asked in disbelief.

"All of us," Carrie assured her. "I feel the same about you. You are my friend. That is all that matters." There was so much to catch up on, but it must happen at a later time. "What is it like here, Alice?" Her heart sank when Alice shuddered.

"It's terrible," Alice whispered. "I know I must look awful."

Carrie wanted to assure her she didn't, but Alice would know she was lying. Instead, she squeezed her hands again. "What can I do?"

"Do?" Alice asked with a hopeless laugh. "There is nothing you can do," she whispered. "I just have to try to survive until I get out of here."

Carrie knew it wasn't necessary to point out Alice wasn't doing so well with that at the moment. "Where do they keep you?"

"In one of the wards. I am in a room with five other women. It's tight, but at least we have beds. I've seen many women sleeping on the floors because there isn't room for everyone."

Carrie nodded. Her brief time in the asylum had revealed it was horribly crowded. She had no idea how far past capacity they must be, but there were far too many people here to be adequately cared for. She thought about what she had learned from Mrs. Packard's books. "How many of the women in your ward seem to be truly insane?"

"Most of them," Alice replied, "but I doubt many of them started that way. There are others, like a woman who was brought in last night, who are as sane as I am." She frowned. "At least for the moment."

Carrie was sickened by the pain and terror etched on her friend's face. "Most people think the insane receive kind treatment in the asylum."

Alice seemed to gather strength from somewhere as she straightened her shoulders. "That's not true," she said firmly. "I have been humiliated and beaten. When I first arrived, I was quite adamant to prove I was not insane, believing they would release me. One of the attendants, Mrs. Bartle, is brought in to handle what they call the *tough* cases. Like me." Her face twisted with painful memories. "On my second night, when I was still trying desperately to convince her I was quite sane, she grabbed me by the hair and yanked me across the room. I was so shocked, and it hurt so badly, that I went with her..."

Carrie closed her eyes as Alice's voice trailed off. "She took you to the screening room," Carrie finished.

Alice stared at her. "How do you know about that?"

Carrie shook her head. "I'll explain later. What happened?" she pressed. She was certain she already knew, but she had to hear it from Alice's mouth if they were to effectively use it.

Alice hung her head. "Mrs. Bartle is quite strong. She picked me up, fully clothed, and plunged me into a tub of icy cold water. I was quite shocked. Before I could struggle to free myself, she pushed my head under water and held it there."

Carrie bit back her cry, but did not try to stop the tears coursing down her cheeks. "Oh, Alice..." she murmured.

"When I thought I would surely pass out," Alice continued, "Mrs. Bartle pulled my head up by my hair and demanded I admit my insanity." She lifted her head proudly. "I would not," she said. "I told her I was quite sane, and that nothing she did could get me to say differently." Alice sagged again. "I don't know how long it went on before I passed out. When I came to, I was lying on the floor of the screening room, shivering."

Carrie moaned. "Has that happened again?"

"No," Alice replied. "She seems content to mostly let me be right now. I think she is confident my roommates will kill me at some point because she knows I won't fight back."

Carrie shivered at the matter-of-fact tone in her voice, desperate to find a way to relieve Alice's plight until she could get her freed. "Alice, we're going to get you out of here."

Alice managed a tight smile. "I want to believe you, but I'm told no one who comes here ever leaves."

"Yes, well they don't know the people working to make this happen," Carrie snapped. "You have very good friends who will not rest until you are free." She paused a moment. "Alice, do you still love Sherman?" She was relieved when Alice stared at her as if she were quite mad herself. She smiled. "I had to ask, because part of our plan is to make Sherman agree to a divorce."

Alice gasped, her mouth a circle of wonder. "I want that more than anything. I could never go back to a man such as Sherman. My great hope is that I will never have to lay eyes on him again." Her head lowered in shame. "I should never have married him," she murmured.

"Did you ever see this side of him?" Carrie asked.

"Never!" Alice cried. "He doted on me, and told me many times how proud he was that his wife was going to be a doctor." She shook her head. "He changed so quickly. I never saw it coming."

"It's not your fault," Carrie said. "There are people who live off controlling others. They will do anything to get them under their dominion. Once they have them there, they reveal who they really are because they believe you have no recourse."

"Like Janie?" Alice asked softly.

"Like Janie," Carrie agreed. "When she married Clifford Saunders, she didn't understand who he truly was." She smiled reassuringly. "But Janie got divorced, is very happily married to Matthew Justin now, and is about to have a baby." She decided Alice could use some good news.

"That's wonderful!" Alice cried, but her eyes filled with tears almost immediately. She took a deep breath and raised her head. "I'm happy for her."

"I know you are," Carrie said gently. "Janie would be here with me now, but her baby is due quite soon." She prayed silently that Janie's child would wait for her to get back to Philadelphia before it was born.

"What now?" Alice asked. "What happens next?"

Carrie knew Alice needed something to hold onto, but before she could say anything else, she heard the key in the lock. She was standing when Dr. Tillerson entered the room.

"I believe you've had quite enough time with this patient," he said coldly.

"I believe I have," Carrie replied pleasantly. "Now I find I need to have a conversation with you."

Dr. Tillerson shook his head. "I am quite a busy man, and I don't believe you have anything of interest to say to me," he said dismissively, and then turned to leave the room. "I will call an attendant to have you escorted out."

Carrie reached into her pocket and pulled out another letter. "I don't think so," she snapped, barely biting back a smile when Dr. Tillerson turned to look at her in amazement. She was quite certain not many dared to contradict the man who held their future in his hands.

"Excuse me?" Dr. Tillerson asked with tight lips and blazing eyes.

Carrie held the envelope up. "I have a letter here from John Hoffman," she said. "I believe you will recognize him as the *Governor* of New York. He was elected in November of last year. He is also quite fond of Mrs. Archer."

"I'm aware of who he is," Dr. Tillerson responded, his eyes taking on a trapped look.

"I'm so glad," Carrie continued in a pleasant voice. "I also have a letter here from David McNeil, the new Inspector of State Prisons. He's quite concerned over Mrs. Archer's situation. I'm suppose you're not aware of how well known your patient is, Dr. Tillerson. I thought it best you should know."

Dr. Tillerson froze. His eyes blazed with a desperate fury, but somehow he managed to keep his voice under control. "What is it that you want, Mrs. Borden?" He made no attempt to reach for either letter.

"I'm so glad you asked," Carrie replied. "I have discovered that Mrs. Archer's situation here is quite untenable. It is necessary for it to change immediately." Her mind raced as she thought of all she had learned in Mrs. Packard's book. "I demand this patient be transferred immediately to a private room in another ward. You know as well as I do that she is quite sane, and merely put here by a vindictive husband." She paused. "A husband who I'm sure is paying you well to keep her here." She knew no such thing, but the mere threat of such an accusation reaching Governor Hoffman would surely make the doctor nervous. The look on his face confirmed her suspicions.

"A private room is quite difficult," Dr. Tillerson said in a clipped voice.

"But not so difficult for *you*, Dr. Tillerson," Carrie said smoothly. "You are a powerful man here. I realize the asylum is grotesquely overcrowded..." She let her voice trail off, allowing it to relay the possibility that this reality would be included in any communications she wrote. Then she smiled brightly. "Which will make it all the more appreciated that my friend will not ever again step foot in the ward where she is being held. She is to be taken directly to her room." She paused. "I will wait while that is done."

Dr. Tillerson stared at her, but didn't argue.

Carrie kept herself from smiling again, enjoying herself despite the gravity of the situation. "In fact, while you get that arranged, I'm going out to my carriage to gather my medical bag. My friend is quite in need of treatment."

Dr. Tillerson met her eyes, his look that of an enraged animal. "You are a *doctor*?"

"I am," Carrie assured him. She saw no reason to mention she would be getting her medical diploma in a few weeks' time. "I would appreciate it if you would address me as *Doctor* Borden from now on." She paused, holding his eyes. "Do not move Alice from this room." She dropped all pretense of pleasantry. "If she is not sitting right here when I return, your name will be prominently displayed in every newspaper in America. You see, one of Alice's closest friends is the renowned journalist, Matthew Justin. I already know he is working on a series of articles about insane asylums. How you handle Alice until we secure her freedom will likely mandate how you are portrayed in his articles."

"Is that a threat?" Dr. Tillerson demanded.

"Why, no," Carrie assured him. "It is a promise. One I would rather enjoy keeping." She turned to leave the room. "I will not need assistance. I know my way out, and I will return in a few minutes. Before I leave, I expect to accompany Alice to her room. I will return tomorrow with more clothes and blankets for her."

Dr. Tillerson dropped his hands in defeat. He straightened, his eyes fastened on Carrie with glittering hatred.

Carrie controlled her shudder. She hoped her confidence in the letters within her possession would provide Alice with the protection she believed they would. If not, she may have just turned her friend's life into even more of a living hell. Either way, she knew they had to get Alice released soon.

Dr. Tillerson turned to Alice. "Wait here. I will return for you."

When Carrie turned back to Alice, her friend was staring at her with amazement.

"How did you get those letters?" Alice took a breath. "I don't know either of those men."

"You do now," Carrie assured her. "I have my ways," she added cheerfully. She put her hand on the doorknob. "I shall be back in a few minutes with arnica and some other treatments that will help you heal. I suspect whatever food you receive here will be abysmal, even in a private room, but hopefully it will be enough to keep you from losing any more weight. You have to promise me to eat whatever you can force down."

Carrie rushed down the halls to the carriage, trying to block her ears to the screams and moans she heard coming from the complex of buildings on the facility grounds. The asylum was housed on close to twenty acres, but it was easy to tell the buildings were overcrowded. The stench in the air spoke of unsanitary conditions. The whole situation made her furious, but right now, her focus had to be on Alice.

Anthony stepped out of the carriage as she drew close. "Did you see her?"

Carrie nodded as she reached into the carriage for her medical bag. "I'll tell you all about it, but first I have to go treat Alice."

Anthony's mouth dropped open. "They are going to let you take your medical bag inside?"

"I didn't give them much of a choice," Carrie said.

Anthony grabbed her hands. "Are you all right?"

His tender question nearly snapped Carrie's rigid control, but she took a deep breath as she straightened her shoulders. "I will be," she said. "I'm having them put Alice in a private room." She raised a hand when Anthony opened his mouth to ask more questions. "I promise to explain everything," she said hastily. "Right now, I have to go before anyone changes their mind."

Anthony stepped back. "I'll be waiting."

Carrie gazed into his eyes, gathering strength to step back into the asylum, and then spun on her heel.

*****

When Carrie left the asylum, every cell of her body was fatigued. She refused to acknowledge it, thought, knowing that whatever she was feeling was nothing compared to Alice's daily ordeal.

Anthony was waiting for her as she neared the carriage. She could tell by the expression on his face that he was concerned, but he remained silent as he helped her step into the carriage. He tucked blankets around her securely before climbing into the driver's seat and heading for the wharf. Carrie sagged back against the seat, grateful for the wind that had chased the morning clouds away. Bright sunlight shone down on her. She basked in it for a moment, and then shivered as she wondered how long it would be before Alice would feel it again.

Anthony tucked her against his side as they stood on the wharf and waited for the boat to arrive, but he remained silent. Carrie knew he was giving her time to come to grips with what she had experienced. She leaned into him, grateful for his solid strength that blocked her from the cold wind blowing in off the river. She closed her eyes, remembering the forlorn look on Alice's face when she had left. Her friend was now in a private room. It was not a protection from screams and moans in the night, but she had to believe the threats, and the letters she had given Dr. Tillerson, would guarantee Alice protection until they could get her out.

Thank you, Alice had whispered when Carrie embraced her one last time.

I'll get you out of here, Carrie had whispered back.

Please hurry, Carrie. Oh...please hurry.

Carrie shuddered as she pressed in closer to Anthony. She could feel him gazing down at her, but all he did was pull her in even more tightly.

It wasn't until they were halfway across the river, the New York skyline beckoning them onward, that she finally found the strength to speak. "It's a terrible place," she said.

Anthony nodded. "I'm sorry."

Carrie could feel the questions pounding in his mind, but she knew he would allow her to tell the story in her own way. Haltingly, fighting tears with every revelation, she told him what she had experienced.

Anthony leaned back to watch her when she got to the part about the letters from Governor Hoffman and David McNeil, the Inspector of State Prisons. "You had letters from those men?" he asked in astonishment. "When did you secure them?"

Carrie flushed. "Last night."

Anthony raised a brow. "I'm afraid I don't understand. Will you enlighten me?"

There was something in Anthony's eyes that said he already suspected the answer, but she knew he would wait for her to speak. "Well..." She hesitated, and then blurted out defiantly, "I'm sure they would have written letters if given the opportunity!"

Anthony's lips twitched. "You *faked* the letters?"

Carrie shrugged. "I realize it was a risk," she admitted. "I decided only to use them if necessary." She scowled. "Anthony, if you could have seen her, you would have done *anything* to help her. Last night, I decided only the threat to their position would force any of the doctors at the asylum to take interest in Alice's care. When I saw her, and heard what they had done to her already, I knew I needed to take drastic action. She simply could not go back to that ward."

Anthony eyed her. "How did you know they had private rooms?"

"I didn't," Carrie confessed, "but the asylum where Mrs. Packard was held has them, so I decided to go with the assumption they did."

"And if they didn't?"

Carrie shrugged. "I don't know, but it doesn't matter, because Alice is now in one," she finished, allowing a triumphant grin to replace her scowl. She sobered quickly. "It's still horrible, but at least she isn't housed with women who will attack her in the night." She peered into Anthony's eyes, trying to read his expression. "Are you disappointed in me?"

Anthony chuckled. "What if I were to say yes?"

"I would be sorry for that, but I wouldn't have changed my course of action," Carrie replied honestly.

Anthony smiled. "Exactly. My opinion doesn't matter, but just in case you're wondering, I find myself in awe of you, Mrs. Carrie Borden. If I had been the one in there, I would have gotten so furious I would have beaten the doctor, and probably found myself confined as a patient. You, however, went in with a well-executed plan to secure Alice's protection." He removed his hat and bowed to her with a grand flourish. "You are an amazing woman, Carrie."

Carrie blushed at the look of love glowing in his eyes. She also felt the burden drop away from her heart. She was not accustomed to deception, but she had decided there were times it was called for. "It *was* rather entertaining to see the look on his face when he saw the letters," she admitted.

Anthony continued to watch her. "And if he checks their validity?"

Carrie shook her head. "I believe he's far too much of a coward to risk questioning them," she responded, "but we have to do everything possible to get her out of there."

"Agreed," Anthony said. "Did you find out anything about Sherman?"

"I did," Carrie said eagerly. "I forgot to tell you. Sherman Archer seems to be rather high up in the management of the Pennsylvania Railroad."

Anthony nodded, his eyes gleaming. "That could work to our favor," he murmured, and then answered the question in her eyes. "The Pennsylvania Railroad is very concerned about public opinion, especially after the rash of accidents they have had."

"Like Matthew and Janie's train!"

"Precisely. They are working hard to turn public opinion in a positive direction. I doubt they would relish a scandal from one of their top people. If it were to hit the papers, it could be a nightmare that wouldn't go away for a long time."

"With Matthew on our side, it should be relatively easy to convince Sherman his life will become a nightmare if he doesn't set Alice free and give her a divorce," Carrie stated, her excitement growing.

*****

Conversation around the Stratford dinner table was spirited and lively. The emotions ran from anger to dismay, to laughter and then back to anger.

When Carrie finished reciting the events at the asylum, she felt drained, but satisfied she had done all she could for that day.

Nancy chuckled again. "I wish I'd been there to see Dr. Tillerson's face when you pulled out those letters."

"It was a bold move," Wally agreed, "but it makes it even more imperative that we secure her release quickly."

Carrie frowned. "There is nothing that could possibly make her situation more urgent than it is at this moment. I did the best I could for her, but she is quite weak. She put on a brave front for me, but Alice has lost far too much weight. Disease is quite common in asylums. She will not have the strength to fight something off if she gets sick. The food is horrible, so I'm afraid she will only grow more vulnerable."

"At least she will be able to sleep now," Nancy said soothingly. She reached out to lay her hand on Carrie's. "You did a wonderful thing today, my dear. Your quick thinking has given her the best chance possible."

Carrie wished that made her feel better, but anxiety still churned in the pit of her stomach. She turned back to Wally. "Is the information I provided about Sherman Archer helpful?"

"It is, indeed," Wally assured her. "We had already discovered he worked for the Pennsylvania Railroad, but knowing he is high in management will make it easier to apply pressure on him. I have a good friend who is a vice president there. I will visit his office tomorrow. I feel certain he will help rectify this situation."

"And you will use Matthew's reputation as a reporter?" Carrie pressed. She was sure this would be crucial to forcing Sherman to take action quickly.

"I will," Wally promised.

"And what will you do now?" Nancy asked Carrie.

"Anthony and I must return to Philadelphia. We're taking the first boat to Blackwell's Island tomorrow morning to deliver clothes to Alice, and then we will catch the early afternoon train. We won't arrive in Philadelphia until late tomorrow night, but I believe I need to be there."

"I can take the clothes to the asylum," Nancy offered. "Michael will accompany me."

"I'll be happy to go with her," Michael confirmed.

"I know," Carrie replied. "I'm grateful for the offer, but Alice needs to see me one more time. I don't know if I will be able to talk with her, but I'm going to include a letter tucked in one of her pockets to assure her everything possible is being done. Right now, hope is the only thing she has to hold onto." She hesitated. "I'm afraid I didn't bring many clothes..."

Nancy smiled. "Since Alice and I are the same size, I suspect mine will be a better fit, anyway. I'll gather some together this evening."

"They will be loose," Carrie said grimly. "She is nothing but skin and bones right now, but at least she'll be warmer."

*****

Carrie stepped onto the train at the station, convinced she had done her best. Alice was now in possession of warm clothes, she had slept through the night thanks to her private room, and the light in her eyes had returned. Her face was still swollen, but the arnica cream had done its job to reduce the swelling greatly. The bruising would turn colors, but at least both eyes were open to more than a slit. She had been able to tell Alice of the plans being made, promising she would return after Janie gave birth.

She had to believe Alice would be out by the time she returned, but she had been careful not to make promises. Wally had warned her that people like Sherman Archer, controlled by their overinflated ego and selfishness, would resist anything that threatened them, refusing to believe they would not conquer in the end. He assured her the pressure he would bring to bear would convince Sherman to release Alice and give her a divorce, but he refused to put a timetable on it. It would be unkind to get Alice's hopes up with a promise that might not be fulfilled.

Carrie had left Alice with hope, careful not to deliver empty promises.

Chapter Eighteen

Carrie slept for long stretches of their journey to Philadelphia, but she could feel the tension growing in her the closer they came.

"What's wrong?" Anthony asked.

Carrie shook her head. "Probably nothing," she replied, even though she didn't fully believe it. She had learned to trust her instincts. "I'm afraid it's Janie."

Anthony nodded. "I want to assure you everything will be fine, but like Wally, I prefer not to make empty promises." He reached for her hand. "We'll be there soon."

Carrie gazed out the window at the darkness as they sped through the night. "The train will be late arriving in Philadelphia. Will there still be carriages?"

"I'll find one," Anthony assured her. "The carriage drivers will know a late train is coming in. There will be someone eager to make the fare, even on a bitterly cold night when most other drivers have gone home."

Carrie prayed he was correct. She forced herself to breathe slowly, knowing worry would do no good. She was getting to Janie as quickly as she could. They had both decided it was the right thing for her to go to New York to visit Alice. Now she could only hope Janie, and her unborn child, would not pay the price for it.

"You told me Janie has an excellent midwife," Anthony reminded her.

"I did," Carrie agreed. "And she does. Martha Sullinger came well recommended. She has met with Janie several times." The vision of the older woman's experienced, calm face gave her a moment of comfort before the worry pressed back in.

"And we sent Matthew a telegram when we left New York. He'll be expecting us."

Carrie nodded again, wondering what difference that would make to Janie if she were in trouble with her labor, but she decided not to point it out. She knew Anthony was saying anything he could think of to relax her. She appreciated the effort.

*****

It was almost midnight, and snow had begun to fall gently, when Carrie and Anthony stepped outside from the station. Anthony craned his neck, but there were no carriages in sight. Evidently, all the drivers had decided late arriving passengers would have to sleep in the station until the next morning. Whatever money they could make from fares was not as appealing as their warm beds. She was disappointed, but she couldn't blame them.

Carrie gripped her satchel tightly and lifted her head. "We'll walk."

Anthony opened his mouth to protest, but closed it and merely nodded. "We'll walk."

They had gotten about a block away from the station when the thud of horse hooves, and the clatter of carriage wheels sounded in the night.

"Carrie!"

Carrie jerked her head around with relief as she narrowed her eyes to see through the snowflakes that had begun to fall faster and harder. "Harold?"

"Yes," Harold called back. "Matthew sent me with the carriage. I was here two hours ago, but left to get something to eat. The train arrived sooner than they had told me. I'm sorry I wasn't here when you arrived."

Carrie climbed into the carriage, followed by Anthony. "What's wrong?" she asked.

Harold peered at her, his blue eyes an exact replica of his twin brother's. "How do you know something is wrong?"

"Just answer her question," Anthony advised. "She has been worried for the last five hours."

Harold nodded. "I arrived this afternoon because I wanted to be here when my niece or nephew arrived. Janie went into labor early this evening."

"What time?" Carrie questioned impatiently, and then took a steadying breath. "I'm sorry," she apologized. "Do you know what time she went into labor?" she asked again, calmly.

"About six o'clock."

"It's not unusual for labor to take far more than six hours," Carrie replied. "What seems to be wrong?"

Harold shook his head. "We don't know for sure. Janie keeps asking for you, and she keeps saying something is wrong."

Carrie frowned. A woman knew her own body better than anyone else. If Janie thought there was a problem, then there probably was. "Is she in pain?"

"Well, the contractions cause her pain," Harold said uneasily. "But, all she keeps saying is that something is wrong."

Carrie managed a smile. She knew it was hard for men to talk about the birthing process in the best of circumstances. "Is Martha with her?"

"Yes," Harold assured her. "Matthew sent for her as soon as labor started."

"Good," Carrie said, wondering what Janie was feeling. She wouldn't know until she got there, but it didn't keep her from dreaming up multiple scenarios. She pushed away any possibilities that ended badly. There had been enough death. "Are my medical supplies at the house?"

"Yes," Harold said again. "Janie insisted they be there. Jeremy carried them up and then went back to the house to be with the twins so Marietta could be with Janie."

Carrie hesitated to ask the next question, but she must know if they needed to stop before they reached Matthew and Janie's house. "Were my surgical instruments brought up, as well?" She had wondered what had prompted her to bring them from Richmond, but she had learned not to question her feelings.

Harold swallowed hard. "They're at the house," he confirmed. "Why? Do you think you'll need them?" His eyes took on a haunted look.

Carrie knew he was thinking of the death of his wife and children. "I hope not," she said firmly, "but it's best to be prepared." She knew she didn't have to ask about hot water. Martha would have made sure there was a steady supply delivered to the room, so it would be there when it was needed.

She peered into the snow, wishing the carriage could move faster, but they were going as fast as it was safe to travel on the snow-covered cobblestones.

*****

Janie stared at her bedroom door, willing Carrie to appear. Matthew had assured her Carrie would be there soon. Her train had been delayed, but she was on the way. She gasped as another contraction hit. Matthew, who had refused to leave her side until absolutely necessary, squeezed her hand tightly until the pain eased again.

Janie looked to Martha. She trusted her midwife with what everyone had hoped would be a normal birth, but she couldn't shake the feeling something was very wrong. "Can you see anything yet?"

Martha glanced at Matthew sternly, and then brought her eyes back to Janie. "I really must insist..."

Janie shook her head. "I realize it is quite out of the norm for a husband to be present during birth, and I agree he should leave when the moment is close, but he is not leaving *now*, Martha." She raised a brow. "This is not a surprise to you. I told you in advance how I wanted this birth to happen."

Martha gazed back at her. "I didn't think you really meant it," she muttered. She smiled reluctantly. "You women doctors are all a little strange, aren't you?"

"We have to be if we want to fight the entire medical establishment," Janie replied. She tried to sound cheerful, but Matthew's worried look told her she had failed. She gripped his hand tightly, terrified to have him out of her sight. "Matthew stays."

Martha shrugged. "Matthew stays."

Janie turned toward the door when she heard it open. Relief flooded her until she saw it was Marietta with another pan of hot water to replace the ones that had cooled. She bit back her disappointment. "Aren't you getting tired of carrying all those pans?"

Marietta smiled, watching her closely as she walked in. "It's easier than what you're doing," she murmured sympathetically.

Janie snorted. "Not all of us can have twins in less than two hours," she declared.

Marietta lifted her shoulders. "I'll agree I was lucky. The pain was intense, but it was over quickly." She walked to the bed to take Janie's other hand. "How is it going?" she asked.

Janie took a deep breath. She was a little embarrassed to continue to be so adamant, but she and Carrie talked often about how women knew their own bodies better than anyone else. "Something is wrong," she repeated for what seemed the hundredth time, though she knew that wasn't true. "I don't know what, but I can feel it."

"Oh..." She moaned as another contraction gripped her, and then gasped with fright as a sharp pain knifed through her. Caught unprepared, she couldn't stop the scream that ripped from her trembling lips.

Matthew jolted straight in the chair. "Janie!"

Martha, who had been standing next to the window to keep an eye out for Carrie, rushed to Janie's side. "What is it?" she demanded.

Janie shook her head frantically. "I don't know!" she cried. Her eyes teared as the pain tore through her abdomen again. All she could think about was how Carrie had lost Bridget. She remembered Rose describing the terrible pain Carrie had been in before she lost consciousness. Janie screamed again as pain ripped through her. "*Where is Carrie!?*"

*****

Carrie sighed with relief when Matthew and Janie's home came into view through the blowing snow. She placed a hand on Harold's shoulder. "I hate to ask you to stay out in this, but I need you to go get Florence."

"Florence?"

"Yes. She lives at forty-three Maple Street. It's a blue, two-story Victorian. Please tell her to come immediately." She understood Harold's puzzled look. "She is a friend, and also a medical student who has been doing her specialty in women's issues and birth. I want her here in case I need assistance."

Harold nodded, a determined look in his eyes. "I'll get her here as quickly as I can."

"She's only a few minutes away," Carrie replied. "I'm sure she'll have to get dressed, but please tell her to hurry." She could feel her own unexplained urgency building.

Carrie and Anthony leapt from the carriage as soon as it pulled up in front of the house. Carrie watched for a moment as Harold urged the team forward, disappearing quickly behind the curtain of snow, and then she ran lightly up the stairs. She heard Janie's scream rip through the house as she walked in the door. Without taking time to remove her coat, she raced up the stairs.

"*Where is Carrie?*"

Janie's panicked cry somehow eased Carrie's own fears. Now that she was here, she was no longer helpless. She prayed for wisdom, opened the door, and stepped into the room.

"I'm right here," she said calmly.

"Carrie!"

Carrie's heart caught at the terrified agony on Janie's face. She glanced at Martha, but could tell by the confounded look on the midwife's face that she didn't know what was going on. She turned back to her friend. "What are you feeling, Janie?"

"Pain!" Janie gasped. "It feels like a knife is cutting me..." She sucked in her breath. "You have to help us...me and our baby."

"I will," Carrie said soothingly as she peered around the room. Her medical bag was placed next to the side of the bed, but it wasn't what she was looking for.

Matthew interpreted her look. "Your other bag is in the hallway," he said quietly.

Janie overheard him. "What other bag?" she demanded before she doubled over in pain again.

Carrie knew being evasive would only deepen Janie's fears. "My surgical instruments," she replied in a steady voice. "I hope I won't need them, but it's better to have them and not need them, than it is to need them and not have them."

Janie met her eyes and nodded stoically. "Do whatever you need to. Just save my baby."

"I'll save you *both*," Carrie said emphatically, opening her medical bag before she turned to Matthew. "It's time for you to leave."

Matthew shook his head. "I'm not..."

"Yes," Carrie interrupted in a no-nonsense voice. "I realize you want to stay, but it will only make things more difficult. Anthony is downstairs. I promise you'll be informed the instant I know anything." She reached out and grabbed his arm, her heart twisting at the look of agony on Matthew's face. "I know you're scared. Marietta will let you know what is going on," she repeated.

Matthew gave a brief nod, and then turned to Janie. "I love you," he said tenderly, brushing a lock of hair back from her frightened eyes. "I'll be downstairs praying for both of you." He leaned over, kissed her warmly, and then left.

Carrie turned to Janie as soon as he was gone from the room. "Tell me what you're feeling," she said. "Besides pain." She grimaced when Janie writhed again.

"There is something wrong!"

"I know," Carrie said. "I need you to describe it the best you can for me."

Janie opened her mouth, but no words came out. Finally, she shook her head. "I don't know how to tell you," she murmured, sweat beading on her forehead.

She shook her head again. "It's like... everything stopped."

"All right," Carrie said reassuringly. She glanced at Martha. "Let's see what's going on."

Martha sprang into action, carrying over the bowl of hot water. "You just tell me what you need."

Carrie spread out her instruments. "I want you to tell me what you know."

"Janie started out her labor like any other woman," Martha reported. "For the first four or five hours, everything seemed to be going fine. Her contractions were getting closer and seemed to be progressing well. Then, suddenly, they slowed down, and Janie started saying something was wrong."

Carrie listened carefully, positioning herself at the foot of the table. "Please place two lanterns to give me adequate light," she ordered. Marietta and Martha rushed to do her bidding. What Carrie saw made her tighten her lips.

"Carrie?" Janie pleaded. "Please tell me what's going on."

"You are dilated, but I don't see your baby. As much as you are dilated, there should be some evidence." She worked as she talked. "I'm going to see if I can tell what is going on in there." She took a deep breath to steady her hands, and then probed gently, relieved when she could feel the baby's head. Her relief dissolved when her hand continued to slide forward, hitting a tight object just below the baby's head. Her lips tightened again when she realized the umbilical cord was wrapped around the child's neck.

She looked up to find Janie's eyes fastened on her. "When the next contraction comes, I want you to do your best not to push," she said gently.

"The umbilical cord?" Janie croaked hoarsely.

Carrie nodded. "I'm going to see how tight it is. If we can get the baby out far enough, I can cut it to make sure it doesn't get any tighter."

"My pushing could tighten the cord before you get it cut," Janie said, her voice trembling.

"Yes." Carrie knew there was no room for anything but honesty.

"Oh..." Janie gasped. She placed a hand over her mouth to muffle her scream, and rolled her head from side to side, but she did not move her lower body.

Carrie was in awe at what a mother could do to protect her child. "That's good," she murmured. She waited for the contraction to end, and then started probing again, dismayed when she found the cord was hard and tight. The baby still felt warm, so she had hope it was alive, but she knew what she had to do. When she looked up, Janie was watching her with knowing eyes.

"Can you do it?" Janie asked shakily.

Carrie wanted to take a deep breath, but she would do nothing to diminish Janie's confidence. She met her friend's eyes squarely. "I can do it."

She turned to Marietta. "Please bring my other bag from out in the hallway." She heard the rumble of carriage wheels, muted because of the snow, and moved close to the window to peer out. She allowed a smile of relief when Florence climbed from the wagon, glanced up at the window Carrie was watching from, lifted her hand, and ran up the stairs.

Carrie turned back to Janie. "I have studied the Cesarean Section carefully since Dr. Wild performed it on me," she said. "Will you allow me to do it?"

"Yes," Janie replied instantly. "I knew something was wrong, and I knew you were the one I wanted to treat me and our baby." Her gaze softened. "I trust you, Carrie..." Her words trailed off as another spasm gripped her.

Carrie prayed with all her might that her friend's trust would be justified. Her mind raced as she thought through the procedure ahead. Suspecting she might have to do this tonight, she had already played it out in her mind during the train ride, but now that the moment was here, she wanted to make sure she didn't forget anything.

Janie looked up when she heard running footsteps on the stairs. "Who...?"

"I had Harold go get Florence," Carrie informed her. She looked at Martha. "I don't want to offend you, but I also don't know how comfortable you are with surgery."

Martha smiled. "Just comfortable enough to be a wonderful assistant."

Carrie smiled in return. "Thank you." She turned to Marietta next. "Please have Matthew and Anthony bring as much hot water as they can. Tell them to leave it outside the door. Let him know Janie needs a Cesarean section, but assure him I know what I'm doing." There was a light tap at the door. "And please let Florence in."

Carrie knew the life of Janie's baby was dependent upon their immediate action. She rapidly explained the situation.

Florence listened carefully and then nodded. "I imagine we need to get started."

Carrie wanted to hug her, but settled for a warm smile. She reached into her surgical bag and pulled out two gowns. She handed one to Florence, removed her own coat, slipped a gown over her clothing, and then went to one of the buckets resting on the table. She plunged her hands into the hot water, reached for the soap Martha handed her, and washed them carefully. When she was convinced they were sterile, she dried them on a clean towel the midwife handed her. Florence finished at the same time she did.

Carrie reached into her bag again. "You can administer the chloroform?"

"Yes," Florence assured her. She turned to Janie. "Are you ready for a rest?"

Janie locked eyes with her, and then turned to gaze at Carrie. "Carrie..." she murmured.

"I'm not going to touch you," Carrie replied, "because I'm going to keep everything sterile, but I want you to close your eyes and feel my hug, Janie. I'll be here when you wake up," she promised. "I'll be waiting with your child." She prayed she would have a live baby waiting for her friend.

Janie nodded bravely, and lay her head back on the pillow. Florence skillfully administered the chloroform. Moments later, Janie's body was limp on the bed.

When Carrie was confident Janie was completely unconscious, she motioned for Martha to pull Janie's gown away from her. She could hear Marietta adding more wood to the fire so the room would stay warm. She closed her eyes, prayed for a moment, and then opened them with set lips and began the surgery. She would have to move quickly.

Carrie carefully cleaned Janie's abdomen with an antiseptic liquid, and used her scalpel to make a six-inch incision in her friend's lower abdomen. Her mind was already moving ahead. Without hesitation, she cut a second incision into the uterus, praying she would find a live child.

Her heart pounded when she saw blue lips on the tiny head encircled by the umbilical cord, but she took hope in the little body's pink flesh. She cut through the cord quickly, lifted the child from the womb, placed it into Florence's hands, and then turned back to Janie.

Janie's little boy was in capable hands, now it was up to her to keep Janie alive. She smiled when she heard a tiny wail come from Janie's son, and then she concentrated on her work. Carrie cleaned out the cavity left behind by the baby's birth, and carefully sutured the incision in the uterus, making tiny, tight stitches. When she was satisfied, she wiped the incision with herbal remedies to be certain it was clean and sterilized, and then sutured Janie's abdomen closed, repeating the sterilization process. She would do everything she could to make certain there was no infection. Finally, she applied and secured a large bandage.

Only then did Carrie straighten and step back.

"Well done," Florence said quietly. "You should never have left surgery."

Carrie met her eyes for a moment, and then turned to search for the baby. "How is...?"

Martha stepped forward. "This is one tough little boy," she said proudly. "You would never know he almost died in there."

Carrie gazed down, her heart swelling with gratitude as a pair of blue eyes stared back at her. The little boy squirmed, opened and closed his mouth, and then went back to staring at her. Carrie laughed. "I believe he's hungry."

Martha looked at Janie. "How long before she's awake?"

"It won't be long," Carrie assured her. "She's going to be sore, but the operation was successful. There is no reason she can't nurse as soon as she regains consciousness." She glanced at Marietta, surprised when she realized she and Janie had never talked about what she was going to name her child. "Do you know what this little boy's name is?"

Marietta shook her head. "They refused to reveal it until the birth."

Carrie smiled. "That sounds like them." She turned toward the door. "I'll be back in a few minutes. I'm going to let Matthew know he is a father."

*****

Matthew had refused to sit down for the last hour. All he could do was pace the room, stare out the window, and throw logs on the fire. The burst of sparks from the fireplace every time he tossed in a piece of dry wood somehow relieved his anxiety. It was as if the explosion of sparks helped release his own explosive emotions. He finally looked over at Anthony. "You haven't said a word."

"Is there something I could say that would help?"

"No," Matthew admitted. He swung away from the window. "I was prepared to not like you," he said abruptly.

Anthony met his eyes. "You were Robert's best friend," he responded. "I understand."

Matthew stared at him, appreciating the steadiness in the man's eyes. "You're in love with Carrie."

"Yes."

Matthew waited for him to say more, but Anthony remained silent. His lips twitched. "You don't talk a lot."

Anthony shrugged. "I talk when there is something that needs to be said."

"Have you told Carrie you love her?" Matthew asked directly.

"I have."

Matthew opened his mouth to press harder, but Anthony kept talking, so he snapped his lips shut, discovering he was grateful for the distraction.

"She told me she loves me, but that she's not ready to consider marriage again."

"Did she say why?"

Anthony smiled slightly. "She is enjoying her freedom and isn't ready to give it up."

Matthew chuckled. "That sounds like Carrie."

Anthony frowned. "Do you think she will change her mind?"

"I would tell you if I knew, but I doubt Carrie knows." He took a deep breath and gazed at the empty staircase before he turned back to Anthony. "She loved Robert very much. It almost killed her when she lost both him and Bridget."

Anthony nodded. "She said you were a large part of her deciding to live."

Matthew closed his eyes, remembering her pitiful condition when he visited the plantation after Robert's murder. "I promised Robert I would take care of her if anything ever happened to him, but it took a lot of people to love Carrie back to the land of the living. In the end, I believe she found a purpose bigger than herself that gave her a reason to live."

"Being a doctor."

Matthew nodded. "Yes. She decided to give it up when she couldn't save her husband and child, but things happened to change her mind. It's given her a reason to live, and it's given her something to put her focus on."

"She also happens to be a magnificent doctor," Anthony stated as a gust of wind down the chimney sent a spray of sparks into the air.

Matthew nodded, understanding Anthony's pain more than he would ever reveal. Some things were meant to remain in the past. "Give Carrie time," he advised. "I was prepared to not like you, but I find that I actually like you enormously." He paused. "Robert would have liked you, too."

Anthony closed his eyes for a moment. They were shining when he opened them again. "Thank you," he said quietly. "I have promised to give Carrie all the time she needs. I fell in love with her the first day I met her, but I completely backed off when I discovered what happened with Robert. I understand her grief because I have experienced it myself. I am prepared to wait."

"Be patient," Matthew advised again. "Carrie has more love to give than you realize. The time will come when she trusts life enough to give it again."

A sound at the top of the stairs caused him to look up just as Carrie started down. The excited look on her face told him she hadn't overheard any of their conversation. He sprang forward, meeting her at the bottom step. "Janie?"

Carrie grinned. "She's fine," she said cheerfully, but then fell silent, her eyes laughing up at him.

Matthew tensed, but realized Carrie wouldn't tease if all hadn't gone well. "If you make me wait, I promise you will pay for it," he threatened.

Carrie laughed. "Janie *and* your son are doing fine, Matthew."

Matthew froze and then threw back his head with a joyful laugh. "I have a son?" He laughed again, and then picked up Carrie to swing her around in his arms. "A *son?*"

Carrie caught her breath when he finally put her down. "A beautiful boy," she confirmed in a soft voice. "He has your red hair and blue eyes."

"We won't hold that against him," Matthew said happily. Then he sobered. "How is Janie? Did you have to do a Cesarean Section?"

"I did," Carrie confirmed calmly. "It went well. She should wake fairly soon and be able to nurse your son. She'll need to rest for about six weeks, but she'll be fine. She can get out of bed and walk around as soon as she feels like it, but she is not to do any lifting or any work," she said sternly. "She has two sets of stitches that need time to heal completely."

"Yes, ma'am," Matthew said solemnly. "I'll make sure she follows doctor's orders." He leaned forward to give Carrie a warm hug. "Thank you," he said in a husky whisper. "I realize I could have lost them both if you had not gotten here in time."

Carrie didn't deny the truth of his statement. "Does your son have a name? We would like to know what to call him."

Matthew hesitated. "Janie wanted to be the one to tell you." He thought for a moment, and then shook his head. "I won't take that away from her. Can I come sit with her until she wakes up?"

"Certainly," Carrie agreed. "I'm quite sure your nameless son would be thrilled to have his daddy hold him while he waits for his mama to regain consciousness," she teased.

Matthew grinned and turned to dash up the stairs.

*****

Carrie watched him disappear, and then turned back to Anthony. "Thank you for keeping him company."

"It didn't take much," Anthony admitted. "He didn't say a word until the last few minutes."

Carrie chuckled. "For a man who likes to talk so much, when Matthew is nervous, he doesn't seem to know how to form a word."

Anthony smiled and opened his arms.

Carrie went into them willingly.

"I'm very proud of you," Anthony said, stroking her hair with his hand.

Carrie closed her eyes, relishing in the embrace.

"Were you scared?" Anthony asked.

"I was scared thinking about it," Carrie admitted, "but once I started, all the fear melted away. I knew what I needed to do, and I knew how to do it." She leaned her head back and smiled up into his face. "It's rather an amazing feeling." She pursed her lips. "I helped save a lot of lives during the war, but there was something sacred about lifting a baby's body from within the womb. I was the first person to ever touch him." She shook her head. "I've never had a feeling like that. I've delivered a lot of babies, but this was different." She paused, remembering Florence's words.

Anthony was watching her closely. "What?"

Carrie hesitated. "It was something Florence said," she finally revealed. "She told me I should never have left surgery."

Anthony continued to gaze at her. "Do you agree?"

Carrie turned to stare out the window, knowing she should get back upstairs. She wanted to be there when Janie came out from beneath the chloroform. "I don't know," she confessed. "I don't regret becoming a homeopathic physician, because I know I'm able to help so many more people that way, but I also can't deny there are times when surgery is the only thing that will save a patient." She took a breath. "That little boy wouldn't be alive if I hadn't been able to perform that operation." She allowed herself a moment of contemplation, and then turned to head back upstairs. No decisions would be made right away. "I must return to Janie." She swung back to him. "You should go to bed. I know you must be exhausted. I'm sure Jeremy is waiting at the house for a report."

Anthony nodded. "I will go let Jeremy know the good news, but I'll wait up for you," he said gently. He held up a hand. "I know you don't need me to, but it will make me feel better."

Carrie smiled, raised on her toes to kiss him warmly, and then ran up the stairs.

She could feel his eyes burning into her back.

*****

Janie was sitting up in the bed, her son nestled in her arms, when Carrie walked back into the room.

"I'm so sorry I wasn't here when you woke!" Carrie cried.

Janie smiled weakly. "They are taking good care of me." Her gaze included Florence, Martha, and Marietta, before her eyes landed on Matthew.

Carrie felt tears mist her eyes when she saw the love exchanged between the two of them. "How do you feel?" she demanded.

"Quite a bit like a pin cushion that has been stitched together," Janie murmured, a smile filtering through the pain. "How long will it hurt this badly?"

"For a few days," Carrie replied, "but you'll feel better soon. You can get up and start walking around as soon as you feel like it, but you have to take it easy," she said. "You can't lift anything, and you're not to do any work. Your incisions must have time to heal properly."

Janie smiled again. "Matthew has already read me the riot act." She shook her head. "Don't worry. I have no desire to move, and I think I will rather enjoy ordering people around. It's about time I got to be the one waited on."

Carrie chuckled and let her eyes settle on the baby. "He's beautiful," she said tenderly. "You have a perfect baby boy."

"Thanks to you," Janie whispered. She reached out with her free hand to grip Carrie's arm. "I don't know how to thank you."

Carrie grinned. "You can start by giving this baby a name," she retorted.

Janie blinked back her tears and pressed Carrie's hand more tightly. She peered down at her son, and then looked back into Carrie's eyes. "I would like to introduce Robert Brady Justin to you, Carrie. We're going to call him Robert."

Carrie held a hand to her mouth. "Robert?"

Janie nodded. "We hope he will be as wonderful as Robert was."

Carrie couldn't stop the tears coursing down her face. "Robert..." she whispered. "He would be so proud."

"He was the best friend any man could hope to have," Matthew said. "His memory will live on through the child you saved."

Carrie felt another piece of her grief dissolve. She had not been able to save Robert or Bridget, but she had saved this little boy.

Robert chose that moment to give a demanding cry, turning to nestle into Janie.

Carrie laughed. "Everyone out," she ordered. "Mama needs to give her son his first meal, and they need to get some rest."

Chapter Nineteen

Wally Stratford settled himself in the chair across the desk from his friend, Ralph Cook. "Thank you for seeing me."

Ralph smiled and sat back, resting his hands on his ample girth. Steady brown eyes that carried both authority and humor gazed at him. Silvery hair topped deep wrinkles. His impeccable dress revealed his wealth. "When I'm visited by one of the most successful realtors in New York City, I always find time." He cocked his head. "Assuming, of course, that you haven't come to tell me I've violated some property code I'm not aware of."

Wally chuckled. "Nothing that dire for you personally." He straightened. "But something much more serious."

Ralph's smile disappeared. "I suspected this was not simply a social call to remind me of some kind of meeting I was about to forget."

Wally shook his head. "No, I'm afraid it's not a social call. Rather than take up your valuable time with idle chatter, I would prefer to get right to it."

"And I would prefer you did," Ralph replied. He leaned forward and placed his elbows on his desk. "What is this about?"

"Sherman Archer."

Ralph's eyebrows rose in surprise. "Sherman Archer? I'm afraid I don't understand."

"You will," Wally promised. "What can you tell me about his position in the Pennsylvania Railroad Company?"

Ralph hesitated. "Something tells me you already know a great deal."

"Perhaps, but I suspect you can tell me more."

Ralph hesitated again. "And when I give you the information you're looking for, you will reveal why you're asking?"

"You have my word," Wally promised.

Ralph gave him another searching gaze, and then began to speak. "Sherman Archer is a fine young man. He's been with the company about five years, recommended by his father who has been a close friend for many years."

Wally listened closely, knowing this revelation would probably make what he had to say more difficult, but he believed it could be used for his advantage.

"Sherman heads up our advertising and publicity division," Ralph continued. "He has played a large role in the rapid growth of the company. I consider him a valued employee." He settled back in his chair. "Now," he declared, "you need to tell me what this is about."

Wally was the one to lean forward now. "I suspect you would not want a scandal involving the Pennsylvania Railroad to come to light at this point in your growth."

Ralph's eyes narrowed. "I'm a patient man, Wally, but you need to tell me what you're referring to."

Wally nodded. "Sherman Archer may be a fine businessman, but he is not such a fine person," he said. He held up a hand when Ralph opened his mouth to protest. "You asked me to tell you why I'm in your office. You need to hear me out."

Ralph nodded curtly and sat back again in his chair. "Continue," he growled.

"Are you aware Sherman Archer is married?"

Ralph looked puzzled. "Yes, of course."

"Do you know Sherman's wife?"

Ralph looked more impatient. "Yes, I've met Mrs. Archer at several social events. She is a fine, lovely woman."

"Did you consider her insane?" Wally asked casually.

Ralph leaned forward in his chair and thumped his meaty hands on the desk. "Wally, I am running out of patience."

"Just answer that last question," Wally insisted.

"Mrs. Archer is a delightful, intelligent woman. We've had several conversations. Do you know she is getting her medical degree?"

Wally nodded with satisfaction. "I do. And are *you* aware that Sherman Archer has had his lovely, intelligent wife committed to the Women's Insane Asylum on Blackwell's Island?"

Ralph stared at him with a shocked expression and then fell back against his chair. "*What?* That's not possible," he protested. He took a deep breath. "Though I suppose you're sure, or you wouldn't be here."

"I'm sure," Wally said. "My wife and I have known Alice for several years. In the last five weeks at the asylum, Mrs. Archer has been beaten, starved, humiliated, and held under water in a freezing tub until she passed out."

Ralph whitened, his dark eyes sparking with distress. "I had no idea," he exclaimed. "No idea at all." He slammed his hands on his desk. "This cannot be allowed to continue." He stood. "I will bring Sherman Archer in immediately."

Wally remained seated, but waved Ralph back to his chair. "I believe we need to be quite strategic about this, Ralph. While Alice is quite sane, I *do* question the sanity of any man who would do such a thing to his wife." He paused, knowing he must be calm, but direct. "We want to handle this so that it has as few consequences for the company as possible."

Ralph sat back down heavily. "What are you talking about?"

Wally shrugged. "If it were to get out that one of your top executives has his very successful, and very *sane* wife locked up in the Women's Insane Asylum, I'm afraid it might undo all the goodwill you have worked so hard to develop after the recent spate of accidents." He watched as Ralph absorbed the impact of his statement.

"Who knows Mrs. Archer is locked up there?" Ralph demanded.

"Quite a number of people," Wally revealed. "One of Mrs. Archer's neighbors was outside with her dog on the night Sherman had three strong men abduct his wife and carry her off to the asylum, holding her mouth closed while she fought them."

"Good God..." Ralph muttered. "I can only imagine the terror Mrs. Archer must have felt." He shook her head. "Or the horrors she has lived in the last weeks." His eyes blazed. "What are we going to do?"

Wally felt a surge of genuine affection for his friend, relieved beyond words that his sense of integrity and his concern for Alice outweighed his concerns for the company. "I believe I have a plan that will work." He met Ralph's eyes evenly. "I don't know how much longer Mrs. Archer will survive in there. We must act quickly."

"Please tell me your plan," Ralph responded. "I'll do whatever is necessary."

*****

Carrie was shivering from the cold when Sarge dropped her off after a long day at the clinic. All she wanted was to soak in a hot tub while she dreamed of escaping the Philadelphia winter. She hoped Marietta had a blazing fire that would take off the worst of the chill.

"You need to take a day off, Miss Carrie!"

Carrie smiled at Sarge's scolding tone as she stepped down from the carriage. "I'm fine, Sarge."

"That be pure nonsense," Sarge snorted. "You be at that clinic every hour of the day."

Carrie took a deep breath, praying for patience as she glanced at the front door that led to warmth and food. "Why did you wait until we got home to start fussing at me?"

Sarge narrowed his eyes. "You don't even know you done slept most all the way home."

Carrie hesitated. She knew she had closed her eyes at some point, but she honestly didn't remember sleeping all the way. She shrugged sheepishly. "I suppose I'm a little tired."

Sarge raised a brow as his lips thinned. "I ain't picking you up in the mornin'. You gonna take a day off, Miss Carrie."

Carrie froze and turned to stare up at him. "You have to pick me up tomorrow, Sarge," she protested. "I appreciate your concern, but I have at least fifteen new patients coming in tomorrow. The flu is hitting Moyamensing badly. We're all working hard to make sure no more die."

"And what if *you* get sick?" Sarge demanded. "You done told me last week to make sure I got plenty of rest so I didn't get this flu. Sounds like you ain't listenin' to your own advice."

Carrie paused, grateful for his concern. "You're right," she admitted. "I promise to get a good night's rest. I won't even stay up and play with the twins. I'll eat and go straight to bed." In truth, that was all she *wanted* to do. She knew the long days were taking their toll on her.

"You promise?" Sarge said suspiciously. "You ain't just sayin' it to make me shut up?"

"I promise," Carrie repeated. "It actually sounds quite wonderful. If anyone wants anything from me, I'll tell them I can't break my word to you."

Sarge peered at her suspiciously for a few moments, and then waved his hand. "Go on in that house and get out of the cold, then. I'll be back tomorrow mornin'." He scowled. "But if you ain't lookin' better than you look right now, I ain't gonna take you."

"Thank you, Sarge," Carrie murmured, stepping close to the carriage to place a hand on his arm. "You're a good man." Sarge ducked his head, but not before she saw the glow in his eyes and the smile on his lips.

"Get on with you," Sarge commanded. "I got me some hot stew waitin' for me at home."

Carrie dashed up the stairs, wondering what Marietta would have waiting for her. She was famished. She pushed open the door, sagging in relief when the warm air enveloped her like a cocoon.

"It's about time you got home," Marietta declared as she appeared in the kitchen door.

Carrie hung up her coat, removed her snow boots, and walked over to put her hands out to the fire. The furnaces were casting heat through the house, but nothing felt better to her than a blazing fire, and it took all of them to beat back the brutal cold gripping Philadelphia. She raised her head and sniffed the air. "Something smells wonderful. What is it?"

"Beef stew and biscuits," Marietta reported. "I'll admit it's wonderful, but not as good as the letter you have waiting for you."

Carrie stepped away from the fire. "Alice?" she asked hopefully.

Marietta frowned. "Not yet, Carrie, but I know it's coming soon. You know Wally said things were moving forward."

Carrie nodded, but was still deeply disappointed. She didn't know how long Alice would survive in the asylum. "Then who is the letter from?"

Marietta shook her head and grinned. "Well, I'm only *assuming* it is similar to the letter I received, though I'm sure yours says more."

Carrie held out her hand. She was far too weary for guessing games.

Marietta shook her head. "You look exhausted. You'll get the letter once you've eaten."

"You're not serious!" Carrie cried. "Give me that letter right this minute." She searched the room with her eyes.

"You won't find it," Marietta promised. "I knew I would need leverage, so I hid it. You promised you would be home by four o'clock. You're two hours late. You are working too much, and you're not getting enough rest." She pointed toward the kitchen. "Go in there and eat if you want the letter."

Carrie chuckled despite her frustration. "You and Sarge," she muttered.

"What? He told you that you're being stupid, too?"

Carrie tossed her head. "I wouldn't go that far," she protested. "He simply said he wouldn't pick me up tomorrow morning unless I promised to get a good night's sleep."

"At least you'll listen to *one* of the men in your life."

Carrie spun around to see Anthony walking down the steps with a rueful look on his face. She put her hands on her hips. "Just why does everyone in my life think they should tell me what to do?" she retorted.

"Perhaps because you don't seem to have enough sense to take all the advice you love to dish out," Anthony retorted back.

Carrie was torn between amusement and annoyance. "I worked far harder than this during the war," she replied, trying to hide the irritation creeping through. "I won't walk away from need when I see it."

"And I can appreciate that," Anthony said evenly, "but business has taught me a few things about being in something for the long haul."

"I would love to hear it," Carrie lied, "but I have orders to eat dinner if I want a letter I am dying to read."

Anthony nodded sagely. "I'm sure it's one you'll be excited about."

Carrie whirled toward Marietta. "Anthony has read my letter?" she cried.

"Of course not," Marietta replied, rolling her eyes for emphasis. "But, he knows what mine says. He was here when it came."

Carrie was suddenly aware that annoyance had won over amusement. She had acknowledged her love for Anthony, but she didn't need, or want, someone else telling her how to live her life. She took a deep breath, hoping her facial expression wouldn't reveal her feelings, and moved toward the kitchen. "I'm starving," she announced. "And I want my letter. I'm going in to eat." She saw the look of concern cross Anthony's handsome features, but she was too hungry and fatigued to care.

She breathed in the wonderful aromas in the kitchen as she dished up a big bowl of soup and sliced two thick pieces of warm bread that she slathered with butter. When she turned toward the table, Anthony was standing next to it.

"I'm sorry," he said quietly.

Carrie shrugged. "I'm just tired."

"No," Anthony replied. "I'm acting like a husband would act. When I started talking, I thought I was being a good friend, but I realize you don't want or need anyone telling you how to run your life. So, I'm sorry," he repeated, his voice remorseful. "I promise not to do that in the future. You are a strong woman who is perfectly capable of making decisions for yourself."

Carrie thought about insisting that it didn't really bother her, but they had agreed to be honest with each other, so she nodded. "Thank you," she said. Then she pointed toward the stew. "Have you eaten yet?"

Anthony accepted the peace offering with a smile. "Yes, but just because I've had one big bowl doesn't mean I don't have room for more. Marietta's stew is wonderful, and she made enough for an army."

Carrie took a bite and closed her eyes, savoring the taste and the warmth flowing through her body. "Oh..." she moaned. "I needed this." She remained silent as she ate the rest of the soup and polished off the bread. Marietta walked in as she ate the last bite. "I have followed orders. Please produce my letter."

Marietta grinned, reached behind the flour canister, and delivered it with a flourish. "My pleasure!"

Carrie reached for the envelope, recognizing the handwriting immediately. "Rose?"

Marietta nodded, but remained silent.

Carrie ripped into it eagerly.

Dear Carrie,

You know that we always say life is what happens after we make our plans. Well, there is some life happening here in Ohio that seems to have changed our plans radically. You know how much Moses has missed the plantation. He never said very much, but I was so painfully aware of it. I know you were, too, along with everyone else.

What came as a surprise is that when we returned to Oberlin after Christmas, I found myself missing it as much as he does. I missed the plantation. I missed family. I missed my school. I missed what I knew was happening there. I was rather surprised with the revelation at first, but I knew I needed to pay attention.

After a few weeks back in Oberlin, I realized my feelings weren't changing. They were only growing stronger. When I accepted how I truly felt, I went to the administration. I wanted to go home, but I knew I wouldn't give up my chance to get my degree. As it turns out, I won't have to!

They told me I was qualified to be a teacher at the school, not a student. They informed me there was really nothing more they could teach me, agreed to let me act as a mentor to young teachers who will come to the plantation to study our model, and informed me I will graduate at the end of the term in April.

We're coming home in April, Carrie! I know I have talked about wanting to teach at a big city school, but the reality of being away from the plantation taught me that it wasn't really what I wanted, after all. I don't care about the prestige. I'm coming home to work with Lillian, and to create as fabulous a school as we can out in the country, where we can give opportunity to students who wouldn't have it otherwise.

I already know what you're thinking. Will they be safe? We've weighed the costs, and agree we want to come home. No matter the risks.

Felicia will stay here with one of the faculty members to finish her schooling. Whenever she comes home, she will be accompanied by a teaching student who wants to visit our plantation school.

I know you have no idea what you will be doing, but at least you can know that when you come home to visit, Moses and I will be there. I can't tell you how happy that makes me. I don't need to tell you how Moses feels about it, and John only wants to get home to Patches.

It's odd... I've worked so hard to get away from the plantation, but now that I've accomplished it, all I want is to go home. Life is funny. I know Mama would cock her head, look at me with those wise eyes, and tell me "life done has a way of teachin' us what be really important!" And, once again, she would be right.

Please tell me you'll be coming home at least for a little while in April. I miss you!

All my love,

Rose

Carrie laughed and clapped her hands with delight. "Rose and Moses are coming home!" She clasped the letter to her chest, her heart expanding with joy. She didn't stop to examine her own decisions about her future—it was enough to know Rose and Moses were following their hearts, and making the decisions that would make them happy.

Marietta grinned. "I knew you would love the letter!"

Carrie grinned back at her, and then looked at Marietta more closely, not able to miss the shadow of worry in her eyes. "What's wrong?"

Marietta shook her head to deny anything was disturbing her, but when she opened her mouth to refute her question, nothing came out.

"Marietta?" Carrie pressed, but she didn't really need her to say anything. "You're worried for them," she said bluntly.

Marietta met her eyes. "Aren't you?" She turned to stare out the window into the dark. "Jeremy and I left our home because we want our family to be safe. Nothing has changed, Carrie. Of course I'm worried for them. Aren't you?" she repeated.

Carrie wanted to deny it, but she didn't see the point. "Yes," she admitted. "As much as I hated them being so far away in Oberlin, at least I knew they were safe." She looked to Anthony. "I've been so busy with the clinic that I really am not paying much attention to anything else." She paused. "Do you know what is going on with the KKK?"

Anthony nodded reluctantly. "It's not good," he said grimly. "Their success in keeping blacks away from the elections last November has emboldened them. The election didn't go their way, but they learned their terror tactics are effective. They are increasing their attacks, and seem to not care who knows." He hesitated. "I think they don't believe anyone will take action to stop them." His face set in grim lines. "I'm afraid they might be right. And, even if action is taken, it will be impossible to control everything in the South."

Carrie sucked in her breath, thinking of all the attacks the plantation had already endured. What were Moses and Rose coming back to? What were they bringing their children back to? She understood their decision to accept the risk, but could she handle the idea of losing someone else she loved to vigilantes? She took a deep breath as worry replaced her delight. She knew worrying served no good purpose, but she couldn't stop the trembling in her gut.

"I'm going to keep my promise to Sarge," she said quietly. "I promised him I would go to bed early tonight. I'm going to do just that."

Carrie could feel the eyes watching her as she walked from the kitchen. All she wanted was to curl up in her bed, go to sleep, and pretend the world wasn't full of horrifying things.

Chapter Twenty

Alice took a deep breath, wishing with all her heart that she could retreat back to the safety of her room, but Dr. Tillerson had insisted she attend the social event planned for her old ward that evening. She suspected he had been compelled to make some degree of improvements since Carrie's visit with letters from Governor Hoffman and the Inspector of State Prisons. Knowing how his mind worked, she was certain he intended to pressure her to make a good report on the ward if she wanted to continue to receive better treatment in her private room.

"I don't wish to attend," she said.

"I know," Miss Wade said sympathetically, "but he was quite adamant. I don't believe you want to defy him," she warned. "You've been hurt enough, Mrs. Archer. Just go along with this, and you'll be back in your room soon."

Alice was grateful they had at least chosen Miss Wade to escort her and not the fearsome Mrs. Bartle. The last two weeks had healed her face, but it had done nothing to eliminate her fear of the ward. She couldn't help being afraid that once back in the confines of her old prison, they would find a way to keep her there. She pulled her coat closer as they neared the ward. The patients confined here were certainly not being any more protected from the numbing cold. She felt guilty for having such a warm coat, but found herself unwilling not to wear it. She sent grateful thoughts to Carrie every day, even while she was wondering why she was still confined in the asylum.

There had been no more communication from anyone. Even if letters had been delivered, she knew she would not receive them if Dr. Tillerson disagreed with something in them. It was easy to envision a pile of letters filling the trash bin in his office.

"What happened to the woman who was hurt the last night I was in the ward?" Alice asked. She needed to take her mind off the fact she may never have any more communication from the outside world. Very likely, Carrie had not been able to convince Sherman to free her. Her brief moment of hope had already faded into resigned acceptance.

Miss Wade cocked her head. "Who are you talking about?"

"I don't know her name. She had arrived just that day, and it was quite clear she was not insane. Mrs. Bartle subdued her in the cold water tub that night. It was her screams and cries for help that had everyone in my room so agitated."

"And your attempt to calm the women in your room was the reason you were hurt so badly," Miss Wade commented.

Alice shrugged. She found it easier if she didn't think of that night. "How is she?"

Miss Wade frowned. "Her name is Beatrice Murray. I'm afraid Mrs. Murray has had a rough time of it."

Alice bit her lip. She needed no imagination to understand what a *rough time of it* meant. Before she could say anything else, they arrived at the ward.

Everyone stopped talking when they entered the room. Alice shifted uncomfortably, her insides trembling more from fear than from the cold. What if Mrs. Bartle refused to let her leave? What if an agitated patient attacked her again? Now that she was freed from the daily reality of life in this cold, dank prison, she found it even more unfathomable that she might end up there again. Surely though, Dr. Tillerson would not be long constrained by the threat of the letters Carrie had produced. As time went on, his fear would diminish and he would take action on the hatred she saw shining from his eyes every time he looked at her. She suspected his insistence about her attendance tonight was simply a reminder and warning of what was waiting for her.

Miss Wade touched her arm. "Mrs. Murray is standing next to the window. I'm sure she would appreciate it if you spoke to her."

Alice's eyes swept the room, noticing the urn of hot coffee and plate of biscuits laid out on a long table in the center. In the realm of social events, this hardly counted as one, but she was glad the women would at least have a hot drink for one night. The atmosphere was blessedly quiet and constrained. She locked eyes with Mrs. Bartle for a moment. The burly attendant, watching from a corner of the room, stared at her with angry disdain. Alice was careful to look back with nothing but calm detachment. There was no reason to antagonize the woman, and every reason to not make her more of an enemy.

Alice turned away in search of Mrs. Murray. Her eyes swept over a woman standing by the window, but she didn't recognize her. She turned to gaze around the room.

"That's Mrs. Murray," Miss Wade said quietly, appearing by her side again. "There, by the window."

Alice shook her head. "That's not possible. I don't recognize her." True, she had only seen her that afternoon before she was moved, but the picture of the delicate, fine-featured woman with frightened, yet sane, eyes was indelibly sketched in her mind. "Dear God..." she muttered, raising her hand to her mouth to stop her cry of distress when the truth dawned on her.

"I told you she's had a rather rough two weeks," Miss Wade said grimly, anger flashing in her eyes. "Mrs. Bartle has taken it upon herself to subdue her."

Alice shuddered and swung her head back to where the woman was standing, staring out the barred sliver of a window, not seeming to even notice the icy wind blowing in. She took a deep breath and slowly walked over. "Mrs. Murray?"

Alice barely contained her shocked gasp when the woman turned to her. "Oh, my dear," she murmured, laying her hand on her arm. "What has happened to you?"

Mrs. Murray stared in her direction through unseeing eyes. "I'm afraid I don't recognize your voice."

Alice was amazed that even after two weeks of horrible treatment, the woman still maintained a grasp of courtesy. "You wouldn't," she said quickly. "I was here the night you arrived, but I was moved the next day."

Mrs. Murray cocked her head. "You're the one who was beaten by your roommate."

"Yes," Alice said softly, and then turned the conversation back to the pitiful excuse for a human standing in front of her. "What has happened to you?" she repeated.

Mrs. Murray grimaced. "What *hasn't* happened to me?" Her cloudy eyes released a single tear that she quickly dashed away.

Alice understood. It was never good to show weakness in this ward. It only made you more vulnerable. She struggled to remember the beautiful woman she had seen enter the asylum two weeks earlier. Mrs. Murray had been lovely—short and tiny, with long, black, beautiful hair. She'd had tender, frightened eyes, and a white, clear complexion. The woman standing in front of her now bore no resemblance.

Mrs. Murray turned toward the window again, seeming to find comfort in the cold air swallowing her emaciated frame. When she spoke, her voice was emotionless. "I have been choked, beaten, kicked, and plunged into that icy tub more times than I can count."

"Why?" Alice whispered.

Mrs. Murray shrugged. "I suppose I shouldn't have mentioned I am a trained dancer or that I am highly educated. I believed, in the beginning, that I could convince people of my sanity. Now I doubt it myself," she said bitterly. "I suppose I should have accepted the inevitable when they started giving me opium to calm me."

Alice groaned. "Opium?" She had seen the results of using opium during her work with patients at school. She also knew, firsthand, the power of addiction because it had consumed her younger brother after his injuries during the war. He had never been the same.

Mrs. Murray still portrayed no emotion. "Mrs. Bartle told me it would quiet my excited nervous system." She chuckled, though there was no humor in it. "Evidently, it had the opposite effect, so they kept giving me more, thinking it would help." Suddenly ,she clenched her fists and leaned toward Alice, hysterical laughter spilling from her lips. "It must not have helped..." she muttered.

Alice sucked in her breath, seeing what she hadn't first been able to recognize in the blinded eyes. She knew excessive amounts of opium could cause insanity. Suddenly, certain she must tell Mrs. Murray's story if she was ever released from the asylum herself, she continued to question her in a calm voice. "What happened to your face?" She was appalled by the open sores and her inflamed eyes.

Mrs. Murray frowned and raised her hand to her face. "Do I look badly? I am told the opium made me quite drunk one night. So drunk I fainted and fell down a flight of stairs." She hesitated, and then finished the story. "When they found me, they poured a large bottle of camphor over my face. It went into my ears and eyes. I have been blind and hard of hearing since then." She paused. "Oh, I can see some shadows – at least enough to get around - but my vision is gone. I can't see a mirror, so I have no idea of what I look like. Not that it matters anymore," she said in a broken whisper.

Alice couldn't control another groan. Camphor could be an effective remedy if used correctly, but too much of it could wreak havoc on skin and on the eyes. "My dear Mrs. Murray. I'm so terribly sorry." She knew her sympathy wouldn't change anything, but she had to at least express it.

Mrs. Murray chuckled, her blind eyes somehow taking on a shine of madness once again. "Sorry. Yes, I am, too. My husband has indeed won."

"Why?" Alice asked. She supposed she should be grateful she was not the only woman trapped here because of her husband, but the knowledge only made her feel ill.

"Oh, Harrison did not like the fact that I was fighting for women's rights." Mrs. Murray's voice became coherent again as she talked about her passion. "Women should have the vote, you know."

"Yes, I know," Alice agreed.

Mrs. Murray brightened for a moment. "I'm quite glad you know. Too many women don't seem to realize we must fight for our rights." She shook her head. "Harrison told me he wouldn't have a wife of his making him look weak and ineffective."

"So, he had you brought here and locked up," Alice stated.

Mrs. Murray looked toward her. "Is that what happened to you? I can't see your face, but you certainly don't sound like the rest."

"Yes. My husband was displeased because I was soon to get my medical degree. He had me abducted one night and brought here."

Mrs. Murray reached out and gripped her hand. "What a horrible man!"

"Just as horrible as Harrison," Alice agreed. Silence fell on the women for a few moments, but Alice knew she had to give the poor woman something to hold onto. Carrie had given her a private room and warm clothes, but her most treasured gift to her had been hope. It was fading now, but she would not diminish its value. "You have to hold on, Mrs. Murray. Things will get better." She had absolutely no basis for her belief, but it was the only thing she could think of to say.

"Hold on?" Mrs. Murray asked absently as another laugh bubbled from her lips. "No, I don't think so, dear. There is but one way to deal with living in this place of horrors."

"Mrs. Murray, I—"

"That's quite enough talking, Mrs. Archer."

Alice felt Mrs. Murray stiffen with terror when Mrs. Bartle appeared at their side.

"Get away from that patient," Mrs. Bartle ordered. "She is nothing but trouble."

Alice wanted to lash out, but knew it would only make things more intolerable for Mrs. Murray. In truth, she had no idea what she would have said to infuse the woman with hope. She feared anything she would have said would have been nothing more than pointless lies. Trapped by the laws of America, Mrs. Murray was at the mercy of her husband because she was nothing but disposable property.

Bile rose in her throat as she walked away from the window, dismayed when she heard Mrs. Murray giggle and turn back to the window again.

*****

Sherman Archer prepared carefully for his meeting with Ralph Cook that morning. He knew his efforts with the Pennsylvania Railroad Company had been producing stellar results. He suspected he was being called in for the announcement of a promotion. His hands shook slightly with excitement as he brushed back his thick black hair, and carefully groomed his moustache. He adjusted the lapel of his suitcoat, straightened the monogrammed handkerchief in his pocket, and brushed away a few specks of lint before turning away from the mirror.

He heard a bell ring in the distance. Sherman smiled with satisfaction as he walked to the dining room. Sending Alice to the insane asylum had been an inconvenience in the beginning, but securing Hettie Holloway as his cook and housekeeper had proved to be a boon. As long as he paid Hettie on time, she had nothing more to say than "Yes, sir," and "No, sir." There were moments when it was lonely without a wife in bed at night, but in truth, Alice had spent much of their marriage at school. It had not been difficult to find other ways to meet his needs. He found he rather preferred single life.

The time may come in the future when he would want another wife; then he would have to deal with the reality of Alice in the insane asylum. He was confident he would be awarded a divorce on the grounds that his once lovely wife was certifiably insane. During a brief moment of doubt, he had offered her a way out two weeks earlier, but she had refused his reasonable request to promise she would never be a doctor.

As Sherman seated himself in front of a plate of hot, steaming food in the dining room, he was confident he had done all a prosperous businessman could be expected to do for a recalcitrant wife. It was his place as a man to control his rebellious spouse. His position as a successful businessman required it.

Feeling secure in his future, Sherman ate his breakfast quickly, and then strode from the house. Even a cold New York wind could not damper his spirits this fine morning. He was about to take a step further into the future he dreamed of.

*****

Ralph Cook exchanged a glance with Wally Stratford when Sherman Archer was announced by his secretary.

"Hello, Mr. Cook," Sherman said heartily as he strode into the room.

Ralph remained seated, merely indicating a chair in front of his desk by a brief nod. "Hello, Sherman."

Sherman hesitated for a moment, his brow lifting when he saw Wally across the room, but smiled and took the seat offered him.

Wally knew that Ralph failing to stand when Sherman entered the room had passed on the message it was intended to. He could see the tension in Sherman's eyes. Perfect. He wanted him on his guard.

"Thank you for coming in today," Ralph began. Now that he had made clear his position of authority, his voice took on a more pleasant tone. "I have called this meeting to talk about the work you have been doing for Pennsylvania Railroad."

Wally understood when Sherman visibly relaxed. No one could dispute the effectiveness of his efforts for the company.

"I hope you are pleased," Sherman said smoothly.

"I'm quite pleased with the increased positive publicity the company has received in the last year," Ralph assured him. "We have discovered that by carefully monitoring the information the media receives, we can overcome negative publicity."

"I'm glad to hear it, sir," Sherman replied. "I have worked quite diligently to accomplish the results you were hoping to achieve." He smiled confidently.

"Yes, you have," Ralph responded. He paused for a long moment. "The problem we are facing now is negative publicity that we cannot control in the media. We find ourselves dealing with something that is quite out of our control, because it is now in the hands of a very prominent journalist."

Sherman stiffened. "What is it, sir? I can assure you I will nip it in the bud."

"Oh?" Ralph asked. "And how will you do that?"

Sherman leaned forward. "I'm not aware yet of what the negative publicity entails, but it can't be anything major or I would be aware of it. First, I will get rid of whatever is creating the negative impression, and then I will meet with the media to assure them it has been dealt with. If there is any media coverage at all, it will be positive because of how we handled it."

Wally smiled slightly, glad Sherman couldn't see his face from where he was sitting. In truth, other than a brief glance and a head nod, Sherman had paid him no attention. It was just as he had planned.

Ralph listened closely and sat back with a sigh. "I wish I believed it would be that simple. As it turns out, it involves someone we consider very important to our company. We want to take care of the problem without jeopardizing this person's position."

"And you believe that is possible?" Sherman asked keenly.

Ralph shrugged. "I suppose it depends on the person. I would hope they value their job enough to take care of the situation quickly, so that we can make it disappear."

"Anyone who doesn't value their job here is a fool," Sherman said firmly, stroking his moustache thoughtfully. "Would you like me to talk to them, sir?"

Ralph shook his head. "That won't be necessary," he said. "I am talking to that person right now." He sat back in his seat, his eyes fixed on Sherman.

Wally watched Sherman closely. He could tell the moment Ralph's statement hit home.

"I'm not certain I understand," Sherman stammered, straightening in his chair as he struggled to regain his composure. "Are you talking about me?"

"I am," Ralph said, dropping all pretense. "It has come to light that your beautiful wife, Alice, was abducted by three men under the cover of night and taken to the Women's Lunatic Asylum on Blackwell's Island. Since I grew rather fond of your intelligent and quite *sane* wife during our social meetings over the last months, I was quite distraught when I discovered this."

Wally allowed himself a satisfied smile as he watched Sherman's mouth open and close silently. He looked like a fish gulping for air while it thrashed on the bottom of a boat.

"To make it worse," Ralph continued, "we have discovered that quite a prominent journalist is aware of this situation, and is preparing to launch a series of articles about it, including the information of your position with Pennsylvania Railroad. I'm sure you can understand what a negative impact this would have on the company," he said harshly. "It would undo all the good you have accomplished in the last year."

Sherman continued to stare at him in shock.

"Have you nothing to say?" Ralph barked after a few moments.

Sherman finally found his voice. "I'm afraid you don't have a clear understanding of the situation," he said stiffly, fighting to regain his dignity. "It caused me great grief to have my wife confined to the asylum, but I found it was for the best."

Ralph waved his hand in the air angrily. "Don't compound your appalling treatment of your wife by lying to me. We both know you chose this course of action because you were threatened by Alice's decision to be a doctor." He shook his head. "What I can't understand is why you believed it was such a threat."

Sherman sat silently for several moments.

Wally could almost see the wheels turning in the man's head as he tried to create a way out of the disaster he had engineered for himself.

"Successful businessmen should never have a wife in a profession," Sherman said formally. "It diminishes their effectiveness in business because of how others perceive him."

Ralph barked a short laugh. "If you believe that nonsense, Sherman, you are even less intelligent than I had already recently decided you are. In case you are not aware of it, more and more women are moving forward in professions. My own daughter is preparing to be a lawyer. I am quite proud of her, and would not allow her to marry a man who had nothing but the utmost respect and appreciation for her intelligence." He leaned forward. "It's really quite simple. You have to fix this."

Sherman nodded eagerly. "I believe I can convince the journalist that it was in Mrs. Archer's best interest to have her committed. I'm sure he must be a reasonable man."

Wally was content to watch as the anger in Ralph's eyes flared to rage. His respect for his friend grew as the older man managed to get it under control.

"That won't do," Ralph said firmly. "Evidently, you heard nothing of what I just said. I believe I mentioned in the beginning of this meeting that I hoped to find a solution to this problem without jeopardizing the person's position in our company." He paused. "Despite your archaic way of thinking, I still would like to do that."

Sherman grabbed on to his last sentence like a life ring thrown to a drowning man. "And how do you see that happening?" he asked quietly.

Wally nodded his head as he saw Sherman finally realize the choices he made in the next few minutes would determine whether he still had a career with Pennsylvania Railroad.

Ralph folded his hands on his desk. "You will go immediately to the asylum on Blackwell's Island and provide the paperwork for Mrs. Archer's release," he said, his voice ringing through his office. "You will leave without seeing her, because that would do nothing but inflame the situation. Then, tomorrow, you will file the papers for divorce, promising to give Mrs. Archer ten thousand dollars immediately."

"Divorce? Ten thousand dollars?" Sherman's features whitened. "That is all the money I have, sir," he stammered.

Wally smiled grimly. Sherman would be appalled at how much they knew about him. His investigator had been quite thorough in the past two weeks.

"That may be," Ralph replied, "but at least you will still have a job." He waited for several long moments of stunned silence and then leaned forward. "Can I count on you to take care of this very unpleasant situation?"

Sherman continued to stare.

Wally knew he was running through all the possible solutions in his mind. It didn't take long for the man's expression to reveal he understood he had no viable options if he wasn't to face complete destruction.

"Where will Mrs. Archer go if I have her released?" Sherman asked.

Ralph narrowed his eyes. "If I thought she was willing to spend even one night under your roof, I would force you to move out and give her your home. As it is, she never wants to step foot through the doors again. I quite agree with her."

"Mrs. Archer will come home with me," Wally said, speaking for the first time.

Sherman swung around to stare at him. "Who are you?" His voice was more bewildered than antagonistic.

"My name is Wally Stratford. My wife and I have known Alice for several years. We will be honored to have her in our home while she rebuilds the life you have tried to destroy."

"I see," Sherman murmured, his eyes flashing around the room like a trapped animal's.

Ralph took control again. "Mr. Stratford will accompany you to Blackwell's Island on the next ferry. Once you have signed the papers for Mrs. Archer's release, he will take you back to the ferry. You will return here, and then go to the courthouse in the afternoon to sign the divorce papers. I'm assured it will not take long, since no one will contest the divorce." He paused for a long moment.

Sherman shifted nervously in his chair.

"When you have done all that, you will return here in the morning and resume your work."

Sherman sagged against his chair. "I will still have a job?"

"You will still have a job, if you return having done those things," Ralph agreed.

Sherman took a deep breath, and then nodded his head in defeat. "I will do as you wish, sir."

Ralph nodded, and then indicated the door. "I have quite a busy morning." He turned to Wally. "I will expect a telegram from you this afternoon confirming Mrs. Archer is safely in your home."

"You will receive it," Wally promised.

Chapter Twenty-One

Alice was startled by a soft knock on her door. She was not usually summoned in the middle of the morning. Sleep had been a futile effort the night before. Every time she closed her eyes, she saw Mrs. Murray's disfigured, forlorn face in her mind. She heard her hopeless voice saying, *there is but one way to deal with living in this place of horrors.* Alice knew what she meant, because she had thought the same thing many times in the weeks of her confinement. She was not being tortured in her private room, but the idea of spending her whole life locked away was intolerable.

Alice walked slowly to the door, wondering if Dr. Tillerson was sending her back to the ward. She considered not answering the knock, but knew whoever it was would just force their way in.

"Hello, Mrs. Archer."

Alice took a deep breath. "Hello, Miss Wade." She fought to keep her voice calm. "Have you come to return me to the ward?"

"No," Miss Wade said quickly, her kind blue eyes softening with compassion. "Nothing like that." She looked around the hallway quickly. "May I come in for a moment?"

Mystified, Alice stepped back. "Certainly." She didn't miss the look of relief on Miss Wade's face as the door closed behind her.

"I'm on my break," Miss Wade said nervously. She reached into her pocket and pulled out a small piece of paper. "You should have this."

Alice reached for it. "What is it?" she asked quietly, certain she knew, but hoping she was wrong.

Miss Wade took a deep breath. "Mrs. Murray had reached the end of her endurance," she said sadly. "She left the social event right after you departed. She returned to her room alone..." Her voice faltered, and then she continued. "She was discovered last night when the other women returned to their room. Somehow, even with her almost blinded eyes, she managed to hang herself from the upper part of her window. She strapped the top part of her dress to the sill somehow, and then hung herself." Tears filled her eyes.

Alice dropped her face into her hands. "That poor woman," she cried. "Poor Mrs. Murray!"

"Yes," Miss Wade said grimly. "What happened to her was quite horrible."

Alice stared at her. "What will they do with her body?"

Miss Wade shrugged. "They have a place in the woods where they bury the dead." Her eyes looked haunted. "I don't know where it is."

Alice remembered the paper she was holding. She looked down and saw her name written on the front.

"I found it in her hand," Miss Wade revealed. "No one knows. I hid it in my pocket, determined you would receive it."

Alice stared at the paper, but didn't open it. She wanted privacy to read Mrs. Murray's last thoughts. "Thank you," she whispered.

Miss Wade, obviously understanding her feelings, stood and walked to the door. She paused, and then turned back to her before opening it. "I will not see you again, Mrs. Archer. I am tendering my resignation today. I will not stay in this horrible place one more moment." She shook her head. "I once thought this was a place that would care for people who find themselves in a very pitiful situation. I wanted to be a part of caring for them." Her face crinkled with dismay. "I realize now that no matter how much I care, I can't protect patients from attendants like Mrs. Bartle. If I don't leave here, I will be the one to go quite mad."

Alice rose quickly and grabbed the woman's hands, pushing aside the somber reality that when she was returned to the ward, as she most certainly would be, this gentle woman would not be there to protect her. "Thank you for your kindnesses," she said. "And thank you for bringing me this letter. I wish you the best." She knew Miss Wade would have a difficult time finding a job in New York City, but whatever she did next, it wouldn't be as bad as enduring the asylum.

"Thank you, Mrs. Archer."

"Please, call me Alice." Alice pressed her hands tightly.

Miss Wade looked down, and then back up quickly. "And my name is Phoebe. I hope you get out of here, Alice."

"Thank you," Alice replied. She stepped forward to open the door. "Let me look out first. It will not be good if they see you coming out of my room. I know you're quitting today, but there is no reason to make it more unpleasant."

"That would be best," Phoebe admitted. She waited quietly for Alice's signal that all was clear. Moments later, she disappeared around a corner.

Alice took a deep breath, stepped back into her room, settled on her hard, narrow bed, and opened the sheet of paper.

Dearest Mrs. Archer,

Thank you for giving me sympathy and caring during my last night among the living. Do not feel badly for me. Whatever is waiting for me cannot possibly be as bad as the Hell I am experiencing on a daily basis. I do believe it will be quite wonderful. I leave this place here on Earth, trusting I go to a better place.

Sincerely,

Beatrice Murray

Alice read the letter several times, wiped the tears from her eyes, and then sat staring out her window. She wondered if she would have the courage to do the same thing if she had found herself in the same situation. People had told her suicide was an unforgiveable sin, but she couldn't believe God would punish a woman who had endured the torture Mrs. Murray had. She chose to believe Beatrice Murray was welcomed to the next life with open arms.

*****

A sharp rap startled her yet again. What was it now? Alice took a deep breath and walked to the door just as it was being pushed open. She stiffened when she recognized her visitor.

"Mrs. Archer."

"Hello, Dr. Tillerson," Alice said calmly. Her mind and heart were racing, but she wouldn't give him the satisfaction of knowing it. She was quite certain she was being taken back to the ward she had been rescued from. Without Miss Wade there to act as a buffer, she needed no imagination to understand the type of treatment she was going to receive at Mrs. Bartle's hands. She fought to control her trembling as she faced the doctor.

Dr. Tillerson stepped back to allow two more women into the room. "Load her things into her satchels," he ordered.

Alice blinked in confusion. Certainly, the doctor would not allow her to take her belongings to the ward, but why was he waiting until they were packed? Why not just force her there, and then come back to dispose of the few clothes Carrie had been able to get to her?

"Come with me," Dr. Tillerson ordered.

Alice complied, knowing resistance was futile. Her confusion increased when they reached a corner and turned away from the ward. She wanted to question what was happening, but the doctor's stony rage made her unwilling to open her mouth.

Dr. Tillerson stopped in front of a door, opened it, and stepped back. "Good-bye, Mrs. Archer," he said shortly, before he turned on his heel and stalked away.

Alice stared after him. What was happening? She looked at the open door, suddenly afraid to walk through it. What if she discovered something in the room even worse than what she had already endured? She had a sudden vision of Sherman waiting to take her home to a different type of prison. She held her breath, wondering if it would do any good to run.

"Alice!"

Alice blinked when a man appeared at the door, and then blinked again, trying to make sense out of what she was seeing. "Mr. Stratford?" Her voice was nothing more than a whisper.

"My dear..." Wally stepped forward and grasped both her hands.

Only then did Alice realize how cold they were.

"You're leaving this place, Alice."

Alice gaped at him, wondering if she was hearing him correctly, and terrified to hope he might actually be right. "How?" she stammered.

Wally held up a copy of the letter Sherman had written. "Sherman left here a short time ago," he said, "after giving Dr. Tillerson this letter, acknowledging that he put you here under false accusations, and demanding you be released immediately."

Alice shrank back. "Are you taking me to Sherman?" she asked fearfully.

"Absolutely not," Wally replied. "You are coming home with me. Nancy has prepared a room for you."

Alice continued to stare at him, trying to make sense out of what she was hearing. The rapid shift from being convinced she was heading back to the ward, to now being offered freedom, was more than she could comprehend. Her eyes filled with tears.

Wally's eyes glowed with compassion as he pulled her into the room and sat her down in front of a flickering fireplace. "I know this is a lot to take in," he murmured. "And I know you've been through a terrible time. I promise I'll tell you the whole story when I get you home, but I suspect you will not be convinced you're free until you are actually out of this place."

"I'm free?" Alice grasped onto the one word that gave her hope. "I'm *free*?"

"You're *free*," Wally said emphatically.

"What about Sherman?" Alice asked.

"Sherman is filing divorce papers this afternoon, and there will be ten thousand dollars in your bank account by the end of the day." Wally's voice was full of satisfaction.

Alice gasped, trying to take in what she was hearing. She glanced at the door. "We can leave now?"

Wally smiled. "We can leave now." He stood, held out his hand, and helped Alice to her feet. "Do you want to wait for your things?"

Alice shook her head quickly. "If you don't mind, I will never again put on a piece of clothing I wore in this place." She hesitated. "I know the clothing used to be your wife's. I am so grateful, but..."

"She will be in total agreement," Wally assured her. He led her to the door. "Let's get out of here."

*****

Alice snuggled beneath the thick layer of blankets in the carriage, basking in the bright sun beaming down on her. She took deep breaths of the first clean air she had smelled in more than two months. The air was still cold, but emerging buds on every tree they rolled under told her spring was around the corner. She wanted to cry and laugh at the same time, but she chose silence. It was the only action she felt she could control.

Wally seemed to understand. He glanced at her sympathetically several times, but remained quiet.

Alice felt a surge of fear. "You're sure the letter was legal? Can they come get me again?"

"They cannot," Wally said reassuringly. "You are *free*, Alice."

Alice stared into his eyes for several moments before she allowed a smile to form. "Thank you. I don't know how this happened, but thank you."

"I'll answer all your questions when we get to the house," Wally promised.

"And Sherman? What will happen to him?"

"He'll be getting what he deserves."

*****

Sherman, still exhausted after a full day of court appearances and filling out paperwork, appeared in Ralph Cook's office the next morning. He had spent a sleepless night attempting to understand how his carefully laid plans had gone so horribly awry.

Ralph looked up when he was ushered in. "Has it all been taken care of?" he asked pleasantly.

Sherman nodded, searching the older man's face for a hint of what was about to happen. His trip out to Blackwell's Island had been quite stressful. Actually walking into the asylum had been shocking. The screams and moans were something he might never forget. Delivering the letter to Dr. Tillerson had been distressing, as well. The disdain on the doctor's face as he read the letter had been unmistakable.

"*You're quite sure you want Mrs. Archer to be released?*" Dr. Tillerson had snapped.

"*Yes,*" Sherman had replied. It had been a lie, but securing his career was worth any price.

Sherman settled down into the chair Ralph indicated. If Alice had but complied with his wishes, none of this would have happened, and yet, he was ready to put it behind him. Filing the divorce papers had actually been quite satisfying. Losing the ten thousand dollars in his bank account was distressing, but his future with the Pennsylvania Railroad Company would replace it, and multiply it many times. He was relieved to be rid of Alice. If he ever married again, it would be to someone more malleable, who was eager to let him lead her. Every man had a right to expect that of his wife.

"Alice is freed?" Ralph pressed.

Sherman nodded.

"The divorce papers have been filed?"

"Yes," Sherman replied. He was quite surprised at how quickly and smoothly it had gone, until one of the secretaries revealed Mr. Cook had been there earlier to meet with the judge.

"And the money transfer has been handled?"

Sherman nodded again. "The bank president had the papers ready. The money has been transferred, and my name has been removed from my ex-wife's account." He was careful to hide his bitterness and anger behind a neutral tone of voice.

Ralph nodded. "Good."

Sherman leaned back in his chair. "I'm glad we can put this all behind us," he said smoothly. "All I've ever wanted to do is create more prosperity for the Pennsylvania Railroad. I'm eager to get back to work." He crossed his legs and placed his folded hands on his knee. "What can I do first?"

Ralph stood, towering over him from behind his desk. "Your office has been cleared out," he said. "I'm giving you twenty minutes to get out of this building. I don't ever want to see you again."

Sherman's jaw dropped as he uncrossed his legs, his heart racing. "What?" he stammered. "What... what are you saying?"

"I'm saying you're done here," Ralph snapped.

"You told me I would still have a job when I returned," Sherman protested, trying to make sense of what he was hearing.

"And you did," Ralph said shortly. "I did not, however, indicate how *long* you would have it. You are now fired. I never want you to darken the doors of this building again."

Sherman continued to stare at him. "You're firing me?"

Ralph stared at him. "You're extremely lucky that is *all* I'm doing," he snapped. "This company means a lot to me. I would never willingly have someone working here that could do the despicable thing you have done to your wife. If I could have you arrested, I would do it with great satisfaction. Having the law behind you does not make it right." His eyes cut into Sherman. "If I were you, I would look for another job far from New York City. I assure you I will do everything within my power to make sure you never secure another position here."

Ralph's eyes narrowed. "And, if you ever go close to Alice again, my investigator will alert me. No matter where you go from here, I'll make sure you never secure another position of any importance." His voice deepened. "Do I make myself clear?"

Sherman stood, slowly realizing everything he had worked so hard for had just crumbled beneath him into a pile of rubble. "My father..." It was his one last desperate attempt to regain control of his future.

"I have spoken with your father," Ralph assured him. "It broke my heart to tell my friend that he has such a degenerate for a son, but once I explained the situation to him, he agreed I could have taken no other course of action." He waved his hand. "Get out of my office. I have a company to run, and you are no longer part of it."

His voice boomed through the room. "You are done here, Sherman Archer!"

Chapter Twenty-Two

Franklin handed the letter to Simon, and then stared off into the fields full of men plowing and working the soil for the seedlings soon to be planted. The fields, carefully fertilized with marl at the end of the season, and then planted in clover for the winter, were evidence of the results of good care. Felicia had given him information about cover crops when they were on the plantation in October. He had been doubtful it would have much impact, but Moses had encouraged him to try it, if only to make Felicia feel valued. Once again, the young girl had been right.

Franklin bent down to lift a handful of rich, dark dirt. The combination of marl and clover had greatly enriched the soil. He knew the tobacco crop would surpass last year's harvest if the weather was cooperative.

Simon put down the letter. "Moses and Rose are coming home to *stay*?"

Franklin said nothing. The letter had made their decision clear. He remained silent as Simon stared off into the distance, already knowing what his friend was thinking.

"They're crazy," Simon finally muttered.

Franklin cocked his head. "Crazy?"

"Crazy!" Simon repeated emphatically. "They're safe up there in Oberlin. Why would they want to come back here?"

Franklin felt a surge of concern as he watched the anxiety tighten Simon's face. "Has something else happened at Blackwell?"

"No," Simon admitted, "but our workers have seen a lot of white men riding by the entrance to the plantation, just staring in. They seem to know my men are on guard, and have been since the attack. It's like they are taunting us with the fact it can happen again at any time. It's maddening because they know our enforced guard means there are less men in the fields," he added with a growl. "If they can't hurt us one way, they can hurt us another."

"Moses seems excited," Franklin observed as he reached for the letter, folded it carefully, and shoved it back into his pocket. "I wonder, though," he confessed, "if they are only coming back because Chooli and I are leaving in a few weeks."

"No," Simon said. "If Moses believed they were supposed to stay up there in Oberlin, he would have worked something else out."

Franklin nodded, hoping he was right.

"When are y'all leaving?" Simon asked.

"The first week of April," Franklin replied. "I'm glad to be leaving," he said abruptly.

Simon regarded him quietly for a moment. "As far as I can tell, this country doesn't treat the Navajo any better than they treat black folk. Do you really think going to the reservation will make things better?"

Franklin hesitated. He would be lying if he didn't acknowledge he sometimes wondered the same thing. "I hope it will," he replied. "I don't guess I believe *any* place in the country is good for either blacks or Indians, but we've got to live *somewhere*," he said ruefully. "I figure our odds will be better out there. The country allowed the Navajo to return to their homeland. After all those years at Bosque Redondo, I don't see the Navajo doing anything to jeopardize it."

Simon nodded. "I saw Chooli before I came out to the fields to find you. She seems very happy to be going home."

Franklin smiled. "She can't wait to see her family again."

"Ajei is growing so fast," Simon continued. "She is a beautiful little girl."

Franklin's smile was wider this time. "That little girl is the light of my life," he said proudly. "Chooli spends all her time trying to keep up with her."

Simon chuckled. "She should be a handful on the wagon train."

Franklin's smile disappeared.

"What's wrong?" Simon asked sharply.

Franklin took a deep breath. "There won't be a wagon train," he said quietly, his insides clenching as he said it.

Simon stiffened. "Why not?"

Franklin tried to shrug casually, but he was sure he had failed. "Seems no one wants a nigger and an Injun on their train."

Simon sucked in his breath sharply. "I thought it was different out there?"

"Maybe not that different," Franklin said bitterly. "Besides, those folks on the wagon train aren't Westerners yet. They're just folks looking for a better life." He paused. "I don't suppose it matters if they are Northerners or Southerners. Prejudice ain't just a Southern thing." He shook his head. "Chooli promises me it will be different on the reservation."

"They will accept Chooli having a black husband?" Simon pressed.

"She says they will because her grandfather and grandmother are so revered." He hid his nervousness with a chuckle. "I didn't have any trouble with them before, but it was a different situation since I was a soldier at Bosque Redondo. What I might have seen as acceptance could have been nothing more than stoic defeat."

"You're a good man," Simon said. "It might take some time, but they'll accept you."

Franklin shrugged again. "I hope so, but regardless, we are leaving for New Mexico in a few weeks."

"How are you getting there?" Simon asked. "You said you can't get on a wagon train."

Franklin sighed, trying to fight back his anxiety. "We didn't have a wagon train when we got here," he reminded his friend.

"True, but you also didn't have an eighteen-month-old," Simon retorted.

Franklin met his eyes, not denying he had the same concerns. "We're going to have to do the best we can."

"You know you could stay here," Simon said. "Even with Moses coming back, there is a place for you. I know he would want you to stay."

"I reckon that's true," Franklin agreed, "but I promised Chooli I was taking her home to her family." His conviction hardened as he remembered the joy on her face when he had promised to take her back to the Navajo homeland. "We're going back to *Dinetah*," he said. "At least this time, we will be able to take the train to Independence, Missouri, and we will have enough money to survive."

"If you don't get robbed," Simon said darkly. He shook his head. "I don't like the idea of you riding horses out there."

"We're not," Franklin said. "We can't get on a wagon train, but I've already got a wagon secured."

Simon looked skeptical. "Won't you be like a sitting duck if you're out there all by yourselves?" he said skeptically. "At least if you were on horseback, you would stand a better chance of escaping an attack." He scowled. "Are you sure you know what you're doing?"

Franklin felt a flare of anger, but it disappeared quickly as the truth raised its head. "No," he admitted. "I'm doing what I believe is right, but I won't say I know what I'm doing." He gritted his teeth with frustration. "Chooli wants a life without prejudice and hatred, especially for Ajei. I can't fault her for that."

"Nope," Simon agreed. "I just hope you live long enough to find it." He forced a smile. "I'm not trying to make things harder, but I'm worried."

Franklin eyed him, finally recognizing the expression in his friend's eyes. He hadn't seen it before because of his own worries. "You'd like to get out of here, too," he stated.

Simon hesitated, and then nodded. "I think Moses is crazy to come back to the South. I understand why you and Chooli want to leave, but I'm not convinced you're going anywhere better." He paused. "I'd like to take my family someplace safe, but I don't know that any place like that exists." He swung off his horse and walked over to scoop up a handful of rich soil. "I love farming, and I enjoy watching how Blackwell Plantation is growing. I'm making more money than I ever thought I would make, but I also lie awake most nights so I can listen for anyone coming after my family," he said angrily. "I'm tired of it."

"I understand. I love New Mexico and the West, but my heart is here in the South. The last year and a half have proven that to me." He gazed out over the fields. "I'm going to miss tobacco farming. I know I can grow crops on the reservation, but it's not going to be the same. Still, I know we'll be happy there."

"How?" Simon demanded.

Franklin understood the anger flashing in his eyes. "Because I am going to *choose* to be, Simon." He shook his head. "I reckon you're right that there ain't anywhere safe for a black man to live. We're always going to have to watch over our shoulder to see what might be coming after us. But that doesn't mean we can't choose to be happy," he said firmly. "No one can take away the right to feel how we want to feel, and to act how we want to act. Sure, I wish things weren't so hard, and I'm going to do all I can to help change it, but I'm not going to wait until then to be *happy*."

"It isn't that easy," Simon growled.

"I don't remember saying anything about it being *easy*," Franklin responded. "There hasn't been much easy about either of our lives. We lived through slavery. Then we lived through a war. Now we're living through vigilantes that want to kill us because we're free." He fixed his eyes on the horizon, smiling when a flock of geese migrating north filled the sky. "I keep remembering what Chooli's family said when they finally got out of Bosque Redondo. They had decided they would not let their past define their future. I've thought about that all winter. I've decided I won't let my past define my *present*, either."

Simon shook his head, but remained silent.

"Why are you staying here?" Franklin demanded.

Simon stared at him. "What?"

"Why are you staying here?" he repeated. "I know you've made real good money the last couple years. You may not make as much money if you leave, but you've got enough to get started somewhere else. If you hate it here so much, why don't you leave?"

"It isn't that easy," Simon repeated.

Franklin was the one to shake his head now. "I've known folks like you all my life," he snapped. "I just didn't figure you to be one of them."

Simon glared at him. "What are you talking about now?"

Franklin met his eyes evenly. "What's happened to you, Simon? You were always one to *make* things happen. Now you're one of those that *talk* about wanting things to be different, but you ain't *doing* nothing to make it happen. You just want to sit around and bellyache about it. When did you become one of those people?"

Simon's lips narrowed with anger for a moment, until his shoulders drooped and he looked away.

Franklin waited, content to watch the geese as they flew out of sight in perfect formation. It was true he had spent all winter pondering what Chooli's family had said when they were finally allowed to return home. He had decided there wasn't anyone in the world who didn't have a reason to want to give up on living. It was always a choice. Just talking about it with Simon had solidified his decision to go back to New Mexico. The journey would be hard, and it might take time for the Navajo to accept him, but he was taking control of his future. That was something to be proud of.

"You're right," Simon finally said, his voice heavy with regret as he shook his head. "I don't know what's happened to me."

"I do," Franklin said sympathetically. "You've done been beaten down. My mama used to tell me all the time that the power of slavery was its ability to beat people down until they didn't have anything in them to fight back. Now that the war is over, those vigilantes are using the same methods they used to keep us living as slaves." He paused as he looked at his friend. "I know you're scared,' Simon, but you can't let them win. Whether you stay here, or whether you leave, you got to make decisions that will make you happy."

"You're right," Simon murmured slowly. "I know you're right..."

"I know you think Moses is crazy to come back," Franklin continued, "but he's making the choice he believes will make him happy. Rose is making the same choice. They know the risks. They have decided not to let the past define how they choose to live their life right now."

"And if they die for it?"

"Then at least they know they didn't let fear control every decision they made," Franklin said bluntly.

*****

Matthew entered the house quietly, listening at the door before hanging his coat and sitting down in a chair pulled close to the glowing embers of the fire. He leaned his head back for a moment, relieved to be home after a long morning. He had left the office early, too disheartened to remain for the day. He took a deep breath and stood to gather wood for the fire. The fact that the flames had died meant Janie had likely gotten Robert down for his afternoon nap, and then used the opportunity to get some sleep herself.

"You home for the day, Mr. Justin?"

Matthew finished piling logs into the fireplace, relieved when they caught immediately, and then turned. "I am, Alma. How is everything?" He thanked his lucky stars every day that Sarge had referred this angel of a woman to them. Janie, while she was getting stronger, was taking longer than anticipated to heal from her surgery. Carrie assured them it was simply because Robert battled with colic, meaning Janie got only small snippets of sleep before Robert's crying woke her again.

"They be all right," Alma assured him. "I'm sorry I let that fire go out. I was in the kitchen fixin' tonight's dinner."

"It's not a problem," Matthew assured her with a smile. "You weren't expecting me home." He glanced at the stairs. "Are they both asleep?" he asked cautiously, afraid to hope for such a miracle.

Alma grinned. "They both be sleeping, sure 'nuff! Miss Carrie came by here about an hour ago with a new remedy. Robert be screamin' his little lungs out until she done gave him some Chamomilla. It weren't long before he stopped that hollering and drifted right off to sleep. Miss Janie was asleep just about as fast."

Matthew smiled. "So why *this* remedy?" he asked. "Hasn't Carrie used other ones?"

"Yep," Alma agreed, "but she says you got to really know how a baby be having the colic before you know how to treat it. Little Robert seems to feel a mite better if you carry him around when he's cryin' and angry. She says that be a sign."

Matthew grimaced. He had not anticipated such an angry and irritable child. Robert looked peaceful and happy when he was sleeping, but as soon as his eyes opened, all the peace disappeared. "Do you think it's because I named him after my best friend?" he asked ruefully. "Robert could definitely have his moments."

Alma chuckled. "That be pure nonsense. That tiny baby up there be too little to be having *moments*," she chided. "He ain't got nothin' but the colic. He's crying 'cause he's in pain."

Matthew ducked his head. "I know he's in pain," he said remorsefully. "I pray every day that he will get better."

Alma chuckled again. "You wouldn't be normal if all that cryin' didn't bother you," she said sympathetically. "Anyway, Miss Carrie had Miss Janie put a warm water bottle on little Robert's stomach last night. That seemed to make him feel better for quite a while. Least, that's what Miss Janie told me. When she told Miss Carrie about that, she knew to give him the Chamomilla. That homeopathic remedy sure 'nuff seems to be workin'. Them two been asleep for a while."

Matthew nodded. "They both need it."

Alma eyed him critically. "Looks like they ain't the only two. You don't look so good, Mr. Matthew."

Matthew smiled. "It's been a long day," he said quietly.

Alma glanced at the ornate grandfather clock in the corner. "Ain't yet two o'clock in the afternoon."

"Yes," Matthew agreed, "but it's been more than long enough."

Alma shook her head. "I 'magine it take a lot out of a man to do what you do. Miss Janie let me read some of the stuff you done wrote for the newspaper. It can't be real easy to write news like that."

Matthew eyed her with surprise.

Alma chuckled. "I bet you thought I couldn't read, Mr. Matthew."

Matthew flushed. "I know better than to make assumptions. I'm sorry," he apologized.

Alma waved her hand. "Ain't no need to apologize. I been learning the last few years, ever since I got set free from the plantation down in Virginia. I got me a ways to go, but I figure I can read pretty good," she said proudly. "I like that book you wrote a whole heap better. It ain't near so hard to read. I like them stories just fine."

Matthew smiled. "*Glimmers of Change*? I'm glad you liked it."

"Yep. The whole world needs to know that it ain't just bad things that happen in this ole world. There be plenty of good out there."

Matthew, needing to hear something besides what he had spent all morning working on, looked at her closely. "Do you really believe that?"

"I sure do," Alma said. "I done learned a lot from some people since I got free."

"Like what?"

Alma pursed her lips in thought. "I learned I got to work hard for what I want, because most things don't come to you without a fight." She thought for a moment. "I learned I got to be strong and brave. And that I got to know I can do anythin' I set my mind to." She turned away for a moment and then looked back at him with shining eyes. "And I learned there always gonna be folks who will put me down or criticize me. I just gots to keep believin' in myself and turn it into somethin' positive."

Matthew raised a brow. "I'm very impressed. Where did you learn all this?"

Alma grinned. "Sarge told me about a school where I been going to learn to read. They don't only teach me to read, though. They teachin' me how to live life as a free woman." She nodded her head decisively. "They told me that one ain't more important than the other. I got to learn how to do both. I reckon they be right."

"I agree with them," Matthew said warmly. "You are a remarkable woman, Alma. I'm so glad you're here to help Janie."

"My help gonna mean a heap more when she can start sleepin' while I be workin'," Alma said. She looked at him more closely. "You need some food, or you want to sleep a while 'fore you eat?"

Matthew considered for a moment. "What's in the kitchen?"

Alma eyed him with amusement. "You such a man... I just finished up a pot of thick onion soup, and there be a whole mess of hot sweet potatoes to go with some ham I sliced."

Matthew was walking toward the kitchen before she finished speaking. "I'll eat first," he said cheerfully, keeping his voice low so he wouldn't wake anyone.

A soft knock on the door made him spin and sprint to answer it before Janie and Robert could be awakened. He smiled when he saw Jeremy standing on the porch. "You're just in time for something to eat," he whispered, pointing at the stairs to indicate his family was asleep. He knew Jeremy would understand immediately.

Jeremy grinned, stepped inside, and shrugged out of his coat. The temperatures were getting warmer, but a coat was still necessary. "Lead the way," he whispered.

Jeremy's grin widened when he stepped into the warm kitchen. "This is more like it," he said cheerfully, talking normally once the kitchen door closed. "The twins were sick last night so Marietta hasn't done any cooking. Not that I'm complaining," he said quickly. "I had some cold biscuits when I got home from the factory. I made Marietta go upstairs to sleep with the twins."

Matthew nodded. "Carrie brought over a remedy that finally worked magic with Robert. He's sleeping soundly, which means Janie is also getting some rest."

"Good!" Jeremy said heartily. "That means we won't have to share this wonderful food."

"Mr. Jeremy," Alma scolded, "you know you best leave enough for Miss Janie!"

Jeremy considered for a moment, and then shrugged. "Fine. She doesn't eat much, anyway."

Alma's lips twitched as she sniffed and turned away to load two plates with hot food.

Matthew's mouth was watering before she placed the dishes in front of them. He stared down at the sweet potatoes topped with a pool of melted butter, thick slices of Virginia ham, and hot biscuits slathered with strawberry preserves. When Alma added a bowl of hot soup to the feast, he almost swooned. "Thank you," he moaned with delight.

Alma nodded, a look of satisfaction on her face, and then eyed him. "You home for the rest of the day, Mr. Matthew?"

"Yes," Matthew answered, understanding instantly. "Why don't you leave early today? You've been here for some long days. I'm sure you would enjoy some time at home."

Alma smiled with pleasure. "Yes'sir, I reckon I would." She hung her apron on a hook and stuffed a few loose hairs back into her bun. "I'll be back first thing in the mornin'."

"Have a good night," Matthew said warmly. He waited until the door closed behind her, and then dug into the food. He could feel the muscles in his neck unraveling as he ate. By the time he finished, the headache that had hounded him for hours was gone.

"Tough morning?" Jeremy asked.

"How could you tell?"

Jeremy shrugged. "I know how to detect the signs of stress."

Matthew looked at him more closely. "I'm not the only one home early. What are you doing here at three o'clock in the afternoon?"

"I was worried about Marietta and the twins. There's no benefit of running a business if you can't leave early once in a while. Since they are sleeping, I thought I would come down here to see why you are home early."

"And you knew that how?"

"I saw you get out of your carriage as I was going into the house."

Matthew nodded, knowing he was stalling.

"So...are you going to tell me?" Jeremy asked.

Matthew sighed. "I get so tired of people's stupidity." His eyes narrowed. "Just when I think things can't get any more ridiculous, they do."

"Care to expound?" Jeremy asked as he soaked up the rest of his soup with a biscuit. "Nothing you can say would surprise me at this point."

"You might be wrong about that," Matthew said darkly. He reached for another biscuit, buttering it slowly as he thought about what he could say. Jeremy was safe, but he still had to be careful. Even one careless word could reveal details of his investigation before he was ready.

"Surprise me," Jeremy invited, his eyes probing.

"Have you ever heard of a book called *The Masked Lady of the White House*?"

"No, but it sounds intriguing."

"Disturbing is a more apt description," Matthew retorted. "You realize that many Americans have yet to realize the true danger of the Ku Klux Klan?"

"I'm aware of their blindness," Jeremy said grimly. "Those in the North want to pretend it isn't true, because they might have to do something about it. Many Southerners continue to make it seem like a joke because they are involved."

"True," Matthew said shortly. "Many newspapers, both Northern and Southern, are playing right into their hands. They seem to want people to believe that complaints of outrages by disguised bandits are simply an attempt to hide *Radical rottenness* behind a cloud of KKK," he said dramatically.

Jeremy stared at him. "I'm assuming that is a quote from a newspaper?"

"It is."

"They believe the attacks happening in the South are being done by *Republicans*?"

Matthew shrugged. "I don't know that they actually *believe* it, but it sure is what they are determined to communicate. The end result is the same." He paused. "The book I was telling you about, *The Masked Lady of the White House*, is written by someone who doesn't even have the courage to identify himself. The author's name is simply, *Anonymous*."

"You're convinced it is a man?"

"Let's just say I feel it strongly in my gut."

Jeremy nodded. "So, what's the book about?"

Matthew sighed. "I read it this morning at the office. The author, whoever he is, has rather pronounced Democratic sympathies. The message of the book is that Southern atrocities by the KKK are the deliberate work of Radical Republicans."

"And the reason for the atrocities?" Jeremy asked.

"Republicans plan to swell their political power through Northern indignation toward a nonexistent conspiracy," Matthew said sarcastically.

"A *conspiracy*? And people truly believe this nonsense?"

"There are people who will believe anything written between the pages of a book, or within the folds of a newspaper. Believing in a conspiracy theory feeds their appetite for intrigue and mystery. It gives them something to talk about, instead of accepting a truth they may actually have to *do* something about."

"And so, blacks, mulattos and white Republicans will continue to be tortured and killed."

Matthew understood Jeremy's bitterness. "Not if I can help it," he said grimly.

"What can you do?"

"I can communicate truth," Matthew replied. "I can challenge other journalists to discover the truth and then make sure people read it."

"And will they care?" Jeremy asked bluntly. "Marietta and I left Richmond for this very reason. As long as the KKK or the vigilantes aren't hurting *their* family, they don't care about anyone else. They just look the other way."

"I have to believe they will care at some point," Matthew said. "People finally woke up to the realities of slavery." He sighed heavily. "I only know silence is not an option. By remaining silent, I am giving unspoken approval of what is being said. Even if what I write does no good, at least I will know I tried. At the end of the day, I have to be able to live with myself."

Jeremy nodded, his eyes flashing. "I saw something in a store on my way home that made me want to be sick."

Matthew waited.

"When I was checking out, the clerk offered to sell me a Ku Klux Knife." Jeremy's lips thinned with disgust. "She was surprised when I turned down the offer."

Matthew narrowed his eyes. "That's one I haven't heard of."

"There are more?" Jeremy demanded.

"Many more," Matthew said angrily. "Saloons are serving Ku Klux Kocktails. Musicians are writing Ku Klux polka dances. Bored postal workers here in Pennsylvania have carved KKK woodblocks, which they are using to cancel stamps." His voice tightened as he thought about all he was learning. "Newspapers are writing stories that make the murders and torture sound like a raucous good time rather than racial tragedy."

Jeremy stared at him. "What's wrong with people? How can they believe it?"

Matthew shook his head. "Unlike newspapers, who are twisting the truth to sell papers and create fascination, but don't really believe it, many people who *read* it believe it completely. America has become a society where people don't take the time to learn the truth." He paused. "In all fairness, the only source most of them have for information is newspapers. The responsibility falls on reporters and editors who are willing to feed untruths and lies to the public." His eyes blazed.

"What else did you learn this morning?" Jeremy asked.

"Isn't that enough?"

"More than enough," Jeremy replied, "but something tells me there's more. You might as well let it all out. I know you're going to write it, and I thank you for that, but carrying it around inside is never a good thing."

Matthew nodded shortly. "I suppose you're right." He reached inside his front pocket and pulled out a folded sheet of paper. "I received a copy of this today. It's a song written by E.C. Buell."

"The comedian and singer?"

"Yes, but there is nothing funny about *this*. The nation seems to be holding its sides with laughter when they hear this song, if the reports are true, but I'm sickened by it. It's called the *Ku Klux Klan Songster*." He unfolded the paper and began to read.

As I went for a walk the other night,
T'other night and got tight,
When I saw a most terrible sight,
'Twas the horrible Ku-Klux-Klan.

With Greeley's white hat for a tub,
There was one dripping blood,
From a hole they had dug in the mud,
To bury a big black-and-tan;
While up at one end of the room,
I saw very soon
Ben Butler hung with a spoon,
By the horrible Ku-Klux-Klan.

What I saw, I'll remember forever,
The thought of it causes a shiver,
The dreaded three Ks, the awful three Ks,

Jeremy sat quietly when Matthew finished, his blue eyes fixed on the kitchen window. "And this was supposed to be funny?" he asked in a strangled voice.

"His audience laughs through the whole song," Matthew said bitterly. "And all the while, the KKK has continued to grow because no one with any authority to stop them is taking them seriously. The people who should be stopping them are doing nothing but throwing wood on a burning fire by turning their backs. Meanwhile, the KKK continues to grow like an infection through our country."

Jeremy turned to him after a long silence. "*You're* going to tell the truth. You're right that you must be a voice. Thank you."

Matthew sighed. "Sometimes I feel like an unheard voice in the wilderness, but I won't quit trying. I can't."

"You changed how the railroads operate," Jeremy reminded him. "When other papers quit writing about the railroads after the Angola Horror train wreck, you kept hammering away. You wouldn't let the public forget. You wouldn't let them ignore they were in danger every single time they got on a train because the railroad companies were being reckless and irresponsible. They were finally forced to change."

Matthew nodded. "They still have a long way to go, but it's better," he admitted. He shook his head heavily. "There are so many things that need changing. It all seems rather pointless and hopeless."

"You've been here before," Jeremy reminded him. "That's why you wrote *Glimmers of Change*. You needed to focus on something different." He gazed at Matthew. "You can walk away any time you want to, but you keep going back."

"I don't have a choice."

"You always have a choice," Jeremy said. "You've decided to be a voice that refuses to be silenced. Sometimes you will see the impact you have. Other times, you may never know. But you're right that there must be voices for truth. You can't give up now."

Matthew remained silent for several minutes before he nodded reluctantly. "You're right. I could never live with myself if I don't speak up." A distant cry made him smile through his frustration. His son had woken from his nap. "Having Robert reminds me every single day that I can't give up the fight. I want my son to have a different world to live in. He's also my reminder that I have to change the world so there are no more senseless deaths."

Chapter Twenty-Three

Carrie walked to her window and opened it wide. March had blown into Philadelphia with a fierce snowstorm that dumped almost twenty inches of snow on the city, but by the middle of the month, warm winds had melted the snow, except for the huge banks plowed from the roads that still looked like charcoal mounds dotting the city. Trees were bursting with buds, and the first crocus blooms dotted the ground. She tried not to imagine how beautiful the plantation would be right now, but it was impossible to block out the images of new foals dancing in the pastures.

She focused, instead, on the telegram that had arrived two days earlier, telling her Alice had been freed from the insane asylum. The house had been full of wild celebration. Elizabeth and Florence had joined them for a victory dinner that night. Now, they were waiting for a longer letter to tell them the whole story. Carrie was happy beyond words that Alice was free, but her heart was unsettled.

She sighed as she stared out at the weary city. She was ready to go home. She turned when there was a knock at the door. "Come in."

Marietta entered the room with a big smile, but her eyes narrowed when she looked at Carrie. "You are *not* wearing that dress for your graduation ceremony."

Carrie looked down and shrugged. "Why not?" The navy dress she was wearing was fine. "It's only going to be Dr. Strikener and a couple of my professors. I would have loved to have Dr. Hobson here, but it is too much to expect he could come from Richmond. It's not actually a real graduation ceremony, but it's the first time I've been willing to leave the clinic long enough to get my diploma." She turned and stared out the window again. "It's funny. I worked so hard, and fought so long to actually get this medical degree, but I think I would rather them just mail me the actual diploma. Perhaps I would feel differently if it were a celebration with all my schoolmates, but this seems rather pointless."

Marietta nodded. "I suppose I can understand that. All the diploma does is give legal confirmation of what you have been doing for a long time—being a doctor. Still," she said, "it *is* an important occasion. Have you forgotten Jeremy and I will be there? And Matthew and Janie?" She put her hands on her hips. "You are simply not going to wear that dress."

Carrie shrugged again. It had been a long morning at the clinic. Carolyn had forced her to leave so she wouldn't miss the ceremony. "You pick something out," she said carelessly.

Marietta grinned. "I will be happy to." She walked straight to the closet and pulled out a soft green gown with white piping around the collar and sleeves. "This will do nicely. It will go wonderfully with your eyes."

"I'll freeze!" Carrie protested.

"It's spring," Marietta reminded her. "You can wear a coat, but you are most certainly not going to wear a winter dress. I won't allow it."

Carrie chuckled. "Are you practicing being a mother for the twins?" she teased. "You seem to get bossier every day."

"That's because you never saw me in my classroom," Marietta retorted. "If you insist on acting like a child, I will have to treat you like one."

Carrie laughed again, feeling some of the fatigue drop away. "I smelled good things in the kitchen when I got home. What are you cooking?"

"You'll find out when we return from the ceremony."

"Tell me," Carrie pleaded. "I might starve before I get my diploma," she complained.

"I doubt it," Marietta said ruefully, "but..." She reached into her pocket. "I brought you a ham biscuit because I knew you would be dramatic about it."

Carrie felt a sudden surge of joy. She wrapped Marietta up in a warm hug. "I'm actually doing this," she cried. "I'm getting a medical degree!"

Marietta stepped back with a satisfied smile. "Now you are acting like someone about to earn the title of *Doctor* Borden."

Carrie froze. "*Doctor* Borden," she repeated. "It sounds rather auspicious."

"It sounds *perfect*," Marietta replied. "You have earned this, Carrie. You'll only have this one time to celebrate your accomplishment. Then, I know you'll go back to working like a crazy woman. For just this one night, you are going to celebrate."

Carrie grinned, but felt a moment of sadness.

"What is it?" Marietta pressed.

Carrie swung to stare out the window. "I wish Robert could see this," she said quietly. "And Father, and Abby..." Her voice trailed away. "I know it's impossible for them to be here, but it somehow doesn't seem right. This wouldn't have happened without them."

"I know they wish they could be here," Marietta said sympathetically. "But," she added firmly, "I believe Robert is cheering you on right now, so excited for you, and so very proud of you."

Carrie nodded slowly, knowing it was true.

*****

Carrie, flanked by Matthew and Janie, and Jeremy and Marietta, stepped from the carriage. She watched Janie carefully. This was her friend's first trip out of the house since Robert's birth, but she seemed to be fine. Her incisions had healed, and her energy increased every day now that her son was finally sleeping. Alma was watching Robert and the twins while their parents joined her for the graduation ceremony.

"Freedom!" Marietta cried. "I love my babies, but it's wonderful to act like a free woman for an afternoon."

Janie grinned, but didn't express the same exuberance.

Marietta laughed. "You've only been a mother for a few weeks. Just wait until you haven't been away from Robert for almost six months. I promise you'll be more excited."

Janie nodded, looking a little wistful as she turned to Carrie. "You're sure he'll be all right? What if he starts crying from the colic again?"

"Hasn't the Chamomilla been working well?" Carrie asked.

"Yes, but..."

Carrie interrupted her with a chuckle. "I know, you wouldn't be Janie if you didn't worry about Robert. Let's go inside. The sooner we get this over with, the sooner you'll get home to your son."

Janie immediately looked remorseful. "It's not that I'm not thrilled to be here," she cried.

Carrie waved her hand. "Pooh! I'm glad you're here, but I'm eager to get it over with, too. I don't know what Marietta is cooking, but it certainly smells wonderful! I'm starved. I really just want to get home to eat." She smiled at Marietta, and then paused. "What is that look on your face?"

Marietta straightened. "What look?" she demanded.

Carrie stared at her. "There was a look," she insisted. "You're hiding something."

Marietta snorted. "I don't know what you're talking about. I do know we're going to be late if we don't get inside." She turned and walked toward the front entrance of the Homeopathic College.

Jeremy took her arm. "Let's go, Carrie. You know all things are revealed in time."

"She *is* hiding something!" Carrie exclaimed. "I knew it!"

"Perhaps, but it's true that only time will reveal what it is," Jeremy replied. "Marietta does know how to keep a secret."

Carrie, knowing he wouldn't reveal anything more, heaved a dramatic sigh and followed him into the building.

"Hello, Carrie."

Carrie smiled brightly as Dr. Strikener approached, his warm, brown eyes glowing with their usual vibrancy beneath thick hair that was now more gray than brown. "Hello, Dr. Strikener. It's wonderful to see you."

"I think since we are soon to be colleagues, it is time for you to call me Lucas, *Doctor* Borden."

Carrie laughed. "That will take some getting used to—both calling you Lucas, and the *Doctor* in front of my name."

"Perhaps, but you have worked hard for it," Dr. Strikener replied. "You, more than any student I've ever had the privilege to teach, deserve that title, Dr. Borden." He took her arm. "We're ready for you in a room down the hall."

Carrie stopped in confusion. "I thought I was supposed to meet you in your office."

"We changed the location," Dr. Strikener replied, continuing forward. "We don't want to keep the other professors waiting. We all have class this afternoon."

Carrie had no choice but to follow, but she didn't miss the look Marietta exchanged with Janie. She could do nothing but gape in astonishment when she walked into the room.

"Surprise!" Abby cried, walking forward to envelop her in a fierce hug.

"You didn't really think we would miss this, did you?" Thomas asked, stepping forward to give his own hug.

"I can't believe you didn't tell me this was happening," Anthony scolded as he grabbed her in an embrace.

"You were in Richmond on business," Carrie protested. "That's more important."

"And that is where you are so wrong," Anthony said. "We all arrived last night."

"You've been here since last night?" Carrie cried. "Where did you stay?"

"At the Continental Hotel," Abby responded. "We wanted to surprise you."

"You succeeded," Carrie assured her, and then turned to the others in the room.

Elizabeth and Florence stepped forward with brilliant smiles. "We're so glad Marietta let us know you're graduating today."

Carrie smiled. "Are you sure it is safe for you to be here?"

"I assured them I wouldn't report them to the enemy," Dr. Strikener said with a twinkle in his eye.

"We've decided to risk colluding with the enemy for one day," Elizabeth said lightly. "Especially for someone who worked the miracle you managed to perform."

"What miracle?" Carrie asked in confusion.

"The one that got me released from the insane asylum."

Carrie gasped, and then turned slowly, not able to believe she was hearing correctly. Her gasp turned to laughs and tears as she sprang forward to wrap Alice in her arms. "Alice! Alice! You're free!"

"Thanks to you," Alice said, tears flowing freely down her own cheeks. She was still thin, but she was gaining weight and her eyes shone brightly.

"Alice wouldn't let me tell you we were coming," Wally Stratford said apologetically as he stepped around a pillar in the room. "When she found out you would be graduating two days ago, she insisted she wanted to surprise you. I know you received your telegram two days ago, but Alice decided to be the letter you are waiting for."

Carrie could hardly find words as she turned back to Alice. "*Surprise* me? I'm surprised my heart is still beating. You'll tell me the whole story later?"

"I'll tell you the whole story," Alice promised.

Carrie hugged her again, and then embraced Wally and Nancy before looking around the room again. "I'm afraid to ask if there are any more surprises. I doubt my heart can handle it."

"I have it on quite good authority that the heart can handle any amount of *good* surprises," Dr. Strikener said solemnly. "I was telling the truth, however, when I said I have classes to teach this afternoon. We need to get this diploma in your hands."

"Wait! Not without us."

Carrie looked up as Carolyn, Randall, Nathan, and Melissa rushed into the room. She stared at them. "What are you doing here? Who is running the clinic?"

"We closed it," Carolyn answered, holding up her hand to stop Carrie's protest. "I know we promised to keep it open, but when our patients found out you were graduating this afternoon, all of them walked out of the clinic. But not before making us promise not to miss the graduation. They love you, Carrie." She smiled brightly. "There is just one more surprise for you." Carolyn walked out into the hallway, and then re-entered holding Faith by the hand.

Carrie laughed and rushed forward to wrap her tightly in her arms. "Thank you so much for coming, Faith," she whispered.

"I wouldn't have missed it for the world," Faith replied. "I owe you a lot, *Doctor* Borden. You have gotten that clinic up and running, and you gave me back a reason for living. Having Carolyn move into that big, old house was just what I needed."

"I'm so glad," Carrie murmured.

Dr. Strikener stepped to the front of the room and cleared his throat. "If we are finally all here for this private graduation ceremony for a *handful* of people, I suggest we get started."

Carrie stared around the crowded room, her heart so full she was finding it difficult to breathe.

Dr. Strikener motioned her forward. "I'm not going to bore everyone with a typical graduation ceremony that goes on endlessly. I'm simply going to say that I have worked with a multitude of doctors over my years in practice, and I have seen many students graduate from both medical and homeopathic colleges. Never have I felt the excitement I feel now as I present you with your diploma and your medical degree, Doctor Carrie Borden."

He gazed around for a moment. "The love and support in this room shows how cherished Carrie is, and it reveals just why she is so extraordinary. No one finishes medical school without the support of family and friends."

"Amen," Carrie murmured.

"Carrie Borden, with the passing of this diploma, you are now officially *Doctor Carrie Borden*."

Carrie slowly reached for the diploma. She had thought receiving the engraved sheet of paper wouldn't mean very much. Now, she discovered it meant more than she could have imagined. She closed her eyes tightly, envisioning Robert's eyes glowing with pride. He had refused to let her join him when he died. He had sent her back to the living. She had not wanted it, and she had struggled for months to discover a reason to live. Staring at the diploma in her hands, she knew she was holding the reason.

"Thank you, Dr. Strikener," she said softly. "Thank you for everything you have done for me."

"You're welcome, Dr. Borden." Dr. Strikener reached out and clasped her outstretched hand with both of his. "Is there anything you would like to share with everyone here today?"

Carrie nodded slowly. "Yes." She closed her eyes for a long moment as her thoughts congealed. When she opened them, she knew what she was going to say. "The road to get here today has been much longer, and much more difficult, than I ever imagined it would be. I remember coming to Philadelphia nine years ago. I had just turned eighteen, and all I wanted to do was become a doctor. I thought if I could get to Philadelphia and talk to someone at the University, they would welcome me with open arms." Everyone laughed when she grimaced.

"Things certainly didn't happen that way, but I met Abby and Matthew during that trip, and they have been constant lights in my life." She smiled brightly at them both. "I would not be standing here without both of you."

"Nothing happened according to plan after that," she mused. "I went home to find my mother ill, a war started, and I ran a plantation."

"Very well, may I add," Thomas said.

Carrie smiled, walked forward, and gave her father's cheek a warm kiss. "You have been my rock for my entire life, Father. You have allowed me to be who I am from the minute I was born. There are not many fathers who would have allowed me to do the things I have done."

"Allowed?" Thomas teased. "I believe *endured* would be the better word choice." His eyes softened. "You have been extraordinary since you were born. All I had to do was step out of the way to let you become who you were meant to be." He paused. "I will admit it was terrifying at times, but I wouldn't change a thing."

Carrie kissed him again and then stepped back. "Every person in this room has played such an important role in my journey," she continued. "Janie, I never would have made it through the war years without you, and I can't imagine life without you now."

Janie smiled as she blinked back tears and nodded.

Carrie turned to Jeremy and Marietta. "I know we are all wishing Rose and Moses were here, but I'm so glad to have my best friend's twin brother and his wife in my life now. You have both taught me so much about courage and tenacity, and Marietta, you have taught me it's never too late to learn how to cook if I ever decide I want to," she added playfully, laughing along with everyone else.

She turned to Anthony, her eyes softening. "Anthony, you have given me the encouragement to become a doctor, and…" Her voice trailed off as his eyes bored into hers with a promise she couldn't miss. "You have taught me… it is possible… to love again." Her voice broke. "Thank you," she whispered. It was true she didn't yet know what she was going to do with the love she felt, but it was time to declare it. She was happy to see her father's delighted smile.

"Elizabeth, Florence, and Alice… I thank you for colluding with the enemy today." She laughed, but immediately grew serious. "We joke about this, but it is going to take people leading the way who can blend the two medical disciplines. I believe both of them are necessary to treat the whole person." She looked at each of them. "Most importantly, you have taught me that friendship is about forgiveness and new beginnings." She let her eyes rest on Alice. "And you, my dear friend, have taught me that we can survive anything."

"Only because you cared enough to fight for me," Alice said in a trembling voice. "I hate to think, now, of how close I was to giving up on life. You gave me hope to hang on long enough for help to come."

"That's what friends are for," Carrie said softly, knowing she and Alice had much to talk about.

She turned to her Bosque Redondo team next. "We went on an amazing adventure we will never forget, and now we are creating an amazing clinic that will touch so many lives. Without all of your willingness to go on the Santa Fe Trail, I wouldn't have met my requirement for my medical degree. I wouldn't be standing here now."

"Going through a blizzard was worth it," Nathan called cheerfully. "Because of you, I get to work with my family and friends down in Moyamensing every single day."

Carrie smiled, nodded, and then turned to Faith. "My dear Faith," she said quietly. "You and Biddy changed my life forever. You both taught me so much—you taught me about my heritage, you spawned the factory in Moyamensing, and now you have created a clinic in the heart of the place you call home."

"You created it," Faith protested.

"No," Carrie corrected firmly. "You and Biddy created it when you first had the vision to give your people what they needed. You created it when you convinced me to return and start it."

Faith was watching her closely. "And now you're leaving." It wasn't a question.

Carrie took a deep breath as she nodded and let her gaze sweep the room. "My work is done here. Carolyn is more than capable of running the clinic now. I have received my medical degree. The future is mine to create. I'm not yet sure what I will do next in the field of medicine, but I do know I'm going home to the plantation to watch the rest of the Cromwell Stable mares give birth." She knew her smile was glowing. "I'm ready to be home again without grief, and without the knowledge I have to leave in a few months. I want to go home. The future will unfold in time."

*****

Carrie was astonished when she walked back into the house and saw the spread of food on two tables lining the walls. They had been pushed out of the way to make room for extra chairs, and to make space for people to stand. "Alma, how did you do all this?"

Alma laughed. "You think I took care of three babies and still managed to put out all this food? You crazy, *Doctor* Borden. Sarge was here for an hour to move the furniture, and I had two of my girls come over to help me. They's in the kitchen now, ready to help serve all this food."

Carrie looked at Marietta. "You made all this food? When?"

Marietta shrugged. "If you hadn't been working around the clock, I never would have been able to pull this off. Alma kept coming down to help me with the twins so I could cook. Sarah Rose and Marcus are now best friends with Robert."

Carrie smiled softly. "Just as it should be."

"Yep," Alma said emphatically. "The circle of life don't stop for nobody. Those little babies gonna create a whole brand new world for us."

Jeremy smiled proudly as he entered the house with Thomas and Abby. "My wife cooked all this delicious food," he boasted. "She cooks as well as Annie! And..." He paused for dramatic effect. "...if anyone dares to breathe a word of that to her, I will deny I ever said it."

"Oh, I'm telling," Carrie teased. "I'll never have to share strawberry shortcake with you again." She understood the flash of pain that filled Marietta's eyes. Now that they lived so far from the plantation, pushed out of the South by fear for their children, the good-natured arguing over strawberry shortcake would not happen very often. "I'm sorry," she whispered.

Marietta shook her head, smiled brightly, and changed the subject. "Did I tell you my parents are coming today?"

"Your parents?" Carrie cried. "I'm so happy to have a chance to meet them."

"The snow finally melted enough for them to make their way to this side of town," Marietta said. "My father's health is not good, so they don't get out very often in the winter. I'm just grateful they are nearby. They moved farther north after the war, but when my father became ill, they decided to return. They were thrilled when they found out Jeremy and I were moving here with the twins."

Carrie eyed her. "I've never thought to ask how old your parents are."

"They are both almost seventy. I'm the youngest of five children," Marietta revealed. "I have four older brothers.

"Good Lord," Alma muttered. "No wonder you always be runnin' around bossin' the world. I reckon I understand it now."

Everyone laughed, including Marietta, as Alma disappeared into the kitchen to bring out more food.

"The youngest child always has to learn how to stand up for themselves," Marietta protested.

"I can assure you that you have learned it well," Janie said. She cocked her head then. "I believe I hear my son calling for me."

"Can I come with you?" Abby asked. "I have yet to meet Robert."

"Of course." Janie's eyes clouded. "I hope he's just hungry," Janie murmured. "He can be rather irritable if he's not."

"Quit worrying," Carrie scolded, knowing she wanted Abby to be immediately taken with a happy child. "He's a model baby now. Just keep giving him the Chamomilla if he seems to be more cranky than normal."

Janie and Abby disappeared up the stairs.

"I'm going to check on the twins," Marietta announced, "and then I'll finish up in the kitchen." She looked around. "Everyone, make yourself at home. The food will all be ready in about thirty minutes."

Carrie caught Anthony's eye, and then glanced at Alice. His quick nod said he understood. She walked over and gripped Alice's arm firmly. "We're going to my room," she said softly. "I want the whole story."

"I'm all yours," Alice responded.

Carrie settled on the window seat and patted the cushion next to her.

Alice smiled as she sat down and crossed her legs. "It's like old times," she murmured.

"Except that we both have had a lot of hard experiences," Carrie said.

Alice reached out to grip her hand. "Wally and Nancy told me about Robert and Bridget. Carrie, I'm so very sorry. I don't know what to say."

"Thank you," Carrie replied. "I won't pretend it hasn't been incredibly difficult, but each day gets easier. Being a doctor has become my purpose for living."

"Not to mention the handsome Anthony," Alice teased.

Carrie smiled. "He's wonderful, but I'm still feeling my way forward." She raised a hand. "Enough about me. I want to know how you got out of the insane asylum."

"You saved me," Alice said. "You saved my life, Carrie."

Carrie shook her head. "I got you put into a private room. Whatever happened after that is what saved your life."

Alice shook her head firmly. "That's not true." Her words came slowly. "You saw me the morning after I was beaten so badly."

Carrie nodded. She would never forget.

"The night before, a new patient had just been admitted. I could tell she was as sane as me." Alice's eyes clouded with sorrow. "Beatrice Murray was a very delicate and beautiful woman. That first night was horrible for her. Her screams of pain are something I will never forget."

Carrie shuddered as she envisioned it. She had finished Elizabeth Packard's book, so she knew exactly what must have happened to the hapless Mrs. Murray.

"My roommates became agitated," Alice continued. "When I tried to calm them, one of them lost control and hit me." She shook her head. "She wasn't trying to hurt me. She didn't know what she was doing." She paused. "Anyway, you came the same day with the fake letters from Governor Hoffman and David McNeil."

Carrie chuckled. "Wally and Nancy told you?"

Alice grinned, but it quickly disappeared. "They did. Thank you," she said fervently. "Without that private room..." Her voice trailed off and then strengthened again. "One of the attendants, Mrs. Bartle, took it upon herself to subdue Mrs. Murray. I know she would have done the same with me if I had remained. She took great pleasure in trying to drive the sane ones into insanity, because it gave her a sense of power." Her eyes filled with pain again. "Mrs. Murray was tortured before they gave her large doses of opium to try to calm her."

Carrie gasped. "Opium?"

"Opium," Alice confirmed in a grim voice. "One night she stumbled and fell down a flight of stairs. The final straw for her was when they poured a large bottle of camphor over her face, and into her eyes and ears."

Carrie groaned with disbelief.

"The last time I saw Mrs. Murray," Alice ground on, "she was almost blind and hard of hearing." She took a deep breath, looking away out the window. "She..."

"What happened?" Carrie asked softly.

Alice met her eyes, her own raw with agony. "She hung herself that night."

Carrie covered her mouth. "No..."

"She gave up, Carrie, because she had no one to give her hope." Alice grasped Carrie's hands tightly. "You gave me hope, and you made sure I had a safe place to live until Wally could figure out how to get Sherman to release me. If you hadn't done that, I'm quite certain I would have made the choice Mrs. Murray did."

"Oh, Alice..."

"I mean it," Alice said in a steely voice. "Actually, I don't think I would have made it as long as Mrs. Murray. The insane asylums are horrible for anyone, but if you are sane enough to know what is happening to you, and have no hope of changing things, you are either driven insane or you give up."

"I won't insult you by saying I understand what you went through in the asylum, but I can tell you I understand what it is like to be in so much pain you want to die," Carrie admitted.

The two friends sat for several minutes, basking in the peace and quiet of the room, and in their shared understanding.

"So how *did* you get out?"

Alice smiled. "That's quite a story..."

Carrie listened through the entire tale. "So, Sherman got what he deserved in the end," she said. "I'm glad."

Alice nodded. "Wally told me yesterday that his investigator has confirmed Sherman went to Chicago. It only took a few weeks before he understood he would never get a good job in New York City. Wally and Ralph Cook made certain of that."

"Do you feel safe?" Carrie pressed.

"I think so," Alice said. "I still have dreams of the asylum every night, and when someone knocks on the door after dark, I run to my room, but things are getting better. I know in my head that no one else is going to come for me now that my marriage is over, but my heart is taking a while to catch up."

"It's wrong!" Carrie said angrily. "It makes me sick to realize how many women this has happened to. To know it is *still* happening is maddening."

"Yes," Alice agreed simply, her eyes expressing the depth of her feelings.

"What are you going to do now?" Carrie asked.

"I'm taking the rest of this term to heal and get strong again. I start back to school in the fall. I am more determined than ever to become a doctor."

"That's wonderful," Carrie said warmly. "Are you moving back in with Elizabeth and Florence until school starts?"

"No," Alice replied. "I plan to in the fall so that we can all finish school together, but I feel safe with Wally and Nancy. And with Michael." She took a deep breath. "That's important to me right now."

"I'm sure it is," Carrie agreed.

"I'm also going to be working with Elizabeth Packard," Alice revealed. "So is Nancy."

Carrie smiled with delight. "Your story should be very powerful in helping get the laws changed. The Illinois legislature listened to her and changed the laws there. Surely, your story will help change the laws in New York."

Alice nodded. "I hope so. Mrs. Packard has warned me it's a long and frustrating process, but she has committed the rest of her life to making sure these atrocities don't happen to other women. I'm going to get my medical degree, but I'm joining her in the fight."

Carrie leaned forward to hug her. "Thank you. It's going to take a lot of women with courage like yours to change things."

"You know," Alice said thoughtfully, "I have always believed women should have the vote, but I never wanted to get involved in the struggle. It's sad that it took me getting committed to an insane asylum before I realized women's rights are the responsibility of *every* woman. Until *all* women have equal rights, none of us do."

Chapter Twenty-Four

Thomas accepted the hot tea Alma handed him with a grateful smile. "Thank you."

"You just sit there and relax a little bit, Mr. Cromwell," Alma said.

Thomas was amused. "Do I look tired?"

"No, but you should be. I figure raisin' Miss Carrie from a little girl be enough to make anyone tired. I ain't never seen anyone go as hard and fast as that girl. Was she always like that?"

Thomas laughed. "She was," he assured her.

"Well," Alma said, "you raised a real special daughter. You sit there and enjoy that tea. Food will be ready real soon."

Thomas smiled again as he leaned back in the chair and closed his eyes, grateful for a reprieve in the activity. Getting away from the factory had been stressful. They had wonderful employees, and their new manager was capable, but it would be a long time before the man would replace Jeremy. With several big orders scheduled to go out, he and Abby had worked long hours to be certain they could take the time away. The train travel, compounded by a three-hour delay because of track problems, had sapped his energy.

"Mind an interruption?"

Thomas nodded, but didn't open his eyes. "You're never an interruption, Matthew. Have a seat."

"Tired?"

Thomas nodded again and forced his eyes open. "It's been a rather intense few weeks," he acknowledged.

Jeremy walked up as he spoke, claiming another of the chairs by the fire. "Are things all right at the factory?" he asked with deep concern.

"Things are fine," Thomas reassured him. Jeremy and Marietta had made the right decision, and he didn't want either of them to worry.

Jeremy eyed him closely, obviously not convinced. "Isn't Pierre working out?"

Thomas sighed. He should have known Jeremy would see right through him. "Pierre is a good manager," he replied, "but it will take him some time to learn everything you know. The business is growing quickly." He paused, thinking of a way to distract Jeremy. "We've got our eye on an abandoned building. It might be time to expand."

Jeremy's eyes widened. "Expand? Now?"

Thomas knew what he was referring to. They'd had a long discussion about this very subject in regard to Moyamensing. They had decided it was far too early to expand in Philadelphia, but the situation in Richmond was different. The Richmond factory was well established and extremely profitable. "We haven't made a decision yet, but we're having to turn away orders because we don't have enough space or employees to do the work. We have the funds to buy the building outright."

"And to equip it for operations without incurring debt?"

"No," Thomas admitted. "That's why we haven't made a decision."

Matthew frowned. "Am I missing something here? If the factory is going well, why not expand? Surely the increased business will pay for the expansion."

Before Thomas could answer, Anthony's voice broke in. "May I join you?"

"Certainly," Thomas said warmly. He had liked Anthony from the moment he'd met him, but now that he had heard Carrie's declaration of love for the young man, his feelings had multiplied.

Anthony pulled up another wingback, claiming the last space in front of the fireplace. He sank into the chair and leaned his head back against the cushioned fabric. "It's nice to sit down for a bit."

"You didn't get enough of that on the train?" Thomas teased.

Anthony made a face. "I found myself pacing the aisles more than sitting," he admitted. "The seats weren't that comfortable, and the old man snoring beside me with drool running down his chin was not that appealing."

Thomas joined in the laughter, grateful for these fine young men in his life. "Did you finish up your business before we left town?"

Anthony nodded, his eyes shining with satisfaction. "I did." He paused for effect. "Once again, every foal at Cromwell Stables has been claimed."

"Already?" Thomas demanded. "Most of them aren't even born!"

"My clients didn't care," Anthony assured him. "These men have seen other Cromwell Stables' offspring from Eclipse."

"*Men*?" Jeremy asked. "How many were there?"

"Five. And, I didn't even have to leave Richmond this time. The five men were all willing to come to me." Anthony grinned widely. "All I had to do was tell them how many foals were expected for sale this year. I asked them for a bid per foal, and then left the room for a little while. When I came back in they all handed me a slip of paper with their bid." He paused again. "I had already done my due diligence on all of them before I allowed them to come, because I know how important it is to Carrie and Susan that all the foals go to good homes."

"Not to mention Amber would have your hide if they didn't go to the best stables on the East Coast," Thomas remarked dryly.

"I'm more scared of her than Carrie and Susan," Anthony agreed. "Anyway, all I had to do was open the sheets of paper and accept the highest bid." He glanced at the stairs. "I haven't had a chance to tell Carrie yet, but the bid per horse is substantially higher than last year, and there are more foals because of the new mares Susan purchased during the summer. It's going to be a very good year for Cromwell Stables," he said happily.

"And a good commission for you," Jeremy observed.

"But of course," Anthony admitted. "I quite earned it." He grinned as they all laughed again, and then looked at Matthew. "When I walked up, you were talking about missing something. Might I be missing it, too?"

Thomas shrugged. "Jeremy was asking me about possible expansion for the factory in Richmond."

"Do you need to?" Anthony asked.

"Well..." Thomas hesitated as he pondered how to answer the question he and Abby had been struggling with for weeks. "It's true that if we want to fulfill all the orders coming in, we should expand."

"But...?" Anthony pressed.

Thomas relaxed. There was no reason to be careful with his words. Jeremy and Anthony were both astute businessmen. Perhaps they could help him with his decision. "But, Abby and I don't want to get overextended. Business is good right now, but that could change quickly. We don't want to put ourselves in a risky position. The extra income would be wonderful because we would both love to hire more employees, but it could backfire on us. We don't want our desire to expand to harm what we have already accomplished."

Anthony nodded thoughtfully. "You're concerned about the railroad speculation and banking decisions having a negative impact on the country's financial position."

"Yes." Thomas was relieved he didn't have to explain the situation.

Anthony nodded again. "I spoke with Abby about this earlier in the year, and I did quite a bit of study of my own. I trust Abby's business instincts, but I find I make the best decisions when I do my own research."

"That's wise," Thomas agreed, his respect for Anthony growing.

"I agree with Abby that the country is going to go through a financial crisis soon, but I suspect it won't be for another two to three years."

Thomas eyed him. "You sound rather confident about that." He didn't share the confidence, but he was intrigued as to why Anthony felt so strongly.

Anthony shrugged. "I am convinced most things in business are based on educated guesses, but the loans the banks have made on land out West won't come due for a couple more years. They are making bad decisions, but I don't think they will bear the consequences right away, which means we won't. I won't go so far as to say I feel confident, but I feel strongly enough about it to expand some of my own ventures."

"Such as?" Matthew asked.

"I've bought three buildings in Richmond," Anthony revealed. "The cost of real estate is still low, and I believe the city is going to recover. I'm making a lot of money from the sale of livestock right now. I want to put it into investments that will last long-term." He paused. "I plan to buy more when the Cromwell foals are paid for."

Thomas listened closely. "And if the economy crashes?"

Anthony raised a brow. "It's not an *if*," he replied. "It's *when* the economy crashes. As far as I can tell from my study, our country goes through cycles of good times and bad times. I'm sure Abby is right that a bad time is coming, but I've bought these buildings at far below what their value will become in the years ahead, andI already have tenants in all of them. And," he said, "I've paid cash for everything. I may make less money during lean years, but I'm not jeopardizing my available resources through risky loans."

Thomas nodded as he stared into the flames, his thoughts spinning.

"Can you buy the expansion space you need outright?" Anthony asked.

"Yes," Thomas confirmed, "but we would have to take out a loan to get it outfitted and ready for operations." That truth was what kept them from moving forward. "We borrowed some to get the factory started, but the economy always strengthens after a war. We decided it was a good risk, and it's proven to be. The loans have been paid in full, and the profits are healthy."

"How long would it take you to repay a new loan?" Anthony asked.

Thomas shrugged. "If orders continue the way they are, and if we put every penny from profits back to paying off the loan, we could do it in about a year."

Anthony whistled. "Impressive."

"It's also impressive how quickly it could drain our reserves and profits from our current factory if the economy crashes," Thomas said.

Anthony thought for a few moments. "I guess it all depends on what is important to you," he said thoughtfully.

Thomas cocked his head. "Meaning?"

"Well, I don't believe you and Abby need more money, so I suspect you are considering expansion as a means to increase employment for people in Richmond."

"That's true," Thomas agreed. "Oh, I won't pretend it wouldn't be satisfying to make more money, but it's also true we would like to quit working quite so hard one day soon." He thought about Carrie's decision to return to the plantation for an extended time. He longed for him and Abby to spend more time there, but if they expanded the factory it wouldn't be possible.

"Then you have to decide what is most important to you," Anthony repeated. "I'm younger than you are, so I have to push harder and take more risks if I want to create anything even close to what you and Abby have created. But..." He shook his head ruefully. "I watched my father work himself into the grave. He was a wealthy man, but that seemed to be all he had. I never saw him do anything but work. He had everything money could buy, but from what I could tell, he had nothing of what really mattered." His eyes darkened. "My mother never saw him, and I'm not sure he even knew all of his children's names."

"And you don't want to be like that," Jeremy said keenly.

"I *won't* be like that," Anthony insisted. "Carrie said earlier that she hadn't told me about her graduation because I had business in Richmond, and she thought that was most important. It's *not*," he said emphatically. "I make money so I can live the life I want, but mostly I make it so I can be with the people I love. If money ever becomes more important than that, I'm going to become just like my father. I've promised myself I won't let that happen."

Thomas took a deep breath. The young man's words had suddenly made everything so much clearer. He and Abby would still make the decision together, but he knew he no longer wanted to consider expansion. He and Abby had done their part in rebuilding the South. He didn't know how much longer he had to live, but he knew he wanted to spend his time doing the things he truly believed were important. He wanted to go home.

*****

Carrie turned toward the door when she heard a gentle knock. She looked at the clock and sprang to her feet. "I bet we're being summoned to the feast," she said. She rushed to the door and opened it.

"May I come in?"

Carrie smiled and hugged Abby tightly, and then pulled her into the room. "Of course. I thought we were being called downstairs."

"We probably will be soon, but I haven't had a moment with you since I got here," Abby replied.

Alice stood. "We're done talking. I'll go downstairs," she said graciously.

"You'll do nothing of the sort," Abby said as she walked over, settled down on the window seat, pulling Alice and Carrie down to join her. She grasped Alice's hand tightly. "I made Nancy and Wally tell me about your ordeal. I can't tell you how sorry I am for what you've been through."

"Thank you," Alice said softly. "I'm glad it's over. I'm also glad you're here, because I wanted to thank you. I know you were the one who contacted Dorothea Dix for the letter that granted Carrie entrance to the asylum in the beginning. Without your influence in getting that letter, Carrie would never have been able to come in to visit me." She rested her head on Abby's shoulder. "I will be forever grateful."

"I'm thankful for the small part I was able to play," Abby replied. "I hear you are working with Elizabeth Packard now." She looked at Carrie. "I've read every page of the book you sent me."

"I've read it, too," Alice revealed. "I will do whatever it takes to make sure more women don't experience what I did. The laws must be changed."

Abby glanced out the window. "The longer I live, the more I understand that hardships often prepare ordinary people for an extraordinary destiny." She released one of Alice's hands to grab hold of one of Carrie's. "When I was growing up, we had a big oak tree that stood alone on top of a hill on our plantation. No matter how many strong storms came, that tree continued to grow. Other trees on our land were toppled by the storms, but not that one. My father used to tell me that it was because that tree stood on top of the hill all alone. The wind would blow, but the tree just kept getting stronger because it had only itself to rely on. It couldn't have become that strong if it was sheltered by other trees. The very force of the wind made it grow big and strong."

"We're all strong trees," Carrie murmured, understanding instantly. Each of them had experienced times of great hardship that would have caused many others to give up.

"We are," Abby said. She looked at Alice for a long moment. "My dear, I believe you will discover that the hardest times of your life often lead to the *greatest* moments of your life."

"I'm going to believe that," Alice said. "I'm going to fight with Mrs. Packard in every state she will allow me to. The money Mr. Cook forced Sherman to give me in the divorce assures I will have the freedom to do that." She grinned. "I'm sure he would be mortified to discover he is financing the war Mrs. Packard and I will wage."

"The two of you will be a powerful force," Abby predicted. Then she turned to Carrie. "I have something for you."

"Oh?" Carrie asked. "Something exciting?"

"We don't know. Susan believed you should have it, so she sent it to me in town."

Carrie was intrigued. "What is it?"

Abby answered by reaching in her pocket and pulling out a letter.

Carrie took the letter, puzzled by the childish handwriting on the envelope. "Who is this from?"

Abby shook her head. "We thought about opening it to find out, but it came through the mail just a week ago. Susan knew we were planning on being here, so she made sure one of the men delivered it to us when they were picking up supplies in town."

"I'll leave so you can open it," Alice said.

"Nonsense," Carrie protested. "But I *am* curious to know who it's from. I don't recognize the writing, and there is no return address." She turned the envelope in her hands, wondering if it would be horribly rude to open it immediately.

"Open it," Alice urged, as if reading her thoughts. "I'll admit I'm curious myself."

"You have no idea the self-control it took to not open that letter," Abby said with a laugh. "I feel like it's been burning a hole in my pocket ever since it was delivered the day before we left. If you don't open it right now, I'm going to do it for you."

"Patience," Carrie replied, holding the letter to the light streaming in the window to see if it would reveal anything.

"I am not patient," Abby retorted. "And I don't *want* to be patient." She reached for the letter. "I warned you. If you're not going to open it…"

Carrie laughed harder and quickly slit the envelope, pulling out the single sheet of paper. Her eyes went to the end of the letter first, and then grew wide with astonishment. "It's from Frances," she cried.

"The young girl from the wagon train who almost died in the blizzard?" Abby asked.

"Yes." Carrie smiled brilliantly, but her smile faded as she began to read the letter. She got to the end and took a deep breath, gathering her composure before she could read it aloud.

Dear Carrie,

You told me I could write you. I guess now is the time for me to do that. Actually, it ain't me writing this to you. I asked a neighbor lady who can write and spell better than me to write it. I hope you don't mind.

Carrie's voice thickened as she thought of the little girl who had so completely stolen her heart on the wagon train. She closed her eyes for a moment, remembering Frances' long brown hair, amber eyes, and sweet face.

I thought things was gonna get better after the wagon train, but my daddy wasn't able to get a job when we finally got back to Illinois. Remember? That's where we came from. Anyway, Mama got some work doing laundry here in Effingham, but things were still real hard. Course, not as bad as they are now.

Carrie, I'm all alone now. The flu came through 'bout a couple months back. It took Mama and Daddy. And it took my little sisters, too. None of them were real strong after that trip West.

Carrie's voice broke as she choked back tears. How much would this little girl have to go through? She could feel Abby's warm hand on her leg, but she focused on the words swimming on the page.

I been staying with a neighbor lady for a little while now, but she don't have enough money to keep me. She found a place at an orphanage for me. Don't you worry about me none, Carrie. I'm gonna be all right. I just wanted you to know what happened to me, cause I don't figure I'll be able to write any more once I get in that orphanage.

You told me I got to have hope and be brave. I want you to know I'm holding on to hope, just like you told me. I don't always feel real brave, but I reckon things gonna turn out all right. I've learned how to do a little reading, and I be learning how to do some writing, but I knew you would read it easier if I let my neighbor write it.

She feels real bad about not keeping me, but things still be real hard up here. Just about every man I see came home from fighting in the war, but there don't be enough jobs for all of them. There are lots of hungry people. I think about that other little girl you told me about, just about every day. I think her name is Felicia. Anyway, losing both parents to the flu is real bad, but I don't figure it's as bad as having them killed right in front of me.

Carrie brushed away her tears.

I want you to know I'll be fine. Thank you for saving my life in the blizzard. I'm gonna try to make it one worth saving.

I love you,

Frances

When Carrie gained enough control to look up, both Abby and Alice had tears in their eyes. "That poor little girl..."

"How old is she?" Alice whispered.

"She would be eleven now." Carrie swallowed the lump in her throat as she thought of Frances all alone in an orphanage. She knew orphanages could be fine places, but she had also heard horror stories of how children were abused or neglected.

"What are you going to do?" Abby asked gently.

Carrie smiled as she looked into Abby's knowing eyes, appreciating that Abby knew what she was going to do before she even said it. "Exactly what you think I'm going to do. I'm going to go get Frances." There had never been another thought once she had read the contents of the letter she was gripping.

"What?" Alice asked with a gasp, confusion swimming in her eyes. "What do you mean? What about being a doctor?"

Carrie shrugged. "I was going to figure out how to do that with Robert and Bridget," she replied, her certainty growing as she talked. "One thing I've learned is that life is what happens to you while you're living," she said. "The Navajo taught me that. You think you know where you're going, and then something happens to completely change your course. The only difference here is that this morning, I had absolutely no idea what I was going to do now that I've received my diploma. All I knew was that I wanted to be home." She smiled, excitement pulsing through her as she talked. "Frances is a special little girl. I wanted to take her home with me from the moment I met her. Now I get to do that!"

Abby looked at her with eyes of warm approval. "She's a lucky little girl," she murmured. "Would you like me to go with you?"

Carrie stared at her, hardly daring to hope. "You can do that? I thought you had to get back to the factory."

Abby shrugged, her eyes bright with determination. "I can't think of anything more important than going with you to get Frances. I'm not willing to wait for you to get home in order to meet my new granddaughter."

Carrie grinned. "We have to make a stop on the way back."

Abby raised a brow and waited, her eyes dancing with anticipation.

"Rose graduates in one week. I want to be there." Carrie glanced at the diploma sitting on her desk. "It meant so much to me to have all of you there to celebrate. Far more than I imagined it would. Rose has worked even harder than I have, and waited longer than I did, to go to school. I can't imagine her graduating without being a part of it."

"On one condition," Abby said solemnly.

It was Carrie's turn to raise a brow. "And that would be?"

"That we keep it a surprise."

"Yes!" Carrie exclaimed, jumping up to do a jig around the room. "I don't know why I should be surprised at how fast life can change, but I always am."

*****

The last of the guests had departed before Carrie found herself alone with Anthony on the porch. She and Abby had agreed to say nothing about Frances or their trip until Carrie had a chance to talk with him. Abby was telling Thomas, of course, but they had decided not to announce it to anyone else. Now that they had finished their scrumptious feast of baked halibut, fried oysters, and more side dishes than she could remember, it was time. "Would you like to go for a walk?"

Anthony looked at her with surprise. "You still have energy for a walk?"

"It's a beautiful night," Carrie replied. "And, I have something to talk to you about."

Anthony cocked his head. "It sounds serious."

"It's certainly important," Carrie acknowledged, wondering why she was nervous, but not denying she was.

Minutes later, they were strolling down a back residential street. It was dark, but a warm front that had moved in that day had turned the night into a balmy spring evening.

"My life is about to take a radical change," Carrie finally said, breaking the silence.

"I'm listening."

Carrie smiled, knowing Anthony was doing just that. Suddenly, she wasn't nervous anymore. She hoped he would respond positively, but she knew it wouldn't change her decision. She was confident in what she was about to do. "Do you remember me telling you about the little girl I saved on the wagon train during the blizzard last year?"

"Frances? Of course."

Carrie stared at him. "You remembered her name?"

"If she's important to you, then she's important to me," Anthony replied.

Carrie took a deep breath. "I received a letter from her today. Abby brought it from home." She told him everything. "I'm going to Illinois to get her," she finished. "I'm going to adopt her and bring her home to the plantation."

"Of course you are," Anthony said quietly.

Carrie stared at him, not able to read his expression in the dark. She didn't hear anger or frustration in his voice, but surely her adopting an eleven-year-old girl changed his perceptions of a possible life together. "I love her, Anthony. I know that sounds crazy after the short time on the wagon train, but I wished the whole time I was with her that I could bring her home with me. She's very special."

"She's also very lucky," Anthony replied.

"It doesn't bother you?"

"Should it?"

All Carrie wanted was a solid answer. "Please tell me what you really think. I appreciate your being understanding and giving me space to make my own choices, but you have also declared your love for me and claimed you will wait for me. Now, I'm adopting a child who will soon be a teenager."

"And you believe that makes me angry?"

Carrie shook her head. "I don't know," she cried, "but I would think it makes you *something*!"

"It makes me more in love with you," Anthony declared, turning her toward him so he could gaze down into her eyes. "It makes me more eager to marry you, but I realize adopting Frances will probably mean I have to wait longer." He sighed. "Carrie, I love you. I want more than anything to be your husband, but I told you I would wait. Do I get impatient? Of course, I do. Do I wish things would happen faster? Yes. Do I have any control of that?" He shook his head. "No."

"You don't *have* to wait," Carrie whispered. "Anyone would be lucky to have you."

"I know I don't have to wait," Anthony assured her. "I realize I have the choice to give up on a future with you, but I'm not capable of making that choice." He tilted her chin up to look into her eyes. "I love you, Doctor Borden. I can't imagine spending my life with someone else. I would rather be alone than settle for another woman just to have a wife."

"It's not fair to you," Carrie protested, secretly thrilled he was not willing to walk away. She felt selfish for wanting him to still love her, but she wasn't yet willing to say she would marry him.

"Life is not always fair," he said gently. "We both know that." He paused for a long moment.

"What? You were going to say something," Carrie probed.

Anthony shook his head slightly, looked over her shoulder, and then sighed. "I know I don't have a right to ask this question, but I'm wondering if you think you will ever have a desire to have more children of your own."

Carrie sucked in her breath. "Is that important to you?"

"I haven't decided," Anthony answered honestly.

Carrie knew she needed to be equally honest. "I don't know if I can." Tears pricked her eyes, but she blinked them away. "My mother almost died when she had me. She was told it would be dangerous to attempt to have more children. I almost died when I had Bridget. I haven't asked, but I suspect it would be dangerous for me to attempt to have more children, as well. I don't know that for certain," she rushed to add, "but I believe you need to know it might not be possible."

Anthony looked off into the distance for a few moments more, and then brought his eyes back to her. "I don't mind not having more biological children," he admitted, "but I have always wanted a lot of children in my home. I suppose it comes from having a lot of siblings. Would you be open to more adoptions after Frances?"

Carrie couldn't hold back the grin on her face. "I would be," she assured him. "There are so many children who need a good home." She hesitated. "I don't know how that would work with my being a doctor, though."

"I don't either," Anthony said cheerfully, "but that doesn't matter right now. We're not married. We're not even engaged. We're just having a conversation. It's enough for me to know you would consider it." He laughed suddenly as he pulled her close. As he lowered his lips, he murmured, "I love you, Doctor Carrie Borden."

Carrie had just enough time to whisper back. "And I love you, Anthony Wallington."

Chapter Twenty-Five

"Frances Harvey!"

Frances raised her hand timidly. Mrs. Akron wasn't mean, but the stern, hawkeyed woman still intimidated her.

"Have you done your homework?" Mrs. Akron asked, her eyes boring into Frances as if she were searching for any hint of an untruth.

"Yes ma'am," Frances said earnestly. In truth, she liked going to school. There were lots of the children in the orphanage who complained about it endlessly, but she remembered every word Carrie had said to her. If she wanted to do something with her life, she had to get an education. Everything she had learned so far was only from a neighbor who had taken pity on her because her mama wouldn't let her go to school—the same neighbor who had been feeding her for the last two months.

Mrs. Sider was a kind woman, but too old and poor to become the mother to an orphaned child. She had wanted to, but had finally decided Frances had a better chance for a good life at the orphanage.

"*Teacher's pet!*"

Frances sighed as Isabella walked close behind her and hissed the taunt in her ear, pinching her arm as she did so. She winced and bit her lip. She knew the pinch would leave another bruise to add to her collection, but she had no choice but to endure it.

The teachers were nice, and the women who ran the home were all kind, but they were overwhelmed with so many children. Frances recognized the same desperate look she had seen in her mama's eyes many times. She had overheard two of them talking the night before. She hadn't meant to, but she'd been told to take the food scraps out to the pigs in the back. When she had carried the bucket of slop to them, she heard two of the women talking. They must not have heard her coming over the squeals of the pigs, but they were talking loud enough for Frances to listen.

The orphanage was supposed to house thirty children. There were close to seventy-five. The war hadn't just killed a lot of men; it had left too many children homeless. Even if their mother was still alive, many of them couldn't afford to feed their children now that their husbands were dead. Desperate, they dropped them off at the orphanage.

"We can't just turn them away," one lady had said. "What are the wee children going to do?"

Frances recognized the soft lilt of the gentle-faced Irish woman she trusted instinctively.

"I pity them," the other woman growled, "but how are we going to feed them?"

Frances envisioned the coarse German woman who belonged to the voice. She was not unkind, but the desperate look in her eyes had grown just in the week Frances had been there. Five other children had been dropped off on the front stoop since she had arrived.

"We plant more gardens," the Irish woman answered. "We'll buy some more pigs. We can't turn them out on the streets to die." She had hesitated, her voice growing more distressed. "I saw that happen back in Ireland. The children were starving during the famine. Only then, we couldn't even grow potatoes to keep them alive. We have to try!"

"It's not like we have a choice," the other woman snorted. "She just keeps letting them stay!"

Frances knew *she* was Mrs. Morrow. She felt deep gratitude to the woman who hadn't turned her away when Mrs. Sider had delivered her here with the story of her parents' and siblings' deaths. Mrs. Morrow's worried eyes had softened with compassion as she nodded her head to indicate Frances could stay.

Frances gritted her teeth when another girl delivered an additional pinch, but she was learning to ignore their meanness. She didn't know how long she would have to live in this place, but Mrs. Sider had told her it would be at least until she was sixteen. Frances was determined to learn all she could. She already had a stash of books hidden under her mattress that she had taken out of the tiny bookshelf in the classroom. She would duck into the sleeping room to read every chance she got, and she had learned to hide behind a large tree where she would go undetected while she read.

It's also where she went to cry. There were moments when she missed her mama and daddy so badly she couldn't hold back the tears that burst forth like gushing water through a broken dam. Her daddy might not have known what to do with her, and her mama might have kept her from going to school, but she knew they had loved her. She hadn't known what lonely felt like until she had watched the bodies of her entire family lowered into shallow graves in the paupers' cemetery.

Frances straightened on the narrow bench, determined not to miss one single word of what the teacher said.

*****

Carrie ground her teeth in frustration. "Will we ever find her?"

Carrie and Abby had spent the last two days searching for Frances. They had tried to locate where she had lived with her parents, hoping to find the kind neighbor who had helped her, but their attempts had been fruitless. There had been so little to actually go on, and Effingham was larger than she had anticipated. Finally, they had turned their attention toward the orphanages in the town.

The first two women who had answered their knock at the door simply shook their heads when she asked for Frances Harvey. Carrie was overwhelmed by the sheer amount of need. The orphanages were full of sad-looking children doing their best to make sense of a life that had gone so wrong. She wanted to take every single one of them home with her.

"We'll find her," Abby answered in a determined voice. "We only have two orphanages left to visit."

"But what if they were full? What if she was taken somewhere else? What if she's not still in Effingham?"

"And what if the sky falls on us while we are looking?" Abby asked with mock alarm.

Carrie managed a laugh, even if she was far from seeing the humor. "You're right. I'm worrying when I have no reason to worry."

"I wouldn't go that far," Abby responded. "I'm worried right along with you, but I'm choosing to funnel that energy into looking for a wonderful little girl with amber eyes." She took Carrie's hand. "We'll find her, Carrie. We won't give up until we do."

Carrie grabbed Abby in a fierce hug. "Thank you for coming with me. I don't know what I would have done if I'd been alone."

Abby shrugged. "You would have done exactly what you're doing now." She grinned. "But, you certainly wouldn't be having as much fun!"

Carrie laughed more naturally and then looked up as the carriage they had hired slowed to a stop.

"This is the next place on your list, ma'am."

Carrie took a deep breath and stepped from the carriage. "Thank you. We'll be back soon."

"Yes, ma'am." The driver's weathered face revealed his age, but his glittering blue eyes belonged to a younger man. "I'll be waiting right here."

Carrie crossed her fingers and sent up a silent prayer as they walked to the front door. Young children were everywhere she looked. She assumed the older ones were in school. None of the children looked mistreated or hungry, but all of them had that same beseeching look as they watched her and Abby arrive. Carrie knew each of them held a wild hope that perhaps they would get to go home with a family that would love them.

She had talked to enough people to know the orphanages were full of war orphans, but far fewer than she had expected had lost both parents. Many of them were considered half-orphans. Their fathers had been killed in the war. Their mothers, still alive, had no means of providing for their children, so they brought them to the orphanage with the desperate hope they would be fed and cared for.

Her knock at the door was answered by a gentle-faced young woman with glowing red hair and soft blue eyes. Carrie knew she was Irish before the woman spoke with the lilt she loved so much.

"What can I be doing for you?"

Carrie took a deep breath, hoping, even while she steeled herself for another disappointment. "My name is Dr. Carrie Borden. This is my mother, Mrs. Abigail Cromwell." She had learned early on that identifying herself as a doctor earned her instant respect. She was not above using any possible advantage to find Frances. "I'm looking for Frances Harvey. Might she be here?"

The woman's face grew thoughtful as she pursed her lips. "Frances Harvey..." she murmured.

Carrie knew that with so many children, not all their names might be remembered. "She's eleven years old," she offered. "Her parents were both killed when the flu swept through here a few months ago." Many parents had died during that time, so Carrie didn't know how helpful the information would actually be. "She has brown hair and amber eyes."

The woman's face cleared. "Little Frances! You're here for her?" Her eyes sharpened immediately. "And just who are you to the wee one? You told me your names, but I know nothing else."

"Of course," Carrie responded, her heart pounding with excitement to have finally found the little girl. "I became close to Frances last winter, when her family's wagon was overturned during a blizzard on their way to Santa Fe. I was able to provide medical care."

"What were you doing on a wagon train to Santa Fe in the middle of winter?" the woman asked in astonishment.

"I was on my way to provide medical care to the Navajo Indians," Carrie said without hesitation. She didn't know if this Irish woman knew anything about the Navajo, or cared at all, but she certainly wanted to portray herself as a caring person. She'd thought a lot about what she would say if she actually found Frances.

"And why are you looking for Frances?"

"I knew her family came back to Illinois after the blizzard. Last week, I received a letter from Francis that let me know her family dies during the flu outbreak." She paused. "I want to adopt her and take her home."

The woman's eyes widened with surprise, but they didn't lose their look of suspicion. "Where is home?"

"My family owns a plantation outside of Richmond, Virginia."

"Virginia?" the woman echoed, her eyes growing more, not less, suspicious. "You're a Southerner?"

"From the look in your eyes, I should probably deny it," Carrie replied, "but the answer is yes. I also happen to love Frances, and I know I can give her a wonderful home." She wondered if every prospective parent had to go through this. She supposed she should be glad, but many children likely went unadopted because of these questions. She had learned a little about the number of children being sent by train to the Midwest from cities like New York and Philadelphia. The number of homeless, orphaned children in the big cities was staggering. They were being sent west with the hope that farm families would give them a good, loving home in exchange for labor. She had heard horror stories, but she'd also learned of well-adjusted children who loved their new families. She was certain there were no perfect answers.

The lady stared into her eyes for several moments. She must have approved of what she saw, because she suddenly relaxed. "Will Frances know you?"

Carrie grinned. "Yes."

The woman nodded. "My name is Colleen Dempsey."

"It's a pleasure to meet you, Miss Dempsey," Carrie said warmly.

Colleen nodded and then reached down to scoop up a toddler clutching at her skirt. "Up you go, Pamela. Let's go to the schoolhouse, shall we?"

Carrie smiled when the curly-haired child beamed brightly and nodded her head vigorously. She exchanged a look of excited victory with Abby as they followed Colleen around the back of the building to another smaller building. Tall trees, just leafing out, provided shade and limbs for many swings.

"Wait here," Colleen said, disappearing through the door.

Carrie took a deep breath, trying to calm her jittery nerves. After everything she had done to find her, she had a brief moment of worry that Frances may wish to stay in the orphanage, rather than return with her to the plantation.

"Relax," Abby whispered, reaching out to squeeze her hand.

Carrie tried, but then stiffened when the door opened again. Colleen appeared, leading the little girl by the hand.

Frances, obviously confused to be pulled out of school, glanced around uncertainly. When her eyes landed on Carrie, they opened wide in shock. "*Carrie!*" she screamed. "Carrie!"

She launched herself forward, almost tackling Carrie to the ground with the force of her embrace.

"I reckon she knows you," Colleen observed.

Carrie clasped the little girl to her tightly for several minutes, content to merely hold her.

Frances finally stepped back and stared up into her face. "What are you doing here? How did you find me?"

"Finding you was a challenge," Carrie answered, "but answering the first question is easy. I'm here because I want to take you home with me." She tipped Frances' face up so she could look into the amber eyes she remembered so well. "If you would be willing, I would like to adopt you."

Frances gasped and raised a hand to her mouth. "You want to adopt me?" she asked in a quivering voice.

"I do," Carrie assured her. "I love you. You are an extraordinary little girl. Nothing would mean more to me than to be your mother."

"To replace Bridget?" Frances asked uncertainly.

Carrie shook her head. "Nothing will ever replace my little girl who died, Frances," she said tenderly. "You're not meant as a replacement, darling. I simply want to love you and be your mother." She took a deep breath. "Would you like that?"

Frances nodded her head so vigorously, Carrie feared it would fall from her shoulders.

"I would *love* that," Francis breathed. "Are we going to your home in Virginia?"

"We are," Carrie answered, curious how she would respond. She and Frances had talked for many hours about the plantation where she had grown up. Last year on the Trail, Frances had never tired of the stories.

"Will I get to ride horses?" Frances asked, her eyes wide with anticipation. "Will I get to see the James River? And see all the tobacco?

"Yes, yes, and yes," Carrie assured her. It was obvious Frances was excited to go back to the plantation, but it was only fair to give her the whole picture. "I don't know how long we will stay on the plantation, though. I don't know where my work as a doctor will take me."

Frances listened intently. "Will you still want me to be with you if you have to go someplace else?"

"Always," Carrie replied firmly. "You are going to be my daughter. Wherever I go, I will want you with me."

"And you're going to be doctoring wherever you go?" Frances pressed.

Carrie nodded.

"Then I reckon that will be perfect," Frances proclaimed, "because I'm going to be a doctor, too!"

Carrie smiled broadly. "You are?"

"Yes," Frances said with absolute certainty. "I watched you save most of my family during the blizzard. I knew if you had been there with your remedies, you would have probably saved them from the flu, too. I want to be able to save people like that, Carrie."

"Then I will do everything I can to help you become a doctor," Carrie said gently, understanding exactly how the little girl felt. "You have my word."

Frances' grin grew wider. Then she noticed Abby for the first time. "Hello, ma'am," she said politely, and then turned back to Carrie. "Who is she? Is she with you?"

Carrie smiled. "This is Abby Cromwell. She is my mother." There was no need to explain the nuances of a stepmother right at that moment. "Once you're adopted, she will be your grandmother. She also happens to be the most amazing woman in the world."

Frances clapped her hand to her mouth again. "My *grand*mother? I ain't never had one of those before! At least not one I ever met," she added. She looked at Abby eagerly, and then her eyes dropped. "Do you *want* a granddaughter?" she asked tentatively.

Abby smiled and stepped forward to lay a hand on Frances' shoulder. "I do," she assured her. "Carrie has told me so many wonderful things about you. I already love you very much."

Frances grinned again before she looked to Colleen. "Carrie can adopt me, can't she?"

Colleen nodded firmly. "Yes. I can only wish every one of the children here would go to such a wonderful home." Her eyes were shining.

"When can I leave?" Frances demanded.

Colleen turned to Carrie. "There are some forms that need to be filled out. I'm afraid you'll have to go to the courthouse."

Carrie reached into her pocket and pulled out a sheaf of papers. "That's already been taken care of. All I need is Mrs. Morrow's signature." She laughed when Frances started jumping up and down.

Colleen laughed along with her, and then pointed toward the main orphanage building. "She's in her office. Let's go talk to her."

*****

Carrie stood on the small balcony of their simple hotel, hardly able to believe they were leaving the next day. She took in deep breaths of the spring air, luxuriating in the smell of blooming lilacs. The trees outside her window were filling out with fresh green foliage. Everything felt fresh and new, just like her life did.

"Carrie?"

Carrie looked down and wrapped an arm around Frances securely. The child smelled like fresh lavender from the bath they had prepared for her in the corner tub. "Hello, Frances."

"Is this really happening?" Frances asked anxiously. "Are you sure you want me?" Her eyes flickered with uncertainty.

"Oh, sweetheart," Carrie said tenderly, as she tucked her closer to her side. "I'm so *very* sure. You know, I was frightened you might not *want* me to adopt you," she confided.

"Really?" Frances breathed. "How could you possibly think that? I've thought about you every single day since I said good-bye to you after the blizzard," she said shyly.

"And I've thought about you," Carrie assured her. They had not had much time to talk since departing the orphanage. "Sit down here with me, Frances." She pointed toward one of the two small wrought iron chairs on the balcony.

"I've never stayed in a hotel before," Frances murmured, staring down from the balcony with wide eyes. "I've never had a lavender bath, either," she confided.

Carrie smiled. "Hotels can be wonderful, but you may have had your fill of them by the time we get back to Virginia." Then she grew serious. "I'm sorry about your parents and your sisters, honey."

Frances' eyes clouded over with sadness. "They were real sick, Carrie. I kept wishing you were there, 'cause I figured you could make them well. I just knew you would have some kind of remedy to fix them." She shook her head. "We didn't have money, so no one would come. Mama died first, but it only took Daddy a few hours to follow her. I don't reckon he wanted to live once she was gone." She swallowed hard. "I did all I could think of for my sisters, but they went the next day."

Carrie gripped Frances' hands tightly, knowing there weren't words to ease the kind of pain the little girl had experienced. She could only imagine the terror she felt while she was trying desperately to save her little sisters – her parents both dead in the next room.

"Why do you think I lived?" Frances asked. "I'm the only one left from my whole family."

Carrie was ready for the question; sure Frances would ask it. "Because you have a very special purpose here," she said.

"Do you think they all would have lived if I had taken better care of them?" Frances asked in a quivering voice.

"I do not," Carrie assured her. "So many people died from this flu."

"Did you help people live?" Frances asked. "Back in Philadelphia at the clinic?"

Carrie nodded a bit reluctantly as she thought of all the people in Moyamensing they had been able to save by administering *Influenzinum.* "We did," she murmured, but then cupped Frances' chin in her hands. "I have knowledge and remedies that a young girl would not have." She thought for a moment. "Were you with your mama and daddy when they died?"

"Yes," Frances answered sadly. "I was holding their hands when they closed their eyes for the last time. Both of them breathed funny for a little while, and then they quit breathing at all." She caught her own breath as she remembered.

"And your sisters?" Carrie asked gently.

"Yes," Frances whispered, tears swimming in her eyes. "I wish I could have kept them alive."

"You gave them a wonderful gift," Carrie assured her. "You couldn't have saved their lives, but you were with them when they died. No one wants to die alone, Frances."

Frances thought about what she said. "Did Robert and Bridget die alone?"

"No," Carrie replied firmly, so glad she knew that was true. "I was holding Robert when he took his last breath." She was even more certain she had made the right decision to ride home to be with him. "Bridget..." Carrie took a deep breath to steady her nerves. "Bridget was dead when she was born. I like to think I was holding her close inside me when she died. I don't believe she ever felt alone."

"Did you hold her when she came out of you dead?"

Carrie bit back her wince. "No," she admitted. "I was unconscious, but Abby held her for a long time. She wanted Bridget to know how much her grandmother loved her."

Frances looked out into the deepening dusk. "I like Mrs. Cromwell," she stated. "She's like you."

Carrie smiled. "We are both very lucky to have her in our lives."

A long silence settled on the balcony. Stars appeared in the sky as tree frogs started singing their spring chorus.

"Carrie?"

"Yes, Frances?

"Can we do something for Mrs. Sider before we leave?" Frances asked. "She was real good to me when my folks died. I would have been in that orphanage a lot longer if it hadn't been for her. And, if she hadn't written that letter for me, you wouldn't be here right now. I reckon I owe her a lot."

"Of course," Carrie agreed. "We don't catch our train until tomorrow afternoon. What would you like to do?"

Frances shrugged. "I don't know..." Her voice trailed off as her face tightened with intensity. "Maybe we could buy her a new dress? She hasn't had one of those in a real long time, I don't think. She would like that."

Carrie smiled. "A dress it is," she agreed. "We'll go shopping in the morning before we catch the train."

"How long will it take to get to Virginia?"

"Well, a little longer than normal," Carrie teased. She had been waiting to give Frances the news, because she suspected she would be very excited. "We have a stop to make before we go to the plantation."

"Really?" Frances asked in an excited voice. "Where are we going?"

"My best friend, Rose, is graduating from Oberlin College in two days. We're going to her graduation ceremony. It's a surprise."

Frances' eyes suddenly grew wide. "Are you talking about Rose and Moses?"

"I am," Carrie agreed, certain now that she had made the connection.

"Aren't they Felicia's parents?" Frances demanded. "The ones who adopted her after her parents were murdered."

Carrie grinned. "They are."

Frances' smile exploded onto her face as she jumped up and twirled around the balcony. "I'm going to meet Felicia?"

Carrie nodded. She knew how much it meant to Frances to meet the girl who had so inspired her. "Felicia will be happy to meet you, too."

Abby stuck her head out of the French doors leading to the balcony. "Are we having a celebration out here?"

"Mrs. Cromwell," Frances cried, "I'm going to Oberlin College to meet Felicia... and Moses and Rose!"

"And Hope and John," Abby added playfully. "We're going to have a wonderful time!"

Frances suddenly stopped spinning, and then looked down at the floor.

"What's wrong?" Carrie asked softly. When Frances lifted her head, she was staring at her with sad eyes.

"I don't have a dress to wear to a graduation ceremony," Frances said, and then her eyes grew even sadder. "I'm afraid I don't really know what one *is*, but I'm quite sure you must be dressed nice. I didn't have much to start with, but Mrs. Sider wouldn't let me bring my clothes when I moved in with her. She was afraid I would bring the flu with me." She shook her head. "I only have my one dress. It's not very nice. I'll be glad to stay in the hotel while you go to the ceremony," she whispered.

"You'll do nothing of the sort," Carrie chided, disappointed in herself that she hadn't recognized the problem sooner. She'd been so excited to find Frances that she hadn't even noticed what she was wearing. "Do you think we're only shopping for Mrs. Sider tomorrow?"

Frances looked up, her eyes flaring with hope. "What do you mean?"

Carrie laughed. "The three of us are going on a shopping spree in the morning!"

*****

Carrie couldn't remember the last time she'd had so much fun. Shopping for a little girl was a new experience for her. Shopping for a little girl who had never owned a new dress was totally exhilarating. She and Abby had probably gone overboard, but the shop they had visited was full of dresses that were so perfect for Frances.

"Look at me!" Frances squealed as she spun around in the middle of the road. Her new pink dress with a white bow twirled around her. Then her face grew serious. "Do you think my mama knows I have new clothes? She always wished she could buy me some, but we never had the money."

Abby leaned down and wrapped an arm around her. "I believe she knows, honey. And, I believe she is completely happy for you. I know she wishes she could have stayed here with you, but since she couldn't do that, I know she wants the best for you."

"Do you really think so, Mrs. Cromwell?"

"I do," Abby said, "but now we have another problem we need to solve."

"We do?" Frances asked. "What's wrong?"

"You can't keep calling me Mrs. Cromwell," Abby replied. "I hope the day will come when you will call me Grandma, or some version of it, but until then we have to come up with something better." She pursed her lips. "I suppose you wouldn't feel comfortable calling me Abby."

Carrie chuckled when Frances shook her head quickly. She knew the little girl was falling under

Abby's spell, but she needed time to deal with all the changes in her life. Aunt Abby wouldn't do, because she truly was Frances' grandmother now that the little girl had been adopted. She fingered the papers in her pocket just to assure herself they were real.

Frances peered up into Abby's face. "My mama was German," she said. "If her mama hadn't died before I was born, I would have called her Oma." She looked down shyly. "If you don't think it's too soon..."

Abby took Frances' hand. "I would love it if you would call me Oma."

Frances looked hesitantly at Carrie.

Carrie knew immediately what she was thinking. "I think Oma is perfect," she said enthusiastically. "And I think you should keep calling me Carrie for now. You had a mama that you loved very much, but you never had an Oma. If the time ever seems right, you can call me something else, but I don't believe that time has to be now."

"You don't?" Frances asked, her lip trembling. "You're not mad at me?"

"Not even a tiny bit," Carrie assured her, giving her a hug. "Now, we have one more store to stop at."

"More shopping?" Frances cried. She looked at all the parcels stacked up behind them on the sidewalk. "I can't possibly need more clothes. I never imagined I would have so many clothes in my whole lifetime."

"No," Carrie agreed with a laugh, "I believe you have plenty of clothes for now. But, we still have to get Mrs. Sider a dress. We have just enough time to buy her something and take it to her house so you can tell her good-bye."

Frances clapped her hands. "That will be wonderful," she said happily. "I'm glad I'm not the only one who is going to have a new dress!"

*****

Mrs. Sider clasped Frances close to her bosom and kissed her cheek. "I'm so happy for you, Frances. You be a good girl. I know your folks are probably dancing a jig up in heaven right now."

"Do you really think so?" Frances asked, leaning back to stare into the old woman's face.

"I *know* so," Mrs. Sider assured her. "Your daddy faced a hard time of it after the war. We may have won that war, but the men who fought it are still fighting a battle here at home. They've come back wounded inside and out. There aren't jobs for them, and not enough help to carry them through." She tilted Frances' chin. "Your daddy was a real good man. He told me one day that he wanted better things for you."

"He did?" Frances asked somewhat doubtfully.

"That he did," Mrs. Sider said firmly. "He hoped to find it in Santa Fe, but losing your brother on the trip during that blizzard took the heart right out of him and your mama. They figured they had failed all of you." Her eyes shone with unshed tears. "I reckon when the flu got them, they didn't have enough heart left to fight it off." She paused. "Your mama wanted you to go to school, you know."

"What?" Frances shook her head. "That can't be true," she protested. "She told me many times that girls didn't have any need of schooling."

Mrs. Sider nodded. "I know she did, but she didn't mean a word of it. She wanted you to go to school so you would have a better life than she did, but there wasn't any money to send you. Rather than have you think badly of your daddy because he couldn't pay for it, she let you think she believed it wasn't important."

Frances absorbed the words. "Thank you, Mrs. Sider. I'm real glad to know that. I'm going to go to school now, you know. As soon as I get to Virginia. I bet mama is gonna be real happy."

"That she will be," Mrs. Sider stated. "That she will be." She turned to Carrie and Abby next. "Thank you for bringing the girl here to say good-bye. That means a lot to me."

"She wanted to say thank you for taking such good care of her," Carrie replied. "I want to thank you, too."

She paused and nodded at Frances, who turned and ran out to the carriage. "Frances has a gift for you."

Frances dashed back into the house, holding three large parcels. "These are for you, Mrs. Sider."

"What is this?" Mrs. Sider demanded, her cheeks flushed with pleasure.

"Open them!" Frances cried, jumping up and down. "I hope you like them. I picked them out myself!"

Mrs. Sider grew red as she opened the boxes. Her eyes grew wide with disbelief as she pulled out two beautiful dresses, both lovely, but serviceable enough to wear on a daily basis. "Oh my!" she gasped.

"Do you like them?" Frances asked anxiously.

Mrs. Sider held the dresses up to her, her eyes glowing with pleasure. "They're beautiful, Frances," she said huskily.

Frances clapped her hands. "Now open the last box. You won't need this one right away, but it will be waiting for you."

Mrs. Sider looked at her curiously before she opened the final parcel. She held her hand to her mouth when she saw a thick, warm winter coat with a pair of gloves and a felt hat nestled on top. "Why, I never..."

"Do you like it?" Frances cried again.

Mrs. Sider dashed away the tears trickling down her cheeks. "I've never had anything so fine in my life," she murmured. Her eyes darkened as she shook her head. "I can't accept things such as these."

"Nonsense," Carrie said firmly. "Most people would have turned their back on an orphan child and believed it was not their problem. Because of you, and especially your kindness in writing the letter for Frances, and then paying to have it mailed, you have made it possible for me to adopt her. I will always be grateful, Mrs. Sider. So will Frances. She wanted to give you something that would make you remember her."

Mrs. Sider turned and pulled Frances close. "I would never forget you, child. I don't need a coat to remind me, but every time I put on one of these pieces of clothing, I will say a prayer for you."

"And will you write me?" Frances pleaded. "I promise to write you back."

"I'll write," Mrs. Sider promised.

*****

Carrie exchanged a satisfied smile with Abby when they pulled away from the tiny cottage with just enough time to catch the train.

Mrs. Sider would find the cash they had stashed in the pocket of one of the dresses soon.

Chapter Twenty-Six

Carrie was trembling with excitement when she stepped off the train at the Oberlin Station with Abby and Frances. The quaint, gabled little station, painted blue and surrounded by a grove of trees, was a charming introduction to the town. She knew her companions were just as excited as she was. It was hard to be so close to Rose and not see her, but Carrie was determined to keep it a surprise. She only had to wait until tomorrow.

"Where are we staying tonight?" Frances asked.

"The Park Hotel," Carrie answered. "It's the same hotel Moses and Rose stayed at with the family when they arrived." She looked around the train station, thrilled to be in Oberlin. She couldn't wait to see Rose's face when she discovered they were here.

"I say we settle into the Park Hotel and find some dinner," Abby said, inclining her head toward Frances.

When Carrie looked over, Frances was making a futile effort to hide a gaping yawn. Carrie smiled, knowing everything was brand new to the little girl. She had refused to sleep during their long train ride, because she didn't want to miss anything. She must be exhausted.

"Good-bye!" Frances yelled to the conductor who had stepped out the back door of the caboose to wave at her. "Thank you!"

The portly conductor waved cheerfully, bowed slightly, and then stepped back inside.

Carrie laughed. "Well, you certainly charmed him."

"He was wonderful," Frances said enthusiastically. "He told me everything about the train, and every town we stopped in. He knows everything!"

Her fatigue seemed forgotten in her excitement, but Carrie knew it would crush down on her soon. She waved a carriage over and climbed in with Abby and Frances, praying there would be no reason for Rose or Moses to be in the same part of town they were.

*****

Rose slid the light blue gown over her head, hardly able to believe she was dressing for her college graduation. She gazed into the mirror over her bureau, wishing with all her heart that her mama were alive to share the day with her.

"What are you thinking about?" Moses asked.

Rose stared into his eyes over her shoulder, and then turned away from the reflection of the mirror to face him. "I'm thinking about Mama," she said softly. "I'm remembering all the nights I taught the secret school in the woods... I'm remembering the times I snuck books out of the Cromwell library, stealing candle ends so I could read at night." Her mind swirled through the memories.

"I'm thinking about teaching at the contraband camp during the war, and then starting the school on the plantation." She shook her head. "The road to this moment has been so long and crooked. Most of the time I had no idea where it was going, though I knew I always wanted it to end up at this very moment in time."

"A college graduate," Moses murmured as he looked down at her. "I'm proud of you, Rose. I could not possibly be prouder of you for making this dream come true."

"*We* made it come true," Rose replied. "I wouldn't be here today without you." She kissed him warmly and then, still enclosed in the circle of his arms, she leaned back to gaze at him. "You really don't mind? You don't mind not getting your degree as a lawyer?"

Moses shook his head. "If I ever decide I need to finish college, I will, but all I want to do now is go home to the plantation and do what I love more than anything. I want to hold you in our bedroom. I want to walk with you on the shores of the James River. I want to go horseback riding with our children through tobacco fields." He chuckled. "All I've been able to think about the last few months was going *home*."

"And now we are," Rose said softly. "I can hardly wait, either." A flash of sadness gripped her.

"What was that look for?" Moses asked keenly.

Rose knew better than to think she could hide her feelings from her astute husband. "I'm so happy to be graduating, but it seems odd..."

"For no one else to be here?" Moses finished for her. "I know."

Rose wondered if she would ever quit being surprised that her husband knew her so completely. "I wouldn't have wanted to go to school anywhere but here in Oberlin," Rose said, "but it's so far away." Her thoughts darkened as she thought ahead. "Felicia will be so far away..."

"Stop," Moses commanded. "We've gone over this so many times. Felicia is doing what she wants to do. She will receive wonderful care here, and she can come home anytime she wants to." He shook her shoulders lightly. "I will absolutely not let you ruin your graduation day by worrying."

Rose smiled. Moses was right. She would tuck her worries away, but she knew she would still feel them. Felicia was her daughter. It was her job to worry about her. "It's really rather amazing," she said with a smile.

"What is?" Moses asked.

"We didn't even know Felicia existed a few years ago, and now it's as if she has been our daughter forever. It doesn't seem like there was ever a time when she hasn't been ours." She paused. "I was so terrified to become her mama, but it has been such a joy, and I'm beyond proud of her. And," she added defiantly, "of course I'm going to worry about her. It's my job to do that. Don't even bother pretending you're not going to do the same thing, Moses Samuels."

Moses shrugged. "I'll worry about her every day," he admitted, "but at least I won't have to for a month.

She's going home with us in two days. I'll have her right where I want her."

"And in just a few days, we'll be home," Rose said happily. "I got a letter from Abby. It said Carrie was heading home to the plantation, as well. I can hardly wait to see her."

"Mama!"

Rose cocked her head. "Felicia is calling us."

"Mama! Daddy! We have company!"

Rose raised a brow and looked at Moses. "Were you expecting anyone?"

"No. You?"

Rose shook her head. "I'm meeting some classmates before the ceremony, but I wasn't expecting anyone here."

"Mama!"

"Mama! Daddy! Come!" John cried.

Rose was mystified. "Whoever it is, they sound excited."

"Only one way to find out," Moses said with a chuckle. He held out his hand. "Madame Graduate, let's get you to your ceremony."

Rose curtsied gracefully, took his hand, and walked with him down the stairs. When she reached the bottom, and looked into the parlor, she froze. But only for a moment. "Carrie? Abby? I don't believe this!" She leapt forward as both of them opened their arms at the same time.

The three women embraced, laughing joyfully.

Rose finally pulled back. "What are you doing here?"

Carrie rolled her eyes. "Did you really think we were going to miss your graduation?"

Rose looked at Moses. "Did you know?"

"No idea," he assured her. "Of course, I have noticed that you are the only one to get a hug."

Carrie laughed and rushed into his arms, followed by Abby. John and Hope danced around the room with joy.

Rose noticed someone standing in the corner of the room. She smiled at the lovely little girl with long brown hair and glistening amber eyes. "Well, hello," she said. "Who are you?"

"I'm Frances." The girl's voice was shy and hesitant.

Carrie stepped away from Rose and walked over to put an arm around Frances. "I'd like to introduce you to my daughter, Frances Borden. I adopted her just a few days ago."

Rose opened and closed her mouth, but no sound came forth.

Carrie laughed. "I know that was mean, but I wanted to see the look on your face when you discovered I have a beautiful daughter."

"It's true?"

"Oh, it's very true," Carrie said, her eyes sparkling with happiness.

Suddenly, Rose remembered, and turned back to lean down and look into the little girl's eyes. "Are you the Frances that Carrie helped on the wagon train last year?"

Frances nodded shyly. "My family died of the flu a few months back."

"All of them?" Rose asked with a gasp.

"Yes, ma'am," Frances answered. "I sent Carrie a letter and told her I was going to an orphanage." An expression of awe filled her eyes. "She came and found me, and adopted me," she said. "We came here so we could see you graduate before we all go home to the plantation."

Rose gazed at her, understanding instantly why Carrie had fallen in love with the little girl with such expressive and intelligent eyes. She had many questions for her best friend, but they would wait. "I'm very glad you're here, Frances," she said sincerely. "Have you met Felicia yet?"

Frances shook her head. "Not yet," she admitted. "She was real eager to get you downstairs when she saw Carrie and Oma."

"Oma?"

"It's German for grandmother," Abby explained happily.

Rose nodded, her mind spinning. A glance at the clock told her they needed to leave for the graduation ceremony. Any more questions would have to wait until later. She put an arm around Frances, and then turned her to meet Felicia. "Frances, I would like you to meet my daughter, Felicia."

"Hello, Felicia," Frances said. "I may just be meeting you, but Carrie told me all about you last year when she saved me during the blizzard. I'm glad to meet you."

Felicia smiled back and moved forward to take Frances' hand. "I'm glad to meet you, too. Will you sit next to me during the graduation? It will be nice to have someone close to my own age."

Frances beamed with pleasure. "I would love that," she replied. She glanced at Carrie. "Is it all right?"

"Certainly," Carrie assured her. "Shall we go?"

*****

Rose linked arms with Carrie and Abby as they strolled along Oberlin's tree-lined streets.

"This is a lovely town," Abby said.

"It is," Rose agreed. "What is truly lovely about it, however, is the opportunity it gives everyone for an education. It's been so wonderful to learn in a college that embraces women and blacks." She shook her head, once again becoming immersed in memories. "I couldn't have even imagined a place like this ten years ago."

"When you were hiding in the woods teaching your little school," Abby murmured.

"Yes," Rose replied. "Sometimes it feels like things will never change, yet it's been less than a decade since I gave up my chance to escape on the Underground Railroad. I was afraid I would spend the rest of my life as a slave on the plantation, but I wouldn't leave Mama. Everything has changed. This country...my life..." She shook her head again. "There are moments when I believe we are quite insane to go back to the plantation, but I have to believe things will continue to change if enough people will fight for it."

"You've learned that here," Abby observed.

"Partly," Rose acknowledged. "I believe I already knew that, but attending a college founded on the belief that educated and committed people could change this country, especially in regard to slavery, has reinforced the knowledge that change only comes when enough people are determined to *make* things change."

"Are you afraid?" Carrie asked solemnly.

Rose glanced over her shoulder to make sure no one could overhear their conversation. Moses was busy with John and Hope, and Frances and Felicia had their heads close together, talking. The sight made her smile, but then it faded. "Sometimes, I'm so scared I feel like I can't breathe," she admitted. "Most of the time I'm not, and I know it's the right thing for us to do."

She looked Carrie in the eye. "How are *you* feeling about being an adoptive mother? I was absolutely terrified when Moses wrote me that he was bringing Felicia home."

"I was more terrified that I wouldn't find her," Carrie replied. "You had never met Felicia. I fell in love with Frances last winter." She glanced back, her eyes glowing with love. "She's very special. I'm lucky."

Rose had a million more questions, but the sight of the college in the distance meant she would have to wait. "We can talk tonight?"

"And tomorrow, and the day after that, and the day after that..." Carrie promised. "I'm so excited we're all going back to the plantation together."

"How long will you be there?" Rose asked.

"What will *tomorrow* bring?" Carrie asked with a laugh. "I've given up trying to imagine what the future will be. I have no idea how long I will be on the plantation. We've talked so many times about how swiftly plans can change once they've been made, but if you had told me a week ago that I would now be a mother, I would have thought you were insane."

Rose frowned, her thoughts spinning when Carrie said the word *insane*. "I got your letter about Alice. It's terrible! Can we talk about that when we're done celebrating?"

"Oh, I think we'll just add it to the celebration," Carrie said with a grin. "I'll give you all the details later, but Alice surprised me by coming to *my* graduation."

Rose gasped. "She's out of that awful asylum?"

"She is," Carrie confirmed happily. "I'll tell you all about it later."

Moments later, their group reached the building where graduation was being held. Rose turned and hugged both her friends again. "Thank you so much for being here," she said softly. "It means so much to me."

"I'm so proud of you!" Carrie cried. "You deserve to be graduating early."

Abby pulled her close again. "You've been an extraordinary teacher for years, my dear, but it's important for the future that you have this degree. I'm so proud of you for making your dream come true."

*****

Rose stood proudly when her name was called. She was still surprised they were allowing her to graduate a year early, but she acknowledged she had earned it. As she walked across the stage, she had a clear vision of her mama's glowing smile and tender eyes. She blinked back tears and looked toward Moses. His eyes were locked onto her, his face illuminated with such pride it almost took her breath away.

The two of them had come such a long way together. Her mind flew to the night she had met him, and his shock at discovering she taught a secret school in the woods. Her husband had gone from being completely illiterate to being a college student, and the very successful co-owner of Cromwell Plantation. Her love for him swelled so large she thought surely her heart would explode.

Her eyes settled on her children smiling at her with such delight, even little Hope who couldn't possibly understand all this moment meant, and then they shifted to Carrie and Abby. She would always be so grateful they had made the trip to be with her.

She finally reached the college dean midway across the stage. "Hello, sir."

"Congratulations, Mrs. Samuels," he said warmly. "You are a complete credit to this school."

"Thank you, Dean Love." Rose accepted the diploma with a steady hand and turned away.

"Wait," the dean murmured.

Rose hesitated, not sure she had heard him correctly. Everyone else walking across the stage had simply accepted their diploma and moved on. She was certain the college hadn't changed their mind, but she didn't know what was happening. "Wait?"

"Yes, please."

Rose remained where she was standing, watching the dean for some indication of what was happening. He met someone's eyes and a look of relief crossed his face. Dean Love motioned for Rose to stay where she was, and then turned to the audience.

"We have a quite extraordinary addition to our graduation ceremonies today. We weren't certain it would be possible, but we have a distinguished guest with us who has made a special request," Dean Love said, his voice ringing through the building.

Rose turned to look at Moses, but his expression showed he was as mystified as she was. When she looked back at the dean, she glanced toward the side of the stage. She couldn't stifle her gasp of surprise.

"I take it you know who she is?" Dean Love asked quietly.

"Of course," Rose whispered, looking toward the end of the stage. She had no idea why she was still standing on it. "I should go sit down."

"No," the dean replied, looking almost as curious as she was. "She asked for you to remain on stage."

Rose watched the stooped old woman make her way across the platform. Once again, she was struck by Sojourner Truth's quiet dignity. It hardly seemed possible it could have been two years ago that she'd heard her speak in New York at the American Equal Rights Association meeting. Now, as she had then, the woman radiated power as she made her way slowly to the center of the stage, her eyes locked on Rose. All Rose could do was gaze back in speechless shock.

The building was completely quiet as everyone waited to see what was about to transpire.

Sojourner Truth walked to the center of the stage, reached out to squeeze Rose's hand for a moment, and then turned to the audience. "I imagine everyone here today knows who I am, so I will not bore you with information. I will also not talk for long, for that is not what today is about. Today is meant to celebrate the end of a student's quest for knowledge. That is something I always applaud."

Every eye in the room was fixed on the woman who had fought for decades for the abolition of slavery, and who had now turned her efforts to women's rights. She was a heroine to everyone there.

"Two years ago," Sojourner continued, "I had the pleasure of speaking at the meeting of the American Equal Rights Association. Whenever I stand in front of a crowd, I always pick out one person who I believe is meant to hear what I'm saying more than anyone else. I like to believe it is because that person is very special, and will someday carry into the future the torch of those of us who fight now." She glanced at Rose and smiled. "Two years ago, the person I spoke to was Rose Samuels."

Rose held a hand to her mouth, not able to believe what she was hearing. She had never forgotten her time in New York, and had indeed felt Sojourner Truth was speaking directly to her. She could hardly believe, however, that the famous woman had felt the same way.

"We did not meet in person that day, but I made sure to learn her name. When I came to meet with a friend here at the college, I heard her name again. Of course, I had to know more." She smiled again. "I was not at all surprised to learn she was graduating early, and not surprised to learn she is going back to the South to teach, because she believes that will have the greatest impact."

She turned to Rose then. "I asked to be able to speak to you today, Mrs. Samuels. I know you're going back to teach your students, but I also know you're going to have students from Oberlin down so they can learn from you." Sojourner's dark eyes glowed with intensity. "Rose Samuels, it is women like you who are leading the way for every woman to come. We face a mighty fight in the years ahead. I can't know if I will see the day women have the right to vote. I'm old, but you're young. You are making sure a whole generation of children know the importance of education."

Sojourner looked up at the crowd. "Education is important because it gives people knowledge. People who don't know things can't change them. It's really very simple. Women have no chance of getting equal rights if the girls of today don't make it their own battle. I am old. Others who have led the way for decades are old. Now it is our job to make sure others care, so that the battle continues."

She turned to Rose. "I can't know all the things you will do in your life, Rose Samuels, just as I couldn't know all the things I would do in *my* life. My word of advice to you today as you graduate, is to keep saying *yes*."

Rose fastened her eyes on the woman's face, drinking in every word she was saying.

"When someone asks you to do something, say *yes*. When you're asked to learn something new, say *yes*. When you're asked to do something you're certain you can't do, say *yes*." Her eyes burned into Rose's. "It's by saying the word *yes,* that I have been to places I never dreamed possible, and done things I never could have imagined. There will be many times you want to say *no*. Many times you'll be certain you are not up to the task." She paused and stared even deeper into Rose's soul. "Those are the very times you have to say *yes*."

Rose, mesmerized by the challenge in the old woman's eyes, just as she had been two years earlier, nodded. "I will," she promised.

Sojourner continued to stare into her eyes until, evidently, she seemed satisfied the message had been received. Then she turned to the audience. "That goes for everyone in this room. I know Rose Samuels, but I feel I know all of you to some degree. You have either just worked hard to get your diploma, you are still studying, or you worked hard to make it possible for one of the young people here to attain it. Either way, you are saying *yes* to the future of this country...to the future of what you believe in."

Rose watched Felicia as Sojourner spoke. She recognized the awestruck expression on her daughter's face, and completely empathized with the bright shine of determination. Her eyes slid over to Frances next. The little girl was listening as intently as Felicia.

She finally let her eyes move to Carrie, finding exactly what she knew she would find. Her friend's eyes were fixed on her. Shining tears of pride and love made Carrie's eyes luminescent. No words were needed to know they were both thinking of all they had been through to reach their graduation days. *Thank you,* Rose mouthed silently.

Carrie nodded. *I love you,* she mouthed back.

Sojourner lifted her arm and swept her hand to encompass the audience. "Too many people are afraid of life. You fear failure. You expect the worst. You let your fears guide you into saying no to life and opportunities." She shook her head. "What a waste," she chided. "I believe every person in this room knows the things you're meant to do. Somehow, you feel it deep in your gut. Let me tell you what I have learned in my many long years on Earth. The chance to do something important doesn't wait for perfect timing, because there *is* no perfect timing. You just got to start before you think you're ready to start."

Rose watched as Sojourner took a deep breath. She realized she was watching one of the greatest teachers alive because Sojourner grasped every available opportunity to make a difference with her words and her voice.

"One more thing," Sojourner continued. "Every time you say no to an opportunity, you're not just saying no to that one thing. You're saying no to all the other opportunities that follow, when you've had the courage to say the first *yes*."

Sojourner looked to Dean Love. "I'm afraid I've taken more time than I should, but I thank you for this opportunity."

"And I thank you for saying *yes* to it," Dean Love replied. "You have given everyone here a great gift."

"Especially me," Rose said. She hugged Sojourner warmly before one of the professors came forward to help the old woman from the stage. Rose finished crossing the platform and found her seat among the graduates, still stunned by what had transpired, and quite certain she would never forget even a breath of it.

Chapter Twenty-Seven

"You're sure you don't want to wait for Moses to get back?" Chooli asked as she tucked Ajei more securely onto her hip.

Franklin nodded. "It's time to leave, Chooli. It's never going to be easy to say good-bye, but we've got a long trip ahead of us."

"I thought I would be able to say good-bye to Carrie," Chooli protested. "And Rose. And Abby. And Felicia." She paused. "And meet little Frances. I'm so glad Carrie sent a letter telling us about adopting her."

Franklin stared at her for a moment. "Have you changed your mind about leaving?" He hated the excited jump in his stomach when he asked the question. He'd thought he was ready to go, but the last weeks had filled his mind with doubt.

Chooli shook her head, but her eyes were uncertain. "No, Franklin. I haven't changed my mind." Then she hesitated, obviously swallowing back words.

"Then what is it?" Franklin pressed, striving to keep his voice patient. He had wanted to leave several days earlier, but things kept coming up to delay their departure.

"I'm afraid," Chooli finally murmured, refusing to meet his eyes.

Franklin softened, hating the fear he saw etched on her face. "What are you afraid of?" he asked tenderly.

Chooli lifted her eyes. "Everything!" she cried. "I still have nightmares from when we came to the plantation. Riding at night through the countryside. Not even being able to ride on the road because we might be discovered. Being chased by vigilantes. Being hungry, and having nowhere to sleep but the ground..." Her voice wavered. "And now we have Ajei. I'm so scared she'll be hurt," she moaned. "I couldn't bear it."

"But we'll be in a wagon, Chooli," Franklin protested. "I told you that already. It's waiting for us in Independence."

"That makes me even *more* frightened," Chooli replied, fear making her large brown eyes even larger. "I read in a magazine Felicia sent me, that this past year has been the worst one on the Santa Fe Trail for Indian attacks. I know my people are on their reservation, but the Apaches are fighting back. It would be bad enough if we were in a wagon train that could protect us some." She shook her head. "If it's just us alone in a wagon, there's no telling what will happen, Franklin!"

Franklin wanted to assure her they would be safe, but in truth, he was as worried as she was. He remained silent, wondering what he could say. He was afraid that whatever words he spoke, they wouldn't carry enough conviction to make her feel confident. He couldn't manufacture a confidence he didn't feel.

"You don't think we should go, do you?" Chooli demanded.

Franklin searched for words before finally opting for the simple truth. "I think it will be dangerous," he admitted. "But," he rushed to add when he saw sadness fill her eyes, "we could go to Independence and wait there until we find a wagon train that will take us on. Surely there will be one that will welcome us."

"And what do we do when we get to Santa Fe?" Chooli demanded. "We still have to cross the territory to get to *Dinetah* on our own."

Franklin lifted his hands. "What do you want me to say? I've told you from the beginning that it could be risky."

Chooli nodded. "I know..." She sighed heavily. "I guess now that it's time to go, it all seems so real. All I've thought about since last October was going home to be with my family. I was so excited about I, I suppose I refused to think about how dangerous it will be." She looked down at Ajei's curly, black hair, and reached a hand up to stroke it gently. "I would never forgive myself if something happened to her."

Once again, Franklin was at a loss for words. He couldn't disagree with her, because he had been thinking the same thing for months. He was not, however, willing to be the one to change their plans. He would not break his promise to his wife.

"Maybe it's too soon," Chooli said.

Franklin caught his breath, looking at her.

"You don't want to leave," Chooli murmured. There was no accusation in her voice, just calm acceptance.

Franklin shrugged helplessly. "I'm torn," he confessed, wondering why they hadn't had this conversation months ago. "I love your homeland, and would love to live near your family. I also love Cromwell Plantation and growing tobacco." He chose not to add that he would also miss everyone on the plantation who had come to be his family, as well. "I'm worried about what it will take to get to *Dinetah*," he finished. He couldn't put voice to the possibility of something happening to Chooli or Ajei. He couldn't bear to think it.

He also wanted to be fair. "Chooli, it's not going to get any easier to leave if we wait longer. I suppose the railroad will go all the way through to Santa Fe in time, but it's not going to be for many years. You don't want Ajei to grow up in the South," he reminded her.

"No," Chooli agreed, "but I do want her to grow up." She looked up at him pleadingly. "We're safe here on the plantation."

Franklin battled with his response. He wanted to agree with her, but he didn't want to lie. "We have been," he said slowly. "But, there is no guarantee there won't be more violence. You know there was an attack on the plantation the night we arrived last fall."

"Yes, but there hasn't been one since," Chooli argued.

"No," Franklin replied, "but Blackwell Plantation was attacked."

Chooli stared at him in confusion. "If you want to stay, why are you trying to convince me to leave?"

"I'm not," Franklin answered, wishing once again they had been able to talk so openly long before this. Perhaps Chooli had to face her fears before she could admit returning to her Navajo homeland was not the best course of action. "I'm trying to make sure we're seeing all sides of our decision." He took a deep breath. "Ajei will face prejudice here," he reminded her.

Chooli looked away for a moment, and then gazed back at him. "And she will face prejudice at home, too."

"But I thought..."

"I told you my grandparents' position with the tribe would protect her," Chooli said. "That is true, but they may not still be alive when we get there. Or they may not live much longer." She gazed down at her daughter. "It will be hard in the beginning for both you and Ajei because you are black. Prejudice can be found anywhere." She took another breath. "Life will be hard on the reservation, Franklin. My people have gone home, but there was much destruction. It will take a long time for them to rebuild the Nation," she said.

Franklin stared at her, trying to absorb what she had said. "What are you saying, Chooli?"

"We're not safe anywhere," Chooli whispered, "but..."

Franklin waited as a long silence filled their cabin. He looked around at the simple structure they had called home since October. It wasn't fancy, but it was cozy. It was home.

"We have a home here," Chooli said. "You have a good job." Suddenly her lips tightened. "Will Moses allow you to stay, now that he and Rose are coming back? Perhaps they won't have a place for you." Panic filled her eyes.

Franklin shook his head. "I'll have a job," he said, glad he could be certain of at least one thing.

"How do you know?"

"Moses wrote me again after telling us he was coming home," he admitted. "I didn't show it to you because we'd already decided to leave."

"What did it say?"

"It said if we changed our minds and wanted to stay, he would have a place for me. He wants to expand operations even more. There's too much for him to oversee by himself."

"You didn't tell me!"

Franklin shook his head. "Of course I didn't. Why would I? It would have just made you feel badly about us leaving. If we're going back to *Dinetah*, it shouldn't matter whether I have a job here or not."

Chooli dropped her lashes. "You're right," she muttered. She looked down at Ajei again, stood, and began to pace restlessly around the cabin. "I don't know what to do, Franklin. I just don't know what to do!"

Franklin remained silent. This was a decision his wife needed to make. He never wanted either of them to feel he had been the one who kept them from returning to her homeland and her people. He loved her and wanted her to be happy.

"Tell me what to do," she wailed.

Frightened, Ajei began to cry.

"Oh, little one," Chooli crooned. "I'm so sorry I scared you. Mama is so sorry." She sank down into the rocking chair in front of the cold fireplace and began to rock her daughter. "It's all right, Ajei. It's all right, *awéé*," she whispered in Navajo. "My baby." When Ajei stopped crying and was once more settled against her chest, Chooli looked up. "We will stay here," she said firmly.

Franklin looked at her, watching sorrow and determination mix in her eyes. "Are you sure?"

"I'm sure," Chooli said. "I will never pretend I am happy about not going home, but neither would I be happy about putting the ones I love most at risk. I love it here on the plantation. We will make this our home now." Tears filled her eyes, but her smile was peaceful. "Perhaps someday we will return to my homeland, but now is not the time."

Franklin ached for his wife. He knew she was thinking of her family.

"You are my family now," Chooli whispered as if she could read his thoughts. "You and Ajei." She smiled softly. "And..."

Franklin tensed when her voice trailed off. He stepped closer to the rocker and knelt down in front of it so he could gaze into her eyes. "And?"

Chooli held his eyes. "And, whoever is growing inside me right now."

"You're pregnant again?" Franklin breathed.

Chooli nodded. "I just realized a couple of days ago. I didn't think it would change anything, because we made the trip here with me pregnant." She chuckled. "I didn't want it to change our plans. Of course, I keep forgetting how miserable I was for most of the trip here."

"And now you do? You want to change our plans? No doubts?" Franklin asked in an even voice. He wanted to jump up and down with joy at the prospect of staying, but he also wanted to make sure Chooli was certain.

"No doubts," Chooli replied, the sorrow fading from her eyes as relief to have finally made a decision took its place. Suddenly, she looked worried. "Are you really all right with staying?"

Franklin finally allowed his joy to show. "I'm fine with it," he promised, as he released a broad grin to spread across his face.

Chooli frowned. "You were going just for me?"

"Not *just* for you," Franklin insisted. "I love you, and I want you to be happy, but I also love *Dinetah*." He paused. "I believe staying here is best for our family right now, though. When that changes, we'll know. In the meantime, we'll make sure our children are safe, and we'll give them the best life we can."

He leaned forward to wrap Chooli and Ajei in his arms, his heart content.

*****

"Do you love the plantation?" Frances asked.

Felicia nodded. "Of course I do."

Frances eyed her more closely. She had discovered in the last several days that Felicia didn't volunteer much information on her own. She didn't seem to mind answering questions if you pushed for it, but she didn't waste words, either.

"You don't like to talk, do you?" Frances blurted out.

Felicia's eyes widened. "What do you mean?"

"Just what I said. You'll tell me things if I make you, but it gets real tiring at times," Frances said bluntly. She liked Felicia enormously, but she couldn't pretend she understood her. Carrie told her it was because Felicia had her mind on so many other things, but she didn't see why that would keep her from talking. Why not just talk about what she was thinking about?

"I'm sorry," Felicia said instantly.

Frances peered into her face. She had to admit she looked remorseful. "Why are you like that?"

Felicia looked troubled. "You're not the first person to tell me that," she admitted. "It's not that I don't want to talk..." Her voice trailed off. "I guess I just don't think about talking."

Frances stared at her. "You don't *think* about talking?" She was glad she and Felicia were alone in the wagon full of supplies. Their driver seemed focused on the spring-rain rutted road. He was nice enough, but he wasn't paying any attention to them. Frances had begged Carrie to let her and Felicia ride in the wagon, since the carriage was so crowded. "How can you not think about talking?"

Felicia shrugged. "I don't know. My mind just starts thinking about other things."

Frances regarded her thoughtfully. "I'm glad I'm not as smart as you are," she said after a long silence.

"You're plenty smart."

Frances was the one to shrug this time. "Maybe, but you don't have any way of knowing that yet. Carrie told me you're one of the smartest people she knows. She told me you would rather read and study than do anything else." She paused, almost afraid to ask the next question. "Is that true?"

Felicia looked off into the distance, and then turned her eyes back. "What if I *would* rather learn? Is there something wrong with that?" she asked defensively.

Frances struggled with her answer. "Don't you get lonely?" She thought of how her desire to learn at the orphanage had earned her nothing but pinches and silence from the other children.

"Sometimes," Felicia admitted, but her eyes were calm. "I'm not like other children, though."

"Really?" Frances asked with a sarcastic drawl, softening the words with a smile.

Felicia chuckled. "It used to bother me, but not anymore. It makes me sad sometimes when people like you think I don't like to talk, but I don't mind being different."

"You really don't like to talk? Or you just don't think about doing it?" Frances asked.

Felicia shook her head. "Does it matter?" she demanded in a frustrated voice. "We're talking now, aren't we? Why do I have to be the one to think about it?"

Frances cocked her head. "I reckon it don't really matter," she admitted. "And I guess you don't have to be the one to think about it." She paused. "Does it bother you that *I* want to talk?"

"No," Felicia said. "Mama tells me that I need to talk more." She met Frances' eyes honestly. "I like you. I like talking to you."

"You do?" Frances asked. "Truly?"

"Truly," Felicia assured her. She turned to stare out at the countryside. "Mama keeps telling me information is a good thing, but that if I don't know how to talk to people about things, all the knowledge won't do me any good."

Frances listened closely. "Do you reckon that's true?"

"I suppose I do. Mama is very smart about these things. She told me she used to be quiet when she was my age, but only because slaves weren't supposed to talk. She and Carrie would talk in Carrie's room at night sometimes, but mostly she was supposed to be seen and not heard. When she started teaching, though, she knew she needed to talk."

"I imagine that would help if you're a teacher," Frances said.

Felicia chucked. "Yes. Mama is a very good teacher."

Frances nodded, and then changed the subject. "Are you afraid to go back to Oberlin and live by yourself?" After three months without a family, she hoped she wouldn't have to live that way again for a long time, at least until she was all grown up.

Felicia frowned. "I am," she admitted. "I don't think I *should* be afraid, though. After all, I'm fourteen now."

Frances felt a surge of compassion that made her grab Felicia's hand. "So what? Fourteen isn't old."

"Maybe not," Felicia replied, "but it was my choice to stay, and I wouldn't change it if I could. Even if I am afraid. I *have* to finish my education."

There was something about the way she said it that made Frances peer at her more closely. "You *have* to? Why?"

"I don't know," Felicia admitted quietly. "I've been thinking a lot about what Sojourner Truth said at the graduation. She said our gut tells us what we're supposed to do. Chooli told me the same thing—that if I'm quiet inside and listen enough, I'll know what I'm supposed to do."

Frances nodded. Carrie had told her all about Chooli. She was looking forward to meeting her. She'd never met a real Indian. "And you believe you're supposed to finish school real fast?"

"Yes," Felicia answered. "I believe I'll know why in time, but I can't say I know right now."

"Why wouldn't your mama and daddy stay there with you while you go to school?"

"They would have," Felicia said. "But they are supposed to be back on the plantation. I know that for sure." Her eyes dropped. "I'm going to miss them terribly, but we have different paths to walk right now."

Frances shook her head. "I ain't never heard anyone talk like you. Especially someone about the same age as me."

Felicia lifted a brow. "Ain't is not a word."

"It is for me," Frances retorted. "I'm trying real hard to talk like all the rest of you, but it's gonna take me some time." She could feel defiance rising in her. "I ain't been to school like you've been. If you don't like me because of that, there ain't nothing I can do about it." Suddenly, she didn't want to watch every word she said. It was tiring.

Felicia shrugged. "It doesn't matter to me, but you better watch out for my mama. She doesn't know how to quit being a teacher. She corrected every word I ever said once I came to live on the plantation. Once you start school, she'll do the same thing to you."

Frances stared at her, seeing nothing but genuine friendliness in her eyes. She relaxed almost as quickly as she had tensed. "I don't mind," she admitted. "I might get tired of it, but I want to talk like the rest of you do. Especially since I'm going to be a doctor." As soon as the words came out of her mouth, she held her breath. She hadn't told anyone but Carrie about her dream. Would Felicia make fun of her?

Felicia nodded solemnly. "You'll make a good doctor."

Frances released her breath. "Do you really think so?" she asked. "Why?"

"Because you know what happens when there isn't a doctor around," Felicia said. "It's been very hard for women to become doctors, but by the time you're old enough to start medical school, it will probably be easier." She grinned. "It won't hurt that your mama is already a doctor."

Frances sucked in her breath again. "I can't call Carrie my mama yet," she said softly. "You think it hurts her?"

"It took me a long time for me to call Rose my mama," Felicia confessed. "I loved my own mama a lot."

Frances listened closely. They had never talked about Felicia watching her parents be murdered. As far as she knew, Felicia didn't know Carrie had told her about what had happened in Memphis. Frances had decided she wouldn't bring it up, because she didn't like to talk about her own parents dying. There were some things you just didn't need to keep reliving.

"My parents died when I was about your age," Felicia said.

Frances nodded, but didn't ask any questions. She just reached out and took hold of Felicia's hands.

Felicia took a deep breath, composing herself, and then smiled softly. "Thank you."

Frances knew that was all that was needed. Both had acknowledged the sadness of their loss. For now, nothing more needed to be said.

*****

Moses drew a deep breath when they rolled between the stone pillars lining the drive into Cromwell Plantation. He had to pinch himself every time to convince himself he was really co-owner. This time, however, was different. He had always been *preparing to leave.*

Now, he had come home to stay.

Rose reached over and took his hand. She squeezed it once, but had to release it quickly to secure little John, who was jumping up and down with glee.

"Home!" John yelled. "Home!" He raised his voice even louder. "I'm coming, Patches. I'm coming!"

Moses laughed, his heart full of joy that his family was now back where they belonged.

"Home!" Hope yelled, her tiny voice full of glee. "We coming, Gramma Annie! We coming!"

Moses gazed at his daughter, and then locked eyes with Rose. As thrilled as they all were to be home, he believed his mama was going to be even happier to have her family back with her again. Cromwell Plantation had truly become her home, and she had never said a word to discourage them leaving, but the glint in her eyes every time they departed told him how hard it was for her.

"I bet your mama is going to have a feast prepared," Rose said.

"You can be sure of it," Moses murmured. He sat back, content to drink in the fresh air as they rolled under the towering oaks spreading over the drive. His mind travelled back to the first time he had come down this road. He had been sitting in the back of a wagon with twelve other slaves purchased that day, nine years earlier. It had been night, but the moon had been bright enough to illuminate the trees they moved beneath. He had believed then, that his life was over. Separated from his mama and sisters on the auction block, there was no way to escape the raw pain ripping his insides apart.

Never could he have imagined...

Carrie, seated next to the driver, looked back at them. Her eyes were wide with excitement. "We're almost home," she said, laughing at John and Hope bouncing around on the seat. "I can't wait to show Frances the plantation."

Moses understood how thrilled she was to share Cromwell with her new daughter. He had felt the same way when he brought Felicia home from Memphis. There had been many times he'd been certain Carrie would never return to the plantation because of the pain of her memories. He was relieved that time was healing them, making room for new memories.

*****

Frances was speechless when they rounded the final curve. She stared at the three-story plantation home, its white paint gleaming in the midday sun. Banks of windows winked at her like shiny eyes. A row of deep green boxwood bushes lined the circular drive, and two huge oak trees stood as leafy sentinels.

When she turned her head, her mouth dropped the rest of the way open. There were several pastures, lined with white wooden fences, full of mares and dancing foals. She gasped as a huge gray horse broke away and thundered down the fence line, his joyful whinnies ringing through the air.

"That's Carrie's horse, Granite."

Frances nodded. She had guessed that already, but actually seeing the Thoroughbred in real life had taken her breath away. She pulled her eyes away from the horses to look back at the house. "That's where I'm going to live?" she breathed.

"I had the same reaction when I saw it," Felicia said with a laugh. "The little shack I lived in with my parents in Memphis was certainly not like this," she said dryly.

Frances continued to stare. "I've heard houses like this existed, but I thought people were making it up."

Felicia laughed as the wagon pulled to a stop. She stood and then jumped lightly from the wagon. "Come on. It's time for you to meet everyone."

Frances froze, overwhelmed and terrified. What had she done? Who was she to live in a place like this? Surely, it would take everyone only moments to know she didn't belong in such a fine place.

"Are you coming?" Felicia demanded.

Frances opened her mouth, but nothing came out. All she could do was shake her head.

"A little overwhelming, Frances?"

Frances gasped with relief when she heard Carrie's soft voice at her side, but she still couldn't speak. She nodded. The fact that the porch of the imposing house was now full of people, did nothing but make her more intimidated. There was no way she was stepping out of the wagon.

"It's your new home," Carrie said gently, reaching out a hand. She nodded to Felicia. "Go on, honey. We'll be there soon."

Frances grasped Carrie's hand like a lifeline as Felicia ran up onto the porch, launching herself into the arms of a black woman, but still she didn't move. "I can't live here," she whispered.

"Why not?" Carrie asked.

Frances shook her head vigorously. "It's too fine for the likes of me."

Carrie squeezed her hand tightly. "It's perfect for you," she said reassuringly. "I'm sure it's probably bigger than anything you're used to, but—"

"Probably?" Francis squeaked, interrupting her sentence.

Carrie laughed. "Will you at least come with me to meet Granite?"

"Your horse?"

Carrie nodded. "He'll be quite upset if we don't come to say hello."

Frances took a deep breath. "The people won't be mad if we see him first?"

"They won't be mad," Carrie promised. "And, I know Granite would like to meet you."

"How do you know that?" Frances demanded, suddenly terrified anew, because what if Granite *didn't* want to meet her. He was a *very* big horse.

Carrie laughed again. "Granite is my best friend. He loves everyone I love."

Frances turned to gaze at her, desperately needing reassurance. "And you love me?"

Carrie stepped close and wrapped her arms around Frances. "I love you with all my heart, Frances. You're safe here. This is your new home." She held her chin and tilted it up so Frances had to look at her. "I know it's overwhelming, but I promise you it will feel like home soon."

Frances couldn't stop trembling, but Carrie's words made her feel better. She leaned forward and allowed Carrie to help her from the wagon. Then, still holding her hand tightly, she walked over to the fence where Granite was prancing in place, his head held high and his tail waving like a flag. Frances had seen plenty of horses, but she had never seen one so beautiful.

Frances held back as Carrie threw her arms around Granite's neck. The horse nickered softly and pulled his head back to nibble at Carrie's head. Entranced, Frances couldn't hold back her giggle.

Carrie turned to smile at her, and held out her hand. "Will you come meet him?"

Frances took a deep breath. Part of her wanted to hold back from fear, but she remembered Sojourner Truth's words, as clearly as if she were standing in front of her speaking them. *Every time you say no to an opportunity, you're not just saying no to that one thing. You're saying no to all the other opportunities that follow, when you've had the courage to say the first yes.*

"Yes," Frances said firmly, as she stepped forward, not missing the shine of approval in Carrie's eyes.

"Hold out your hand," Carrie said. "Like this." She held out her palm.

Frances followed her example.

Carrie smiled, pulled something from her pocket, and laid it in Frances' hand.

Frances stared at the orange object. "You have a carrot in your pocket?"

Carrie grinned brightly. "May gave it to me this morning when we left Richmond. She knows they are always the first thing Granite wants. She harvested it from the garden last night."

Frances held her breath as Granite lowered his head. He nibbled the carrot gently off her hand, and then blew on her softly.

"He likes you," Carrie said.

Frances released her breath and tentatively put her hand out to touch Granite's nose. The horse stood completely still, his eyes fixed on her. "He's wonderful!" she breathed. "Oh, Carrie, he's wonderful."

*****

The sun was setting when Carrie noticed Frances fighting off sleep. She smiled tenderly, pulled her up from the rocker, and led her upstairs to the room that would be hers. Felicia would be sharing it with her while she was visiting, but she was still in the kitchen with her Grandma Annie. She pulled a nightgown from the bag Moses had carried up earlier, helped the sleepy little girl put it on, and then pulled back the covers.

Frances, barely able to keep her eyes open, crawled into bed. "Thank you for bringing me here," she murmured.

Carrie smiled. "You're welcome, honey." Once Frances had gotten over her initial fear, she'd had tremendous fun getting to know everyone. Felicia had shown her around the house, but Amber had stolen her away and introduced her to all the horses, and to Clint, Susan, and Miles. It had been so wonderful to sit on the porch with lemonade while she listened to Frances' laugh float to her on the breeze.

Carrie tucked the girl in and kissed her on the cheek. "Good night, Frances. I love you."

Frances smiled. "I love you too, Carrie," she whispered. Moments later she was asleep, her lashes fluttering as her breathing grew steady and even.

Carrie gazed down at her for several minutes, hardly able to believe she was at the plantation with her *daughter*. Tears filled her eyes. "I wish you were here, Robert. I wish you could meet Frances," she whispered, not wanting to disturb the little girl's sleep.

A surge of peace was all the answer she needed.

Chapter Twenty-Eight

Thomas took deep breaths of the late spring air, wishing it didn't carry the smell of smoke and exhaust. It was bad everywhere throughout the city, but down along the river where the factory was located, it was worse. He bit back a sigh.

"You're missing the plantation," Abby remarked.

Thomas shrugged. There was no reason to deny it, but he didn't want to fixate on it.

"What happened in Philadelphia?" Abby pressed. "I've only been home for two days, but I can tell something has changed."

Thomas considered her question. He'd thought he was doing a good job of concealing his feelings, but obviously he had been mistaken. "Did you go look at the new building today?"

Abby raised a brow. Evidently, he wasn't ready to answer her question. "I did."

Thomas waited a few moments, but she didn't offer anything else. He bit back another sigh, knowing this was her way of saying two could play the game of concealing information. He smiled half-heartedly. "I deserve that."

"You do," Abby said calmly.

"I don't know what I'm feeling," Thomas said, watching the bustle of the city as they traveled the road back to their home on the hill. Richmond seemed to get crazier with every passing day. He knew the city needed the growth and activity to recover from the war years, but it was increasingly exhausting.

"I think you do," Abby probed.

Thomas gritted his teeth, wishing she wasn't right. "Perhaps," he said. "I'm sorry." He shook his head in apology. "I just don't know how to communicate it."

"May is fixing strawberry shortcake tonight," Abby said. "We'll wait until we've had dinner to discuss anything. Strawberry shortcake should loosen your tongue," she predicted.

Thomas managed a chuckle. "Perhaps."

Abby eyed him for a long moment, and then answered his earlier question. "The building is fine. I believe it would be perfect for expansion, if we decide to do that."

Thomas turned to her. "Is it what you want to do?" He didn't want to put the decision off on her, but he very much wanted to know how she felt.

"I believe it will have to be a mutual decision," Abby replied carefully.

Thomas hoped he was concealing his impatience when he answered. "Of course. I'm just curious as to what you think."

Abby shook her head decisively. "We'll talk about it tonight, after strawberry shortcake."

Thomas knew there was no pressing her when she had that look in her eyes.

*****

"Care to go out on the porch?" Thomas invited.

Abby nodded her head quickly. "That sounds lovely. The world smells delightful tonight."

Thomas bit back the reply that wanted to escape his lips. Perhaps to a Philadelphia city girl, Richmond truly did smell delightful. All he could smell was the odor of smoke and coal fires mingled with lilac and the honeysuckle climbing the fence along the property border.

Abby settled on the porch swing, smiling graciously as she accepted the tray with two cups of hot tea that May handed her. "Thank you," she murmured. She waited until the door swung closed behind May, and then turned to Thomas. "We're alone now. Please talk to me."

Thomas took a deep breath, knowing the conversation could no longer be avoided. "Anthony and

I had a conversation in Philadelphia," he began. "We were talking about expanding the factory." He paused, knowing Abby would remain silent while he formulated his thoughts. "When I expressed reservations about moving forward with the expansion, he told me I needed to decide what was important to me."

"And have you?" Abby asked.

"I have," Thomas admitted, but was seized with sudden anxiety. What if Abby felt differently? He would never dream of forcing her out of the life she loved.

"I would like very much to hear it," Abby pressed.

Thomas sighed. Once he said the words, there would be no taking them back. "I've spent my life focused on making money," he began. "Anthony said something that struck me quite hard. He said that he makes money so he can be with the people he loves, and he is determined that money will never become more important than that." Thomas took a deep breath. "I'm no longer interested in expanding the factory, Abby. I believe we've done our part in rebuilding the South. I don't know how much longer I have to live, but I do know I want to spend whatever time I have left, doing the things I believe are important." He looked up and met Abby's eyes squarely. "I want to go home."

"Thank God."

Thomas blinked, not sure he had heard correctly. "Excuse me?"

"Thank God," Abby repeated. "I believe it would be a smart business move to buy the new building, and I believe we could make it profitable quickly enough to make it a viable business decision, but there is not one single particle of me that wants to do it."

Thomas furrowed his brow. "Do you truly mean that?"

"I do," Abby said firmly. "I've been feeling for a while that I'm ready to slow down and spend more time on the plantation, but knowing that I now have a granddaughter, as well as so many other people that I want to spend time with, has made that more of a reality." She reached over and took Thomas' hand. "I know we will continue to spend time in Richmond for a while, but I also believe we can spend more time on the plantation."

Thomas watched her closely as he made his next statement. "And perhaps work toward finding a buyer for the factory?" he said slowly.

"Yes," Abby agreed. "I've worked hard for the last twenty-five years, Thomas. I would like to think I've earned the right to step away from business."

Thomas slipped an arm around his wife's shoulder and pulled her close. "I was afraid you would be upset."

"Far from it," Abby assured him. "But I understand the fear. I was afraid *you* would be disappointed when you discovered I wasn't interested in expansion."

"Far from it," Thomas chuckled.

They sat in silence for a long while, letting the peace of the night wrap around them. The sun slipped low on the horizon, and then dipped beneath it, unleashing a canopy of stars that still managed to glimmer through the hazy air.

"We need to come up with a plan," Abby said after a long while.

"I agree," Thomas replied. His thoughts were spinning again. Deciding to step away, and actually doing it, were two different things. He didn't want to make any decisions that would put the factory at risk. Too many families were dependent upon the income. He and Abby could live off the money they had made all their lives, but families would be destroyed if they lost jobs. "Have you ever sold one of your factories?"

"No, but we're going to get a lot of experience," Abby said cheerfully. "We're smart enough to figure out the right ways to do it, and I can trust God that the right buyers are waiting who will follow in our footsteps."

Thomas sucked in his breath. "Do you really believe that?" He wished he could be so certain.

"I have to," Abby declared. "I've not given my life to create businesses that treat employees with respect and dignity, only to see some greedy person steal that away. I'm not worried about Philadelphia," she mused. "Jeremy is there. We can sell him the factories if he and Marietta want them, allowing them to pay us out of the profits. He can hire and train a new manager for Moyamensing in time. It will create a steady income for us, and it will give him a foothold he would not have otherwise. I trust him implicitly."

"As do I," Thomas agreed. "The Philadelphia factories could not possibly be in better hands. And yet, what if he and Marietta feel it is no longer safe for the twins? They may decide to move farther north."

Abby shrugged. "We'll cross that bridge if we come to it," she said casually. "Right now, we are making decisions we believe are right for *us*. None of us has the ability to predict the future. We'll just have to see what happens." She sipped from her tea as they swung gently back and forth. "I'm not sure what to do about Richmond, though," she admitted. "Pierre is learning to be a good manager, but I don't believe I trust him with the factory, or with all our employees," she said, gauging his reaction.

Thomas agreed. He had been watching their new manager closely. He liked Pierre, and he wanted to believe he was a good man, but he suspected the manager position was more than he could actually handle. Putting the entire factory in his hands was not something Thomas would even consider. "What do you think about Willard?"

Abby drew back with surprise. "Willard? He's been at the factory for only a year. And he has no business experience."

"Neither did you when you took over for your late husband," Thomas reminded her. He had been watching Willard Miller for the last several months. He and his wife, Grace, had become regular guests for dinner since Harold had done the interview with them for *Glimmers of Change*.

"That's true," Abby said. "But surely Willard is not ready for such a huge responsibility."

"Not now," Thomas agreed, "but I believe he could be. He's quite intelligent. He's pouring through the books I gave him."

Abby cocked her head. "The books you gave him?"

Thomas nodded. "Willard wants to be a businessman. He asked several months ago if I would share some books with him, so I sent him home with a stack." He took a breath. "I've been meeting with him on a weekly basis to mentor him. He asks quite keen questions, and he's very quick to pick up on things. He's even made some suggestions I've implemented in the last week while you were gone."

"You didn't tell me!" Abby exclaimed. "What a wonderful thing to do."

Thomas smiled. "He's a fine young man."

"So, you've been training him for this all along?" Abby asked, a hint of disappointment in her eyes.

Thomas understood immediately that she thought he had been hiding his plans from her. "Absolutely not," he said. "Until last week, I had every intention of expanding the factory and staying here in town to run everything. I was simply helping Willard because I've grown so fond of him and Grace." He took Abby's hand. "I would never do anything behind your back, my dear. I have far too much respect for you."

Abby sighed and laid her head on his shoulder. "Thank you, Thomas."

Another long silence enveloped them.

"You really believe Willard could take over the factory?" Abby finally asked.

"Perhaps it's wishful thinking," Thomas admitted, "but I believe he could." Thomas considered his next words carefully. "We could find many people with more business experience, but I doubt we could find anyone who would feel the way we do about running the factory. I've watched him with the other employees. He makes friends easily, and he treats everyone the same. It doesn't matter if they are black or white. He's eager to learn from everyone, and takes on jobs no one has given him to do. When I ask him why, he says he wants to learn everything in case we need his help in the future."

"What about Pierre?"

Thomas was struggling with that aspect of the decision. "I like Pierre, and I think he could be a good manager, but I don't believe I would ever feel comfortable leaving the factory in his hands," he admitted. "I can't imagine selling it to him one day. He's fair to everyone who works there, but I sense an edge to him around the black workers, especially if he doesn't think I'm watching." He shook his head. "There's something about him that I can't quite put my finger on. I just know I'm not comfortable with it."

Abby nodded. "I've felt the same thing," she admitted. "I don't spend as much time on the factory floor as you do, but I can sense the tension among a lot of our workers when he's around. That tension was never there when Jeremy was the manager." She frowned. "Have you talked to Marcus about it?"

Thomas nodded. Marcus was from the Black Quarter. He was a friend to the entire family, but he and Jeremy were especially close, and had worked closely together at the factory. "He hasn't said a whole lot, but he has told me we should be careful."

Abby looked at him sharply. "That's unusual for Marcus. He's usually very direct."

"I know," Thomas agreed. He had thought perhaps he was overreacting, but Abby's response made him realize he had been right to be concerned. "I'll talk to Marcus about it again in the morning."

Abby nodded and went back to the earlier part of their conversation. "Can we go out to the plantation soon?"

Thomas smiled. "I would like that. I probably need a few days here to take care of some things, but why don't I have Spencer take you out tomorrow?"

"I can't do that," Abby protested. "I just returned from the trip with Carrie. It wouldn't be fair to you. We'll do what needs to be done together, and then we'll go out."

Thomas waved his hand in the air. "Nonsense. I won't be far behind you. It would give me great pleasure if you would go."

Abby gazed at him. "I probably shouldn't agree, but I'm going to." Her eyes brightened with happiness. "I want you to spend more time with Frances," she said eagerly. "She's a very special little girl."

"I'm looking forward to it," Thomas agreed. "I want to ride with her all over the plantation like I did with Carrie when she was that age. Of course," he chuckled, "Carrie knew the plantation better than I did by that point. She only let me think I was showing her new things."

*****

Eddie opened the door of his home when he heard the quiet tap he was expecting. He remained silent as Marcus walked in, but his eyes widened when he saw that Marcus was not alone. "Who's this?" he asked sharply.

"Willard Miller," Marcus replied. "He's a good man. We want him here tonight."

Eddie wanted to argue, but he didn't have any facts to argue with. He'd never seen the white man standing in front of him. Willard was young, but he had the sharp look that said he had seen battle, and probably more pain than a man deserved to have. Eddie pushed down his misgivings. "Hello, Willard."

"Thank you for letting me be here, Eddie," Willard replied.

Eddie, who had learned to be cautious, merely nodded, careful to keep his face a mask. He trusted Marcus, but anyone could be fooled. His three years in Castle Thunder Prison had taught him that.

"Is Carl joining us?" Marcus asked.

Eddie nodded. "He'll be home in a few minutes. He was finishing up at the restaurant. Opal has a meeting at the church tonight." They had planned their meeting for this evening for that very reason. His wife was strong, but there was no reason to alarm her with suspicions. He knew their suspicions were justified, but it was too early to talk about them with anyone else yet.

"And Clark?"

"My brother is on his way home," Eddie replied. "Opal made a strawberry pie this morning before she left for the restaurant. You two want some?"

"Of course," Marcus said eagerly. He turned to Willard. "Opal is the best cook in Richmond."

Willard nodded. "That's what the Cromwells tell me."

Eddie eyed him sharply. "You friends with the Cromwells?"

Willard returned his gaze with unflinching eyes. "I'd like to think I am," he said. "I've been at the factory for a while, but last year I did an interview with Harold Justin for the book he and Matthew wrote."

"*Glimmers of Change*?" Eddie broke in to ask.

"That's the one," Willard answered. "Me and my wife, Grace, got along fine with Harold, so he took us back to the Cromwells for dinner that night. We have dinner there about once a week or so."

Eddie continued to gaze at him. He looked like he was telling the truth, and since Marcus worked at the factory, he would know if the man was lying.

"His wife, Grace, is at the meeting with Opal at the church," Marcus offered.

Eddie stared at him. "At the church? But..." There were certainly white people who came around the Black Quarter, but none of them went to the church meetings.

"Grace is black," Marcus said.

Eddie swung his eyes back to Willard.

"Grace is the finest woman I know," Willard said quietly. "I grew up in Alabama. I served in the army, but ended up the guest of Rock Island Prison in Illinois for most of the war."

Eddie understood the shadows in Willard's eyes. "Go on," he said.

"When the war was over, I was told to walk back home to Alabama. I was doing that, but got real sick. Grace and her family found me on the road. They took me in and saved my life." He smiled. "Grace and I fell in love. Now we're married."

Eddie gazed at him. "You picked an interesting place to live," he said bluntly. "Folks don't take too much to mixed-race marriages around here."

"Nope," Willard agreed, "but as far as I can tell, there is nowhere in the country that does. When I got a job at Cromwell Factory, we decided to take our chances."

"How'd you get the job?" Eddie asked. He was relaxing, but you couldn't know too much about a man if you were supposed to trust him with information that could end up with you dead.

Willard smiled. "I met Matthew Justin during my travels. He helped me get the job."

Eddie relaxed the rest of the way. Matthew Justin was one of the best judges of character he had ever met. "I'm glad you're here," he said warmly.

"You may not be when I tell you what I have to say," Willard said darkly.

Marcus held up a hand. "We're waiting on Carl and Clark. I say we have some of that strawberry pie."

Eddie was worried by the look he had seen glinting in Willard's eyes, but he agreed with Marcus' decision to wait on his brother and son. "I'll dish it up," he offered. Knowing Clark and Carl would want some, he filled four plates with the delicious pie.

Willard moaned when he took his first bite. "This is wonderful," he said. He looked at Eddie with narrowed eyes. "How do you stay so skinny with a wife who can cook like this?"

Eddie chuckled. "It don't matter how much I eat," he said ruefully. "Opal has been trying to put weight on me since we got married. I am her constant disappointment. She says I'm very bad advertising for her restaurant."

Carl breezed in through the back just as Eddie finished speaking. "Not bad enough to keep the place from being packed, Daddy, so I wouldn't worry about it."

"I don't," Eddie agreed. "As long as she tries to fatten me up, I'll always have plenty of food. After three years in Castle Thunder, I don't ever want to be hungry again."

Willard eyed him with interest. "I've heard real bad things about that prison."

"You know of one that anybody says *good* things about?" Eddie retorted.

"Can't say as I do."

Eddie introduced Willard to his son. "My boy, Carl, is seventeen." He understood the reservation that sprang into Willard's eyes. "He's been working with us for the last two years," he assured him. "You ain't got nothing to worry about."

Willard nodded slowly, but his eyes remained cautious.

Carl took a bite of pie and smiled. "I watched my Daddy taken off to prison when I was just a kid. It was the same day my mama died in an explosion at the armory during the war. I know the risks, but I ain't going to sit back and do nothing. My daddy taught me to be real careful."

Eddie was proud of the humble confidence in his son's eyes. Carl did, indeed, know the risks of the work they did.

The front door opened again.

"Hello, Clark," Marcus called. "This last plate of pie is yours, but I'm on my last bite. If you don't grab it fast, I'm going to claim it."

Clark snatched his plate and dug in. Then he saw Willard sitting across the room. His eyes shuttered as he looked at Eddie.

"It's all right," Eddie said. "Marcus brought him. Willard Miller works at the factory. He's friends with the Cromwells and Matthew Justin."

"You sure about that?" Clark asked suspiciously.

"I'm sure," Eddie said. "He's got news for us."

"What kind of news?" Clark asked as he shoved another forkful of pie into his mouth.

Eddie looked around the room. "We're all here. I say we get started. Marcus, why don't you begin?"

Marcus put down his empty plate and stretched his long legs in front of him. He leaned back against the rungs of the wooden chair that was far too small for his muscular body. "There be something wrong at the factory," he said bluntly.

"Why do you say that?" Eddie asked, alerted by the tension in his friend's eyes.

Marcus hesitated, searching for words. "It's more a feeling than anything," he admitted.

"I agree with his feeling," Willard said. "Things haven't been right since Jeremy left."

Eddie had a strong feeling there was something wrong as well, but more concrete information would certainly be helpful. He'd talked to several of the men who worked there. All of them were uneasy. "Anybody would have a tough time taking Jeremy's place," he argued. "Is it the Pierre fella you're worried about?"

"Yes," Marcus said. "It's nothing that jumps out at me, but everything in me says we got to be careful."

Eddie considered his words, but he was more affected by the look in his eyes. "We've learned to listen to our guts," he said. "What do you suspect?"

"I wish I knew," Marcus growled.

"I think he's here to harm the factory," Willard stated.

Eddie swung his eyes to him. "Why?"

Willard shrugged. "It's more of a feeling, but I got reasons for feeling it."

"Why?" Eddie repeated. He respected what their feelings were telling them, but he needed more facts if they were supposed to do anything about it.

"Pierre is not who he says he is," Willard said slowly. "It's not real obvious things that he does, but I don't know a black person in the place who is comfortable with him. I think if it were up to him, there wouldn't *be* one black person in the place."

"Have you told Mr. Cromwell how you feel?" Eddie asked sharply.

"Not yet," Willard admitted. "I meet with him every Thursday night, though. I've been watching until I could decide if my feelings seem justified." He sighed. "I'll meet with Thomas in two nights. I'm going to talk to him then."

"Why do you care?" Eddie demanded.

Willard met his eyes evenly. "My wife is black," he said, "and she's pregnant. Having a mixed-race baby made Jeremy and Marietta leave Richmond. I don't want to have to do the same thing, so if I want things to be different, I have to change them." He paused. "Changing them means making things better for every race. The thing is, I understand how the white men feel. Most Southern white men are hurting as bad as black folks. They're having a hard time getting jobs, and they feel like their whole life was destroyed."

Tension crackled in the room.

Willard held up a hand before the others could respond. "I didn't say I think they're right. I'm just saying I understand. I'm trying to help the whites at the factory see a different way to handle things." He pursed his lips. "I think Pierre is here to stir things up."

"Why?" Eddie demanded again, his mind whirling.

"Because not many people like the fact that Mr. and Mrs. Cromwell have as many black people working in their factory as white people," Willard said.

"He's right," Marcus added. "There has been talk floating around that there is a plan to hurt the factory."

"How?" Eddie snapped. The Cromwells had been very good to his family. He was not going to let anything happen if he could help it.

Both Marcus and Willard shrugged, frustration filling their faces.

"All we know to do is watch," Marcus said helplessly, his eyes flashing with anger.

"And we set up guards," Eddie snapped, a plan taking shape in his mind. "Every black man who works at that factory lives here in the quarters. They will all be willing to help."

"And start a fight if someone comes to hurt the factory?" Marcus demanded. "That could end up going very badly."

"If need be." Eddie stayed firm. He knew none of them wanted that, because it would bring the wrath of the police down on them, but what choice did they have? If the factory was destroyed, the loss of income would hit the Black Quarters hard.

"How can I help?" Carl asked.

Eddie wanted to tell his son to stay out of it, but one black man's fight was *all* their fight. "Listen. You know we hear a lot of things in the restaurant. Most white folks talk too much. It's like they think we can't hear or we're too stupid to understand them." He managed a chuckle. "So, we use it to our advantage. I'm going to have a group of men go down to the factory every night for a while, until we figure out what is going on. Willard, let us know what Thomas says after you talk to him. We'll also talk to some of the other men who work there and see if they suspect anything." He met each man's gaze around the table. "If something is going on, we'll figure it out."

Clark stood. "I'm meeting with some of the militia tonight. Many of them work at the factory. I'll start setting up units to go down every night."

"Tell them to stay out of sight," Eddie said sharply. "They should be close in case anything happens, but if they get spotted, it could bring a heap of trouble down on us."

The five men all nodded solemnly.

Chapter Twenty-Nine

Abby smiled with joy when Frances dashed out across the porch and down to the carriage.

"Oma! Oma!"

Abby felt tears choking her throat as Frances' arms wrapped around her neck. She had dreamed of a granddaughter for so long. The pain of holding Bridget's tiny, dead body in her arms after they pulled her from Carrie had haunted her for months. To have a living granddaughter was such an answer to her prayers. She hugged Frances hard, and then held her back. "You've already grown!" she exclaimed. "How is that possible?"

Frances giggled. "Annie says she is gonna put more meat on my bones."

Abby felt her throat thicken again. She had never heard the little girl *giggle* before. "If Annie says she will, then she will," she assured her.

"I've never seen so much food before," Frances confided, lowering her voice almost to a whisper.

Abby knew that was true. "Do you have a favorite food yet?"

Frances frowned. "A favorite food?" She scrunched up her face and thought deeply. "I suppose it would have to be fried chicken. I ain't never had it before I come here."

Rose walked out onto the porch as she was talking. "Ain't isn't a word, Frances. It wasn't a word yesterday, and it's not a word today."

Frances sighed. "I had to start school, Oma. Felicia told me Miss Rose would start correcting everything I said. She was right."

Abby laughed. "You'll survive, my dear," she said teasingly. "Do you like school?"

Frances brightened. "I do! All the other children are real nice," she exclaimed, and then hesitated.

"What is it?" Abby asked gently. She wondered if Frances was having trouble being in a school with black children.

"It makes me sad that not all the children eat as well as I do," Frances said. "I know some of them are hungry. Not all of them even bring a lunch."

Abby locked eyes with Rose over the little girl's head. She knew they were both touched by her compassion. She also knew that Frances must have spent many days hungry in the past.

"I have an idea to help them," Frances continued.

"You do?" Abby asked in amazement, wondering how many children were in the school. Frances had only been here for two weeks, and she was already looking for ways to make things better.

"Yes," Frances replied. "I talked to Miss Lillian about it. She's going to have a lot of the parents come to plant a big garden outside the school. I know most of them have gardens at home, but there must not be enough for them to bring to school, so we are going to grow it ourselves."

"What a wonderful idea! That will make a big difference," Abby said warmly.

"I hope so," Frances said. "Carrie is gonna give me all the seeds to plant the garden. Parents are gonna help, but mostly it will be students who do everything."

Abby looked up when Rose cleared her throat.

Frances grinned. "Miss Rose clears her throat when I say something wrong." She thought intensely for a moment, and then her eyes cleared. "Going to," she said triumphantly. "I said gonna. I should have said *going to*."

"Very good," Rose congratulated her. "And I love your idea. Lillian told me she wanted to talk to me about something, but we haven't had time yet."

"That's only part of it," Frances said, her voice a bit uncertain.

"Oh?" Abby asked, leaning down to look into her eyes. "What is the rest of it?"

"Well..." Frances murmured, "the garden is a good start, but we need more for everyone to eat. Miss Lillian and I decided cornbread would be a good thing, because it fills up stomachs."

"That sounds like a good idea."

Frances continued to gaze at her. "I think so, but it will take quite a lot of cornmeal to make that much cornbread, Oma."

Abby hid her smile as she continued to listen.

"Miss Lillian said there are parents who will cook it all and bring it to the school, but..." Frances hesitated, seeming to suddenly be floundering.

"You need money for the cornmeal," Abby finished.

"Yes!"

Frances eyed her expectantly, but didn't say anything else. Abby just looked at her. She was quite impressed with how the little girl had worked her way around to asking for money, but she needed to finish what she had started.

"Oma...?"

"Yes, Frances?" Abby smiled softly, trying to make it easier for her.

"When I was at the orphanage, they had something they called patrons. From what I could tell, it meant they gave money so everyone could eat."

"Yes, that's what it means," Abby replied, once again catching Rose's eyes. She could tell they both were fighting laughter, but Rose had the advantage of being *behind* Frances. She bit her lip harder.

Frances took a deep breath. "Oma, would you be a patron for the school?" she blurted. "Will you give us money to buy cornmeal? Just for the kids who can't eat?"

Abby pretended to ponder the question, before she slowly nodded her head. "Why, yes. I believe that would be a very worthy cause."

Frances' face split with a broad grin. "Really, Oma? Really?"

Abby laughed now, and reached down to give Frances another hug. "I'm happy to do it. I do believe you're going to be very good one day at asking for money."

Frances frowned. "Maybe, but I think it would probably be more fun if I was the one being asked. I'd rather make lots of money, and then give it away."

"That is certainly more fun," Abby agreed solemnly. She slid her arm around Frances' waist. "Where is Carrie?"

"At the clinic," Frances said. "She told me I could go with her when school is out for the summer."

Abby cocked her head. "You're not in school today."

Frances sighed. "I'm not in the school *building*, but Miss Rose turned the *house* into a school," she said dramatically. "She is helping me catch up."

"Good for her," Abby said. "What are you learning?"

"Arithmetic." Frances sighed and rolled her eyes.

"I thought you *wanted* to learn and go to school," Abby reminded her.

"I do," Frances insisted, "but..."

"But what?"

"But Amber was going to take me riding today," Frances blurted out, her eyes shining with pleasure. "Carrie has been teaching me how to ride."

Abby read the rest of the story in the little girl's eyes. "And now it's all you want to do."

"Exactly!" Frances said, a triumphant expression on her face as she glanced back at Rose with an impish grin. "I knew you would understand."

"Oh, I do," Abby assured her. "I understand that the faster you learn your arithmetic, the faster you will get to go riding." She laughed and waved her hand toward the house. "It's time for you to go back to school, young lady."

Frances' triumphant expression faded, but she chuckled. "Felicia told me it wouldn't do any good to try and get out of it."

"You should listen to her," Abby answered. She looked up at the porch. "Hello, Annie. How are you?"

"I'm doin' right good, Miss Abby," Annie said. "I see Frances be tryin' to work her charms on you, too."

"I wouldn't want to be left out," Abby said lightly. She eyed the tray Annie was holding. "Do I see molasses cookies?" she asked hopefully.

"And lemonade," Annie answered.

Frances spun around, her eyes wide with delight. "Molasses cookies?"

"Which ain't for you, little lady, till you be done with your schoolwork," Annie scolded. "Get on back into that house."

Frances scowled. "Ain't is not a word, Annie," she said primly.

"Ain't is *my* word," Annie retorted, her eyes dancing with fun. "Ain't no little girl who tells me how to talk is gonna eat my cookies."

"Gonna isn't a w—" Frances snapped her lips closed. She looked to Rose for help.

Rose grinned. "There are some battles that aren't worth fighting. Especially with a woman who can cook like my mother-in-law. Unfortunately for you," she continued, "you have nothing to trade for the right to speak incorrectly, so you have to learn to do it correctly."

"It ain't...It's not fair," Frances protested.

Abby hid her smile again, knowing it was this very spirit that had enabled Frances to endure all she had been through. She was quite certain Carrie had been just this way when she was a child. "Go on and finish your schoolwork," she urged. "I would love to go riding with you later."

Frances brightened immediately. "Really? You know how to ride a horse?"

"Certainly," Abby retorted. "I can outride you, granddaughter of mine."

"We'll see about that,' Frances teased before she turned and raced into the house, letting the screen door slam behind her. Rose grinned, following not far behind.

Annie shook her head. "I declare. That little girl be somethin', all right."

Abby allowed laughter to shake her body. "Carrie is going to have her hands full," she agreed.

"I don't know 'bout that. She gives the rest of us a hard time, but she done worships Miss Carrie."

Abby smiled softly. "Carrie saved her."

"I don't think she'll eber forget that," Annie replied. "And besides, that little girl got a heart of gold. There ain't a one of us that ain't in love with her." She laid down the tray, and turned toward the house. "You enjoy that, Miss Abby. I got to go in and finish cookin' supper for everyone."

Abby relaxed into a rocker. It was not very often that she could sit on the porch with only her thoughts for company. She closed her eyes, allowing the soft spring air to wrap her in its comforting embrace. The raucous caws of blue jays mixed with the sound of buzzing bees and the playful whinnies of the foals in the fields. Wonderful aromas blew in from every direction. The smell of fresh cut hay, the first of the season, wrapped around her like a blanket. She sighed, so very glad she had agreed to Thomas' insistence that she come to the plantation early. She could hardly wait, though, until he got here and could spend more time with Frances. She dreamed of the hours they would spend riding together.

*****

Abby was still resting on the porch when Carrie rode up on Granite.

Carrie smiled and waved, handed off Granite to Amber, and then ran up on the porch. "What are you doing here?"

"Is it too soon for me to be here?" Abby teased.

"Hardly," Carrie retorted. "You and Father spend far too little time here. I keep hoping that will change, but I know you two are married to the factory."

"Not as much as you might think," Abby replied.

Carrie gazed at her for a minute and then sank down in one of the rockers. "What are you talking about? I can always tell there is more than you are saying when you use that tone of voice."

Abby smiled, and then explained briefly. "Your father and I are going to spend much more time here," she finished. "We hope within six months to come home, making short trips to Richmond only when we need to."

Carrie's mouth opened, but no sound came out.

"Surprised?"

"Shocked would be more appropriate," Carrie finally replied. "Father is really coming home? Back to Cromwell Plantation?"

"He's never quit loving it, Carrie."

"I know," Carrie said quickly, "but you remember how hard it was for Father to be here after my mother died. Ever since the war, he seemed so content to be in Richmond. I know he enjoyed his visits, but it felt like he was most comfortable in the city."

Abby nodded. "I suppose that was true for a while." She paused. "I guess the same thing was true for me," she said thoughtfully. "We were focused on building the factory, and on doing what we could to rebuild the South."

"What has changed?"

"We have, I suppose," Abby said. "We're getting older..."

"You're not old!" Carrie protested.

"I didn't say we were old," Abby laughed. "I said we're getting *older*. There is a difference, my dear."

"I will concede that point," Carrie replied. "But what has made you change?"

Abby shrugged. "I told you on New Year's Day that I wished we could slow down and spend more time on the plantation."

"And then you talked to me about your plans for expanding into a new building in Richmond," Carrie said. "That didn't sound like slowing down to me."

Abby chuckled. "I will concede that point." She sobered. "I suppose it was two things. The thing that changed it for me was your adopting Frances. I have a granddaughter now. One I very much want to spend time with. Thinking about Frances made me realize how much I want to spend more time with all those I love. I don't know how much time I have left," she said.

"None of us do," Carrie said solemnly.

Abby nodded, knowing she was thinking of Robert.

Carrie looked pensive for several moments. "You said there were two things," she reminded her.

"I did," Abby agreed. "Anthony said something to your father that made him realize he wanted to come home."

"Anthony?" Carrie echoed.

Abby revealed what Thomas had shared with her. "Your father has decided to spend the rest of his life doing what he believes is most important, Carrie. Spending time with you...getting to know Frances...being home on the plantation. It's what he wants more than anything."

"I have one more thing to thank Anthony for," Carrie murmured.

"Do you love him?"

"Yes," Carrie replied. "He's a wonderful man."

"But...?"

"But I don't know what I'm going to do with that yet," Carrie said, her words more hesitant now. "Sometimes, I think I should go ahead and marry him, but then something inside stops me."

"Is it Robert?"

Carrie met her eyes evenly. "I don't think so. I would have said yes at first, but I don't feel that way anymore. I believe Robert would want me to be happy. If marrying Anthony would make me happy, I believe he would want that for me."

"You're not sure it would make you happy?" Abby asked gently. She believed Anthony was a wonderful man, but only Carrie could know what was right for her.

"I don't know," Carrie said. "It's really that simple. I don't know. I would think I would *know*, really know, if marrying Anthony would make me happy. Since I don't, I'm not ready to make that decision."

Abby smiled. "You're comfortable with yourself." The knowledge made her very happy.

"I suppose I am," Carrie acknowledged. "I loved Robert with all my heart, but there was also a part of me that thought I needed to marry him in order to be truly happy. I'm glad I did, and I have no regrets, but..."

"You know your life can be wonderful and fulfilling without a man," Abby finished for her.

"Yes," Carrie said softly. "I'm glad you understand. Most women would think I was quite mad to not jump at the chance to marry Anthony."

"He loves you," Abby replied. "He'll wait for you."

Carrie looked at her oddly. "Will he? I'm not sure how I feel about that. I don't want to think I'm holding him back from finding a woman who will love him in return."

"I'm afraid that's not your choice, my dear," Abby said gently. "Anthony will be here in a few days." She hid her smile at Carrie's look of total delight. Her daughter might not be ready to make a commitment to marry Anthony, but she clearly loved him very much.

"He will?"

"Yes. He's coming with your father. We received a telegram yesterday, saying he was coming to Richmond. Your father is finishing up some business before he leaves. Anthony will come with him."

Carrie smiled. "I'm glad. I want him to meet Frances."

"He'll love her," Abby assured her.

"How could he not?" Carrie asked lightly. "Everyone loves Frances."

"That's true." Abby didn't say anything more. She was quite confident the day would come when Carrie was able to acknowledge that she wanted to spend her life with Anthony, but she needed to come to it in her own time, and in her own way.

*****

Carrie was startled out of her thoughts when the front door slammed open and Frances ran out onto the porch. "Whoa! Is there a fire somewhere?"

"No," Francis replied with a broad grin. "But I finished my arithmetic. I wanted to escape before Miss Rose decided I need to learn something else." She clasped her hands and looked toward the barn. "Is it time to go riding? Oma said we could all go riding."

"Oh, she did, did she?" Carrie teased. "I've had a long day at the clinic. I'm not sure I want to go." She stretched her arms above her head and yawned.

Frances peered into her face for a long moment, and then shook her head. "Nope. I can tell you want to go."

Carrie smiled, her heart melting. "You think you know me that well, do you?"

Frances grinned again. "Yes." Then a look of uncertainty crossed her face. "Am I right?"

"You're completely right," Carrie agreed. "Let me change out of this ridiculous dress. I've got someplace special to take you today."

Frances clapped her hands and jumped up and down. "Can I go out to the stable and help Amber get the horses ready?"

"Absolutely. Tell Amber I want to ride Granite again. He hasn't had enough exercise today."

"All right," Frances agreed. "Who should I ride today?"

Carrie hesitated, but decided it was time. "Why don't you ride Peaches?"

"The beautiful palomino mare that Moses brought home two nights ago?" Frances asked in a voice of disbelief. "Really?"

"Really," Carrie answered. "She's a lovely mare, has good gaits, and is quite gentle. I want to see if she is as perfect as her owner said she is."

Frances stared at her. "And you trust me to ride her?"

"I do," Carrie assured her. "Should I not?"

"Oh, no," Frances said hastily. "You can trust me. I would love to ride her!"

"Then go get her ready," Carrie directed. "Abby and I will join you in a few minutes."

Frances dashed off the porch. "Hurry!" she called back over her shoulder.

Abby was already moving toward the door. "I'm going to change, too. Spencer carried my bag up before he drove back to the city."

"Spencer has already left?" Carrie was disappointed. "I hoped to talk to him tonight. I thought he would go back in the morning."

"I tried to talk him into it, but he insisted he had to get back," Abby responded.

Carrie stared at her when she hesitated. "What aren't you saying?"

Abby shook her head. "Nothing. I'm a little uneasy, but I have no reason to be."

Carrie stiffened. She couldn't help looking around for anyone lurking in the trees. She supposed she would always have that reaction. "Uneasy about what?" she demanded.

Abby shook her head again. "I don't know," she admitted. "I think it's just that I'm not used to playing hooky from my life. I'm glad I'm here, but I will admit it feels rather odd to not be at the factory."

"You seem to be forgetting how well I know you," Carrie muttered. "Will you at least promise to tell me when you know what is bothering you?"

"I promise," Abby said. She reached for the door handle. "But right now, I'm going to change so we can take our beautiful girl for a ride!"

*****

Frances stared around in awe when they broke out into the clearing by the river. "It's so beautiful!" she cried. "I've never seen anything so beautiful in my life."

Carrie could not have agreed with her more. Her special place by the river was beautiful in any season, but it was even more spectacular in May. Spring had exploded throughout the entire South, but it seemed to be making more of a statement in this place she loved so much.

Wisteria spilled purple blooms from the trees, their heady fragrance perfuming the air. Virginia bluebells crowded the ground, while columbines waved their coral heads in the breeze. Delicate white spring cress gave a touch of elegance among the brilliant fire pinks. A light breeze tossed the limbs of the trees, making the leaves dance in time with the whitecaps breaking on the river.

Carrie took a deep breath, feeling the expected magic fill her heart. She looked at Frances' face as her daughter gazed around with a reverent hush. Carrie had always dreamed of sharing this place with Bridget. It relieved her to know sharing it with Frances brought her just as much joy.

"What is this place?" Frances asked. "It's very special."

"How do you know that?" Carrie asked.

Frances shook her head. "I can just feel it." She turned to look at Carrie. "Is it a special place?"

"The most special place in the world," Carrie answered, reaching out to hug her daughter close. "I found this place when I was your age. My parents didn't know I used to go out riding on my own. It would have scared my mother to death, and I didn't want Father to have to hide it from her. By the time I finally got permission, I had been coming here for over a year." She laughed. "I probably shouldn't be telling you this..."

"You're certainly giving her ideas," Abby acknowledged wryly.

"How did you find it?" Frances demanded.

"Just roaming around," Carrie answered. "My most favorite thing to do was to find deer trails through the woods so I could follow them. I never knew where they would go. One day, I followed a new deer trail that brought me here."

"And you've been coming here ever since?" Frances looked around again. "I used to dream of a place like this," she said quietly.

There was something in Frances' voice that made Carrie look at her more closely. "What do you mean?"

Frances turned to stare at her, uncertainty making her gaze waver.

"Go ahead," Carrie encouraged her. "What do you want to say?"

Frances still hesitated. "You'll think I'm silly," she protested.

"I won't," Carrie promised. "I used to dream about all kinds of things, too. I still do," she admitted.

Frances took a deep breath. "I didn't use to dream of a place *like* this." She lifted her amber eyes to look into Carrie's. "I dreamed of *this* place. I feel like I've been here before." She took a deep breath and waited for Carrie's reaction.

Carrie took a deep breath of her own as she felt warmth spread through her. She gripped Frances' hands tightly. "I have no trouble believing that."

"You don't?" Frances breathed with a look of relief.

"No," Carrie assured her. "I have a feeling God knew you would become my daughter a long time ago. Don't you think God would want you to feel at home here?"

"So, you think I had the dream so I would feel at home here?"

"Don't *you*?" Carrie asked gently.

Frances nodded, slowly at first, and then more firmly. "I do," she agreed. She pulled away from Carrie to walk around the clearing. "I love it here," she whispered. "Can I come here whenever I want to?"

Carrie smiled. "I want you to get more comfortable riding first, but then yes, you may come here whenever you want."

Frances grinned. "I think I'll get comfortable riding Peaches very quickly," she proclaimed.

"Oh?" Carrie asked with a raised brow. "Why do you think that?"

"She fits me," Frances said earnestly. "She's so gentle, and she's so smooth." She paused. "I think she really likes me, and I already love her," she proclaimed.

"I'm glad to hear that," Carrie said lightly, "especially since I bought Peaches for you."

Frances had turned to stare at the river, but now she swung slowly back. "What did you say?"

"I said I'm glad to hear you love her, because I bought Peaches for you." Carrie gazed at her daughter with love, remembering the day her father had presented her with Granite.

Frances turned to look at Abby.

Abby nodded. "If Carrie says Peaches is yours, it's true."

Frances looked back at Carrie, her expression saying she still wasn't at all convinced. "Peaches is *my* horse?"

"Well, only if you want her," Carrie teased. "If you don't, I can do something else with her."

"No!" Frances cried, rushing into Carrie's arms. "I want her! Of course, I want her."

Carrie was alarmed when the little girl's voice choked with tears. "Honey, what's wrong?"

Frances took a deep breath. "Nothing is *wrong*," she said. "Everything is right. It is so right."

"And that's making you cry, because you never thought your life could be like this," Abby said.

Frances turned to look at her Oma. "That's right," she said, glad to not have to find words to explain what she was feeling. "I got real used to things being bad. I just kinda expected that things would go wrong. That way I wasn't surprised.

Abby wrapped an arm around her granddaughter. "There will always be things that don't go the way we want them to," she said softly. "Hard things will happen that cause us pain. But," she said, "there will always be enough good things to balance them out."

"Always?" Frances asked.

"That's been my experience," Abby replied.

"And mine," Carrie added.

"What about losing Bridget? Do you think enough good things will happen to balance that out?"

Carrie thought for a moment and then began to smile. "Frances, I know that's true. Many good things have happened since losing Robert and Bridget, but you becoming my daughter has been the best thing of all. The joy of you being my little girl has balanced everything out." Tears filled her eyes as she realized how true it was. She knew she would always miss Bridget, but the thought of her daughter no longer caused her pain.

Chapter Thirty

Anthony swung from the train. He was glad to be back in Richmond, but he was mostly excited because he would be leaving for the plantation with Thomas tomorrow. He could hardly wait to see Carrie again and have a chance to meet Frances. He looked toward the carriage row eagerly, disappointed to discover it was empty. He considered walking to Thomas' house with his luggage, but didn't relish the idea of trudging up the hills on a hot spring day. He dropped his bag, and settled back to wait. Richmond was getting busier every day.

As Anthony waited, he thought about the fact that there were not enough carriages. His thoughts began to form into a plan, congealing in his mind with seemingly little effort. He smiled slightly as he realized his frustration could actually be an opportunity. His smile widened as he glanced down the row of other stranded businesspeople checking their pocket watches with impatient looks. He began to calculate how much it would cost to buy wagons and hire drivers. He would need a place to stable them, but certainly he could find enough stalls. In time, he could build his own stables, making sure his horses received the best of care.

Even if the economy took a dive, there would always be need for transportation in a growing city. The investment would be relatively low, but the returns would come in for a long time. He already knew that if he treated his drivers fairly, making sure they were compensated better than any other drivers in the city, he would never run out of people eager to work for him. The Cromwells had taught him that valuable lesson.

His thoughts were interrupted by a carriage rolling to a stop in front of him. "Church Hill?" Anthony called.

The driver nodded, jumped down from his seat, and grabbed Anthony's bag. "I'll get you there quick as I can, mister."

Anthony was already calculating how long it would take to get this new business venture up and running. The one thing he had learned well from his father was the value of building a business that didn't require your constant presence and involvement. He wanted to make money, but he also wanted to live a good life. He was certain it was possible. All one had to do was keep their eyes open for the right opportunity.

"What you do, mister?" the driver asked once they had pulled away from the station.

"I'm a businessman," he informed him, making a rapid decision as he spoke. "I'm starting a new carriage service here in Richmond." There was no time like the present to discover if his idea had as much validity as he believed it did.

"That right?" the driver drawled. "I reckon we need another one. There sure ain't enough of us to get everybody where they need to be."

"It certainly looks like that," Anthony agreed. "Do you have any friends looking for work?"

"I might," the man answered shrewdly. "Guess it depends on how much you be paying them."

"I'm still working that out," Anthony admitted, knowing the man driving the carriage was his best source of information. "Can you tell me what a good wage is?"

The man cocked his head. "I don't know that I would call it a *good* wage," he stated, "but I'll tell you what I get paid."

He named a figure much lower than Anthony would have anticipated. "Is that what everyone pays?"

"Pretty much," the man grunted. "It ain't real easy to get a job in this city, so we gots to take what they pay us."

"I see," Anthony murmured. He continued to calculate rapidly in his head. When he was sure of his figures, he said casually, "I'm prepared to pay more than that."

The man eyed him keenly. "How much more?"

"I don't believe paying by the hour is the best way to do business," Anthony replied. "I also believe that men who are willing to work hard deserve to be paid more."

"How do you do that?" the driver asked.

"I still have some final calculations to make," Anthony responded, "but I figure I need to make a certain amount from every carriage I buy. The rest of the money made that day would go to the driver."

"How much you need to make?" the man demanded.

Anthony appreciated the calm caution in the man's eyes. He also understood why the driver's eyes widened in disbelief when he named the figure.

"And the rest would go to the driver?" he asked with astonishment.

"That's right," Anthony answered, more sure than ever that his plan was solid.

"That's almost triple what drivers make right now. Why you gonna pay that much?" the man demanded.

"Don't you think you're worth it?"

The man cocked his head. "I am," he said, "but I can't say that about every driver. There be a lot of lazy men driving carriages." He shook his head. "As hard as jobs be to come by, it seems right stupid to me to not work hard, but I ain't got no say what anyone else does."

"Which is exactly why I'm doing things the way I told you," Anthony answered. "If a driver is working hard, they will make a lot more money than they can make now. If they're not working hard, and they don't take as many passengers, they won't make as much. Regardless, I will make what I need to make from every carriage."

"That's smart," the man admitted. "It could work."

"But," Anthony added, "I'll expect certain things from my drivers."

"Like what?"

"They have to treat the horses well. If I learn anyone has mistreated a horse, they will be fired immediately."

"Seems right," the man drawled. "The horse be the one doing all the work."

Anthony was pleased the driver was in agreement. A thought took form in his mind as he continued to talk. "I also want them to treat their passengers well. It's not enough to just take them where they're going. I want the drivers to be friendly, and I want them to tell their passengers things about Richmond." He paused. "When someone needs a carriage, I want them to look for ours first because they've heard good things about my company."

The driver nodded again, but had to focus on a traffic snarl on Broad Street.

Anthony sat back, pleased with what he had learned. He would talk with Thomas more about it that evening. He was sure Thomas could direct him to the best stables, and the best places to buy carriages. He could handle purchasing the horses on his own. He already knew the first places he would visit. Cromwell horses were far too fine to pull carriages, but he'd made connections with horse traders who dealt with lower quality stock that would meet his needs perfectly.

Ten minutes later, when traffic was moving smoothly again, the driver turned back to him. "What's the address on Church Hill?"

Anthony provided it, and then added, "By the way, what is your name?"

"Norris. Norris Bass."

"It's a pleasure to meet you, Norris. My name is Anthony Wallington."

"Pleased to meet you, Mr. Anthony," Norris replied. "I'm thinking about that address. Do you be going to Mr. Thomas Cromwell's house?"

"That's right," Anthony responded. "He's a good friend, and I live there with him and his wife when I'm in town on business."

Norris nodded his approval. "They be real good people," he said. "There be lots of my friends that work for that factory." He paused. "If you be friends with Mr. Cromwell, now I know why you be willing to pay so well. You know how to treat people right."

"I hope so," Anthony answered. "Besides the fact that it's the right thing to do, I believe it's smart business. I'll make more money if my employees work hard and are happy."

"Yep, I sure 'nuff figure that's true," Norris said. "You asked me a while back if I might know of some folks who would like to work for you. I figure I can get you all you need, but..."

Anthony waited for him to finish.

"...but I have one condition."

Anthony hid his grin. "And what is that condition?"

"I want to be the first person you hire."

"I could do that," Anthony answered. "With one condition."

Norris pulled up behind a wagon stopped in the middle of the road, and then turned to face him. "What that be?"

"You've got to hire and train all my drivers. I'll pay you well to do so." He named a figure.

Norris gasped and stared at him with disbelieving eyes. "That much?"

"You having a job will depend on the success of the company," Anthony replied. "I believe you would find me the right men, and that you would train them well." He had learned to trust his instincts. His instincts told him he was right about Norris Bass.

"You can count on that," Norris said. "I know the men who wants to work hard, and they know I won't put up with nonsense."

"Then your wage is fair," Anthony said, glad he had all the money coming in from the sale of the Cromwell horses. This was the perfect way to invest it – much better than more real estate. "I'd like to meet with you in two weeks, if possible." He would be back from the plantation, and all the funds would be available. "I'll be ready to start putting everything together then. You talk to your friends while I'm gone. I'll start with twenty drivers, and we'll go from there."

Norris nodded. "What kind of hours you want them to work?"

"We'll have two shifts," Anthony answered. "One will go from six in the morning until two o'clock in the afternoon. The second shift will go from two o'clock until ten o'clock in the evening. No one will have a terribly long day, but passengers will have more options."

Norris eyed him. "And what if some of the drivers want to work both shifts, so they can make more money?"

Anthony frowned. "That's a very long day."

Norris smiled. "We all used to be slaves, Mr. Anthony. We know what long days are. Sittin' in a wagon ain't that hard when you're used to working in fields. It ain't been so long since we could actually make money. We gots a lot of catching up to do."

Anthony stared at him. "I suppose you're right," he said thoughtfully. He realized they had just turned onto the street where Thomas' house was. "I'll consider it. We'll talk about it in two weeks."

"Good enough," Norris said cheerfully. "Just one other thing, Mr. Anthony."

"What would that be, Norris?"

"Be careful while you're here in Richmond."

Anthony cocked his head, wondering at the sudden discomfort in Norris' eyes. "Why?"

Norris looked even more uncomfortable. "I been hearing things," he answered evasively.

"What things?" Anthony asked. "There's no use in warning me if you're not going to tell me what you're warning me about." Norris pulled the carriage to a stop, but Anthony didn't get out.

Norris sighed. "We don't rightly know yet," he admitted. "I'm part of the militia from the Black Quarter. We be expecting trouble, but we don't know where it gonna come from."

"What makes you think *I* should be careful?" Anthony probed. "Richmond is a very large city, with a large number of people. Why me?"

Norris shifted in his seat and glanced toward the house. "You promise you won't say nothing to Mr. Cromwell?"

Anthony hesitated, not sure it was wise to make a promise like that, but he needed to know what was going on. "I promise," he said reluctantly.

"Me and the boys are watching the factory every night," Norris revealed. "We been hearing things that make us think there gonna be trouble." He raised a hand. "I don't know nothing more than that, but I would keep Mr. Cromwell away from the factory at night. We figure if something gonna happen, it's gonna happen then."

"But if I warn Thomas, he could put more of a guard around the factory," Anthony protested, already regretting his promise.

Norris shook his head firmly. "That's not a good idea," he insisted. "We suspect the trouble is from *inside* the factory. If Thomas posts a guard, he ain't ever gonna know the truth. At least not before it might be too late."

Anthony took a deep breath.

"Mr. Anthony, we gonna watch things real good. Most of the men in the militia work for Mr. Cromwell. None of us wants something to happen to the factory."

"All right," Anthony reluctantly agreed. "Thomas and I are leaving tomorrow for the plantation, anyway."

"You are?" Norris asked. "I reckon that's good. We'll keep an eye on things."

"Have you talked with the new manager about this?" Anthony pressed. "Pierre should know."

"He knows all he needs to know," Norris said evasively. "I gots to get going, Mr. Anthony. I'll see you in two weeks."

Anthony nodded. "Come here to the house two weeks from today."

Norris jumped down, pulled Anthony's bag out to deposit it on the walkway, and then leapt back up. Moments later, he was rolling down the road.

Anthony watched him for several long moments before he turned and went into the house.

*****

Moses walked up the porch stairs, still finding it difficult to believe he was home on the plantation for good. He had been thrilled to discover Franklin, Chooli, and Ajei were staying. He had just finished riding through the fields with Franklin, discussing more expansion. Now he was starving.

"The tobacco looks real good, Daddy."

Moses gazed down at his almost six-year-old son, his heart about to burst with pride. John had ridden through the fields with his father, never once complaining. Indeed, he had seemed to enjoy every moment. "It does, John. Everybody has been working hard."

John looked toward the barn. "I know you want me to come eat dinner now, but I'm going to go check on Patches after that. I want to make sure he's all right."

"Amber will take good care of him," Moses replied.

"I know, Daddy, but Patches is *my* pony. He's mine to take care of."

"You're right," Moses said solemnly. "You can go out as soon as we're done eating."

John turned to him with an earnest expression. "Daddy?"

"Yes? What is it, son?"

"Are we really staying, Daddy? We're staying here on the plantation?"

Moses stopped and sat down on the front step, pulling John down to join him. "We are, son. How do you feel about that?" He realized, much to his chagrin, that he and Rose had been so focused on how Felicia felt, that they had neglected to ask John. They'd assumed he would be eager to come home, but it wasn't fair that he hadn't been asked. He had been only four years old when Robert was murdered during the attack on the plantation, but he wasn't too young to remember it.

"Oh, I'm real glad, Daddy. This is where I belong."

Moses gazed at his son's intense expression, recognizing himself in John's face and rapidly growing body. "How do you know that?"

"I want to be a farmer like you, Daddy," John said. "There ain't any use to live somewhere else."

"Ain't is not..."

"You're right," John said quickly. "There *isn't* any use to live somewhere else."

Moses hid his smile. His son was the best spoken almost-six-year-old he'd ever known, but he wasn't surprised since Rose was his mama. She turned everything into a game so their children would enjoy learning, but she was quite serious about the games, and she was adamant that they speak well. "Are you sure you want to be a farmer? There are a lot of things to do out there in the world."

"I'm sure, Daddy," John insisted. "I'm old enough to learn more things this year," he added. "Can I work out in the fields with the men?"

Moses hesitated, not sure how Rose would react. "Why don't I talk to your mama about that?"

John sighed. "That's always what you say when you're getting ready to say no."

Moses chuckled. "That may be true sometimes," he admitted, "but not always. Sometimes it means I don't want to make a real big decision without talking to your mama."

John cocked his head. "Is my wanting to work with the men a real big decision?"

"It is," Moses assured him. "If we say yes, it means you're growing up. I'm not sure I'm ready for that."

"It happens to everyone," John said patiently.

Moses choked back a laugh. "I suppose that's true."

"Daddy?"

Moses could tell John's next question was serious by the look in his eyes. He knew Annie had supper ready, but it could wait a few more minutes. Having time to talk with his son was what made riding the fields with him so wonderful. "Yes, son?"

"I think I have a bigger problem."

Moses raised a brow. "And what is that?"

John sighed. "It won't be too long before I'm too big for Patches," he said sadly. "Grandma Annie says I'm growing as fast as you did, Daddy. What am I going to do when I'm too big for Patches?" His expression was distressed. "I don't *ever* want to be too big to ride him."

"I know, John." Moses truly did understand his son's dilemma, because he knew just how much John loved his black and white pony. "It's going to happen though, son." He didn't see any reason to beat around the bush. "Can you imagine *me* riding Patches?"

"No!" John exclaimed. "You would hurt him!" As soon as the words came out of his mouth, his eyes grew even sadder. "How long before I'm too big, Daddy?"

"I don't know, son, but I think you'll know. And, I'm quite sure Miles will tell you."

John's lip quivered. "But what will I do with him? I could never get rid of him."

"Of course not," Moses agreed. "Patches is part of our family." He thought for a moment, pretending he hadn't already given this some consideration. "What if you were to give Patches to Hope? You've done such a good job with him. Don't you think he would be perfect for your little sister?"

John stared off into the distance with a serious expression before he turned back. "Hope isn't ready yet, Daddy."

"Nope," Moses agreed easily. "She is only three and a half. But maybe when she's four. That's when we got Patches for you," he reminded his son.

"And you think I'll be too big for Patches by then?" John asked.

"Unless you figure out a way to quit growing," Moses said with a chuckle. "I think you're going to be bigger than I am."

John stared up at him and shook his head. "That's going to take a real long time."

"Not as long as you think," Moses said, realizing just how true it was. "So, what do you think about giving Patches to Hope?"

"And I'll get another horse?" John asked, his eyes both sad and excited.

"Of course," Moses replied.

"Then I'll give Patches to Hope," John said decisively. He eyed his Daddy. "On one condition."

"There's a condition?" Moses asked with surprise, fighting to control the smile twitching his lips.

John nodded. "Miss Abby has been teaching me how to negotiate." He said the word slowly, feeling his way through the many syllables.

Moses groaned. "God help me." He took a breath, slightly alarmed at how fast his little boy was growing up, but the alarm was mixed with pride. "What is your condition?"

"I want to pick out my next horse on my own."

"From one of the foals?" Moses asked, expecting the answer to be yes. He was surprised when John shook his head.

"No, I don't want to be a horse trainer, Daddy. I just want to be a farmer." He paused. "I would like to go with you to a sale and pick out my horse. I want him to be big enough so that I'll never have to give up another one."

Moses hesitated. "That's going to be a very big horse, son. I'm not sure you'll be able to handle something that size right now."

"That's not true," John said earnestly. "Carrie told me I'm not that much smaller than she was when Mr. Thomas got Granite for her."

"But she was quite a bit older," Moses protested, still resisting the idea of his young son on top of a horse the size of Granite.

"Age shouldn't matter, Daddy," John argued. "I'll go to the sale with you. We'll make sure I can ride the horse before we buy it."

Moses threw his head back with a laugh. "You talked this through with Miss Abby already, didn't you, John?"

John grinned. "I might have," he admitted.

Moses laughed again. "You should have told me that from the start. If I'd known you and Abby cooked this up, I would have just said yes from the beginning. I would have known I was going to eventually give in."

John smiled, but nodded solemnly. "I'll remember that in the future."

"Are you sure you're only five?" Moses asked.

"I'm almost six, Daddy," John answered. "Miss Abby is going to teach me more about negotiating."

Moses groaned again before he stood and walked to the house. "Now I really need some food."

*****

Carl heaved the heavy can of trash onto his shoulders and opened the back door to the alley behind the restaurant. It had been a long, hard day, but the restaurant had been busy from the time they opened the door. The success of Opal's Kitchen was even more than they had dreamed, but he still struggled with restlessness. He thought of going West on a daily basis.

"Carl!"

Carl looked up, his eyes picking out his best friend, Leo, walking toward him down the alley. He immediately tensed. "What is it?" he asked. He lowered the can onto the ground and looked around to make sure they were alone.

"There ain't be nobody else out here," Leo assured him. "I been waitin' out here for you."

"Why?"

Leo took a deep breath. "I only been waitin' a few minutes. I figured I oughta talk to you first."

Carl gritted his teeth, fighting for patience. "Tell me what it is, Leo."

Leo nodded, barely visible in the dark. "I heard some white men talking down on the wharf."

"About what?"

"It was hard to hear what they said 'cause boats kept blowing their whistles, but I could tell they were angry, and I heard them say Cromwell Factory a few times."

Carl stiffened. "When was this?"

"About an hour ago," Leo answered. "I had to finish up my work before I could get here." Suddenly, he frowned. "I almost forgot. I heard them say the name Thomas a couple times. That mean anything to you?"

Carl dashed to the door of the restaurant, flung it open, and ran inside. "Opal, where is Daddy?"

Opal looked up calmly, steam from the stove making her skin shine. She was busy starting a huge pot of collard greens that would simmer all night. "He left a little while ago, Carl." Her eyes sharpened. "Why? What's wrong?"

"I ain't got time to explain," Carl said, frantically looking around. Everything inside him told him there would be trouble tonight. He suspected that had been the real cause of his restlessness all day. "Where did Daddy go?"

Opal looked nervous now. "I don't know, Carl. Can I do anything?"

Carl shook his head, not wanting to frighten her any more than she already was. "No." He thought quickly. "If Daddy comes back, tell him I've gone over to the Cromwells' house. He'll know what it means."

"The Cromwells' house?" Opal gasped, genuinely alarmed now. "Why? You tell me what's going on right this minute."

Carl shook his head. "I can't," he insisted. "I got to get there. I'm going to send Leo to find Daddy and Uncle Clark."

"What should I do?" Opal asked, fighting for control.

Carl hesitated. He hated to create more fear, but it wasn't fair to leave her unprepared. Besides, Opal had been a spy during the war until she had to take him and his siblings out to the plantation. "I would go home, Opal," he said. "Go home and stay inside. I would tell everyone you see to do the same thing."

Opal opened her mouth to ask more questions and then snapped it shut. "Go," she urged. "Be careful."

Carl turned and ran out the back door again. Leo was waiting right where he left him. "Go to my house," Carl ordered. "Find Daddy and Uncle Clark, or anyone else in the militia. Tell them what you told me. Let them know I've gone over to Mr. Cromwell's house to make sure he's all right."

"By yourself?" Leo demanded. "That ain't smart, Carl."

"I'll be fine," Carl responded, knowing it was true. "They ain't coming after him in his house. I just got to make sure he don't go anywhere. Now go!"

He turned and disappeared into the shadows, running as fast as he could.

Chapter Thirty-One

Anthony paced the porch, staring into the darkness with every sound he heard.

"Where is he, Mr. Anthony?" May asked, wringing her hands as she stared out into the night with him.

"I don't know," Anthony replied, grinding his teeth with frustration.

"It's not like Mr. Cromwell to miss dinner," May insisted. "At least not without sending a message."

Anthony knew she was right, but he felt the need to calm her. "We're leaving for the plantation tomorrow. Perhaps he's finishing up work before we leave."

"Without sending a message?"

"Perhaps he couldn't find someone to deliver it," Anthony said lamely. Then he realized what was wrong with that statement. "Where is Spencer? Isn't he Thomas' driver?" Spencer would have come to let his wife know if Thomas was going to be late so she wouldn't worry.

May sighed. "Mr. Cromwell gave him some time off since he drove out to the plantation this week. He's over in the Black Quarters tonight. Somebody else be driving Mr. Cromwell."

"Who?" Anthony demanded. He looked at May more closely. Her eyes were more frightened than he suspected they would be under normal circumstances. "You're not telling me something, May."

May shook her head. "I don't know anything, except that I'm real worried about Mr. Cromwell."

Anthony wasn't convinced. "May, if you know something, you need to tell me."

"I don't know nothing," she insisted, dropping her eyes. "I been feeling like something is wrong, but

Spencer won't tell me anything. I've been pestering him with questions all week, but he just shuts up like a clam and says things are being taken care of."

Anthony's alarm grew. He remembered what Norris had said about being careful, and his insistence that he keep Thomas away from the factory at night. Well, it was night, and he had no idea where Thomas was. He tried to tamp down images of him injured or dead, but they wouldn't be controlled. He clenched his fists and stared once more into the night, trying to decide how he was going to get to the factory. He couldn't just stand on Thomas' porch and not do something.

A sudden movement in the shadows put him on alert. He turned quickly, and pushed May through the door. "Stay inside," he hissed. He turned to meet whatever danger lurked just beyond the range of his vision. He took deep breaths, wishing he had grabbed one of Thomas' guns earlier in the night. What good would he be unarmed?

"Who's there?" he called sharply.

A figure slowly emerged from the darkness beneath the magnolia tree. "Is that you, Mr. Wallington?"

Anthony frowned. The voice was familiar, but he couldn't place it. "It is. Who's out there?"

The figure moved close enough for him to recognize the teenager who had served him at Opal's Kitchen when he had lunch there with Carrie. He searched his brain to come up with a name. "Is that you, Carl?"

"Yes." Carl stepped onto the porch, the outline of his body showing how tense he was. "Is Mr. Cromwell here?"

"No." Anthony ground his teeth harder. He had hoped Carl was here to deliver a message from Thomas. "Why? Are you looking for him?"

Carl looked around nervously. "Can we go inside?"

Anthony opened the door, waited for Carl to enter, and then joined him in the foyer. "Why are you looking for Thomas?"

Carl sagged. "He really ain't here? I came to tell him to make sure not to go anywhere tonight."

"Why?" Anthony was aware May was listening from just inside the dining room.

"There's going to be trouble tonight."

"At the factory?" Anthony snapped.

Carl stared at him. "How did you know that?"

"Norris told me," Anthony said.

"Norris Bass?"

Anthony nodded his head impatiently. How he knew didn't matter. The only thing that mattered was what they were going to do about it. "How long will it take to get to the factory?"

"I ain't got no wagon," Carl responded.

"I know that," Anthony snapped again. He took a deep breath to control his frustration. "We'll have to go by foot. How far is it?"

Carl took a deep breath. "It's a couple miles, I reckon. I know all the backways, though. I guess it'll take about thirty minutes."

"Not if we run." Anthony dashed into the parlor and chose two revolvers from Thomas' gun case. He checked to make sure they were loaded, stuck them into his waistband, and then headed to the door. "Lead the way," he said. "We've got to get to the factory."

He and Carl were running before they hit the road.

*****

Thomas finished signing the last papers and slowly straightened. Only then did he look at the clock. "What in the world?" he muttered when he realized how late it was. A quick glance out the window told him it was already dark. He knew May would be worried, and Anthony was probably wondering why he had left him on his own for dinner, but it couldn't be helped. Leaving for the plantation so soon after returning from Philadelphia had meant a tremendous amount of work must be done. He had just finished creating orders and finalizing shipping reports.

He turned to file the papers, acknowledging what was really bothering him. Pierre's paperwork had been done shoddily, which was bad enough, but the bigger issue was that many of the numbers simply didn't add up. It had been so long since he had done the bookkeeping, that it had taken him longer than usual to go through everything. He had left all of this to Jeremy for over a year, counting on him to give reports on a monthly basis. For the past hour, he had been cursing himself because he had assumed he could expect the same capability and integrity from Pierre.

He blamed Pierre, but he also blamed himself and Abby for allowing this to happen. They had not been paying close enough attention to what was going on.

He extinguished the lanterns and looked out his office window, frustrated when he didn't see a carriage waiting for him. Granted, the hour was late, but his driver was well paid to adhere to his schedule. He sighed, wishing he had not given Spencer the night off.

With no other choice but to walk home, he grabbed his briefcase. As he reached for his office door to pull it closed behind him, a loud noise down on the factory floor made him freeze. He held his breath, waiting for his eyes to adjust to the darkness. The one thing he was certain about was that no one should be in the factory this late at night.

He stood silently, pondering his best course of action. He didn't know if the sound had been caused by one person or a group, but he had to assume there was more than one. His thoughts spun as he considered his options. Leaning over, he set his briefcase against the wall and removed his shoes, leaving him in just his stocking feet. He intended to find out who was in his factory, but if they didn't already know he was there, he certainly did not want to alert them. Evidently, he had extinguished his office light before whoever it was had entered the building. He prayed that would give him an advantage.

Thinking quickly, he spun back to his desk. Easing open the top drawer, he sighed in relief when it pulled out silently. He felt for his revolver in the almost total darkness. When his hand hit cold metal, he pulled it out carefully. It would be unwise to encounter an intruder when he was unarmed.

Grateful he knew the layout of the factory so well, Thomas eased soundlessly to his office door and stood in the opening, listening as hard as he could. Nothing but silence met his ears for several minutes, but he had learned to trust his instincts.

Every instinct said someone was in the factory.

He crept out onto the office landing and looked down into the blackness of the factory floor. Something was down there. Thomas was content to wait until whoever it was revealed themselves.

Nothing moved.

Just when he had decided to walk down the steps to the floor below to inspect things more closely, he heard a scuffling noise below him. He stiffened, craning his head out further to detect any movement, but the darkness continued to conceal whoever was down there.

Another sound, this one to his left, made him move behind the large square column reaching to the roof. Someone was on the landing with him, but he couldn't see a thing. He could only hope they were having the same problem. He had a sudden realization that only someone very familiar with the factory could be moving around so quietly. Whoever was in the factory must also work there.

Thomas held his breath, not wanting to make a sound that would give him away. When a match flared in his office, he gripped his revolver and forced himself further back into the narrow opening between the column and the wall. He peered around the column, his insides clenching with fury when he recognized the face illuminated by the match. *Pierre!*

Something made him stand quietly as Pierre rifled through some of the files, obviously searching for something. Thomas thought of all the files he had removed tonight, intending to take them home with him for closer inspection during his time at the plantation. He was quite sure they were what Pierre was searching for. He smiled grimly at the frustration on Pierre's face as he lit match after match, searching through the papers. Finally, the man used one of the matches to light a lantern. Warm light filled the room.

Thomas was preparing to step out of hiding to confront his manager when he heard several loud noises from below. He shrank back as Pierre stalked out onto the landing.

"I said to keep it quiet down there!"

"Sorry, boss," one man muttered.

Thomas heard a hissing sound as another match ignited below him. Knowing he was risking detection, he shifted to allow himself a better view. He wasn't afraid, but he did want to figure out what was going on. His alarm grew as he counted ten shadowy figures on the factory floor, each of them clothed in black.

"What the..."

Thomas swiveled his head back toward his office when he heard Pierre's muffled exclamation. Pierre picked up his briefcase from where Thomas had left it against the wall. As soon as he opened it, his manager would be aware Thomas was in the building. He quickly decided being on the offensive was preferable to the defensive.

Thomas raised his revolver and stepped over to the open door. "Looking for something?"

Pierre cursed and swung toward him, reaching for his gun as he did so.

"I don't suggest touching that gun," Thomas said in a steely voice, realizing the sound of their voices would have alerted everyone below. He couldn't know if they would run or attack, so he had to assume the worst. Whatever he was going to do, he must do it quickly.

Pierre's eyes widened. "Mr. Cromwell! What are you doing here?" His tone switched to one of surprised innocence. "You startled me. I...I forgot some paperwork that I need to finish tonight."

"And you need all the men down there to help you carry it?" Thomas asked sarcastically.

Pierre flushed with fury and dropped all pretense. "You're not supposed to be here tonight," he said coldly, his eyes calculating as they scanned the office.

"I can see that," Thomas said calmly, thinking through his options. He realized he didn't have many. "What are you really doing in the factory, Pierre?"

Pierre narrowed his eyes as he considered his response. "I'm your manager. I can be here anytime I want," he said defensively. "I called these men in to do some needed work."

"In the dark?" Thomas demanded, almost amused that Pierre couldn't come up with anything to say that remotely made sense. "And, let's be clear. You *were* my manager," Thomas corrected. "After going through the reports tonight, I am quite aware you either have no idea what you're doing, or you came here to deliberately sabotage the factory." He was suddenly very confident that had been Pierre's plan all along. "Who are you really?" He raised the gun and put his finger on the trigger. "I would prefer the truth."

"What's going on up there?" a man called.

"Pierre has been captured," Thomas called back, careful to keep his eyes trained on the man in front of him. "I suggest you leave before I discover who you are." He smiled tightly as curses rang through the building. "Pierre and I are just going to talk for a while."

Pierre stiffened as his eyes searched the room for a means of escape.

"Only one way out," Thomas said calmly. "You'll have to get past me and a bullet." He cocked his head. "Who are you Pierre? Why are you in my factory?"

Pierre's only response was to curl his lips back into a snarl.

Thomas stared, hardly able to believe the man had hidden such intense hatred for so long.

"I was sent here to do a job," Pierre snapped. "One I aim to finish. You were warned, Mr. Cromwell. You were told if you kept hiring niggers that we were going to set things right."

Thomas nodded, surprisingly unbothered by the revelation. "By destroying my factory?"

"That's right," Pierre retorted.

Thomas smiled, and then raised his voice enough to be heard by everyone in the building. "I'm going to assume the men on the floor also work here. I wonder if they realize that by following your directions, they are also destroying their own lives. Jobs are hard to come by in Richmond. There are none that will pay as well as Cromwell Factory. I wonder if they've thought about how they will feed their family when they don't have a job."

All noise on the floor had ceased. The men had either left, were listening, or were creeping upstairs to kill him. Thomas chose to go with the second option. He could only hope they would listen to reason.

Pierre looked desperate now. "What does it matter?" he growled. "People like you have to be stopped. We can't let you destroy the South."

"Destroy the South by giving good-paying jobs to two hundred white men?" Thomas asked coldly.

"And two hundred niggers," Pierre shot back.

"You're stupid, Pierre," Thomas said derisively. "Destroying the factory won't make it possible for me to hire more white people. All it will do is make sure the two hundred white people who work here won't have a job at all." He paused. "Of course, I know you don't really care about that. You're just going to crawl back into the hole you crawled out of when you showed up here. Whoever sent you here will make sure *you* have money, but what about all the men you're leaving behind?" He talked calmly, praying the men listening were rational and intelligent enough to recognize the truth. He realized hatred could make you incapable of reason, but talking was his best course of action right now. He knew he couldn't single-handedly stop whatever the dozen men below him had come to do.

"Don't listen to him," Pierre shouted. "I gave you a job to do. You'd better do it if you want your families to live through the night!"

Thomas suddenly understood. Pierre had played on the men's prejudices to get them to agree to his plan, and then threatened their families if they didn't follow his orders.

"Don't believe him!" Thomas yelled, his voice bouncing off the rafters. "He can't hurt your families."

Even when the words came out of his mouth, he knew he had no way of being certain of that. White vigilantism was spreading everywhere. For all he knew, the families of every single man below him could be under the control of angry vigilantes who would not hesitate to hurt people to fulfill their agenda.

Evidently, the men below him knew it as well.

There was a long silence, and then he heard matches being struck again. He waited only a moment before the glow of flames was enough to know the men were setting fire to the factory. He clenched his teeth and glared at Pierre. "It's going to be hard to get out from up here."

Pierre glared back. "I'm prepared to give my life for the Southern cause," he snapped. "Men like you simply can't be allowed to destroy our way of life."

Thomas stared at him. "I believe you actually mean that nonsense," he said wearily. "What happened to you, Pierre?" He wanted to understand what was fueling the ignorant hatred exploding in the South.

"The same thing that happened to most Southern men—at least those of us who lived through the war," he said bitterly. "The niggers have destroyed our country."

Thomas heaved a sigh. Nothing he could say would change the man standing in front of him, at least not in the few minutes he had to escape the factory. And he most definitely was *not* willing to give his life for it. He prayed someone would notice the flames and alert the fire department station nearby.

First, though, he had to get out of the building alive.

He thought about leaving Pierre there to die, but realized he didn't want to stoop to the same level as the man willing to kill him. He waved his gun toward the open office door, coughing slightly as the smoke began to rise. "You first," he snapped.

"I'm not leaving," Pierre growled.

Thomas shrugged. "That's your choice." He knew he was running out of time to escape. As he stepped forward to lift his briefcase, knowing there were papers in it that he would need, Pierre leapt toward him.

Caught off balance, he didn't have time to pull the trigger before the man's bulk crashed into him. He grunted and fell against the desk, the hard wood knocking the air out of him.

*****

Anthony and Carl ran as fast as they could, dashing down empty roads and through dark alleys. Just enough light spilled from windows to make it possible to avoid potholes and trash cans. Dogs barked, but none ran out at them.

Anthony concentrated on breathing, counting the blocks as they ran. He kept his thoughts focused on Thomas. He had grown to love Thomas and Abby, but more than anything, he couldn't imagine Carrie having to face another loss. Losing her father to an act of violence was not something he was going to let happen. Not if he could stop it. Lungs burning, he willed himself to run faster.

He prayed Carl was right that there were men guarding the factory. Surely, they would be able to stop whatever was going to happen tonight, but he couldn't count on it.

"We're almost there!" Carl gasped as they rounded another corner into a long alley wedged between tall, brick buildings.

Anthony recognized they were now in the commercial district down by the river. He gritted his teeth, and kept running. *I'm coming, Thomas*, his mind screamed. *I'm coming!*

*****

Thomas gathered enough air and strength to push Pierre off him.

Pierre recovered and cocked his arm back.

Thomas saw it coming, but was still too stunned to dodge the fist Pierre aimed at him. He grunted as it smashed into his face. Blood spurted from his nose as smoke filled the office. Fighting to maintain consciousness, he realized he still had the gun in his hand. He shifted slowly, trying to steady the shaky pistol.

Pierre chuckled, a wild look in his eyes as he grabbed for the gun.

Thomas fired.

He fell back as Pierre ripped the gun from his hand and continued to laugh maniacally. The man was clearly mad, and truly was willing to die to destroy the factory. Abby's face filled his mind. Then Carrie's. Thomas grunted as he fought to push himself up again. The smoke and pain were making it almost impossible to move.

Regret filled him as he realized he would die that night.

*****

Anthony rounded the corner just as a contingent of men rushed toward the factory, the glow of flames flickering in the windows. "No!" he yelled as he ran forward, determined to reach the building first.

"Daddy!" Carl yelled. "Mr. Cromwell is in the building!"

Moments before Anthony reached the doors, they were pushed open from the inside. Close to a dozen men, clothed in black, ran out onto the street.

"Get them!" Anthony yelled over his shoulder as he dashed into the building. "I'm going after Thomas!" He knew someone had entered the building behind him, but he didn't have time to find out who it was. He ran through the smoke to the stairs leading up to the office, glad he knew the building. He barely registered the flames devouring wooden tables and material laid out to be made into clothing the next day.

"*Thomas!*" he hollered.

A loud gunshot boomed through the factory.

Anthony pounded up the stairs. Just as he reached the top, another gunshot exploded.

*****

Thomas cried out as a searing pain burned through his leg. Pierre stumbled toward him and then launched himself through the air.

Pierre crashed down on top of him, his hands reaching for his neck. Thomas fought to push him off, but he could feel himself losing consciousness. "I'm sorry, Abby," he whispered. "I'm sorry, Carrie..."

Just before he slipped into the blackness, a shadowy figure appeared at the office door. He waved his hand weakly, and then closed his eyes.

*****

Anthony stood at the door for a moment. He saw a flicker of movement in the smoky air, but had no idea who had made it. All he was certain of was that Thomas was at the bottom of the pile. It took only a moment to realize the man on top was Pierre. The factory manager was still alive, and had his hands around Thomas' neck.

Anthony grabbed Pierre, punched him savagely, and then tossed him aside. Then he spun back, still uncertain whether the man who had followed him in was friend or foe. "Help me get Thomas!" he shouted as he ran back and knelt beside his friend.

"I'll take his knees," the stranger gasped.

Anthony peered through the smoke at a tall, skinny black man, who he figured must be part of the black militia that had been standing guard. Anthony's instincts told him the man could be trusted. He reached down, wrapped his arms under Thomas' shoulders, and picked him up.

The black man grabbed Thomas under his knees and lifted him easily. "We got to get out of here," the man snapped.

Suddenly, two more men appeared. One of them laid a wet towel over Thomas' head to protect him from the smoke. The other one handed wet towels to Anthony and the tall man.

Anthony laid the towel across his mouth and took a few deep breaths before pushing it aside. "Let's move!" Praying Thomas was still alive, he surged toward the door, wondering how they would get through the flames that must have consumed the stairs by then.

One of the additional men supported Thomas' torso as the three of them rushed down the landing with his limp body.

Anthony gasped with relief when he saw more men pour into the building, all of them armed with large buckets of water. They heaved the water in unison at the stairs, putting out the flames just enough for them to push through the acrid smoke.

"Run!" they hollered.

Anthony ducked his head and ran, sucking in fresh air when they burst through the door.

He could hear the clanging of a firetruck bell in the distance.

"Keep going!" one of the men yelled. "Get Mr. Cromwell out of here. We don't know what is going to happen!"

Anthony drew deep breaths as they continued away from the building. They stepped back into shadows as the first firetruck rounded the corner. The horse plunged to a stop as ten men leapt off the truck, pulling a hose with them. More clanging bells revealed more help was on the way. He was sure every volunteer fire company in Richmond would soon be there. There was not a single person who didn't remember the fires that had consumed almost the entire business district at the end of the war.

Anthony laid Thomas down gently and removed the wet towel, terrified they had been too late.

"He's still breathing!" the thin man said triumphantly.

Anthony stared at Thomas' battered face. His stomach clenched in knots, however, when he looked down and saw blood seeping from his pant leg. "He's been shot," he said grimly. As he ripped the material away from Thomas' leg, he saw the large, bloody wound gushing blood.

The man stood up and pulled off his shirt, quickly ripping it into strips. "Move back," he ordered.

Anthony stepped back, praying Thomas would make it.

The stranger expertly wound the strips of cloth around the wound. "This should stop the bleeding," he announced. "Willard, go get Spencer. Tell him we got to get Mr. Cromwell out of here, and to the hospital."

"Who are you?" Anthony asked.

"I'm Eddie."

Carl raced up just then. "This is my daddy. This is Anthony Wallington, Daddy."

Eddie eyed Anthony. "You the one sweet on Miss Carrie?"

Anthony managed a tight smile. "Guilty as charged." He understood, now, why Eddie had worked so hard to save Carrie's father. The Cromwell family had done a lot for him. Anthony looked back at Thomas and asked the question he was afraid to verbalize. "Do you think he'll make it?"

"I think so," Eddie said, "but I'll feel a whole heap better when we get him to a hospital."

Spencer materialized from the darkness. "I'll get him there," he said firmly, and then looked at Eddie. "We found Morton knocked out in the bushes. They only took the carriage and the horse a few blocks, though. I found it."

"Is Morton gonna be all right?"

"He'll have a nasty headache in the mornin', but he'll make it." Spencer looked at Anthony. "Can you help us get Mr. Thomas into the carriage?"

"Certainly," Anthony replied. "And then I'm going to the hospital with you, Spencer."

"Wouldn't expect nothing else," Spencer replied. When Thomas was laid out on the carriage seat, his head resting in Anthony's lap, Spencer turned to Eddie. "Will you go by the house and let May know what happened? I reckon she is fit to be tied. You tell her Mr. Cromwell gonna be just fine."

Eddie hesitated. "You reckon that be true?"

Spencer nodded. "He's a strong man. He's gonna make it." He picked up the reins and clucked to the horse. "Git on," he called.

Anthony looked back at the factory, flames shooting from the windows. He doubted the firefighters could save the building, but if they could stop it from spreading to the other structures, they would be heroes. He was thankful for a night with no wind. He prayed it would stay that way. Then he turned his prayers to Thomas.

"Please let him live," he muttered. *"Please let him live..."*

Chapter Thirty-Two

Eddie was waiting outside Thomas' house when Spencer rolled up in the carriage. He stepped from the shadows of the barn once Spencer had stabled the horse and given it a ration of grain and hay. "Mr. Thomas gonna be okay?"

Spencer didn't look surprised to see him. "The doctor figures he will be. He swallowed a lot of smoke, but your stopping the bleeding in his leg was probably what saved his life. That bullet busted up an artery pretty good," he said. "If y'all hadn't got him outta there, he wouldn't have made it."

Eddie sighed with relief. "Had he come to when you left?"

"No, but the doctor didn't seem much worried about that. Anthony is with him."

Eddie raised a brow. "They let him stay?"

Spencer chuckled. "Don't know they had much choice. He made it clear he weren't leaving Mr. Thomas there by hisself."

"Anthony a good man?" Eddie asked. "I hear he be sweet on Miss Carrie."

"I reckon he is. And, yes," he added, "he be a real good man." He changed the subject. "Did you catch them boys that done did this?"

"We did," Eddie replied. "Willard went for the police while the militia rounded them all up. We figured they would listen to a white man before they did us."

Spencer frowned. "Probably just this one time. Now that they know that white man be friends with us, they probably won't listen again."

Eddie shrugged. "Maybe, but at least we got the men who set that fire."

"Factory workers?"

"Every one of them," Eddie said angrily. "They kept spoutin' off that they didn't have no choice." He shook his head with disgust. "They destroyed their jobs right along with everybody else's."

"What about Pierre?" Spencer asked.

Eddie shrugged. "He didn't make it," he said shortly. "By the time they could get firefighters back up them stairs, I guess the smoke done did him in."

Spencer thought about what Anthony had told him on the trip to the hospital. "Had he been shot?"

"Nope," Eddie replied. "I heard those two gunshots, but I don't reckon we'll know what happened until Mr. Thomas tells us."

Spencer nodded wearily. "Go home, Eddie. You did real good tonight. Without you makin' sure there be a guard there, it would have been a whole lot worse."

Eddie shook his head with disgust. "I didn't do real good," he said bitterly. "Those men should have never got in there. I still don't know how they snuck past the guards. And I don't know how they missed the fact that Mr. Thomas didn't leave the factory. Clark and I wouldn't have been there if Leo hadn't come to find us." He tightened his lips. "It coulda been a whole lot worse, but it should never have happened in the first place."

"Things happen," Spencer replied, reaching out to lay a wrinkled hand on his friend's shoulder. "Without you there, Mr. Cromwell would be dead." He frowned. "Course," he added gravely, "it is a worry how they got past our guard."

Eddie looked at him sharply. "Go on. What are you thinking?" He was certain it was the same thing he was thinking, but he couldn't bring himself to give words to it.

"I'm thinking they had to know where our guard was hiding," Spencer said. "There be only one way for them to know that." He shook his head. "I hate to be thinking it, but..."

Eddie nodded, his stomach clenching. "I'll find out the truth," he said. "We gots to know who sold us out. And, why they did it."

Anthony dozed fitfully in the hard chair next to Thomas' bed. The hospital staff had insisted he couldn't stay. He had made it clear he wasn't leaving, so they had finally left him alone in the dark room. Every time he woke, he listened until he could hear Thomas' breathing. Only then could he fall back asleep. Eddie had come by early that morning, only getting in because he had a friend working the front desk. They had talked briefly in the hallway, and then Anthony had gone back to sleep.

"That can't be real comfortable."

Anthony jolted awake when a voice broke into his dream of fire and smoke. He opened his eyes and blinked rapidly several times to clear his vision. "Thomas?" He was relieved beyond words to see Thomas' eyes were open. "Thank God."

"Indeed," Thomas agreed ruefully. He coughed and looked around him. "I take it I'm in the hospital?"

Anthony nodded, reaching for the pitcher of water next to Thomas' bed. He poured a glass and handed it to him. "I imagine you're thirsty after swallowing so much smoke."

Thomas reached for the glass eagerly. "I could use some water," he agreed. He drank thirstily, coughed several times, and then drank some more. Finally, he put the glass down. "What happened?"

"We were hoping you could tell *us*," Anthony answered. "I can only tell you that you scared me half to death. The building was on fire, and very smoky when I got there. I heard two gunshots when I ran inside. When I got upstairs, I saw you lying under Pierre. He had his hands around your neck." The memory almost took his breath. "We pulled him off you and got you out of there."

"Pierre?" Thomas asked.

Anthony met his eyes. "Pierre didn't make it."

"I see," Thomas murmured. "How did he die?"

"From smoke," Anthony answered. "Eddie was here earlier. He told me they pulled out his body late last night."

"Was he shot?" Thomas demanded.

"No," Anthony answered. "You weren't so lucky, however."

Thomas blinked, and then lifted his cover to stare beneath it. "That's why my leg hurts like the dickens."

"Bullets seem to have that effect," Anthony said wryly. He gazed at his friend. "What happened?"

Thomas explained, pausing when he came to the end of his recital. "Did the factory make it?" he finally asked in a hoarse voice.

Anthony shook his head slowly. "The brick walls are still standing, Thomas, but everything else is destroyed. All the machinery. All the material. The loading dock burned. All your equipment is gone."

Thomas stared blankly at him, trying to absorb the information. "What happened to the men who set the fire?"

"The black militia caught them," Anthony replied. "They're all in jail. No one took kindly to them setting a fire in the business district."

Thomas stiffened. "How many other buildings burned?" he asked in a strained voice.

"None," Anthony assured him. "Eddie told me that by the time it was all over, close to two hundred men worked to put the fire out. All the fire engines were there, and they had several bucket brigade lines leading down to the river. Everybody worked hard."

Thomas sagged back against his pillow. "I'm glad," he said with relief. Sorrow filled his face. "So many jobs have been lost," he said thickly. "How could those men have destroyed their own jobs? What will their families do now?"

"And all because you dared to give jobs to black men," Anthony said quietly. "It just doesn't seem possible that people would be so short-sighted."

"Oh, I think maybe those men got caught up in it," Thomas said slowly. "I think in the end, they didn't want to do it."

"Then why did they?" Anthony snapped. "Surely you don't feel sorry for them!"

"I feel sorry for the entire South," Thomas replied wearily, reaching for the glass of water again. When he was done drinking, he turned back to Anthony. "I'm fairly certain Pierre threatened their families if they refused to set the fire."

"They were stupid," Anthony said angrily.

"I agree," Thomas said, "but men have done worse things for far less reason than protecting their family. I suspect they felt trapped."

"Well, now they're trapped in jail," Anthony replied. "They have no jobs, and no way to feed their families. I imagine they will be there for a while. They hardly *protected* their families."

"No," Thomas said sadly. He turned to stare out the tiny window next to his bed. "Prejudice and hatred never make sense, Anthony. I should know. I used to think black people had no value at all."

Anthony eyed him with surprise. "You?"

"Me," Thomas answered. "I sincerely believed they were a lower species that required the white man to keep them in slavery for their own good."

Anthony stared at him with astonishment. "What changed you?"

"Carrie," Thomas said simply. "She refused to let me live in my ignorance. It wasn't until I found out about Rose and Jeremy, however, that my heart truly changed. My prejudice took on a human face. Once it did, I realized how untrue my beliefs were. It was a hard lesson. I'm disappointed in those men, but I'm not angry with them. I used to *be* them."

"And Pierre?"

Thomas frowned. "He got what he deserved. He was there simply for the purpose of destroying the factory. I don't know who finagled him into getting the job, but I'm going to find out." He paused. "Not that it will do any good," he admitted. "He fulfilled his purpose."

Anthony considered his next question. "What are you going to do now?"

Thomas shrugged. "I'm going out to the plantation to let my daughter make me well." He looked as if his own words surprised him, but his eyes grew more certain. "I can't imagine a carriage ride will be very comfortable with this bullet wound, but it will be worth it once I get home." He looked thoughtful. "Will you bring Willard and Marcus to the hospital this morning? I don't imagine the doctor will let me out today, and I need to talk to them."

Anthony nodded. "Certainly. Are you going to rebuild the factory?"

Thomas met his eyes. "I don't know yet. Abby and I decided just a week ago that we were going to fire Pierre, put someone else in charge, and work toward selling it."

Anthony's eyes widened. "I had no idea."

"I have you to thank for it," Thomas answered.

"Me?" Anthony asked in astonishment, and then he remembered their conversation in Philadelphia.

"It took me a little while to realize what is truly important to me," Thomas replied thoughtfully. "Last night, I was certain I was going to die. The idea of never seeing Abby and Carrie again broke my heart."

"As it would break theirs," Anthony said softly.

Thomas nodded. "I know." He looked out the window again. "I hate the idea of all our workers being without a job for good if we don't rebuild the factory, but I also can't imagine starting from scratch, and..."

"And, you're not sure you want to make that investment again right now," Anthony finished.

"That's true," Thomas admitted. "Rebuilding the factory in a solid economy would be risky. Rebuilding it when we already know the unwise financial decisions being made by our government and by banks..." His voice trailed off again. "Rebuilding it now would be stupid," he finished. He paused for several moments, and then nodded. "I believe I've made my decision." A look of relief filled his eyes.

"Carrie will be thrilled," Anthony said. "So will everyone else on the plantation."

"No more than Abby and I," Thomas admitted.

Anthony hesitated before deciding to say what he was thinking. "Will losing the value of selling the factory be a problem for you and Abby?"

Thomas considered the question. "We had certainly hoped to have that for the future, but we'll have plenty. We'll get something from the insurance company, though not what we could have made in the years to come, or what we would have made if we sold it. We still have the factories in Philadelphia. We're planning on selling them to Jeremy, but they will create income for a long time. And," he added, "the plantation is doing well." He looked at Anthony more closely. "What are you thinking? I have the feeling you're leading up to something."

Anthony smiled and explained his plan to start a carriage business in Richmond. "I calculated the business expenses and profits last night, while I was waiting at the house. It's solid," he said confidently. "I have enough to invest in ten carriages and hire twenty drivers. I'm fine with starting there, but..."

Thomas was listening intently. "But there is enough business to handle starting with more if you had a partner," he said shrewdly.

"That's true," Anthony admitted. "I realize now is not the best time to talk about launching a new business, Thomas. You need to rest."

"It's the perfect time," Thomas said quickly. "And the answer is yes."

Anthony blinked. "It is?"

"On one condition," Thomas answered. "Four hundred good people lost their jobs last night, but some of them mean more to me than others. I would like to have Norris at least consider hiring them first. He will have final say, of course."

"Done," Anthony agreed.

"Thank you." Thomas smiled. "I'll run it past Abby, of course, but I already know what her answer will be. It's a brilliant idea, and it will require far less involvement than the factory did. We will invest the fire insurance money into the carriage business."

"It will require zero personal involvement," Anthony said. "I'm prepared to handle everything. You will be a partner in the profits, but I won't need you to do anything. Simply being able to start on a larger scale will make all the difference in the world."

"Then my answer is an even bigger yes," Thomas said with a grin. He sobered quickly. "But first, I have to finalize things with the factory." He grimaced. "Will you get Willard and Marcus here for me?"

Anthony stood. "Certainly." He hesitated a moment. "Are you sure you want to go out to the plantation tomorrow? I can have someone ride out there to let Abby and Carrie know you've been delayed."

Thomas eyed him shrewdly. "Do I look that bad?"

Anthony smiled. "Only if having a broken nose, two black eyes, and a bullet in your leg might be alarming."

Thomas frowned, and then shrugged. "No more alarming than other things Abby and Carrie have dealt with. They'll want me there, and there is nowhere I would rather be." He looked at Anthony. "I would appreciate it if you would help me get home."

"Home it is," Anthony responded. "Besides, surely you know how much I want to see your beautiful daughter."

Thomas grinned ruefully. "I was confident it wouldn't take too much to convince you."

*****

Thomas was propped up in the bed with a fresh bandage on his leg when Willard, Marcus and Eddie walked in.

After greetings, Willard was the first to step forward. "You don't look as bad as I thought you would."

Thomas grinned, determined not to wince at the pain any movement caused. "Do you lie very often, Willard? I looked in the mirror a little while ago. Anthony was right when he told me I looked like I had been on the receiving end of a very large baseball bat."

Willard chuckled. "Now that you mention it, he could be right." He sobered. "How are you, Thomas? We were all terrified you weren't going to make it."

"I had my moments of the same thoughts," Thomas admitted. "My doctor assures me I will be fine, however."

"You'll be fine faster when you get out to Miss Carrie," Eddie said.

"You're right," Thomas agreed. "Anthony and I are headed out to the plantation tomorrow."

Willard frowned. "Tomorrow? With that bullet wound?"

Thomas nodded. "Carrie will give me some magic potion that will make it heal faster. It will be worth the pain of getting there."

"*Agony* of getting there," Marcus muttered. "Thomas, I don't think you realize how much it's gonna hurt."

"Probably not," Thomas said, suddenly wondering if he had made the right decision. "But all I want to do is go home to the plantation." Just saying the words made him realize anew that he was willing to endure whatever it took.

"Then you should," Marcus said quickly. His eyes grew very serious. "You know the factory was destroyed?"

Thomas nodded. "Anthony told me this morning. I wanted to thank all of you for saving my life last night, and for trying so hard to protect the factory."

"You're welcome, Mr. Thomas," Eddie replied, "but we failed. I went by there this morning. There ain't nothing left."

Thomas sighed, but forced a smile. "We can't undo what has already been done," he said. "Now we just have to figure out how to look ahead to the future."

"Are you rebuilding?" Willard asked.

Thomas shook his head, knowing how hard his next words would be for these men to hear. "No." He explained his and Abby's decision to step back from working. "We don't have it in us to start from scratch," he admitted. He looked at Willard and Marcus. "I already know this is going to hurt our employees," he said heavily, not missing the tension filling the two men's eyes.

"Yep," Marcus agreed.

Thomas knew how much that simple answer conveyed. "I'm going to pay all our workers for two months."

Marcus stared at him. "What?"

"I'm going to pay them all for two months," he repeated. "I wish I could do more, but I'm hoping it will give everyone time to at least make other plans."

"That's real good of you, Thomas," Willard said.

"It's the least Abby and I can do," Thomas answered.

Eddie broke into the sudden silence. "Besides the men sitting in jail, there will be one more man you won't have to pay."

"Oh?" Thomas asked, watching fury ignite in Eddie's eyes.

Eddie nodded. "Me and Spencer were talking last night. We was wondering how those men got in to burn the factory without our guard seeing them."

Thomas remained silent. He had wondered the same thing, once he'd been told about the militia maintaining a guard, but he hadn't brought it up. He didn't know that it mattered now, but he would admit he was curious.

"I was wondering the same thing," Marcus said angrily, and then froze for a moment. "Are you telling me that...?" His voice trailed off.

Eddie sighed. "It was Brian. He told the fellas who burned the building that we didn't have a guard on the shipping dock. They snuck in that way. That's why the guard didn't see them."

"Brian Hansen?" Marcus snapped. "You saying he sold us out to that Pierre fellow?"

Eddie nodded.

"How do you know?" Marcus pressed. "I can't believe that be true!"

"Believe it," Eddie said heavily. "Castle Thunder taught me that anyone can sell you out, Marcus."

"But why?"

"We ain't never gonna know," Eddie replied. "By the time I talked to everyone else and figured it out, he was gone."

"Gone?" Marcus echoed, his eyes wide with disbelief.

"Gone," Eddie repeated. "I went to the boarding house where he had a room. The man who runs it said he dashed in there last night, stayed for a few minutes, and then ran back out."

"He knew we'd figure it out once all the white workers who set the fire got caught," Willard guessed.

"Yep, that's what I figure," Eddie replied. He looked at Thomas. "I be real sorry about that, Mr. Thomas."

Thomas shrugged. "It happens."

Marcus stared at him. "Ain't you angry?"

Thomas shrugged again as fatigue pressed down on him. "What good will it do? The damage has been done. The factory is gone. So is Brian. I hate what he did, but I'm not going to waste my energy on thinking about him." He eyed the three men. "We just have to figure out what comes next."

"Okay," Willard said slowly, obviously struggling with anger. "How do we do that?"

Thomas marshaled his flagging energy. "Eddie, you're fine because you have the restaurant." He fixed his eyes on Marcus and Willard. "I appreciate all my workers, but the two of you mean a great deal to me and Abby. I've been thinking all morning about what I can do."

"Ain't your job to take care of me and Grace," Willard objected.

"No, it's not," Thomas agreed, "but what if you could do something for me, that would also help you?" He knew Willard had a lot of pride.

"That might could work," Willard said cautiously. "What do you have in mind?"

"You told me one time that you love horses, Willard."

"I do," Willard responded with shining eyes. "I figure horses are the finest animals on the planet. I've worked with them every chance I had."

Thomas nodded, glad he had remembered correctly. Then he turned to Marcus. "Jeremy told me once that you love horses, too. Is that true?"

Marcus nodded. "That was my job on the plantation where I was a slave. It was the only thing I liked about that place." He got a faraway look in his eyes. "I still miss some of them horses."

Thomas smiled. "Then I think the two of you will be perfect."

Silence filled the room until Willard broke it. "Perfect for what, Thomas? You're not being very clear." His eyes filled with concern. "Do they got you on some kind of medicine?"

Thomas chuckled, but knew he was quickly getting too tired to talk. He briefly outlined the carriage business he and Anthony had discussed that morning, glad he had already run what he was about to say by his new partner. "At first, we thought we would stable our carriage horses in someone else's stable, but our profit margin will be higher if we have our own. We want to buy a stable, and have the two of you run it. We'll pay you well—more than you were making at the factory. In time, if you like it, and if it's going well, we'll sell it to you. You can make payments on it until you pay it off." He took a breath to gather his remaining energy. "Of course, the two of you will have to work together. Do you see that being a problem?"

"Ain't no problem with me," Marcus said quickly.

"Or me," Willard added. His eyes were shining. "Me and Marcus have been working real close on things at the factory, anyway. We knew Pierre wasn't handling business, so we've been taking care of some things."

Thomas had a moment's curiosity about what those things were, and then realized it didn't matter anymore. The revelation did, however, cement his belief that he had chosen the right two men to run the stable.

"Where are you going to buy the stable, Mr. Thomas?" Marcus asked.

Thomas was suddenly completely exhausted. "Could we talk details in a couple weeks?" he asked wearily.

"Of course," Willard replied instantly. "You need to get some rest."

"I believe that's true," Thomas replied. He laid his head back against the pillow as pain shot through his leg, making even his eyes and nose hurt worse. He bit his lip to keep from groaning.

When he opened his eyes again, the three men were gone. Grateful, Thomas sank into a deep sleep.

Chapter Thirty – Three

Carrie and Rose trotted slowly down the shade-dappled road, content to do nothing but listen to the calls of songbirds, and watch butterflies do a carefree dance among wildflowers.

Carrie was the first to break the silence. "Any regrets about not returning to Oberlin?" She could hardly believe they'd been back on the plantation for almost three weeks. The time had flown by so quickly. She and Rose had spent time together, but moments for heart-to-heart talks had been few.

"Not a one," Rose said. "I knew I was ready to come home, but actually teaching here in my school again has meant more than I expected."

"Why?"

Rose pondered the question. "I suppose it's because I'm doing something very few other people are doing," she said. "I love teaching both black and white students together. It has changed all of their attitudes so much." She paused, thinking deeply. "You know, almost every day I think about teaching my secret school in the woods before the war. Almost ten years later, it seems my life has come full circle, except now I know that I'm where I'm supposed to be. All I could think about back then was getting away from the plantation so I could be free. After the war, all I could think about was leaving the plantation again so I could go to college." She paused. "I remember the day in Oberlin when I realized I just wanted to come home. For the first time, I truly felt I had control of what was going to happen with my life. When I no longer felt I had to resist life here on the plantation, I was free to understand that this is home."

"I'm glad you're so happy."

"But you're not?" Rose asked.

"No," Carrie said quickly, "I *am* happy. I'm glad to be home, and I love having Frances here." She smiled. "Every day with her is a miracle."

Rose smiled, too. "You're a wonderful mother, Carrie. I knew you would be."

"She's such an easy child," Carrie murmured, surprised when Rose laughed loudly. "Why are you laughing?"

Rose was almost doubled over in the saddle. "Frances is a true joy, but she is every bit as hardheaded as you were at that age." She straightened, but couldn't stop laughing. "I think your mother is up in heaven laughing with me."

Carrie smiled at Rose's warm laughter, but shook her head firmly. "I don't think I was hardheaded," she responded. "Neither is Frances. We both know what we want out of life, and are determined to find a way to get it."

"That's a fact," Rose proclaimed. "Frances did her best this morning to convince me that arithmetic is completely unnecessary because she could learn it more quickly if I would allow her to help Susan with the stable books. She kept repeating that practical application was *preferable*." She laughed again. "And she said it just like that."

Carrie cocked her head. "She's probably right."

"See..." Rose sighed. "You two are just alike. You were like that when you were her age. Your mother and father almost pulled their hair out convincing you that you had to learn the lessons your tutor gave you." She paused. "What they don't know is that the only reason you showed up for most of those lessons was because I made you go, so that I could learn them myself. You may have thought it was a waste of time, but it was the only way I had a chance to go to school."

Carrie smiled as the memories swarmed her mind. "You and I were always so different about education."

Rose cocked her head and looked thoughtful. "What would have made it better for you?"

"Arithmetic?" Carrie asked. "Letting me handle the books for the stables," she said promptly. "If I could have seen a practical application for what I was learning, I believe I would have seen it as more than just a waste of my valuable time."

Rose stared at her for a long moment. "So, I should tell Frances that if she does well in her arithmetic, she can help Susan with the books?"

"Yes. Frances is smart, but she's not like you and Felicia. She doesn't care about learning just for the joy of learning. She will want to learn when she discovers there is a *reason* for learning." Carrie continued to think. "I learned my lessons because if I didn't, my mother wouldn't let me ride, but I didn't learn to love knowledge. It wasn't until I started medical school that I loved learning because every single thing I learned meant I could help someone. I couldn't learn things fast enough then. Frances has a lot of catching up to do since her parents never had her in school, but she's working hard."

Rose grinned, her eyes bright with excitement. "Thank you!"

Carrie stared at her. "Thank you? For what?"

"For showing me how important it is to teach different students in different ways. You've given me a lot to think about."

Carrie shrugged. "You're already an amazing teacher, Rose."

"Yes," Rose agreed, "but it's when I think I know it all and quit learning that I'll quit being an amazing teacher."

"I'm happy to let my daughter challenge you," Carrie said with a smirk. "I suspect she'll be good at that for the rest of her life."

"Like mother, like daughter," Rose agreed.

Carrie laughed, and then looked back as a carriage rattled up behind them. "Anthony!" she called. Then she froze. Where was her father? They were supposed to be together. As the carriage drew closer, she saw the strained expression on Anthony's face.

"Carrie!" Anthony called, relief evident in his eyes. "Your father is ill!"

Carrie and Granite covered the remaining yards to the carriage in seconds. She gasped when she looked down at her father, lying prostrate on the seat. His eyes were barely open, and she could see he was feverish. "What happened to him?" she asked, alarmed by his battered face. "Were you attacked on the way here?"

"No," Anthony assured her. "I'll tell you the whole story, but we have to get him inside. He seemed to be fine when we started from Richmond, but then he started feeling very badly about an hour ago."

Carrie's thoughts whirled as she tried to decide whether they should go home or return to the clinic. "Tell me what happened," she commanded. "I need more information!"

Anthony hesitated, and then told her quickly about the attack on the factory.

"He was shot? Two days ago? And he's in this carriage?" She stared at Anthony in disbelief. She would have to process the information about the factory later. Right now, she had to focus on her father.

"I know. I tried to talk him into not coming, but he wouldn't listen. He just said he would be better on the plantation, and that you would take care of him."

"Stubborn fool," Carrie said with a sigh. She couldn't be angry, though, because she would have done the same thing. She looked at Rose. "Go back to the plantation and get Abby and Polly," she ordered. "I'm taking Father back to the clinic. If his leg has gotten infected I'll need my supplies there to help him." She didn't mention her fear that the doctor who treated him hadn't gotten all the bullet fragments. "I'm going ahead to get things ready," she told Anthony, feeling a surge of compassion for him. "He'll be okay," she whispered.

Then she turned and galloped back in the direction she had come, praying she hadn't just told a lie.

*****

Carrie was exhausted when she walked out into the clinic waiting room, vaguely registering that it was now dark outside.

Abby sprang to her feet, and Anthony spun away from the window. "How is he?" Abby asked, her voice strained and shaken.

Carrie smiled in an attempt to alleviate her fears. "Father is going to be all right," she said firmly, "but I'm not moving him from the clinic for a couple of days. I'm sure the doctor who treated him at the hospital did the best he could, but he didn't get all the bullet fragments out of his leg. Infection set in before he and Anthony could make it here."

She gazed at Anthony sympathetically. "You couldn't have known," Carrie assured him, "and neither could Father. If the wound had been clean, the trip out here would have been grueling, but he would have been fine."

"And now?" Abby asked anxiously.

"He's still going to be fine," Carrie said soothingly. "It's just going to take a little longer."

Abby stared at her. "I want the whole truth, Carrie. Don't hide anything."

"I wouldn't dare," Carrie replied with a smile. "I truly believe he's going to be fine, but it will take a couple of days for his fever to come down. I won't move him from the clinic until that has happened."

"I'm staying here with him," Abby declared.

"Polly is making up the extra bed for you now. I knew you wouldn't leave him," Carrie replied. "I'll be sleeping in the other room so I can keep an eye on him, but I don't expect any more problems. He just needs time to heal." She met Abby's eyes squarely, relieved when she saw Abby begin to relax.

"Can I go in now?" Abby asked.

"Yes. I don't expect he'll regain consciousness for a few hours or more. He'll be happy to have you there when he wakes up."

Abby rushed forward to engulf her in a hug. "Thank you," she whispered, and then hurried into the room.

Only then did Carrie turn to Anthony. She smiled when he opened his arms, and walked straight into them, sighing with pleasure when they wrapped around her.

"You're really something, Dr. Borden," Anthony murmured.

Carrie rested her head on his solid chest for several minutes before pushing back to look into his face. "And so are you, Anthony Wallington. Father was conscious for a few minutes before I performed the surgery. He told me you carried him out of the burning factory." Her throat clogged with tears. "Thank you," she whispered.

"I wasn't the only one," Anthony said modestly.

"Eddie told my father the truth," Carrie replied. "That you ran all the way from the house. That you got there firs,t and burst into the factory through the flames to get to him."

"I love your father," Anthony replied. He tilted her chin up. "And I love you, Carrie."

"I love you, too," Carrie said with a sigh, burying her head back into his chest. She had been terrified by the image of her father's waxen face staring at her from the carriage. His leg had already been angry with infection when she got him to the clinic. She had fought fear of him dying while she had worked to save him. The dual battle had exhausted her.

Carrie looked around. "Where is Rose?"

"She returned to the house to get food. She should be back any minute."

The mention of food made Carrie realize she was starving. "Good!"

"And he'll really be all right?" Anthony pressed.

"I promise," Carrie replied, grateful beyond words that she was certain this time.

*****

Abby was watching Thomas when his eyes blinked open. "Welcome back," she said softly.

Thomas turned his head toward her, blinking several more times. "Abby?" he asked hoarsely.

"Yes, my dear." Abby lifted a glass of water to his chapped lips. "Drink this. It will help."

Thomas sipped the liquid, and then made a face. "What's in that?"

Abby smiled. "Some of Carrie's magical remedies," she said lightly. "She warned me you wouldn't like the taste, but she said to show you no mercy."

Thomas managed a chuckle. "That sounds like my daughter."

"Who also just happened to save your life," Abby informed him. She knew Thomas couldn't have known there were still bullet fragments in his leg when he decided to ride out to the plantation, but she still wasn't over her terror.

"I'm sorry," Thomas said. "I didn't mean to frighten you."

Abby sighed. "I know, Thomas. The only thing that's important now is that you're going to be just fine. You have to stay here in the clinic because Dr. Borden refuses to release you, but you'll be home in our bed soon."

Thomas held her eyes. "There is nothing more I want in the world besides that," he said.

Abby closed her eyes for a moment, feeling the truth of the statement engulf her. They were both home on the plantation, right where they wanted to be.

"We need to talk about the factory," Thomas said groggily.

"Not now," Abby replied. "It can wait."

"I want to," Thomas insisted.

Abby eyed him. "Only if you drink the rest of Carrie's magic remedy."

Thomas reached for it. "Give it to me," he grunted.

Abby watched to make sure he drained every drop before taking the glass back. "You may talk now."

Thomas stared at her for several moments before he spoke, pain etched into his face. "The factory is gone, Abby."

"I know," Abby replied. "Anthony told me what happened."

"I don't believe it makes sense to rebuild," Thomas said slowly, watching for her reaction.

The long night had given Abby plenty of time to think. "I quite agree with you, my dear. I regret so many people losing their jobs, but we've done our part. It's time for us to be finished. We've already talked about this. We weren't planning on the fire, but what's done is done."

"Do you really mean that?"

"With all my heart," Abby said firmly. "We have our fire insurance to recoup a large part of the loss, but I believe that part of our life is over."

Thomas continued to watch her. "You've been on the plantation for two weeks. Do you really think you can be happy here?"

Abby laughed lightly. "I've never been happier," she assured him. "The only thing it will take to make it perfect is for you to be here with me all the time."

"I believe you mean that," Thomas said with relief.

"Completely," Abby assured him. "I love every minute I spend with Carrie, and Frances is a complete joy. Annie taught me how to make strawberry pie yesterday, and I went riding into the tobacco fields on my own a few days ago. I'm becoming quite good friends with many of the plantation workers. I'm discovering I quite enjoy being the plantation matriarch," she said with a grin.

Thomas laughed, and then grimaced.

"Enough talk, my dear. Carrie warned me you would try to overdo it." She laid a hand on his forehead. "Your fever is better, but it's not gone. I'm not saying another word until you have had some more sleep." She smiled. "When you wake up, there will be some more special water for you."

"Joy," Thomas muttered, and then closed his eyes. Moments later he was sound asleep, his features relaxed, and his breathing even.

Abby leaned over to kiss him, and then laid down on her cot. Thomas would sleep for several hours. She breathed a prayer of gratitude before she drifted into a deep slumber.

*****

Carrie was waiting in the kitchen when Frances came barreling downstairs the next morning, Felicia on her heels.

"How is Opa?" Frances demanded. "Miss Rose wouldn't tell us hardly anything last night because she didn't know much. She said he was going to be all right, but I couldn't sleep all night."

"Me either," Felicia proclaimed, her eyes wide with distress. "How is Thomas?"

Carrie smiled. She loved hearing Frances call her father Opa. Abby had assured the little girl that he would love it. She also knew how much Felicia loved her father. He had taken a special interest in her from the day she arrived, wide-eyed and frightened, from Memphis.

"I promise you he is going to be fine," she said. "That's why I came back to the house this morning. I knew you would be worried."

"What happened to him?" Felicia asked.

Carrie sighed. She was not eager to explain this part of it, but she was determined to get it out of the way before her father came back to the house. She didn't want the two girls pestering him with questions. She opened her mouth to begin, but was interrupted by the door swinging open.

"Mr. Anthony!" Felicia cried. She jumped up to give him a hug.

Carrie smiled at him warmly, and then turned to Frances, who was watching with wide eyes. "Frances, I would like you to meet Anthony Wallington."

Anthony smiled and walked over to take one of Frances' hands. "Hello, Frances. You're as beautiful as Carrie told me you were. I'm so glad you're here. You've made Carrie a very happy woman."

Carrie bit back a smile as she watched her strong-willed daughter melt beneath Anthony's charm. Rose had been right; like mother, like daughter.

"Hello, Mr. Anthony," Frances said shyly, gazing up at him. "It's very nice to meet you."

"Now that Mr. Anthony is here, will you tell us what happened to Thomas?" Felicia pressed.

Carrie nodded and took a deep breath. She had debated all night how much to tell them, ultimately deciding the truth was the best thing. Attempting to shelter them from the realities of life would do nothing to help them prepare for living with them. "The manager at Cromwell Factory was a bad man," she began. "He was not who everybody thought he was."

Felicia nodded wisely. "Like the policemen in Memphis who murdered my parents."

"Yes," Carrie agreed solemnly. "He talked some of the workers into setting fire to the factory."

"Why would they do that?" Frances asked with astonishment. "Weren't they burning the place they work?"

Carrie nodded. "They were," she agreed. "People don't always think through the consequences of their actions," she said sadly.

"But how did Thomas get hurt?" Felicia asked. Then she gasped. "Was he at the factory?"

Carrie exchanged a look with Anthony. "He was," she confirmed. "He was there much later than usual, so no one expected him to be there. He had a fight with his manager." She took another deep breath. "He was shot."

"Shot?" Frances echoed, her eyes filled with horror.

"Shot?" Felicia cried angrily.

Carrie understood when Felicia's anger faded quickly, only to be replaced by fear. Felicia would never forget watching both her parents be gunned down. "He's going to be fine, Felicia. I promise." She waited until the fear began to fade from the young girl's eyes before she continued. "We all have Anthony to thank for saving his life."

Both of the girls spun to face Anthony.

"You saved Opa?" Frances cried. "Thank you!"

Felicia rushed forward to give him another hug. "Thank you, Mr. Anthony."

"I had help," Anthony replied modestly. "But, you're welcome."

Frances looked back to Carrie with a question in her eyes.

"Anthony saved him," Carrie repeated firmly. "He was the only one who knew Father was in the factory. He ran all the way from Father's house, and then raced into the burning building to pull him out. He carried him out of the factory, and went to the hospital with him." Her heart swelled with gratitude once again as she envisioned the scene.

Frances eyed Anthony for a few moments, and then rushed forward to wrap her arms around him. "Thank you, Mr. Anthony," she murmured. "I hardly know my Opa at all. If you hadn't saved him, I wouldn't get to know him better."

Anthony returned the embrace, his eyes latched on Carrie.

Carrie knew from the expression on his face that he was already falling in love with Frances. She wasn't surprised, but the knowledge did something odd to her heart.

*****

Thomas was sitting up in bed when Carrie arrived at the clinic after breakfast with a basket full of ham biscuits and preserves. Abby had already made coffee.

"Well, look at you," Carrie said cheerfully, putting down the basket and placing a hand on his forehead. "Your fever isn't gone quite yet, but it's better than I expected."

"My fever doesn't stand a chance against whatever is in the water Abby keeps making me drink," Thomas complained. "I sure could use a cup of coffee." He eyed the pot simmering on the stove hopefully.

"You're talking to the wrong person for pity," Carrie retorted. "If you hadn't been so set on being here on the plantation, and had stayed in the hospital an extra day as recommended, you wouldn't have gotten so sick."

Thomas sobered, but shook his head. "I disagree. Abby told me you had to perform another surgery on me. I believe I fared far better right here than I would have in Richmond." His eyes glowed with love as he looked at her. "Thank you, Dr. Borden."

Carrie leaned over to hug him. "I would appreciate it if you never scare me like that again," she scolded.

Thomas chuckled. "So says the young woman who has made me old before my time with some of the decisions *you* have made."

Carrie couldn't help laughing. "You may have a point," she conceded. "The important thing is that you are going to be fine." She looked toward the waiting room. "Do you feel like a little company? I won't let them stay long, but you have two young ladies who will probably not give me any peace until they have seen with their own eyes that you're going to be all right. I also pity Rose and Lillian if I send the girls on to school without their getting proof."

Thomas grinned. "Frances and Felicia? Please let them in."

Carrie walked out into the waiting room. "Remember what I told you," she reminded them. "You can only stay a few minutes because he needs to rest."

Felicia nodded solemnly. "Yes, ma'am."

"I promise," Frances said quietly.

Carrie stood back and waved for them to enter. Both girls rushed to the door, but then slowed to a sedate walk when they entered the room.

"Opa!" Frances cried as she walked to stand beside the bed. Felicia took a position on the other side.

Thomas reached out to grasp their hands tightly. "Hello, Frances. Hello, Felicia. Thank you for coming to visit me."

Felicia had her eyes fastened on the bedspread that was lumped up above the bandage. "Did you really get shot?"

"I did," Thomas acknowledged, "but lucky for me, the man was not a very good shot."

Carrie pursed her lips as she exchanged a long look with Abby. Anthony had told her that Eddie's quick action to staunch the bleeding was what had saved Thomas' life after they rescued him from the burning building. They had decided the girls didn't need to know everything.

"How long will it be before you can go riding with me and Carrie and Oma?" Frances asked eagerly. "I have my very own horse now, Opa!"

Thomas raised a brow. "You do?"

Frances nodded. "Carrie bought Peaches for me, just like you bought Granite for her when she was my age."

Carrie watched Felicia carefully, relieved there was no jealousy in the older girl's expression. Felicia rode, but only when she was forced to. Her connection with Thomas was in the library.

"That's wonderful," Thomas said, "but..."

"But he won't be riding a horse for at least six weeks," Carrie said firmly. "We have to give his leg time to heal."

Frances nodded, but couldn't hide her disappointment.

Felicia smiled brightly. "I brought home some books you'll want to see, Thomas. I've been studying business, just like you told me to. There is so much I want to talk with you about."

Thomas smiled. "I can't wait to do just that. We'll have lots of time for long conversations," he promised. He looked thoughtful for a moment, and then turned to Frances. "I may not be able to ride a horse right now, but do you like to have stories read to you?"

Frances nodded shyly. "My folks never did because they didn't really know how to read, but Carrie has read me a few stories. I like it."

"Then I'll read you stories every day," Thomas replied. "Have you ever heard of *Little Women*?"

Frances frowned. "Is that a book?"

"It is," Felicia said excitedly. "My mama brought me home a copy before we came to the plantation, but I haven't had a chance to read it yet." She paused. "Would it be all right if I listened while I'm here?"

Carrie watched her father's face ignite with joy.

"Of course," Thomas agreed.

"What's the book about?" Frances asked.

Abby was the one to answer. "It's about four sisters. Their names are Meg, Jo, Beth, and Amy March. The book is about how they grow from little girls to women. It was published last year, and is already quite popular."

"Have you read it, Oma?" Frances asked.

"Not yet," Abby replied, "but the author, Louisa May Alcott, is a friend of mine."

"That's right," Carrie murmured. "I remember you telling me about her. She was an abolitionist, and is fighting now for women's right to vote. What I know most about her is that she was a staunch advocate for homeopathy."

"Yes," Abby replied. "She is quite remarkable. I've heard wonderful things about the book."

Francis edged closer to her. "Will you join us when Thomas reads it to us?" she asked hopefully.

Abby smiled brightly. "There is nothing I would rather do, Francis."

Francis rewarded her with a beaming smile.

"And now," Carrie announced, "it's time for two young ladies to go to school. My father needs to rest."

Thomas frowned playfully. "She's a very bossy doctor."

"She should be," Frances said seriously. "I'm going to be just like her when I become a doctor." She started to walk out, and then turned back. "Opa?"

"Yes, Francis?"

"I heard you asking if you could have coffee when we were out in the waiting room." She placed her hands on her hips. "You can't have coffee right now," she said earnestly. "Carrie explained on the way over that you need to drink lots of the remedy she mixed so you will get better quickly. That's what you need to do."

Carrie turned her head to hide her smile.

"Yes, ma'am," Thomas said seriously, but made a face. "It doesn't taste very good."

"I know," Frances said. "I didn't like some of the remedies Carrie gave me on the Santa Fe Trail when she saved my life, but I'm sure glad I drank them. I wouldn't want to miss being here with all of you."

Carrie's heart melted a little more. She strode forward to give Frances a warm hug. "Thank you, honey," she whispered. "Go on to school now. I promise he'll drink it all."

Thomas watched the two girls leave with a bemused expression. "She is just like you were at that age," he said quietly. He watched the two girls walk over to the schoolhouse, and then smiled. "Both of you are very lucky."

"I'm reminded of that every day," Carrie agreed.

Claim a *FREE* copy of <u>*The Bregdan Principle!*</u>

You'll receive it in high resolution and full color – a file you can print directly on your own printer, or send to have it done. Just join my mailing list!

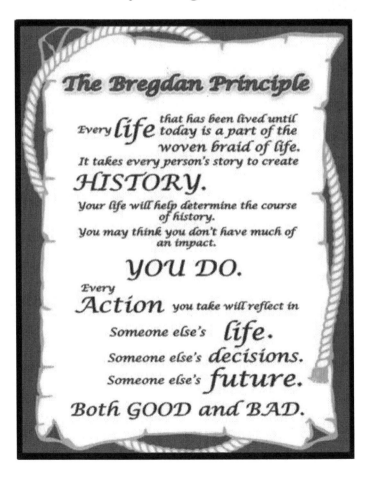

An Invitation

Before you read the last chapter of Storm Clouds Rolling In, I would like to invite you to join my mailing list so that you are never left wondering what is going to happen next. ☺

I will also GIVE you a free copy of The Bregdan Principle that you can print or your computer, or have printed for you.

Join my Email list so you can:

- Receive notice of all new books & audio releases.
- Be a part of my Launch celebrations. I give away lots of gifts! ☺
- Read my weekly blog while you're waiting for a new book.
- Be part of The Bregdan Chronicles Family!
- Learn about all the other books I write.

Just go to www.BregdanChronicles.net and fill out the form.

I look forward to having you become part of The Bregdan Chronicles Family!

Blessings,
Ginny Dye

Chapter Thirty - Four

Carrie and Anthony walked out to the barn two days later with Frances skipping between them.

"You're sure you know how to ride?" Frances teased as she glanced up at Anthony.

"I can outride you, little girl," Anthony scoffed. "I'll be sure to take it easy on you."

"Take it easy on me?" Frances cried, peering up at Carrie for defense. "Tell him how good I am, Carrie!"

"I suggest you *show* him," Carrie responded lightly. "Miles taught me how to ride years ago. He taught me a lot of other things, as well. One of the things I remember best is him teaching me that instead of telling people what I'm going to *do*, that I should remain silent until I could tell them what I had *done*." She cocked a brow. "Rather than boast about what you can do, Frances, I suggest you just do it."

Frances considered her words. "I suppose that makes sense," she said somewhat reluctantly.

"I'm so glad you think so," Carrie said wryly, her lips twitching as she tried to control the laughter bubbling up inside her. She lost the battle when she met Anthony's amused eyes. "Come on, Frances," she said in between laughs. "I want to go see the new place you and Amber discovered this afternoon."

Minutes later, they were trotting down the road between tobacco fields.

"I love this time of year. June is one of my favorite months of the year." Carrie gazed out at the green plants stretching as far as she could see.

"The tobacco is beautiful!" Frances cried. "I love all the pink flowers."

"Me too," Carrie agreed. "Enjoy them as much as you can though, because they'll start topping the plants in the next week or so."

"Topping them? What does that mean?" Frances asked.

"It means they'll cut off the tops of the tobacco plants," Anthony informed her.

"Why?" Frances cried. "They'll cut off all the flowers. Then they will all just be the same boring green."

"I felt just that way when I was your age," Carrie said. "Actually, I *still* feel that way, but they have to do it to make the tobacco grow strong. When they top the plants, all the food and energy goes to the leaves. That's important, because the leaves are what they harvest."

"It seems wrong that the flowers have to die in order for people to make money," Frances said sadly.

"Again, I agree sweetie, but if it makes you feel any better, the flowers would die off on their own in another few weeks," Carrie replied.

Frances stared out at the plants. "I suppose it makes me feel a little better," she admitted. "Miss Annie told me the other day that when I find things to be happy about, I got to suck all the life right out of 'em, 'cause I never know when it will end." Her imitation of Annie's voice was remarkable.

"She's right," Carrie agreed with a smile. "Annie is a very wise woman."

Frances nodded. "I'm going to ride out in the tobacco fields every day until they top the flowers. That way, I'll be able to hold them in my memory for when they're gone."

"That's a very good idea," Anthony said huskily. "That's what I'm doing right now."

"What do you mean?" Frances asked.

"I love riding out here with you and Carrie. I'm going to do it every chance I get while I'm here, so that I can hold it in my memory."

Frances eyed him. "I'll go riding with you anytime you want, Mr. Anthony."

"Thank you," Anthony responded. "Right now though," he grinned as his eyes sparkled with fun, "you just need to see if you can keep up with me." He leaned forward, signaling Master, the bay gelding he was riding, to break into a gallop.

Frances whooped with joy and urged Peaches forward. The mare tossed her head and took off at a controlled gallop.

Carrie smiled. Peaches wouldn't catch Master, but she knew Anthony would hold the gelding back so that Frances wouldn't feel too bad.

"Try and catch us, Carrie!" Frances called back over her shoulder with a taunting laugh.

"Want to show them what you have, boy?" Carrie murmured to Granite. He snorted, and then sprang forward into a dead run as soon as she released the reins. She laughed happily as they flew down the road. It took only moments to pass Peaches, with Frances cheering her on, and then she gained on Master.

Anthony glanced back over his shoulder with a grin, and hunched forward in his saddle, letting Master have his head.

Carrie held Granite neck-and-neck with Master for about a minute, and then gave Anthony a cocky grin. "You never had a chance!" she called as she released Granite again. Her Thoroughbred was far in front before she pulled him down to an easy canter, slowed to a trot, and then let him drop to a walk.

It was several minutes before Anthony caught up. They both pulled to a halt until Frances and Peaches joined them.

Frances had a smile on her face, but she was clearly frustrated. "I'll never win a race on Peaches!" she cried.

"Don't be so sure," Carrie said calmly.

"She never runs really fast," Frances retorted.

"Her owner told me Peaches is a very smart horse," Carrie informed her. "He was right."

"What do you mean?" Frances demanded.

"He told me Peaches would be perfect for you because she would never outrun her rider."

Frances just stared at her. "Am I supposed to know what that means?"

"No," Carrie replied with a chuckle. "What he meant is that Peaches won't run faster than your ability to ride her or handle her. The better you learn how to ride, the faster she'll run for you."

Frances stared at her with suspicious eyes, and then turned to Anthony. "Is that true?"

Anthony shrugged. "I've never heard of such a thing, but if Carrie says it's true, I would probably believe her. She knows more about horses and riding than both of us together."

Frances swung back to gaze at Carrie again. "Is that really true?" she demanded again.

"It is," Carrie assured her. "Think about it like this. Wouldn't I know that you wanted to go faster and faster on Peaches?

Frances nodded, but her eyes were still mutinous.

"Do you think I would get you a horse that you would want to trade for a faster one someday?" Carrie asked.

Frances thought hard, and finally shook her head. "No. You would get me a horse that I could have forever, just like you've had Granite since you were my age."

"That's right," Carrie replied. "Peaches is as perfect as you think she is. She may never beat *Granite*," she said a little smugly, "but she'll give him a good race someday."

"How soon?" Frances demanded impatiently.

Carrie chuckled. "That will be up to you and Peaches, Frances. Keep listening to everything we teach you. Miles is the best teacher I know, and Susan and Amber will help as well."

"I'll work hard," Frances promised. "Riding is certainly more fun than arithmetic!"

"I couldn't agree with you more," Carrie said with a laugh. "Now, where is this place you and Amber discovered?"

Frances grinned and turned toward the river. "It's down by the water." She trotted ahead eagerly, leading them down a narrow trail through the woods.

Anthony raised a brow. "You let her and Amber ride around the plantation on their own?"

"Reluctantly," Carrie replied. She understood his surprise. There had been too many attacks on the plantation to assume the girls would be safe. "We've told them they can't explore the woods around the school, and that they can't go toward the gate. We've limited them to the area between the house and the river." She shook her head. "I don't want them to live with fear all the time. Amber is smart enough to be careful. I finally decided that if she can be brave enough to ride on her own after being with Robert when he was murdered, I have to be brave enough to let her do it." She smiled. "Within reason."

Anthony eyed her for several long moments, and then his lips twitched. "Which means one of the plantation men always have them in view?" he guessed.

"That might be a possibility," Carrie said demurely. "They have freedom, and the rest of us have sanity. I believe it's a fair arrangement."

Anthony chuckled, and then broke into a canter to catch up with Frances. "Let's go see what they've discovered."

Several minutes later, they broke out into a clearing along the James River. Carrie smiled when she realized where they were. Deep in conversation with Anthony, she had not paid attention to the trail Frances took them down.

"Have you ever been here before?" Frances asked eagerly.

Carrie thought about telling her she hadn't, but in truth, she had explored every square inch of the plantation. She pointed to a large rock out in the river instead. "See that rock?"

Frances nodded.

"Rose and I started meeting on that rock when we were younger than you, to celebrate every New Year's Day. We sat out on that rock and watched the sun rise."

"And told each other what your dreams were for the year," Frances guessed.

"That's right," Carrie replied. "We only stopped doing it a couple years ago."

"Why did you stop?"

Carrie gave her a mysterious look. "Because now we meet somewhere else."

"Where?" Frances demanded.

"I'm afraid that's a secret," Carrie murmured. She planned on sharing the tunnel with Frances soon, but she wasn't ready to talk about it with Anthony. The tunnel was hardly a family secret anymore, but it was still something very special.

"A secret?" Frances cried. "You have to tell me!"

"I will," Carrie promised.

"When?"

"Soon," Carrie said with a laugh, amused at France' imperious tone.

Frances stamped her foot, and put her hands on her hips.

"You're in trouble now," Anthony said with amusement. "Any time a female puts her hands on her hips, she means business."

"Is that right?" Carrie asked. "I'll be sure to remember that."

"When?" Frances repeated.

Carrie opened her mouth to answer, but was shocked into silence when Frances' defiance disappeared as quickly as it had appeared, only to be replaced with heartbreaking vulnerability that made the girl's eyes glimmer with tears. Carrie dropped to her knees. "Frances, what's wrong?"

Frances shook her head, trying to control her trembling lips. "I don't mean to be too pushy," she stammered. "Please don't send me back."

Carrie grabbed her shoulders. "Send you back? To the orphanage? I would *never* send you back. What would make you say that?"

"My teacher at the orphanage used to tell me that no one liked pushy little girls," Frances said quietly as she kept her eyes on the ground, her cheeks flaming red. "She told me if I ever wanted to be adopted, that I had to be different. I tried real hard to be different while I was there, but sometimes I still forget."

"I hope you forget *all* the time," Carrie murmured, stroking the little girl's hair back from her hot cheeks.

"Your teacher was very wrong, Frances. You are perfect just as you are." She pulled her close and whispered in her ear. "I have a secret for you."

"Wha...What?" Frances stuttered.

"I love pushy little girls," Carrie confided. "Do you know why?"

"Why?" Frances was still staring at the ground.

"Because I was one, too. And you know what else?"

Frances shook her head, but had raised her eyes now, and was looking at Carrie intently.

"I'm a pushy *woman* now," she said firmly. She lifted Frances' chin so she could meet her eyes. "The world has all kinds of rules about how women are supposed to be, but you don't have to live by any of them."

"I don't?" Frances breathed.

"You don't," Carrie stated. "I'm a doctor because I didn't live by the rules. Rose is a teacher because *she* didn't live by the rules. Oma is a successful businesswoman because *she* didn't live by the rules. The only rules you have to live by, honey, are the ones you set for yourself inside."

"Do you have rules for yourself?" Frances asked, her eyes bright with interest.

"I do," Carrie responded. "One rule is that I always have to live with integrity. Another is that I will let grace and compassion rule my life." She paused. "The second one is not always easy, but I keep trying. I have other rules, too..."

Frances kept staring at her. "What are they?"

"Well," Carrie said slowly. "Those are going to have to wait until we go to the secret place together."

Frances froze, and then her eyes began to shine. "You're still going to take me to the secret place?"

"Of course," Carrie said. "I've planned on it all along. I'm just waiting for there to be a full moon."

"A full moon? Is that part of what makes it special?" Frances asked, her eyes wide with anticipation.

"Definitely," Carrie answered, leaning forward to kiss Frances' cheek. "The moon will be full in two weeks. When it's full, I will share the secret with you." She prayed there would be no clouds to diminish the experience. They didn't really need a full moon, but she knew it would make the night even more memorable for her daughter.

Frances gave a glad cry and flung herself into Carrie's arms. "I love you!"

Tears filled Carrie's eyes as she pulled her close. "I love you, too, Frances."

*****

Carrie walked out onto the porch after supper. A few minutes later, Anthony appeared at her side.

"Care to go for a walk?" he asked. "It's a beautiful night."

"I would love to." She glanced over at her father and Abby sitting side by side in the rockers. Their hands were entwined, and her father's leg was elevated on a stool. He was getting stronger every day. It made her happy to see them relaxing together on the plantation.

Abby glanced at them, her face full of contentment. "You two have a good time."

Carrie breathed in the fresh air as they strolled through the gathering dusk. There was nothing as magical as a summer night on the plantation. It was warm, but early June didn't deliver the same searing heat as late July and August.

Crickets and tree frogs were stringing up their orchestra, as whippoorwills sounded their evening serenade. Fireflies lifted from the ground in response to the encroaching darkness, dancing through the trees as they flashed their lights on and off. The heady fragrance of honeysuckle mingled with wild roses.

"How do you stand to ever be away from here?" Anthony asked.

"It's hard," Carrie admitted. "Much harder than it used to be. There was a time when all I wanted was to leave the plantation and make my way in the world. I never thought it would be a war that would take me away. Then, I left again to go to medical school." She hesitated. "I was happy here with Robert, but when he was murdered..." Her voice trailed off. "At first, I thought I would never leave again because I felt close to him here, but soon, all I wanted to do was get away again. That's what took me on the Santa Fe Trail," she admitted, thinking back to the chaos of feelings she had endured after Robert and Bridget's deaths.

"And now?" Anthony asked.

"And now," Carrie said quietly, "I want to stay...but I have to leave again." Saying the words out loud made her heart clench.

"Why?" Anthony asked, clearly startled.

Carrie paused. "I haven't told anyone else about my decision yet."

"I'm honored to be the first," Anthony said, and then waited.

Carrie continued walking a few paces before she turned to him. "Can we go back to the place by the river where Frances took us this afternoon?"

"Certainly," Anthony answered, and then hesitated. "Can you get us back in the dark?"

Carrie laughed. "I could get us back if I was blindfolded," she assured him.

Nothing more was said as they walked through the woods. Carrie smiled when Anthony reached down to take her hand. She could smell the river before they reached it. She drew in deep breaths, letting memories carry her back to all the big decisions made by the James River. Its flowing water had been part of her life for as long as she'd been alive.

The sun was just sinking below the horizon when they reached the river. Water whispered through the small rocks lining the shore as small waves advanced and receded. A bank of pink and purple clouds caught the golden rays of the departing sun, splitting them into dazzling shafts of light that seemed to reach all the way to the heavens.

"Spectacular," Anthony breathed when the sun finally dipped far enough below the horizon to release its hold on the clouds. "Care to tell me your decision now?"

"I've made two, actually," Carrie replied, praying she would have the right words, and that the whispering waves would give her courage. "The first, is that I have to go back to medical school." Anthony turned to her, but she didn't see the surprise she had expected.

"Because you want to be a surgeon, as well as a homeopathic physician," he said quietly.

Carrie gaped at him. "How did you know that?"

"Because you're a natural surgeon," Anthony replied. "You performed a Cesarean Section on Janie under less than ideal conditions. You saved your father by removing the bullet fragments a less capable surgeon left behind. The first day I met you, you saved the lives of three vigilantes who attacked the plantation." He gripped her hands. "You're a very gifted surgeon, but can you combine the two practices?"

Carrie shook her head. "I don't know. I don't even know if I'll find a medical college that will have me now that I've embraced homeopathy."

"Do you regret it?"

"No," Carrie said quickly. "I went to school to help people. I'm still convinced homeopathy is the best way to treat the majority of illnesses, but there are times when only surgery is the answer." She paused. "I've gotten away with what I've done so far, and conditions during the war made people look the other way, but it's not going to be that way in the future. If I want to continue practicing medicine the way I want to practice it, I have to go back to school."

Anthony thought for a moment. "It's not like you have to tell the medical school that you happen to *already* be a doctor."

Carrie smiled. "I've certainly considered that." Then she shrugged. "I believe I'll find the right school."

Anthony nodded. "What about Frances?"

"She'll come with me, of course," Carrie answered. "When I adopted her, I told her we may not always be on the plantation because of what I do."

"And she was all right with that?"

Carrie smiled. "She said it was perfect because she's going to be a doctor, too."

Anthony chuckled. "She's an amazing little girl."

Carrie cocked her head. "I'm glad you think so." She paused, trying to figure out how to say what she wanted to say next. She had no idea how to make her next pronouncement blend with the first, but she was certain of her feelings. "My father told me about the carriage business you're starting in Richmond. It sounds wonderful."

"I believe it will be profitable," Anthony replied, "and it will give a lot of good men a good job."

"So, you'll be staying in Richmond?" Carrie asked, feeling her way forward.

Anthony shrugged. "I don't know. I decided to start this business because once it is up and running, it will require little of my time. Norris will be a good manager. Willard and Marcus will take excellent care of the horses." He paused. "I'm doing my best to create sources of income that will give me freedom. I told your father in Philadelphia that my own father worked so hard that he did nothing else, and hardly knew his family. I know I don't want my life to be like that." He looked at her more closely. "Why are you asking, Carrie?"

Carrie took a deep breath and met his eyes. "At the beginning of this conversation, I told you I had made two decisions."

"I remember," Anthony replied. His eyes were fastened on hers.

Carrie's heart was beating so fast, she wasn't sure she was going to be able to speak. She cleared her throat, turned to stare out at the river for a long moment, and then turned back, her heart calming. "The second decision... is that I would like very much to be your wife."

Anthony's eyes opened wide, and his face bloomed in a joyous smile. "You mean it?" he demanded. "You want to marry me?"

"If you still want me," Carrie murmured with a smile. "I know we have things to figure out, but I love you, Anthony." She thought back to her earlier conversation with Frances. "I hope I'm not being too pushy."

"If I still *want* you?" Anthony asked. "It's all I think about." He laughed. "And just for the record, I happen to love pushy women. Especially you." He laughed again and pulled her to him, pressing his lips to hers with a kiss of joyous promise and passion.

*****

Moses climbed the steps to the house, every muscle aching with weariness, and his heart filled with contentment. He smiled at Thomas and Abby, claiming a rocker when Abby waved him over.

"Long day," Thomas commented. "You missed supper."

Moses shrugged. "Mama always keeps food for me." His face lit in a smile. "Franklin hired ten new men last week. They've already started on clearing more land. I rode out there to take a look. It will be ready to go under a cover crop this winter. We'll plant next spring."

Thomas whistled. "Very impressive."

Moses nodded. "It's amazing how fast men will work when they know they share in the profits of what they're creating." He looked at Thomas more closely. "How are you feeling?"

"Like six weeks of not riding is going to be unbearable," Thomas said ruefully.

"I told you I would drive you out through the fields in the carriage," Abby reminded him.

"I know, but it's not the same," Thomas replied. Then he shook his head. "Self-pity is not flattering," he acknowledged, and then squeezed Abby's hand. "I may not be able to ride out into the fields, but it's my pride that's keeping me from seeing them. I'm sorry, my dear."

Abby smiled. "I'm sure I would feel the same way."

"Probably, but I would be happy to go for a carriage ride tomorrow," Thomas said firmly.

Abby leaned over to kiss his cheek. "And, I'll be happy to take you."

Moses eyed him. "When you feel up to it, I could use your suggestions on some things I'm thinking about in regard to our plantation. Do you feel up to it?"

"I had a bullet in my leg, not my head," Thomas said wryly. "I doubt if I can tell you anything you don't already know, but I'll try." He grimaced. "There I go again." He shook his head. "I'm not made to be an idle man."

Moses eyed him. "You're a lucky man," he said quietly.

"Lucky?"

"Yes, lucky," Moses repeated. "You've worked hard all your life. Now you have a chance to sit back and enjoy what you've created."

Frances ran out onto the porch with a book tucked under her arm. Felicia was right behind her. "Opa! Are you ready to read some more of *Little Women* to us? You quit reading last night right when Beth was real sick with scarlet fever. We have to know what happens!"

"Of course, we could just read it ourselves," Felicia said coyly.

Thomas scowled. "I hardly think so," he retorted, reaching for the book. He turned up the flame on the lantern sitting on the table next to him. "I want to know what happens, too."

Moses watched them for a moment. "Lucky," he repeated.

*****

Carrie and Anthony approached the porch hand in hand. She was happy to see Abby and her father were still there, and even happier to see Frances, Felicia, and Moses sitting with them in the warm glow of lantern light. As they were climbing the steps, Rose, Susan, and Annie walked out. Annie was carrying a tray piled with cookies.

"Is that for me?" Carrie asked brightly.

Annie raised a brow and eyed her keenly. "I see that gleam in your eyes, Miss Carrie. You got something to be celebrating?"

"I might," Carrie said evasively, reaching for a cookie.

"Oh no you don't, young lady," Annie said, pulling the tray behind her back. "You ain't gettin' no cookies until you spill the beans."

"She's right," Abby said in a lilting voice. "Spill the beans."

It took only a glance at Abby's glowing face to know she already guessed what Carrie had to say.

"Spill the beans!" Frances cried, jumping up from her chair. "What are we celebrating?"

Carrie turned to meet Rose's eyes. She saw the bright happiness she was hoping to see. "Anthony and I are engaged," she said joyfully. She held up their linked hands as evidence.

"She may live to regret saying she'll marry me," Anthony stated, "but I'm not going to give her much time to change her mind."

Cries of congratulations rang through the air.

Thomas waved Anthony over and shook his hand firmly. "Not that you need it, but you have my complete approval. If you think you can handle this daughter of mine, I am happy to give my blessing."

Frances snorted. "Anthony won't be *handling* her, Opa. Carrie is a pushy woman."

Carrie laughed, glad she had told her father and Abby about the conversation earlier that day.

Frances walked over to stand in front of Anthony. "Does this mean I am going to be *your* daughter, too?"

Anthony knelt down. "I hope so, Frances. If you'll let me become your daddy."

Frances stared at him. "Are you sure you're all right with pushy girls?"

"I'm sure," Anthony said. "I already know you're perfect just the way you are."

Frances nodded, a bright smile blooming on her face. "Then it's all right with me if you marry Carrie." She looked around the porch with a dazed expression. "Sometimes it seems like a dream that I was in an orphanage with no family. Look how much family I have now!"

Carrie brushed away her tears, unsure how her heart could contain so much happiness. There were plans that would have to be made, but her decision to marry Anthony felt completely right.

She looked toward the barn, a smile bursting forth when a half moon slid up to rest on the trees. Its glimmering light illuminated the horizon, beckoning her forward into a future she never would have dreamed possible.

To Be Continued...

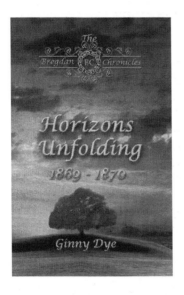

Coming Winter 2018!

Would you be so kind as to leave a Review on Amazon?

Go to www.Amazon.com

Put Looking To The Future, Ginny Dye into the Search Box.

Leave a Review.

I love hearing from my readers!

Thank you!

The Bregdan Principle

Every *life* that has been lived until today is a part of the woven braid of life.

It takes every person's story to create

HISTORY.

Your life will help determine the course of history.

You may think you don't have much of an impact.

YOU DO.

Every

Action you take will reflect in

Someone else's *life*.

Someone else's *decisions*.

Someone else's *future*.

Both GOOD and BAD.

The Bregdan Chronicles

Storm Clouds Rolling In
1860 – 1861

On To Richmond
1861 – 1862

Spring Will Come
1862 – 1863

Dark Chaos
1863 – 1864

The Long Last Night
1864 – 1865

Carried Forward By Hope
April – December 1865

Glimmers of Change
December – August 1866

Shifted By The Winds
August – December 1866

Always Forward
January – October 1867

Walking Into The Unknown
October 1867 – October 1868

Looking To The Future
October 1868 – June 1869

Many more coming... Go to DiscoverTheBregdanChronicles.com to see how many are available now!

Other Books by Ginny Dye

<u>Pepper Crest High Series - Teen Fiction</u>

Time For A Second Change
It's Really A Matter of Trust
A Lost & Found Friend
Time For A Change of Heart

<u>Fly To Your Dreams Series</u> – Allegorical Fantasy

Dream Dragon
Born To Fly
Little Heart
The Miracle of Chinese Bamboo

All titles by Ginny Dye
www.BregdanPublishing.com

Who am I? Just a normal person who happens to love to write. If I could do it all anonymously, I would. In fact, I did the first go round. I wrote under a pen name. On the off chance I would ever become famous - I didn't want to be! I don't like the limelight. I don't like living in a fishbowl. I especially don't like thinking I have to look good everywhere I go, just in case someone recognizes me! I finally decided none of that matters. If you don't like me in overalls and a baseball cap, too bad. If you don't like my haircut or think I should do something different than what I'm doing, too bad. I'll write books that you will hopefully like, and we'll both let that be enough! :) Fair?

But let's see what you might want to know. I spent many years as a Wanderer. My dream when I graduated from college was to experience the United States. I grew up in the South. There are many things I love about it but I wanted to live in other places. So I did. I moved 42 times, traveled extensively in 49 of the 50 states, and had more experiences than I will ever be able to recount. The only state I haven't been in is Alaska, simply because I refuse to visit such a vast, fabulous place until I have at least a month. Along the way I had glorious adventures. I've canoed through the Everglade Swamps, snorkeled in the Florida Keys and windsurfed in the Gulf of Mexico. I've white-water rafted down the New River and Bungee jumped in the Wisconsin Dells. I've visited every National Park (in the off-season when there is more freedom!) and many of the State Parks. I've hiked thousands of miles of mountain trails and biked through Arizona deserts. I've canoed and biked through Upstate New York and

Vermont, and polished off as much lobster as possible on the Maine Coast.

I had a glorious time and never thought I would find a place that would hold me until I came to the Pacific Northwest. I'd been here less than 2 weeks, and I knew I would never leave. My heart is so at home here with the towering firs, sparkling waters, soaring mountains and rocky beaches. I love the eagles & whales. In 5 minutes I can be hiking on 150 miles of trails in the mountains around my home, or gliding across the lake in my rowing shell. I love it!

Have you figured out I'm kind of an outdoors gal? If it can be done outdoors, I love it! Hiking, biking, windsurfing, rock-climbing, roller-blading, snow-shoeing, skiing, rowing, canoeing, softball, tennis... the list could go on and on. I love to have fun and I love to stretch my body. This should give you a pretty good idea of what I do in my free time.

When I'm not writing or playing, I'm building Millions For Positive Change - a fabulous organization I founded in 2001 - along with 60 amazing people who poured their lives into creating resources to empower people to make a difference with their lives.

What else? I love to read, cook, sit for hours in solitude on my mountain, and also hang out with friends. I love barbeques and block parties. Basically - I just love LIFE!

I'm so glad you're part of my world!

Ginny

Join my Email List so you can:

- Receive notice of all new books
- Be a part of my Launch Celebrations. I give away lots of Free gifts!
- Read my weekly BLOG while you're waiting for a new book.
- Be part of The Bregdan Chronicles Family!
- Learn about all the other books I write.

Just go to www.BregdanChronicles.net and fill out the form.

53933880R00291

Made in the USA
San Bernardino, CA
02 October 2017